Happy Creatures

ÁNGELA VALLVEY

Translated by Margaret Jull Costa

PENGUIN BOOKS

PENGUIN BOOKS

Published by the Penguin Group
Penguin Books Ltd, 80 Strand, London WC2R ORL, England
Penguin Group (USA) Inc., 375 Hudson Street, New York, New York 10014, USA
Penguin Group (Canada), 10 Alcorn Avenue, Toronto, Ontario, Canada M4V 3B2
(a division of Pearson Penguin Canada Inc.)
Penguin Ireland, 25 St Stephen's Green, Dublin 2, Ireland
(a division of Penguin Books Ltd)
Penguin Group (Australia), 250 Camberwell Road, Camberwell, Victoria 3124, Australia
(a division of Pearson Australia Group Pty Ltd)
Penguin Books India Pvt Ltd, 11 Community Centre, Panchsheel Park, New Delhi – 110 017, India
Penguin Group (NZ), cnr Airborne and Rosedale Roads, Albany, Auckland 1310, New Zealand
(a division of Pearson New Zealand Ltd)
Penguin Books (South Africa) (Pty) Ltd, 24 Sturdee Avenue, Rosebank 2196, South Africa

Penguin Books Ltd, Registered Offices: 80 Strand, London WC2R ORL, England

www.penguin.com

Los estados carenciales first published in Spain by Ediciones Destino, S.A., 2002
This translation first published in Great Britain by Viking 2004
Published in Penguin Books 2005

1

Grateful acknowledgement is made for permission to reproduce extracts from the following:
Winesburg, Ohio by Sherwood Anderson, published by Jonathan Cape, reprinted by
permission of the Random House Group Ltd
'Ithaca' from *The Complete Poems of Cavafy*, copyright © 1961 and renewed 1989 by Rae
Dalven, reprinted by permission of Harcourt Inc.

Typeset by Rowland Phototypesetting Ltd, Bury St Edmunds, Suffolk
Printed in England by Clays Ltd, St Ives plc

For my daughter (Érika),
for my husband (Jenaro),
for my neighbours on the seventh floor (M. and Mme Krozack)
and my dog (Yeltsin),
despite whom
I managed to write this novel . . .

Although this book is – as all books ultimately are – for you, the reader, for all those who have ever asked themselves: 'What is happiness?', or who are perhaps searching for happiness or believe themselves to be unhappy . . .

. . .first, be aware of your own good fortune, because, even though you may not know it, you are undoubtedly fortunate. Look around you and see how much there is to discover. Don't go thinking how difficult it is to be happy in the times we live in, because they are no worse than any other times, past or future.

In *The Campaigns of Alexander*, Arrian wrote that, in the sphere of human happiness, it is the general rule that, eventually, everyone will suffer some misfortune. You are troubled by the conflicts and deficiencies in your life, you say, but did you really expect to find no misfortunes in your path? Did you really think you would be the exception? Or are you perhaps suffering only because you know that, one day, you *will* suffer? But isn't it absurd to suffer now simply because you are going to suffer later? Avoid whatever pain may come your way because that *is* 'real', and cheerfully begin your apprenticeship of life, but never ever think it is over. And enjoy reading this novel, for, to paraphrase Montaigne, this, dear reader, is a book of good faith.

So you lost the empire of the world.
Do not distress yourself, it was nothing.
So you gained the empire of the world.
Be not too joyful, it is nothing.
Griefs and joys all pass.
Everything in the world passes and is nothing.
> (from the Persian 'Anwari Soheili',
> quoted by Schopenhauer in
> *Parerga and Paralipomena*)

If love is the answer,
could you rephrase the question?
> Lily Tomlin

Contents

I. What we represent

Ulysses arrives at the Academy

The prudent man aspires not to pleasure, but to the absence of pain.

Aristotle, *Nichomachean Ethics*

There are some things it is better not to know and others which it would be wise not to forget. Or so he thought when it was all over – if, of course, anything ever is over.

However, on that gloomy September afternoon when part of his destiny was just beginning to be forged, Ulysses Acaty wasn't thinking about memory or about forgetting. At nearly thirty-seven, alone with his young son and a few debts, he preferred to occupy his mind with less abstract subjects.

The sky was preparing for the coldest months of the year and was, as always, indifferent to human passions. The baroque Plaza Mayor in the part of the city known as Habsburg Madrid was looking decidedly decadent in the velvet light of the setting sun. Here, beggars and gentlemen, charlatans and judges, noble ladies with powdered faces and grimy maids in threadbare clothes had once gathered to witness ceremonies and celebrations, from royal weddings to autos-da-fé, from church processions to public executions. Now the statue of Philip III was surrounded by an equally colourful crowd: tourists; the hopeless poor with no roof or floor to call their own; the long-term unemployed; idlers loitering outside the antiquated window displays in the arcades; executives, immigrants, crazy adolescents, housewives and terrorists.

Ulysses looked fondly at the façade of the Casa de la Panadería and said to himself that things probably hadn't changed very much since it was built. Only now, of course, everything was far more expensive.

He hurried on, but it was hard to make a great deal of progress when pushing a buggy with a child inside.

When the boy had been born, signalling the end of the good times, his wife had said without hesitation, without even blushing: 'We'll call him Telemachus. It's not a very common name, but then you know how I hate common things. And given that you're called Ulysses and I'm called Penelope, it makes perfect sense.'

As he was smiling confidently down at Telemachus, who was looking back up at him with his funny, gap-toothed smile, he only just missed colliding with a young woman.

Ulysses walked on, determinedly pushing the buggy in which his son, who had just turned two, was gleefully kicking his legs, as if he had discovered that this was his sacred mission in the world and that nothing and no one would prevent him from carrying it out. Telemachus was a fortunate creature: the very image of the absence of pain.

Ulysses glanced at his watch. He would be late for class, and Vili, his father-in-law, would shoot him his usual reproachful yet forgiving look.

Ulysses hadn't, in fact, the slightest wish to go to the Academy of Don Viliulfo Alberola – known to everyone as Vili – or to endure another moment of his talks about happiness, but Vili had subtly threatened Ulysses when he had suggested that it might be a good moment for him to stop coming to the meetings. (For heaven's sake, it was the worst possible time for him to have to leave the house, just when he should be doing the washing and preparing Telemachus's supper!) And although Ulysses was not easily cowed, he had preferred not to provoke the good professor's rage and so had continued to keep his weekly appointments with Vili and with the motley crew of nutters who followed Vili with sectarian zeal. It was, he supposed, Vili's way of keeping tabs on him, and of getting to see Telemachus on a regular basis. Although he was, officially, only Telemachus's step-grandfather, Vili had always been very much the grandfather and clearly loved the child. On the other hand, Ulysses had the feeling that old Vili was less and less at ease in his own personal life, and he had a pretty good idea who was the cause of all the stress. The poor man's teachings were proving of little use, since he seemed unable to apply them rigorously to himself, at least when it came to his relationship with his wife.

Ulysses wondered what laws were for if they did not apply to the law-givers. Not that he was a great fan of laws, sharing as he did Napoleon's observation that their sheer number meant that no legislator could ever guarantee that, sooner or later, those same laws would not eventually get him banged up in prison as well. Vili's laws were not like judicial legislation, he called them *rules*, and they were, if such a thing were possible, even more disturbing, because Vili believed that anyone who followed them could find happiness.

For Ulysses, the fact that someone like Vili should theorize about happiness and philosophy was not in itself particularly commendable. Vili could afford to devote himself to it because he was rich. No, he wasn't a millionaire; anyone could be a millionaire, but to be as wealthy as Vili was not within the grasp of just anyone. He was possessed of a fortune administered by several teams of lawyers and managers, who only bothered him a couple of times a year so that he could sign a few documents. He owned houses in so many parts of the world that Ulysses was sure Vili could not possibly remember them all, far less have visited them all. And yet he devoted himself to teaching the people who came to his Academy; to living in his apartment – a vast place, admittedly, but not at all luxurious – in the heart of Madrid (for here, he said, he had found

5

his agora); and to putting up with his wife, Valentina, with a stoicism that mingled perversity and selflessness.

Happiness.

Yes, happiness.

But what was happiness?

Ulysses again peered at his son over the hood of the buggy. Telemachus was shouting and laughing, kicking and gabbling nonsensically and looking around him with the joy of someone seeing the world for the first time and feeling pleased with everything he sees. And this was precisely what he did feel. Ah, how happy little Telemachus would be, as Virgil might have said, if he knew he was happy.

Ulysses ruffled the child's hair with his left hand. The little boy craned his neck so that he could see his father; his eyes were as wide and bright as two fresh hazelnuts cut in half, and he bestowed on Ulysses a huge, satisfied smile. He was a lovely, funny, playful child, and no one would ever have thought that he lacked for a mother.

Ulysses tiptoed into the lecture room, holding Telemachus in his arms. The session had already begun.

'Of course you're a good person. And a fortunate one too . . .' Carlota Rodríguez said, smiling soothingly at her fellow student. She had lovely thick red hair, and behind her glasses her eyes were a bright methylene blue.

Roberto Olazábal returned her smile, but his smile emerged more like an involuntary wink and this made him pause before he spoke. He didn't want her to get the wrong idea. He glanced at her, but her face showed no signs of unease or irritation, rather the opposite. Good, he thought.

Ulysses sat down as quietly as he could, placed the child on his lap and gave him a plastic toy to play with.

6

'It's true,' said Roberto, this time addressing Vili. 'I mean, I get up every morning and I say to myself: God, you're a lucky bastard. You've got so many advantages, you know. In the whole of the universe, which is a big place, you happened to be born on Earth, a small planet on the outskirts of a medium-sized galaxy, but which has an atmosphere, hot and cold running water and supermarkets. And in the whole of the Earth, you happened to land up in Europe, Spain, Madrid. H'm. Not bad for starters. And then you've got a job, a fantastic job – well, given the way things are nowadays, a brilliant job. Not only that, you're white as well, which, considering the circumstances, is the best colour to be. Anyway, that's what I tell myself every morning when I get up.'

Roberto sat back in his seat and scratched behind his ear. He took a breath before continuing. 'Because the fact is that if I lacked even one of these advantages, I'd be up shit creek. I mean, if I didn't have a job, or if I was black, or if I lived in Uganda . . . You'd just have to take away any one of my advantages and I'd be finished. They're only advantages, you see, as long as I have all of them.'

Vili nodded wearily.

'H'm, yes . . .' he murmured.

Next, it was Chantal Porcel's turn to speak. She was fifty-four and lived with her mother. When someone asked her ex-husband why they had got divorced, he referred to his mother-in-law, using the same words that Lady Di had used on television, touching the hearts of the world: 'There were three of us in the marriage, and it was rather crowded.'

'Well . . .' She fidgeted nervously in her seat. She hardly ever knew what to say. She hated speaking in public, and yet she was very chatty on the phone. She was also prone to occasional attacks of brazenness. 'I feel terrified every time I have to get on a plane. I say a prayer as I go up the steps. I ask God to make sure, if the plane does crash, that my body is so badly burned that no one notices I didn't have time to shave my legs before I got on board.'

Vili raised his eyebrows and laughed as he stretched out his legs, crossing his left ankle over his right and leaning back in his comfortable red leather armchair.

'But what's that got to do with what we've been talking about?' asked Jacobo Ayala, shaking his head, mystified.

Chantal stared down at the floor, pretending to look for something, half embarrassed, half myopic. 'Nothing really, I suppose,' she admitted. 'But I just wanted you to know . . . in case it helped.'

Irma Salado was also divorced, although she was still only thirty-one and had recently started going out with a nice Greek guy.

'In order to survive,' she said, twining a few locks of platinum blonde hair around her fingers, 'I relativize everything. That's the secret: relativity. Just ask Einstein. For example, I say to myself: All right, so you're not a natural blonde, but at least you can dye your hair, and even though the dyes aren't all they're cracked up to be, at least you've *got* hair.'

She looked at her companions one by one, in search of approving looks. 'And yes, I admit I haven't got a fantastic job like Roberto over there, but at least I've got a job and, although it's not exactly glamorous or easy, at least it pays the bills. All right, I'm not very tall, but I can always wear heels, can't I, and, although I've already twisted my ankle three times because of the damned things, it just proves that before I began wearing heels every day, my ankles weren't twisted to start with.'

She paused for breath, proudly pushing out her chest before she went on. 'OK, I haven't got any money, but I've got pockets waiting to be filled, which means I've got a jacket which I managed to buy despite my empty pockets. No, I don't lead a very exciting life – after all, the most exciting thing I do each day is watch the TV news. It's true that my life isn't very thrilling, but at least I have a life, which means that I'm alive, which is not something to be sniffed at, given that, if I wasn't, I wouldn't be able to complain about anything at all . . .' she shrugged and filled the ensuing pause with a troubled sigh, '. . . because I'd be dead. Don't you agree?'

'Aren't we taking this a bit far?' said Jacobo Ayala, who had been blind since birth, and who was, as ever, shaking his head in disapproval.

Ulysses stroked his son to keep him quiet, then automatically touched his own ear. Every time Jacobo spoke, Ulysses seemed to hear the nasal twang of the BeeGees, which buzzed inside his ear until it tickled. At least the BeeGees sang in tune, which was more than could be said for Jacobo.

Ulysses then turned his attention to Irma. He noticed her rosy fingers. She had small, nervous hands. From the viewpoint of Pure Art, Irma was neither pretty nor ugly, but she had her own style and her own peculiar way of seeing things, and that, in itself, was something.

A few weeks ago, Ulysses had asked her how she was and about her job in a crèche. 'Oh, it's not too bad,' she had said, glancing warily at Telemachus, 'although most of the time the children behave like absolute bastards.'

While she spoke those words, her breasts rose and fell, moving about beneath her tight black linen top; he looked at them again now with growing interest.

His friend, Jorge Almagro, also divorced, who worked as a tax inspector and who was addicted to net-sex, edged his chair closer to Ulysses.

'Irma's wearing a very plunging neckline today,' he whispered, startling Ulysses with his breath, which was laden with a mixture of menthol and nicotine. 'If I was in a position to simply kick over the traces, I'd invite her back to my place and show her my book of handy household hints.'

Ulysses gave him a bemused look and removed Telemachus's hands from the lapels of his friend's crumpled jacket.

'You know what I mean . . . my habits,' Jorge said distractedly, his eyes still fixed on Irma's long blonde hair. 'Because, in case you hadn't noticed, habits are stronger than passion. And I lead an ordered, middle-class life. Women find that attractive, it makes them feel secure. I would take Irma home and show her my torso bronzed by UV rays. My old bidet. And my cock yearning for conjugal duties. But it's so big – my cock, I mean . . . she probably wouldn't even see it. My cock, I mean. That's what happened with my ex-wife, she could never bring herself to look at my cock. She said it was like a large, blunt instrument, too alarming for any woman to contemplate.' With a gesture of his hand, he brushed the blurred image of his ex-wife from his mind, and winked mischievously. 'Nevertheless, I could show Irma a few new things, amongst them my cock, which I'm quite sure she's never seen before. My domestic eccentricities would probably prove fascinating to someone like her.'

Ulysses smiled.

'Oh, yeah. Look, when it comes to sex, it's not novelty that counts, but how you do it, so you're always in with a chance, with her or whoever. You should have a go. Less talk and more action. Although I've an idea Irma has been going out with someone for a few weeks now.'

Jorge went on: 'If I still had all my hair – an eventuality I have not enjoyed since my divorce – I'd be tempted to see how the land lies with the girl. If my bonce was fully covered and protected by hair, I'd have the courage to approach a woman like Irma.' He folded his arms and looked at the person about to speak, pretending to listen, as if he were sitting at his desk in primary school. 'But she – my ex – got everything. Everything. My courage, my house in the country, my heart, my current account, my grandmother's sideboard, Jorgito . . . As you well know, all she left me was a case of galloping alopecia. And the few hairs I had up until yesterday have gone with the wind because I'm forced to drive around on a motor scooter with no helmet, because she, of course, kept the car.'

'Now, now,' said Ulysses, 'stop feeling so sorry for yourself. We're here to look for happiness, aren't we?'

'Happiness?' Jorge grimly pursed his thin lips. 'Oh, yes, of course, happiness.' He half-closed his eyes as if sunk in thought. 'I'd really like to find it one day – in fact, I'd give almost anything to get my hands on the son-of-a-bitch.'

Ulysses was struggling to keep hold of Telemachus, who was trying to get down from his lap.

Outside, night had fallen, and the street lamps were filling the one vast window with a patina of threadbare artificial light.

'We're all so terribly alone in the world!' Ulysses heard someone near him say in a dull voice.

He turned round and saw a middle-aged man he did not know; this was presumably the man's first visit; unless, of course, Ulysses had simply never noticed him before. He was wearing gloves, and his frightened, wary face seemed to presage some imminent horror.

Ulysses could not possibly know how accurate this presentiment was, but he would soon find out.

He glanced at the man – a ragged-looking individual, with curious hollows in his temples apparently worn away by the constant, anxious pressure of his fingers. Ulysses studied him for a few moments, but was unable to concentrate, what with Telemachus's wriggling.

The dream of happiness

Here are two words that you should keep in your heart; observe how they control you and watch over you; you will be perfect and will live in peace. Those two words are *Endure* and *Abstain*.

Aulus Gellius, *Attic Nights*

There were about forty people in the room that evening. They were all keen to learn something, to find out what the others had to say and, more especially, to hear Vili; they were all bewildered, anxious creatures in search of clarity and some indication, however provisional, that living was not absurd.

None of them was happy. Too much loneliness – or frustration or information or resentment or repression or fear – kept them all, in varying degrees, paralysed and confused in the face of the strange intensity that living requires.

'I'm not sure Telemachus is a truly Christian, or even a very proper, name to give to a child,' sighed Jorge, grabbing the boy by one arm and hauling him out from underneath his chair. 'What will you call him for short, do you think? Tele? Macca? You should be ashamed of yourself, giving him a name like that!'

Ulysses sat for a moment, distracted, staring at Jorge, who was struggling to control the boy. He thought to himself that, in the hesitant light of that room packed with worried people, and viewed from where he was sitting, Jorge seemed like a product of what Hugo von Hoffmansthal termed 'neurotic idealism'. Jorge's colour came and went, and Ulysses had the bizarre feeling that the edges of his friend had grown suddenly blurred.

'Will you tell your son to keep still!' whined Jorge, the rosy crown of his bald head glinting with a few scattered beads of sweat.

'Have you ever stopped to think,' Ulysses said slowly, drawing his son to him, 'how difficult it is for anyone to be completely still? I think we are all in some way condemned to perpetual motion.'

'I hate it when you go all metaphysical. You're like a character out of one of those old psychological novels.'

'Well, at the moment I would give my kingdom for a nice cold beer. And the hand of the queen mother in the fairy tale for a cheese sandwich.'

'Which fairy tale?'

'Oh, God, I hate it when you play the tax inspector.'

'But I *am* a tax inspector.'

'I rest my case.'

Someone nearby told them to stop talking, and Ulysses clutched the small, quietly protesting Telemachus to him.

Vili stood up. After listening to his disciples' slow litany of complaints for more than an hour, the moment had come for him to speak. He was a rather short man, a man of restless, agile gestures, with bright, shining, dark brown eyes, which resembled two small windows opening on to an autumn landscape. He had a prominent belly which he disguised with a dark, impeccably tailored shirt, adorned with large sweat stains under the arms and in the middle of his slightly bowed but still sturdy back. His clothes were obviously not cheap, although they were hardly shown to best advantage on his tired, fifty-plus body, or perhaps he merely transmitted to his clothes a kind of startled scruffiness, a paroxysm of wrinkles that inscribed on everything he wore the crazy script of his habitually restless gestures.

'You're always complaining about life,' he said, stretching out his arms theatrically and then rubbing his hands together as if to relieve some stubborn itch, 'and I, like Boethius, offer you the consolation of philosophy. But philosophy can do nothing for you if you think not like philosophers, but like frantic children who allow yourselves to be carried away by your own caprices or like animals blinded by your own instincts.'

'It's easy for you to think like that, Vili, but not for most of us,' said Hipólito Jiménez. He was a 32-year-old painter and decorator. Almost everyone there knew that his biggest problem in life was knowing that he was the son of his mother, an old prostitute, once a familiar figure around Puerta del Sol, or, to be more precise, in a particularly grotty boarding house in Calle Carretas.

'That's why we're here, Hipólito. So that you, and people like you, can learn to think,' replied Vili, taking a deep breath.

'For many of us happiness is just a dream, an unimaginable luxury,' insisted Hipólito, 'because it's hard enough for most of us just to live, to get by.'

Johnny Espina Williamson, a pale-skinned, heavily bearded Latin American, shifted in his seat, silently shaking his head, a look of bewilderment on his face.

'We understand perfectly how you feel, Hipólito,' he said, rubbing the thick, curly growth under his chin. 'We know that, in your case, it must be difficult to live knowing that you can never take offence when someone calls you a son-of-a-bitch, but . . .'

Hipólito turned pale, and his face contracted with incredulity and rage. He was a handsome, well-built young man, and had pretty, almost feminine lips and a faraway look in his eyes, eyes which, when he heard Johnny's malicious words, burned with anger and grew as thick as soup that has been boiling for a while over a high flame.

'Fuck you!' he shouted, pointing at Johnny with one large, trembling hand.

Johnny didn't even blink, although he was probably only half the painter's height and weight, and, if not twice his age, a lot older.

'I'd be careful who you fuck, Hipólito!' he advised, a sly, malevolent smile spreading over his face.

'I'll fuck whoever I like, you bastard!' The veins on Hipólito's neck were standing out like electricity cables, and Vili, visibly upset, went over to him to calm him down.

A general murmur of disapproval, mingled with a perverse feeling of excitement at this confrontation, grew and bounced off the bare white walls of the Academy.

'Fuck you! Fuck everyone!'

'Careful now,' muttered Johnny in an unpleasantly jovial tone. 'You might end up fucking your own father.'

Luz's marriage

I will tell you a secret that will make others love you with no need for herbs or spells: 'Love and you will be loved.'

Lucius Annaeus Seneca, *Moral Epistles*

Luz Sanahuja – who had recently celebrated her forty-fourth birthday – had married Pedro nearly twenty-two years ago. They did so on a spring morning full of sunshine, birds, children and flowers, in the church of Las Salesas Reales in Madrid, the same church in which Luz had been baptized and where, a few years later, she took her first Communion dressed in a fairy-tale tulle dress. Around midday, she said 'I do' and, at that moment, there was a strange stillness in the clear, cool air surrounding the couple, a silence filled with such pure, simple happiness that you could touch it with your hands.

The orange blossom with which the church was decked had burst into the fraying shreds of a delicious, all-enveloping perfume. Pedro's hair shone as never before; he looked like a twelve-year-old, filling every inch of his morning coat with youth, health and symmetry. His face and neck were as close-shaven as a marine's, and, embarrassed by the look of wonderment in his bride's eyes, he bowed his head and began to recite the Lord's Prayer.

Luz could not help gazing devotedly at her new husband, with radiant eyes that shone with a fine, oily film of tears. She felt full of tenderness and empty of all anxiety. She thought that if that moment were to last for ever, her spirit would be unable to resist this overdose of pleasure and would explode with fullness, ripeness and perfection. It would burst and stain everything around with large drops of beauty, subtle sensuality and pure joy.

When she looked back at that moment now, with bleak nostalgia and just a touch of rancour and fear, she told herself that it had been the happiest day of her life, that she had never experienced anything so exquisite ever again.

Shortly before the end of the marriage service, however, she had felt a kind of tension grip her whole body, from her neck down to her ankles, and, a moment later, she felt a tiny, warm trail of sticky blood between her legs, soaking her delicate white, petal-soft underwear, trimmed with lace and brocaded in silk.

The sudden arrival of her period was not enough, though, to alter one iota her sense of well-being. She knew she was young and beautiful, that she had an iron constitution and a resplendent heart that harboured innumerable ways of giving love. And she had complete confidence in herself.

Her father was an engineer and would have preferred his daughters – he had two – to have found husbands who were graduates; in the case of his eldest daughter this was not to be. 'But Papa,' said Luz when she first started going out with Pedro, 'if that's what's worrying you, his family owns an ironmonger's with a staff of three, on Calle Serrano. And Pedro is an only child. When his father retires, the ironmonger's will be his, I mean . . . ours. Anyway, what's the point of further education? Look at you. As I recall, you were never home. Whenever we needed you, you were always away somewhere travelling. I'd rather have an ironmonger as a husband – at least he'd come home every evening.' They did not discuss the matter further.

Pedro and Luz were soon making plans to get married. He was twenty-three, tall and handsome, affable, hardworking and as strong as an Icelandic whaler. She was in love and lived in a kind of gooey daydream far removed from the world, a half-moon heaped with lilies, marital beds and infinite manly caresses on her thighs and neck, on her skin the colour and texture of mother-of-pearl.

They spent their wedding night in Paris, in Montmartre, in a little hotel heavy with dark velvet curtains, the same colour as the blood that had soaked the petticoats of her bridal gown. Alone in their room, they got undressed and put out the lights. They opened the windows, and the yellowish streetlamps outside covered them in a luminescent blanket of delicate abandon.

Although a virgin, she was not afraid of having sex with her husband. She had seen his red, erect penis countless times, had stroked it with a kind of bored submissiveness and had experienced, as she did so, just the remotest flutter of disgust in the darkness at the back of her throat. Pedro was young and healthy, and he respected her wish not to have sexual relations before marriage, but whenever they went out together – which was every evening – he always, rather slyly, managed to steer her towards some suitably secluded spot.

'Go on, touch me,' he would ask Luz pleadingly, and she would look into his eyes and see a profound darkness, like churning, marshy waters, in their green depths.

The honeymoon in Paris should have been the moving, much-heralded ceremony of the mingling of their skins, of long-postponed desire at last set free. And yet Luz wanted to put off the moment for as long as possible.

'It's all right,' whispered Pedro, his mouth on her mouth, as they lay on the soft, old Parisian bed, 'don't worry, you won't feel a thing . . .'

She frowned and stammered: 'What? What do you mean? I thought . . .'

Pedro's freckled face, the face of a young libertine barely out of adolescence, reddened. 'I just meant it won't hurt,' he said by way of clumsy apology.

But, of course, it did hurt – a persistent, slippery pain that travelled all the way to her kidneys and formed into a knot in her belly. It was as if some ancient wound inside her were being cauterized beneath a small, intense flame. Despite everything, she learned, very gradually, to teach Pedro, and to make the best of his clumsiness, his haste, his wandering, fumbling fingers. She instructed him in the exact science of the caress, in the dramatic technique of penetration, and in the philosophy of sensitivity.

Pedro was never a master of these arts, but what Luz got from him was enough for her to feel satisfied and loved for many, many years. They had two beautiful children, both very like Pedro – Ana, who had just turned twenty, and Pedro Jr, who was eighteen.

It was twenty-two years since Luz had been the hopeful, excited bride and since she had abandoned her language studies to share her life with an attractive ironmonger. For twenty-two years she had believed that the world was a delightful place beneath a sky of warm stars hanging motionless in the tranquil nights, like her own state of perfect domestic order. Then one day – she couldn't say precisely when – she discovered that her dreams had withered and that cracks were beginning to appear in her hitherto round, indestructible sky.

Her children had grown up. Her husband had put on weight and grew more silent with each day that passed. Her hopes had dried up along with her skin.

'But what did you expect?' Vili would say to her. 'Everything deteriorates, everything tends to disorder and corruption, it's just a matter of time. Beauty, youth, purity, water, wine ... even our atmosphere is a chaos. Those two fine astrophysicists, Murray and Holman, say that even the planets farthest from the Sun are partly governed by chaotic forces due to subtle interactions between their respective orbits. Jupiter, Saturn and Uranus spin and dance to the rhythm set by Mr Chaos. Any system made up of three bodies is, by definition, chaotic, and that includes the family. My dear Luz, if Newton had suspected such a thing, he would have died, trembling with horror. And if even he would have been astonished by such an idea, it's hardly surprising that you find it horrifying too. That's just how things are.

'So what? What do you hope to gain with all your gratuitous moaning and groaning? Don't keep stoking the fire just to make the madness worse. That's life. That's how it is: ashes and confusion, but prodigies and grandeur too. Napoleon knew that we live and die amongst marvels. You should know this too, that flowers are born out of the mud, and that you can draw not just depression from your sadness, but strength as well. We are mortal flesh, but, as Pindar said, mortality is made for mortals. Make the most of your mortality, drain your time here to the dregs. We are like blind men trying to understand the rainbow – but, Luz, what does it matter, what does it matter? Can't you feel life seething all around you?'

Luz admired Vili's wisdom and listened to him and watched him completely entranced. 'You ought to write all these things down in a book, Vili,' she would say.

'Oh,' said Vili, 'don't think I haven't thought about it. I've even made notes and sketched out a plan. But I'm not sure that I should. After all, anything I might say has already been said before and far better.'

'Well, say it again, then, as you do out loud at the Academy. Sometimes you have to keep repeating things until people understand,' insisted Luz, 'until *we* understand.'

In Vili's Academy she had found, if not the lost happiness of her wedding day, at least a great source of consolation for a period of her life in which her children were no longer her children, merely people who shared her house and her table, but who did not need her any more; her husband was just a bore with a beer belly, and the iron that was his trade had tattooed a kind of greenish rust round the edges of his fingernails – the colour, ridiculously enough, matched his eyes – and she felt that she had lost her life, a life she would never be able to recover.

She started taking tranquillizers. She stole a box of Tranxilium from her parents' house – her mother was getting on a bit, and the doctor kept her blood pressure under control with mild sedatives. Luz began with just the occasional pill, when her anxiety reached unbearable limits, and it took her three long, sad, stupid, sterile years of narcotic torpor and painful self-pity to admit that she was an addict.

When you turn out the lights

You young people, unhampered by laws, modesty or prerogatives, think now of the old age that is to come, and then you will not waste a single moment. Enjoy yourselves while you devour the years of your youth, for time flows past like water.

Ovid, *The Art of Love*

'We are such fools, constantly pretending, failing, falling into madness; and sometimes, life seems to us so dangerous and despicable, yet we carry within ourselves a hidden desire to survive at all costs, a murky fascination for the banquet of life which awaits us at every moment with its barbs and its dark, bewitching enigmas. We want to free ourselves from the flesh, from these poor, tattered remnants clinging to our skeleton, and from the empty spaces that inhabit our spirit, but without all that, where would we go? What would become of us without the wild, famished pack of hounds that are our needs, our miseries? Would we have a Shakespeare, a Mir space station, a Michelangelo? Would we know in detail about the enthralling life of bacteria? My friends, we must learn to look towards the red glow on the bright horizon; and every day, regardless of whether it is reasonable or advisable, we must each of us weave our own story, because we are straw and like straw we can light mighty fires,' Vili had said one evening in early September.

Luz was remembering these words – though perhaps not exactly – as she was walking up Atocha. Near the Centro de Arte Reina Sofía, she saw a familiar figure amongst the hurrying crowds of

22

people trying to cross at the lights or catch the local buses or push their way past the other people filling the city centre at that hour.

For women, thought Luz, there was always something very touching about seeing a man holding a little child. It gave you a feeling of security. It was an oddly exciting image, and its potency lay in a strange and ancient female power: the strength – which she had forgotten – that came from being and feeling oneself to be a woman.

Luz imagined the young father's talents for pleasure, his hands hanging limp and inert over the side of the bed at night while he slept. She imagined the cot beside him, in case the boy woke in the early hours wanting a drink or because he had had some childish nightmare, the kind in which vast, sinister, black stains threaten to crush the defenceless little bodies of children. She blushed at her own thoughts, but quickened her step until she had caught up with Ulysses, who was carrying his son in his arms; then, timidly, but resolutely, she touched his shoulder.

Ulysses swung round, startled, and as if defending himself from some surprise attack, grabbed Luz's trembling hand and was about to twist it.

'Ow!' she cried.

Ulysses immediately released her hand and tried to apologize.

'Oh, dear God, I'm so sorry. Did I hurt you?'

Luz lied and said no, it was nothing.

Telemachus pointed at her with one small, sticky hand, in which he was clutching the dissolving remains of a red lollipop. God knows what it is that sweet-manufacturers mix with the candy to achieve that almost supernatural aroma of strawberries, but it clearly has nothing remotely to do with strawberries.

'Bad lady, Daddy?' asked the little boy, indicating Luz, who was rubbing her bruised wrist.

'No, she's not a bad lady at all, she's a nice lady, she's a friend of

Daddy's. Her name's . . . Well, anyway, she's a friend of Daddy's.' Ulysses gave Luz an apologetic half-smile. Her face seemed familiar.

'Luz. My name's Luz. From Vili's Academy . . .' she said.

'That's right, of course, Luz,' said Ulysses, although he had not been quite so certain a moment ago.

She must be one of the women who came to listen to Vili, but who rarely spoke. Perhaps that was why he hadn't really noticed her before.

She wasn't bad-looking, a somewhat faded Natalie Wood, although somewhere deep in her eyes – so timid and embarrassed and blue – he could see a spark, an ember that was about to go out, but still had the potential to glow like molten metal. It would just take someone to blow on it to coax the flame into life again.

He wondered if she was married. He deduced that she was from the ring on her finger, and – once he had put his son down and taken her wrist in his hand and started massaging it softly with his fingers – from the look on her face.

'Hello,' said the little boy. He had his father's charming smile. Cheeky and subtle, but with just a hint of malevolence, as if he knew some dreadful secret of hers which he was considering announcing to the whole world.

Ulysses' art of love

> In order to be happy, we must rid ourselves of our prejudices, be
> virtuous, enjoy good health, have interests and passions, and be, by
> nature, hopeful, for most of our pleasures we owe to hope. . .and alas
> for those who lose it!
>
> Madame du Châtelet, *A Discourse on Happiness*

'Anyway,' said Ulysses, taking a long sip of his vermouth, 'my wife
clearly suffered greatly after our separation, so much so, in fact,
that, as far as I can see, she's gone up three cup sizes and entirely
lost her postpartum spare tyre.'

Ulysses pressed his lips together and smiled at Luz while he fed
Telemachus a crisp. He was wondering vaguely just how far he
was likely to get with this woman. She seemed nervous and disoriented, like a dog trying to cross the road alone, but she was also
eager to please and to make the world believe that she was strong
and confident. He liked her long nails, unvarnished but glossy, her
small chin, her dark, clearly delineated eyebrows, and her eyes –
two large, unexplored, blue spaces. He imagined her warm flesh at
night, in bed, huddled on the edge of the mattress so as not to
brush inadvertently against her husband's body; he imagined how
her left breast would pulsate to the faltering rhythm of her heart.

Luz had bloomed and was reluctantly beginning to fade without
anyone fully appreciating her beauty. This, thought Ulysses, had
made her sad.

He loved women, but, after thinking about the subject long and hard, he had finally concluded (as had so many men before him) that, as a whole, the female sex was an impenetrable mystery which defied all attempts to unravel it; he never knew what to make of women or precisely what was going on in their heads. He did sense, however – based on his own experiences with Penelope and on a few books – that what they needed most was to be respected and appreciated, because when they weren't they became so cold they could part the sea with one hard, dissatisfied, reproachful look.

All women, without exception, believed they were a treasure to be cherished at every moment. Women believed they were princesses. Far be it from him to contradict such a belief, however ridiculous it might seem, because they might well be right, the wretches.

'Oh, who knows . . .' he said, immersed in his own thoughts, taking his wallet out of his pocket. 'Anyway, I don't want to bore you with my problems. Besides, it's all water under the bridge now.'

He looked at the clock above the bar and signalled to the waiter to bring them the bill.

'Oh, you're not boring me in the least!' replied Luz, who had barely touched her drink, some sort of diet thing, full of bubbles, the colour of dirty water. 'Besides, as Vili says, hearing about other people's troubles makes our own much more bearable.'

Ulysses got to his feet and picked up his little boy, who managed to grab a handful of crisps before being hoisted up into his father's arms.

The bar was decorated with reproductions of old advertisements: 'Use Juanse's Special Powders. Thanks to Juanse, the pain has gone'; 'Diarrhoea? Use Juanse's Diarrhetil, price 0.40 *céntimos*'; 'Breathable red sticking plasters – El Elefante' . . .

'What unhappiness could possibly befall a woman like you, someone as . . .' and he bestowed on her one of his most seductive

26

looks, '. . . beautiful as you.' Then he got a firmer grasp on his son, removed a dangerously large and crunchy crisp from his mouth, and said, 'I'm really sorry to have to interrupt such a pleasant conversation, but the time has come to give this little devil some food.' He left a few coins on the table, on the stainless steel saucer that a fair-haired young man wearing an apron had just brought. 'If you like, you can come home with us and we can carry on talking. We live just around the corner, in Calle Santa Isabel.'

'Oh, I don't want to be a bother . . .'

'It wouldn't be any bother, would it, little man? We could do with a bit of female company.'

Luz surprised herself by accepting and getting to her feet, thinking as she did so: 'Now what? Now what?' Nevertheless, she decided to join them. She liked the look of stunned rapture with which he regarded her, as if she were the first woman he had ever seen. By his side, she felt special, she glowed like a pearl, and her lips formed into smiles that her brain had not instructed her mouth to make.

She was not to know that Ulysses looked at all women like that. Frankly, it didn't matter. She wouldn't have minded anyway.

They went out into the street, which was full of the roar of traffic; the sky had clouded over – a metallic sheet blackened by the exhaust fumes from the cars racing madly round the Glorieta de Atocha. Looking up at the thick clouds that hung about the buildings in dense, sooty skeins was enough to dishearten anyone. A storm was about to break. Ulysses buttoned up the boy's little woollen jacket and hurried on.

'I should have brought the buggy, but I always have the feeling that we make faster progress when we leave the ghastly contraption at home. And Telemachus weighs more than a bad conscience. Still, it's good exercise for me. People can say what they like, but being a house-husband certainly keeps you fit.' Ulysses adjusted his hold on the child, who seemed restless and was doubtless hungry.

'I think we'd better run for it, if we don't want to get a soaking. Don't worry, it's not far.'

'Hungry,' whined the little boy.

They were going down Calle Santa Isabel when the first warm, fat drops of rain began to fall, bouncing furiously off the pavement.

Ulysses took refuge from the downpour in the doorway of his house. Luz stood beside him, tentatively tidying her hair. The rain was falling now as if someone were hurling great pitchers of water down from the sky purely to annoy people.

Ulysses pushed open the heavy, probably eighteenth-century street door that led into his building. They went up the worn stairs, polished to an antique, whitish gleam, to the third floor. As with so many old buildings in Madrid, there was no lift. She was expecting to find a cramped, shabby apartment. She imagined Ulysses slaving away in an ancient kitchen, heating up the little boy's milk in a cracked saucepan and, in winter, rubbing his hands together to combat the cold air wafting in through the cracks in the dark window. She was already feeling sorry for him. The thought of a young man, probably little skilled in household tasks, living alone with a demanding, hungry child always hanging about his legs, was enough to arouse the more perverse imaginings of any housewife.

So she was amazed when Ulysses opened the front door and she found herself in a cosy home painted in warm brick reds and browns, with woven wood blinds and parquet flooring.

'Warm brick red tones,' Penelope had assured him before she left, 'are never overbearing, they're welcoming and evocative of rural life, of farmsteads owned by large, cheerful, well-to-do families who never quarrel and are always happy because they lack for nothing and because they have health, wealth and love in abundance.'

She was the one who had bought the art deco oak dining table, the one who had supervised the workmen when they were putting up the hessian dado along the corridor, and which Penelope herself had finished off with the kind of braid that upholsterers use for trimming sofas. It was Penelope who had bought the mohair blankets for the baby's cot, and she who had overseen the work involved in knocking through the kitchen, utility room, living room and dining room. The apartment was, at most, seventy square metres and it was as untidy as any home that has a child running about in it all day and every day. Nevertheless, despite the ominous darkness of the storm filtering in through the balcony windows, it was such a warm, delightful place that it made one feel like staying the night.

Ulysses told her to sit wherever she liked, and Luz sat down in an armchair from which she could watch the rain deluging the street.

There were only two bedrooms – as well as a studio, the door of which, as Ulysses informed her, was kept locked – and Telemachus went unsteadily about his business, swaying like a slightly seasick passenger, newly disembarked. He looked for a toy with which to entertain himself and distract his complaining stomach while Ulysses made his lunch. He was a very pretty child, with rosy cheeks, very fair hair and a ready smile, but Luz felt no desire to pet him or make a fuss of him. For a moment, she felt sorry for the poor little chap. His mother had abandoned him, and now not even his father's occasional female visitors felt the impulse to coo over him, even, if only hypocritically, in order to please Ulysses.

She felt positively cruel, yet she still didn't go after the boy, but stayed in her chair.

'Would you like some wine?' She saw Ulysses opening and closing cupboards and placing on the worktop a bottle of red. 'You are going to eat with us, aren't you?'

'Yes, I mean, no. Yes, well . . . I . . .'

Ulysses filled a glass and held it out to her with a smile.

'Are you in a hurry?'

'No, not really.'

'Well, then, if you've nothing better to do, you can eat with us. Or, rather, with me. Because first, I have to feed my son and heir. We're running half an hour late as it is, and he'll go to sleep straight afterwards. It won't take long. He gobbles his food up like a little pig. I think he suspects that I might snatch the plate away from him at any moment, so he doesn't bother with any of the niceties.'

When Ulysses carried Telemachus off to his bed, the little boy was moaning and rubbing his eyes with tiredness. Then this single father with the curly brown hair and the burning eyes prepared lunch: warm bread with anchovies and olives, a fricassee of endive and clams, and a bit of cold chicken left over from the previous day.

They finished the second bottle of wine and realized that they were both rather tipsy, but they nevertheless opened a third; and as Luz's spirits rose, so her defences crumbled like a sandcastle licked by the waves.

'So you're a painter,' she said, indicating the studio door, firmly locked so that Telemachus could not get in there and wreak havoc.

'Less and less, but yes, I am, just about,' said Ulysses, pouring himself some more wine.

'And how long have you been painting?'

'Well, if you'll forgive the rather crude, er, analogy, it was much the same with painting as it was with masturbation, in that I started practising it as soon as I learned how and I haven't been able to stop since.'

Luz blushed, then they both burst out laughing. (Though he laughed the loudest.)

'And are none of your paintings here?'

'No. My ex-wife, Penelope, was in charge of the decor. I just paint. I'm not very good at knowing when a picture goes or doesn't go with the upholstery.'

'And what do you paint? Abstract art, figurative, or . . . ?'

'I wish I could produce those huge canvases full of large areas of paint in which every brush-stroke is the symbolic representation of something terribly profound. I'd like to produce the sort of stuff I learned about in art school, and which I've pretty much forgotten now. You know the kind of thing, a black splodge surrounded by a few jagged edges: an affectionate parody of the *comédie humaine*; some splashes of red on a pale green background: an allegory of sullied *arte povera*, et cetera . . . But I don't have the imagination, and my thoughts don't tend much to the metaphysical, being mostly taken up with a constant anxiety to satisfy my primary needs: sex, food, shelter, little things like that . . . So I just paint what I see, mostly my son, household objects, people who appear in magazines, the light coming in through the window. Even you, why not? After all, Luz, you're a light that came in through the door.'

She cleared her throat and shifted uneasily in her chair; she didn't, in fact, feel particularly embarrassed, but Ulysses' presence so close to her, an awareness of his smell, of being able to reach out and touch his face and of the surprising degree of intimacy that can suddenly spring up between two perfect strangers, troubled her far too much for her to be able to control what she was saying and to attempt to be amusing, perceptive and brave.

'And how would you define it?'

'Define what?'

'Art, painting . . .' said Luz timidly, not knowing what to talk about.

'Um . . . I don't really know,' he said. 'Perhaps something you can hang on the wall?'

Luz took a sip of her wine. She had the strange feeling that all the bones in her heart had been broken.

'Do you sell much?'

'The current art market is in a bit of mess. You have to find a good dealer, and it's best if you belong to some movement: pop art, minimalism, Fluxus, the new figurativism, body art, *arte povera*, land art . . . there are so many of them, I can't remember them all. Let's just say that the money I earn, plus what my ex-wife gives me for Telemachus, is enough for us to get by on. That way we more or less manage to keep our small dysfunctional family afloat.'

'Aha.'

She said 'aha' and felt stupid because she wasn't able to say anything else, so she went on drinking until her legs were trembling with desire.

She made love with him. Her blood boiled as if she had been put on a high flame to heat up. She giggled foolishly and experienced an animal pleasure, which, although only a shadow of the first happiness – so innocent and simple – of her wedding day, nevertheless comforted her and gave her such intense delight it took her breath away.

This was the first time she had ever been unfaithful to Pedro. She might never deceive him again. But she realized how much she had needed this new experience. This encounter was what might be accurately termed 'an illusion', and she knew it was only transitory. But what did it matter if it wasn't real happiness, only pleasure? It had been a long time since she had felt life buzzing around her so clearly and emphatically.

She was alive, she really was. Yes, dear God, she was alive. And just when she had stopped believing in miracles.

When they had finished, Luz was as satisfied as she was grateful. However, she told Ulysses that this would be the first and last time, that she had to consider her husband (and her children too, a little).

'Fine, if that's what you want. But you're so lovely, so perfect,' he replied and buried his face in her right shoulder, where the skin was so fine, it felt as if it might break if you so much as stroked it.

'What do you say, then – shall we make love for the last time one last time?'

A couple of hours later, Luz was back home. She went into the bedroom she shared with her husband. The apartment was empty; neither Pedro nor her children had come home yet. She got undressed, lay down on the bed and carefully sniffed the skin of her arms and her knees. After a while, she got up, went into the bathroom and took various bottles of pills out of a small lilac-coloured wash bag. She tipped the pills into the toilet bowl and flushed them away. Then she took a long bath, full of bath salts, essential oils and perfumes. She stretched out her legs in the water and smiled foolishly at the blank of the wall tiles.

Scenes from the married life of a philosopher

> When Socrates was asked if it was better to marry or not to marry, he replied: 'Whatever you do, you'll regret it . . . But get married anyway. If your marriage works out well, you'll be happy; if it turns out badly, you'll be a philosopher.'
>
> Diogenes Laertius, *Lives, Teachings and Sayings of Famous Philosophers*

Vili was troubled that evening, but it wasn't the fault of the weather, which was violent, cold and stormy, just like his domestic life. He had the weird feeling that he was living in what is known in physics as a potential well. His marriage was going through a very rough patch. Valentina, his wife, was clearly losing her grip.

He was sitting in his comfortable leather wing chair, restlessly leafing through a copy of *Elle*. Occasionally he would scribble something down with a sky-blue ballpoint pen, or add a cheery moustache to the face of one of the splendid models photographed in exquisite, horribly expensive clothes.

From his vast penthouse above the Gran Vía, he could see the rain falling like an implacable curtain of darkness on the incessant traffic in the street below.

He put the magazine down and picked up another with a much less alluring cover – one of many bought by his wife describing the evils perpetrated by the male sex on the angelic female sex – the cover of which declared that penetration (the sexual variety) was an act of macho profanation and irresponsibility, the equivalent, to a practising Catholic, of urinating in the stoups of holy water at the entrance to churches and then running away.

He gave a worried frown. He flicked through a few unsavoury articles peddling the infamous idea that since men were an unnecessary luxury in the natural world and a real nuisance to women, it would be best to eliminate them from the face of the earth in order to ensure the early creation of a promised land inhabited solely by Amazons, liberated at last from the filthy detritus of penises and all their appurtenances, which – according to these illiterate rants – were many, each more disgusting than the last.

He let out a resigned sigh and, without realizing what he was doing, began answering a questionnaire entitled: 'Are you happy with your hormones?'

To the question: 'Do you dread menstruation?', Vili unhesitatingly ticked the box saying 'Yes, a lot', ignoring the boxes for 'Quite a lot', 'A little' and 'Not at all'.

By the time he had got as far as the third question, Valentina had entered the living room and, as usual, was in a foul mood. Vili wondered where, at the age of fifty-five, she had managed to dredge up the energy to feed such resentment against the world in general and against him in particular.

There was nothing left of the woman he had met thirty years before, a sweet-natured single mother, her eyes bright with *joie de vivre*, her lips moist and parted in expectation of a kiss. At the time, she could have been mistaken for an advert for Coca-Cola. And she was so beautiful!

She still retained some of her beauty, but she was incapable of seeing this and of enjoying it. Now, thought Vili, her eyes glittered with rage, and were as pale and transparent as diarrhoea. Rage made her ugly.

Valentina, the same woman who had once been the light of his life, had gradually, before his very eyes, become transformed into its greatest vexation. Vili felt, however, that if Socrates could put up with the domestic torments of living with Xanthippe, *his* wife, as a form of discipline, then he could endure with fortitude Valentina's day-to-day cruelty.

Ah, how well he understood the son of Sofroniscus the sculptor and the midwife Phaenarete – old Socrates, who had probably been about as fat as he was and possibly far uglier, and who deployed the weapons of reason and irony against a bunch of loonies who concluded that the best way to deal with a septuagenarian philosopher was to serve him a hemlock cocktail, as if his wife hadn't poisoned his existence enough already.

Valentina strode past him in her peasant clogs and flowery skirt, leaving behind her a penetrating trail of Armani perfume that struck the nose like a whiplash. She poured herself a glass of Absolut Citron vodka and downed it in one. She had read somewhere or other – though doubtless not in a book by Kant – that top models drank vodka, and she had drawn the ridiculous conclusion that vodka wasn't fattening. She had been drinking it ever since. Vili wasn't sure it was entirely good for her, even if the wretched stuff wasn't fattening.

'What are you thinking about?' she said, pointing at Vili with her newly emptied glass.

'I've thought so much that I've reached a point when, frankly, I don't know what to think any more,' he said, putting on his glasses and returning to the questionnaire in the magazine.

'You're probably looking at my magazines and thinking that I only read rubbish. I can tell. I can almost see your dirty little neurones whispering to each other about me.'

'Don't start, Valentina.'

'Don't start? And what, may I know, have I started?'

'We can't, we can't, we can't . . .'

'Can't what?'

'Go on living like this. It's the same every day. A stand-up fight between you and me. A meaningless war. Wouldn't it be better if we tried to get on with each other? Wouldn't we both stand to gain from that? Even if we were to lead separate lives. You know I love you, Valentina. You've always known it, so why do you do this to me?'

'You know, Vili, when I first met you, longer ago than I care to remember, you seemed to me an intelligent, mysterious man. Do you know what my mistake was?'

'No.'

'Going to bed with you. Once you've sucked a man's cock, all his charm disappears in a trice. Admiration is the basis for respect, but carnal knowledge puts an end to any admiration one might feel for the male of the species.'

'I asked you to be my wife and, at the time, you liked the idea.'

'Oh, I did then. Now I don't find being your wife any fun at all – did you know that?'

'I was beginning to get that impression, yes, but I really don't believe that I'm the problem, Valentina. The problem lies in you – there's something inside you that is poisoning you, something that can only be inside you, because I believe . . .'

His wife turned and stalked over to the vast windows that let in the reddish light from the neon signs in the street, a light tinged with the blackness with which the rain was impregnating the air.

'Ha! *You* believe! You've even got your own Creed!'

'All I mean is . . .' Vili sighed, filling his chest with air and calmness. He wasn't setting out to make himself the victim, but he had an awful suspicion that this was precisely what he was.

'Ha!' Valentina spun round, interrupting him. 'Let me tell you something. The first thing to bear in mind is that I'm a woman, right? My chromosomes are XX. The other thing we mustn't forget is that you're a man, right? So your chromosomes are XY. Those, my dear, are the male chromosomes. What we must also bear in mind is that the Y chromosome, the male chromosome, is merely a genetic residue the sole purpose of which is to make testicles. Your testicles, for example, as well as the great mound of other testicles walking around out there, filling up the world and making it a more brutish and stultifying place with each day that passes, as if things weren't complicated enough as it is. So . . .' Valentina paused for breath, sounding rather tired and hoarse, 'since that's the way it is, why should I want to hear anything that *you* have to say?'

Vili stood up. This time he was the one to go over to the windows, and he did so with a defeated look which was beginning to be his habitual expression.

'This is what the defenders of Sparta said to the commander of the Roman army: "If you are a god, you will not harm those who have never harmed you. If you are a man, advance, because you will encounter men of your own stature."'

'What did you say?' asked Valentina, one hand on her hip and a cynical smile frozen on her purple-painted lips.

'Nothing, I was just quoting Plutarch. My dear Valentina, I'm trying to make you understand that if you insist on fighting with me, if you insist on making me your enemy, in the end, I will have to defend myself.' Vili slowly rubbed his eyes; he was tired and his head was aching.

She walked over to the kitchen door.

'Don't you start playing the worried little man about to have a heart attack because of his harpy of a wife. You don't fool me!' she said, looking at him coldly. 'And for your information, I've decided that I won't make love with you again until . . .'

'*What*?' This time Vili's face betrayed real irritation. 'We haven't made love for over a year!'

'Oh, really?' Valentina stood poised, about to go into their luxurious kitchen. 'Well, then, you've got a fair idea of what to expect from now on,' she said and slammed the door behind her.

The dysfunctional Holy Family

A Spartan, when rebuked for going into battle despite being lame, retorted that his aim was to fight not to flee.

Valerius Maximus, *Memorable Deeds and Sayings*

It had been raining non-stop in Madrid all week. No one had seen the blue of the sky since, days before, a few large, gloomy, water-laden clouds had censored their view of the morning sun and, at night, of the small number of stars normally visible beyond the glare of the street lighting. The colour grey quite suited the city, but the rain continued to pelt down and was an invaluable aid in creating vast, tenacious traffic jams and in exacerbating the ill temper of the citizens who found their daily lives in the big city made even slower and more difficult than usual.

Despite this, Vili's disciples still managed to get to his classes at the Academy on time.

Elena Urbina, a weary housewife, came to the classes whenever she could, although not as often as she would have liked. She was slightly younger than Valentina, although she looked much older and was far less well groomed.

'Go on,' said Vili, looking at her fondly and making a swift comparison between the two women, from which Elena emerged the winner.

'I don't really know what Goodness is,' said Elena, sighing. 'It's such a big word.'

She was clearly overweight and not particularly attractive physically, but she used part of her minimal free time to help out at a charity involved in the fight against Aids.

Valentina, on the other hand, was not involved in the fight against Aids; at most – thought Vili – she was engaged in the fight against wrinkles.

'The fact is, sir,' (Elena was one of the people attending the Academy who called Vili, 'sir',) 'I'm not always very sure that Goodness exists at all. I see too much pain around me. Illness, loneliness and death. Not to mention my husband . . .'

There was a chorus of laughter from the other people in the room.

'Now don't get me wrong.' She put on a look of utter innocence; she obviously enjoyed working an audience. 'My husband's not a bad person. He's never mistreated me or anything like that. And he'd better not try either. But, seriously, he wouldn't hurt a louse, even if it had taken up permanent residence in his crotch. He makes a lot of work for me, though, simply because he's so useless. When I married him, I had to teach him how to do the simplest things – like, for example, taking the clothes hanger out before putting on his jacket.'

Elena rode the wave of collective hilarity. Despite the cramped space, she even took a few steps towards the other people seated nearby on the chairs arranged in a semicircle around a platform. Vili usually sat in an armchair on the dais, although now he was leaning on the back of the chair where Jacobo, the blind man (he would never let anyone refer to him as 'visually impaired'), usually sat.

'It's just that, sometimes,' Elena continued her peroration, 'if the food isn't on the table when it's time to eat, he cups his hands and thumps his chest – tocotoc, tocotoc – like that. Exactly the way orangutans do. I know because I saw it once on a nature programme on telly. But . . .' She smiled at Vili and let her arms drop theatrically

41

on either side of her broad, matronly hips, 'but as I understand it, this isn't a sign of aggression amongst gorillas, it's just a way of releasing tension. And if that's how it is with gorillas . . .'

There was a burst of group laughter that echoed round the Academy at the same time as a rumble of thunder outside ushered in a snaking, galvanic flash of lightning.

Elena waited until the noise of her colleagues' laughter and of the electric storm had died down.

'If that's how it is with gorillas, why shouldn't it be the same with my husband?'

When Elena sat down again, slightly pink-cheeked and with a little smile of satisfaction on her thin lips, it took everyone else a while to return to the question they had been discussing in the last few sessions: What is happiness and can it be achieved through Goodness? They had not as yet reached any conclusion, although since they rarely did, no one was very worried.

David Molina, a young father who dressed with casual elegance and moved like a catwalk model, took the floor.

'I know exactly what Elena means,' he said, patting his jacket pocket and taking out a finely embroidered red handkerchief with which he gently wiped his cheek, 'because I have the dubious good fortune of having a husband at home just like hers.'

While David was talking, Jorge Almagro, seated as usual at Ulysses' side, gave a long, melancholy sigh.

'How can they do it, Ulysses?' he whispered. 'It's a complete mystery to me.'

'What are you talking about?' asked Ulysses. Telemachus was asleep in the buggy beside him, and every now and then, Ulysses would gently touch his forehead. He was afraid the boy's temperature was rising. Hardly surprising really. Taking a child his age out and about in these storms, in a Madrid flailed by rain and by what seemed to be an unexpectedly early winter, pretty much guaranteed catching a cold.

'I mean David and other men who are that way.'

'What do you mean, "that way"?'

'You know!' Jorge waved his arms about affectedly and made various languid gestures with his right hand.

'You mean homosexuals.'

'Call them what you like, but remember I wasn't the one who said it.'

'Don't be so homophobic, Jorge. Perhaps you should try it. Maybe "that way" you might change your mind.'

'What do you mean?'

'Since you can't find a girlfriend, perhaps you'd have more luck finding a boyfriend.'

Jorge stared at Ulysses, a look of pure horror etched on his pupils.

'You are a bastard sometimes!' he cried despondently. 'Thank you, but no. I could never be a fairy. I've always hated suppositories.'

It seemed to Ulysses that Jorge presented a reasonably faithful portrait of educated lust, and that the disgusted faces he pulled were a mixture, in equal parts, of foolishness and refinement. Ulysses was fond of this besuited and betied man, because he knew that imprisoned inside his outward appearance of a man of order was a soul shrouded in the darkness of the most primary masculine angst.

Jorge took out a packet of chewing gum and offered it to Ulysses, who rejected it with a shake of his head. Jorge started chewing furiously, making audacious little noises that evoked inexplicable sensations of moistness and melancholy.

'I need to think clearly,' Jorge said, filling his chest with air. 'I think chewing gum is excellent for that,' he whispered to Ulysses confidentially.

'For what? Tooth decay?'

'No, it's sugar-free. It helps you think because it oxygenates the brain. I read somewhere that when you chew for a long time, the oxygen gets into the cerebral cortex more easily and makes your synapses work more efficiently.' He sighed and put his leather briefcase between his legs, under the chair. 'That's what I read anyway. And, as you know, I have a natural tendency to believe any nonsense I read in a magazine. Even if it's in *Hustler*.'

Vili and David were discussing the latter's family. David was complaining that his wasn't a normal family, or that, while it suffered all the defects and miseries of a normal family, it enjoyed none of the advantages. That's why he was doubly unfortunate. He felt like a lame soldier caught up in a battle. The ferocity and harshness of the fray were the same for all the combatants, but he had to face them while suffering a physical disability.

A normal family? What family was, in fact, normal? Vili asked. What was normality? Could anyone tell him? The word 'normality' struck him as being a slippery, thorny, distinctly psychiatric-sounding concept, difficult to define.

Besides, was there a perfect model of the family that one could imitate?

'Let's try and think,' said Vili, 'of the best family we can imagine, something that will serve us as a prototype, as a reference point.'

People offered various examples.

'The royal family,' said a dark-haired girl; her ears were adorned with enormous silver hoop earrings and she was smiling vigorously.

'Yes, but are we all kings and princesses, everyone of us without exception?' asked Vili.

'No,' she admitted, smiling with slightly less intensity than before.

'Since we cannot describe them as an ordinary family, we cannot, therefore, use them as a model to emulate, isn't that so?'

'No, you're quite right, we can't.'

44

'So we'll have to reject them as a model, then. Has anyone any other suggestions?'

'The family in *The Little House on the Prairie*,' called out a man sitting near Ulysses and Jorge; his dark hair was combed back in a ponytail and he was wearing an unusual pair of glasses with green lenses. 'They were a perfect family, always united in the face of adversity, and always up to their necks in disasters.'

Vili smiled and smoothed his unruly, grizzled hair, less abundant than it had been thirty years before, but far more abundant than it would be in another thirty years' time, if he was lucky enough to live that long, he thought, as he carefully removed a couple of hairs that had remained entwined around his fingers.

'But if I remember rightly, that family . . .' he coughed and then thoughtfully scratched his chin, 'was a TV family, not a real family but a fictional one. We live outside the small screen. We live and die here, in the world.'

David got to his feet again.

'I've just thought of a family that can't be improved upon. An example of perfection and humanity.' He was an attractive lad who, for some reason, or lack of it, seemed to be much given to tears and to fidelity. 'The Holy Family. That's the example I propose. The Virgin Mary, St Joseph and the baby Jesus. A classic model, a prototype that has remained unrivalled for more than two thousand years now. There you have it, sir, the ideal universal family.'

'Agreed,' said Vili. He got up from his seat and moved about amongst the chairs around him, his hands interlaced behind his back, looking for all the world like a noble, vigorous carthorse. 'It seems to me an excellent example, David. I congratulate you on your choice.'

Some of the other people there whispered amongst themselves, but a sense of anticipation soon silenced them and made them focus their attention on the two speakers.

'Thank you.'

'But let's see . . .' Vili went over to David, who was almost a foot taller. 'Let's see in what way your family differs from the Holy Family we have chosen as a paradigm.'

'Well, for example, my mother says that my family is odd, abnormal, meaningless and against nature. She says it's because I'm married to a man and not to a woman. And when I say "married", I mean that my partner, Óscar, and I are a genuine couple and are registered as such in the records office in Alcobendas. For my mother, the fact that I've paired up with a guy with a moustache instead of a girl with blonde plaits is something so terrible that she can only cope with it by dint of large doses of Christian resignation. For my mother, knowing that we have a son, conceived by artificial insemination using a surrogate mother, a child who is mine alone and not Óscar's, just proves that we are a pair of degenerates who don't fit in with the grand plan that her Catholic God had for the universe, that we actually pervert and obstruct that plan by our mere existence.' David shrugged and his lips trembled slightly.

'That's just your mother's opinion,' said one of the other people there, a man with a kindly face who looked like a former factory worker. 'And as Clint Eastwood said, opinions are like bottoms, everyone's got one. Take no notice of her, my friend.'

'Yes, it may just be my mother's opinion, but a lot of other people would agree with her,' said David. 'And obviously I care about my mother's opinion. I can't just ignore it.'

'OK, OK, but let's get back,' suggested Vili, 'to our model family. The family of Jesus Christ. What kind of family was it?'

'A good family, of course.'

'Yes, agreed, but was Joseph Jesus' real father?' asked Vili.

'No, he wasn't,' replied David. 'His real father was God.'

'Ah, so Jesus was the son of God, but his actual father, i.e. God, wasn't married to his mother, the Virgin Mary.'

'No, he wasn't.'

'So, perhaps the Virgin Mary was a bit like a surrogate mother for God,' concluded Vili. 'Just like the surrogate mother that you and Óscar looked for to bear your son, I might add.'

David stared down at the floor.

'I hadn't thought of it like that,' he admitted, blushing slightly.

'And how was Jesus conceived?'

The girl with the hoop earrings joined in again.

'He was conceived by the grace of God! Through the Holy Spirit in the form of a dove!' she said, as if that particular Biblical episode filled her with especial glee.

'Really?' Vili smiled and his sly face took on a sulphurous hue. 'A dove, eh? Well, well . . . You know, that sounds awfully like artificial insemination, which is exactly what you and Óscar did with the mother of your child.'

'Yes, I suppose it is,' agreed David. 'Except that we did it in a clinic and used a kind of syringe. Without a needle in it, obviously. A couple of doctors and various nurses took charge of everything else.'

Jorge gave David a long, wary look, his irises glinting like two pieces of coloured glass. He felt a pang of envy. It drove him mad listening to David's complaints. He could hardly bear it. Not only was this whining poofter tall, handsome, rich and healthy – and had all his own hair – he also had a husband and baby waiting for him at home every night as if he were the most important and desirable person in the known universe.

'Of course, doves, syringes, it's all the same . . . Science has made giant leaps since Year One BC,' Jorge muttered wearily from his seat next to Ulysses. 'And David's child is very like the Christ child. A little babe born amongst the lower wanks, so to speak . . .'

'*What*?' Ulysses stared at Jorge uncomprehendingly.

'By artificial insemination, I mean,' whispered Jorge, stretching like a bored snake in the sun.

'So,' Vili looked at David, a triumphant smile on his face, 'I don't really know what you're complaining about. If God himself created a highly dysfunctional Holy Family, *quod erat demostrandum*! What's good enough for God should be good enough for you, and, more especially, for your mother, if she's so religious. Tell her so, as soon as you get the chance, David.'

David weighed up the matter in silence.

'But I still feel like a lame man caught up in a battle,' he said at last. 'A cripple in the midst of the barbarity of war.'

'Lame?' Vili was quick to respond. 'Fine, so you feel like a lame man, but I thought you intended to fight, not give up and go scurrying off at the first opportunity. I thought you wanted to defend your family, to give them a good start. You don't need to be able to run to do that, all you have to do is fight. So what does it matter if you're lame? What matters is that you're prepared to do battle, and, without moving from the spot where you are, to unsheathe your sword and confront the enemy.'

The sublime indifference of the hero

It is more praiseworthy to be able to make good use of wealth than of weapons; and more glorious still than making good use of wealth is not to want or need it.

Plutarch, *Life of Gaius Marcius Coriolanus*

Ulysses put a new jacket on Telemachus, a blue fleece, very cosy and smart; then he put a hat on his head and picked him up in his arms as if he were a large, fidgety, life-size silicone doll.

Two days before, Penelope had sent round a courier bearing an enormous parcel full of over-priced children's clothing. There was everything, from Calvin Klein socks and vests to tiny pairs of Gucci jeans with fringes down the side à la Apache Indian. He decided that, since his wife was a highly successful fashion designer, it probably wasn't that expensive for her to get hold of the Loewe and Ralph Lauren outfits she sent every season. In the year and a half since she had left them, she had done this four times: in spring, summer, autumn and winter, never, of course, coinciding with the meteorological seasons, but with the far more advanced seasons of the catwalks.

Anyway, thought Ulysses, even if it did, even if the children's clothes did cost her a fortune, she could easily afford such fripperies. Telemachus was, after all, her son.

The little boy, however, was not always happy with the colour and appearance of the finery chosen for him by his distant, sophisticated mama. He might still only be a little shrimp, but he seemed to have very firm opinions when it came to clothes.

'S'orrible . . . Don't wannit, don't wannit! Don't like it!' he had declared a few minutes before, pointing, with evident distaste, at a delicate yellow jersey, hand-embroidered on the chest and around the sleeves with little ducks, each of which was smiling a furious, orange, silk-thread smile.

'No, it's not horrible,' Ulysses corrected him, starting to get irritated with his son's obstinacy. 'It's just . . . horribly expensive.'

'Don't wannit,' insisted Telemachus.

'I don't *want* it,' enunciated Ulysses.

'Me neither.'

'No, I meant that you should say "I don't want it" not "Don't wannit". Oh well, if you really don't want it, I'll wear it.' He picked up the tiny garment and gazed at it enraptured, as if thrilled to have been presented with something that would improve his life at a stroke.

'No, 'smine. Not yours. Mine!' Telemachus angrily grabbed the jumper from his father.

He ran out of the room, swaying slightly as he made his way to his bedroom. There, he took a teddy bear out of the wicker basket in which he kept his toys and tried to put the jersey over its head, leaving it hanging between the bear's ears and chest, like a somewhat eccentric, dishevelled turban.

In the end, they both agreed that it would be best if Telemachus put on an old fleece sweater, bought in the local flea market, which had Superman emblazoned across the front, except that now there were only a few faded traces of the superhero's once dazzling image.

As they were preparing to leave, Ulysses held the little boy close to button his jacket, then picked up the umbrella and slung over his shoulder a bag containing a bottle of water, an extra set of clothes – in this case, a child's track suit designed by Ágatha Ruiz de la Prada (he always took extra clothes in case something happened and the boy got himself dirty or wet himself) – some nappies and two spare dummies.

'Let's go and see your granny,' he said to Telemachus.

'Yeees!' said the little boy, clapping, and then he clung to his father's back, giving him a tender and entirely unaltruistic hug.

Ulysses closed the door of the apartment and went carefully down the stairs to the street. They would catch the bus. It dropped them at a stop very near the old people's home where Araceli lived. She was Penelope's grandmother, Valentina's mother. He was deeply fond of her. And she was so alone.

When he thought this, he remembered for a moment the faint voice of that man at the Academy, some days before, when the storm was rumbling across the sky and the rain was hammering down on the street like a black haemorrhage, sullying still further the already complicated urban landscape. 'We are all so terribly alone in the world!' the man had said in his anxious, faltering voice. It had sounded like the fearful cry of a child – or of a rat.

He shuddered to think of it and made himself more comfortable, with his son on his lap, both of them installed now on a seat on the bus crammed with people who were all drenched to the soul by the downpour and as grumpy as they had been on previous days.

The rain lent the faces of the passers-by a blurred opacity, making them look like the main protagonists in some drunken, feverish dream.

Lately, the atmospheric conditions in Madrid had been at their harshest (and conditions in Madrid could be very harsh). It even reminded him of his childhood in Maur, a tiny village near Zurich. His father used to say that the climate there could be divided into nine months of winter and three months of wind and cold weather.

'Sweetheart,' his mother would say to him, making her usual encouraging noises. 'Stop complaining and go out into the street and get a bit of rain since there's no sun to be had.'

Ulysses' father had been secretary of the Spanish consulate in Zurich for eleven years. There he had married a plump, guileless woman, a Swiss German with a round, tranquil face – the woman who would soon become Ulysses' mother – and he was reasonably happy with her and her sausages and their two children (Ulysses and his younger brother, Héctor), until one night, just after dark, Henriette felt unwell, heavy-limbed and lethargic, and two months later, she succumbed meekly to cancer, never uttering a word of complaint during her brief illness, but having completely forgotten that she had two sons of six and eight, and a husband who didn't even know how to open the fridge.

'Oh dear God, my wife!' said his father in the hospital, when they wheeled her out on a trolley, covered with a white sheet, to take her to the morgue. He placed a final kiss on her stiff, dead lips, and was unable to shed a single tear, even though he had enough saved up to fill the ancient, lion-footed bathtub in which, every other day, she used to treat herself to an overly perfumed bubble bath. 'Death is such a democratic bastard!'

Ulysses had never heard his father swear before. He could feel sadness floating in the air, like a bird with a grave face and dull, sunken eyes, grown weary of fighting for life; and he sensed that, from that moment on, things would not go well.

A few months after the funeral, he, his father and his brother all returned to Madrid. His father was never the same again. He stopped complaining and he barely ate. He worked a lot and delegated the domestic chores to a rather stupid, scatterbrained maid who tirelessly cooked them disgusting celery purées which she always served lukewarm.

The first day at school in Madrid, Ulysses had his box of coloured pencils stolen. He even knew who the thief was, but he couldn't prove it – everyone seemed to buy their writing and painting materials from the same stationer's, the same brand too.

He loved painting and drawing, and those pencils were his sole means of maintaining his childish, circumscribed happiness.

The incident hit him hard; it seemed entirely unjust. In the afternoon, after school, he ran home to wait for his father and give him the bad news.

'Sort it out yourself, I don't want anything to do with it,' was his father's laconic response when confronted by this vast, terrible childhood tragedy.

Ulysses realized then how much his life had changed.

He no longer lived with his smiling mama in a Swiss postcard full of lakes and mountains.

The next day, when the other boys in his class went out to play, he managed to steal all the coloured pencils, wax crayons and felt-tip pens he could find in his classmates' desks. He took them home (they lived only two blocks from the school, in Chamberí), went back to the playground, and still had time to play a ten-minute game of football, thinking all the while that sorting things out for himself wasn't nearly as difficult as he had imagined.

No longer sweet sixteen

Cato said to a malicious old man: 'Old age brings with it so many unpleasant things, why make it worse by adding cruelty?'

Plutarch, *Life of Marcus Cato*

South Madrid is very different from North Madrid. Heading south, beyond the grubby, puny Manzanares river, the landscape becomes progressively dustier and more industrial as the Plaza Elíptica disappears in the bus's rear-view mirror; as you leave behind you Plaza de Castilla and Alcobendas and head northwards, however, the Madrid mountains bloom before you and delight the eye with their Mediterranean vegetation of scrub and pines.

Ulysses and Telemachus were heading south. Their bus turned on to the N-401 and stopped outside the local morgue. Not surprisingly, the people who got off there never seemed very glad to have reached that point.

Five stops further on from the morgue, Ulysses and Telemachus struggled off the bus and stood in the mud oozing from the flooded bits of lawn that edged the pavement opposite the old people's home. A few yards away from the bus stop stood a red-brick building with aluminium-framed windows. It could have passed for a school or the local library if it wasn't for a sign in ostentatious gilt lettering that announced: The Retreat – Residence for the Elderly.

Araceli was waiting for them, sitting neatly in the pastel-flecked armchair in her room, next to the window that looked out on to the street. Despite the fact that the heating was on throughout the building, and the temperature was probably in excess of 22°C, she was wearing a thick blue woollen jacket. She held out her arms to Telemachus, without getting up from her chair.

'My baby!' she said in a warm, somewhat tremulous voice, and her watery eyes filled with tears, until they were two black plums pulsating with life.

Telemachus freed himself from his father's arms and ran to her, pressing his face against his great-grandmother's old legs and smearing her black skirt with crystalline drool.

'Gramma, grammama!' he babbled, his words half-drowned by happy laughter.

'Hasn't my little boy grown! Why, you've grown at least three feet since last week!' she exclaimed proudly, tousling the boy's silky, fair hair.

Ulysses kissed her on the cheek and asked her how she was.

'I'm fine, my dear, fine. Sit down,' and she indicated a canvas rocking chair near the bed. 'Bring it over here, beside me.'

Noticing how pleased his son was to see his great-grandmother, Ulysses remarked on the fact that Telemachus clearly adored her.

'He loves me a lot because he knows that I love him a lot too, isn't that so, sweetheart? Telemachus and I are very alike, we have to say what we feel.' She planted a tremulous kiss on the boy's pink cheek. 'We old folk are just like babies, helpless, tiresome creatures who desperately need other people. If we weren't kind and affectionate to those around us, no one would put up with us and we'd be abandoned en masse at motorway service stations.'

They had left the door of her room open, and they could hear the murmur of conversations in the corridor and in some of the neighbouring bedrooms. Discussions about the side effects – which tended to attack the eyes and the large intestine – of certain unpleasant medicines which, alas, after a certain age, were absolutely vital if you wanted to continue waking up each morning; about a particular doctor from the university hospital, whom several elderly people suspected of being a serial killer with a morbid predilection for the very ancient; about when, precisely, the longed-for family visits would occur and how best to fit these in around their daily activities. 'I won't be able to go to the Internet class on Thursday because my grandson from Zamora is coming to see me', or: 'Who's going to want to come out on a day like this just to watch a few old frights like us slowly dying?'

Suddenly a figure filled the doorway. It was a man in his seventies with a bulging stomach, who was wearing a jaunty Tyrolean hat and a red pullover with a pattern of beige diamonds.

'A very good day to Araceli and her guests,' he said, bestowing on them a broad smile that revealed, to the full, a set of superb, very new false teeth.

'Good day,' replied Telemachus cheerfully.

'Oh, hello, Anselmo,' Araceli said, shooting him a short, sharp glance. 'Aren't you supposed to be having a massage?'

'Yes, that's where I'm off to now, but I just thought I'd pop in and say hello first.'

'Fine, well, now you have. Goodbye, Anselmo. Enjoy your massage.'

'Oh, yes, sorry. I can see you're busy. I'll catch up with you later, over coffee.'

When he had disappeared up the corridor, Araceli pulled a face.

'They're turning the old people's homes in this country into Sodom and Gomorrah,' she whispered in a soft, confiding, slightly crazed tone.

'What?' Ulysses blinked in astonishment, then examined her face closely.

'Yes, the madmen who run these places,' explained Araceli, as she petted the little boy, 'employ sexologists who are constantly urging us into promiscuity.'

Ulysses looked at her, amused.

'It's true.' She sighed and pointed cautiously at the door. 'Of course, the reason they're doing it is because they know we can't get pregnant, otherwise . . . They're always going on about a healthy sex life, free love and a lot of other outdated piffle. They like to think they can keep us quiet with a bit of sex, a lot of tranquillizers and a dash of telly. But I think that, at my age, a healthy sex life doesn't mean a busy sex life, it means a sex life without the sex. A bit of peace, I mean. And no urinary infections, thank you very much!'

'Finding a partner isn't all bad, Araceli,' Ulysses suggested shyly. 'A bit of love brings with it a bit of company too.'

'Oh, I'm not saying it's a bad thing,' she replied, pursing her dry lips, which were touched with just a hint of pink gloss, 'but you have to admit that, at my age, a good man is very hard to find. Especially when most of the ones I like are dead.'

'What about Anselmo?'

'Anselmo? Ha! He's ten years younger than me and six inches shorter. Besides, you saw him, you saw that huge belly of his. He's got a sign on his forehead saying: "I'm going to die of overeating."'

'Well, he seems very interested in you.'

'Yes, but I'm not interested in him,' said Araceli firmly. 'I mean, you've seen him. He dresses like a demented clown and talks like Ronald Reagan. I'm not even the tiniest bit interested.'

'If you say so.'

'Worst of all, he's got bad breath, which doesn't surprise me in the least, given how much he eats. He changes his false teeth every year, but it doesn't help. I can't understand how it's possible for anyone's mouth to smell that bad nowadays. Or perhaps it's his bum.'

Telemachus suddenly started sneezing violently, his eyes began to water. He looked almost frightened. Araceli immediately made as if to get to her feet, and Ulysses helped her to complete the manoeuvre.

'Febreeze Fabric Refresher,' she said indignantly.

'I'm sorry?'

'Let's get out of here. The child is sneezing and it's all becàuse of the Febreeze.'

'The what?'

'It's the spray they use to perfume the curtains and the bed-clothes.' She grabbed his arm and muttered in confidential tones: 'You know, disposable nappies aren't always enough for a lot of people our age. So they perfume everything. They spray Febreeze everywhere. I can only assume that the manufacturer must have bribed the director of this dump. But I read on the Internet that it's dangerous stuff. It's got some kind of poison in it. Dogs drop like drunken flies after one whiff of it. Hamsters keel over. And I don't need to tell you what happens to cats. Let's get the child out of here, he's too small to survive in this extermination camp. He's only about the same height as your average domestic animal.'

Ulysses picked up his son in his arms and the three of them slowly left Araceli's bedroom, closing the door behind them.

Everything in its place

Happiness is no easy matter: it is difficult to find in ourselves and impossible to find anywhere else.

Sébastien Roch Chamfort

A woman about the same age as Penelope, whom she had met on business in Italy once, had given her a brief summary of her life. According to her, when she was five she had said to one of her little male friends at nursery school: 'If you give me your Action Man, I'll let you kiss me.' When she was ten, she announced to a classmate: 'If you do my social science homework for me, I'll let you go with me to the toilets. I'll drop my knickers and you can see what I've got underneath', although it must be said that, at the time, she didn't have anything much worth seeing. At sixteen, she suggested to a boy in her group of friends: 'If you take me for a ride on your motorbike all round the neighbourhood, I'll let you touch my left breast for three whole minutes.' At twenty-two, she cornered a young lecturer in the Department of Economics – who had been lusting after her since she was a first year, but who kept failing her in the exams – and made a deal with him: 'If you pass me in the exam, I'll do you a little manual favour in the toilets, wearing a glove, mind.' When she was twenty-five, shortly after getting married to her first husband (she was now on her third), she suggested to her dull, innocent spouse: 'If you buy me that chesterfield sofa, I'll give you a blow-job tonight.' And while she was talking to Penelope, on the eve of her thirty-fifth birthday, she smiled fondly and wondered out loud: 'Do you think I'm a bit of a tart?'

This extraordinary woman confessed that, on her journey through life, she had reached just one practical conclusion as regards personal relationships: that every woman should be a bit of a tart now and then. Just a bit. And only now and then. But tarty. And a little bit motherly too. It seemed to her that this, for a woman, was the best way to get on.

Penelope heard all this with a frown on her face, upset by such existential assumptions.

'Men are crying out for it, Penny, you just have to look around you,' said the woman. 'What they want in a woman is a mother and a whore: when they don't need the former, they need the latter, and that's all men require from women. And if you can play both roles at the same time, your partner won't want to let you out of his sight. I haven't had a particularly wonderful time with men myself, because I've got stuck in the role of whore, you see. It's what I'm best at. I've started to get the hang of it now, although it's taken me all my life. But I just can't get into the role of mother. I don't know why. Oh, well, nobody's perfect. And, of course, all my marriages have ended in disaster.'

Penelope had never thought of it in these terms, but her marriage had foundered too.

On a visit to Ulysses and her son, after she had left them, her husband had said bitterly: 'You've got no heart', and she had retorted in her usual common-sense way: 'Well, I've got X-rays that prove otherwise, darling.' And with that, she had slammed out of the apartment, her little son's whimpering still audible through the door.

Before, when she had left them for good, she had written a farewell note to Ulysses, which she had stuck on the oven door

60

with a kitchen magnet: 'I'm leaving. If you want any supper, there's some rat poison in the fridge.'

And the best thing was that she really had prepared him some rat poison in a plastic Mickey Mouse bowl, carefully wrapped in aluminium foil and lovingly placed on the middle shelf in the fridge, alongside a few cartons of milk, three baby's bottles of sterilized water and a half-rotten cabbage languishing stoically in the vegetable drawer.

Shortly after leaving them, she had landed a job as assistant designer with one of the best fashion houses in Spain.

She was interviewed by the head of the fashion house – an ageing, terminally ill homosexual, as sensitive as he was feckless, who combined the mind of a pre-school child with the artistic and commercial instincts of a genius. He had been poring over her designs for some days, and now had a few personal questions to ask her.

'How tall are you?'

'Five foot six.'

'And how much do you weigh?'

'Um . . . before or after I've shaved my legs?' Penelope asked back.

'Are you married?'

'Yes, but I've just left my husband and son, and all I require of life is that it doesn't place any more husbands and sons in my path ever again. I have no family obligations, if that's what's worrying you,' she lied, although it wasn't so very far from the truth.

'How old are you?' asked the ageing *enfant terrible* of Spanish haute couture; his voice was so theatrical and strident that he always gave the impression of being terribly embarrassed, no matter who he was talking to.

'Well,' she said, 'physically, as you can see, I'm twenty-five. Mentally, though, I'm pushing fifty-six. And spiritually I've just turned twelve. So let's just say that I'm thirty-three.'

The chief designer allowed his face to betray the barest hint of an expression, which looked more like the mark left on his face by some ancient wound. The corners of his lips took on a fossil-like stillness, and only after a few seconds did Penelope realize he was smiling.

She got the job, but then she deserved it; they weren't doing her any favours – she had real talent. Not that she had acquired this at university, of course, since all she had got out of the School of Fine Arts was a useless degree and an equally useless, graduate husband. No, her abilities were born in some complex, recondite place inside herself. And no husband – or even son, flesh of her flesh – would prevent her from dragging them out into the light and taking full advantage of them.

Ah, women. The eternal prisoners of biology and culture, spiders caught in their own web.

The same drama, in varying degrees of poignancy, had been acted out through all eternity.

And Penelope was not prepared to let herself be trapped inside it.

She was in the hallway of her apartment, looking long and hard at a Chinese elm-wood chair which she had bought the previous year in an antiques shop. For some months she had kept it in the hall, beside a black-stained teak wine rack, in a corner behind the front door, beneath a lurid, pop-art collage made by a young artist from the Malasaña district of Madrid. There the chair had almost blended in with the wall, and its delicate symmetry, the wonderful filigree work of the carved back, went unappreciated. Now, however, in its position beneath the large window in the living room, near the fake fireplace, it shone like a small, bright, private jewel.

She had undergone a similar process to that of the chair. In the apartment where she had lived with Ulysses and her son, she used to feel like (and therefore probably was) a fat, lazy, amiable servant.

Her brain was full of that grey fluff that lurks underneath sofas. Her skin smelled of beer and the grease from fried chicken. The mere idea of having to plan the next day's meals brought on a nightly panic attack. And there was that recurring dream in which she had to perform complicated mathematical operations – because her life depended on it – with a piece of black chalk on a blackboard in total darkness.

'Things look different,' thought Penelope as she carefully drew on her stockings, 'when we put them in a different place. And the same applies to people.'

Community spirit

Diogenes' only slave, Manes, ran away. When Diogenes found out where he was, he made no attempt to get him back because, he said, it seemed foolish; after all, if Manes could live without Diogenes, why shouldn't Diogenes live without Manes?

Lucius Annaeus Seneca, *Philosophical Treatises*

In the 1950s 'togetherness' was the name given to the 'community spirit' enjoyed by a few, theoretically fortunate, model couples. Couples who presented a united front in every aspect of life, who shared everything, even the most terrible of feelings. Political ideas, culinary tastes, professional ambitions, television programmes, dark sexual desires. Husbands and wives who would say to each other: 'I understand your disappointments as if they were my own, my dear'; 'I can read your mind as if it were an open book'; 'I know exactly what you must be feeling right now, my love'; or 'I don't need to explain to you what went through my mind at that moment, because you know better than I do.' They were spouses who spent every moment together, who, whenever possible, breathed the same air (apart from those hours devoted to work, of course), who went walking together, did the shopping together, went to sleep and woke up together.

Laura Yanes and Francisco de Gey were one such couple – a fused identity, two entwined, unindividuated souls, whose only independence from each other was that forced on them by their individual physical needs. Total love devoted to total mutual enslavement. They were not two, but one; not twin souls, but Siamese twin souls, as if they were afraid to exist on their own account, filled by a strange atavistic fear of freedom, that dense, black ball that weighs heavier than a death sentence.

They were the total couple, down to the most desperate corner of their being. Or at least they had been until recently. 'The real indicator of a married woman's character is her husband's current account,' opined Francisco, a thin, nervous fellow in his forties, who was a regular at Vili's academy (not only was it situated opposite his house, it was free); he went there, he said, in order to get inspiration for the great novel he was writing, the European magnum opus of the new millennium and the post-industrial era, the novel that would doubtless change the direction of Western literature.

Literature, women and bank accounts were his main problems. They all had to do with his need to feel some sense of power and control over what – as he was painfully beginning to suspect – was his failure of a life. The fact was that his current account wasn't at its best at the moment, if it had ever known a best.

At the same time, his wife was gradually drifting away from him, to the point where Francisco was afraid that Laura might start to be herself rather than just the obverse or reverse of the spiritual and carnal union they had once formed.

And literature, for which he professed a religious idolatry – and for which he felt the vocation of a monk or a vassal – kept slipping through his fingers like water, for he had never been capable of writing anything.

He noticed with clear-eyed horror how that infernal machine, the laptop – a present from Laura – sent out malevolent waves that forced him to keep his distance. He tried using a typewriter – a 1950s Underwood that had belonged to his grandfather – but this had the same repellent effect, and lacked the charm of the laptop, which he could at least plug in, then open up files and admire the bright little icons blinking at him from the desktop.

With a ballpoint pen, he got no further than sketching out a few possible titles and the opening sentences of his future great novel.

In the corridors of Vili's Academy, before the session began, he would sometimes bump into Johnny Espina (a scurrilous, cantankerous type, and another Great Writer in the making). They would often argue about literature. One evening, Johnny, his usual mordant self, recited a few lines from Martial which, as he affirmed with a sly smile, suited Francisco perfectly: 'Sertorius never finishes what he starts, Though he begins a hundred things each day. And even when he fucks, I ask myself, Does he always pull out early?'

'God, you're a sick bastard,' Francisco said to him reproachfully.

'Look, I was just trying to provoke you, to make you decide once and for all what you want to do, regardless of how it turns out.' Johnny straightened up and drew his hand across his perspiring brow. 'Anyway, you've no business talking to me like that; remember, I've written sixty-five books of poetry, whereas you haven't managed to finish a single one of the books you've started. Frankly, I think I deserve a little more respect.'

'But how many have you published, eh? Tell me that.You've written loads, according to you, but how many have you published?'

'What's that got to do with anything?'

'Everything,' laughed Francisco, 'absolutely everything. You're always going on about how you're an artist, but what's so artistic about you, apart from having a nose like John Lennon's?'

Johnny flew into a rage, not that this was anything unusual. He pressed his lips together, trying to contain his anger and giving the impression to those watching him that his teeth had all come loose and were floating blithely around inside his mouth, while he struggled clumsily to keep them in.

'You're a pathetic little wanker,' he said to Francisco at last, before turning on his heel and striding off. 'But you're not going to get me to argue with you, you moron. As Vili says, and as Socrates would say: If a donkey kicks me, I'm not going to go to the bother of suing him.' He gave a long, calm out-breath and strode over to the door of the Academy. 'Go fuck yourself!'

Love – what a wonderful word. For ten years, love had been Francisco's refuge. He believed in love.

According to Seneca, the good thing about pain was that if it lasts, it's nothing serious, and if it's serious, it doesn't last. Precisely the same could be said about love. His had lasted for ten years. It wasn't much. Nor was it very little. Perhaps it had been neither a big love nor a small one. Now he felt that it would be much easier to write a thousand love stories than actually live one of his own. The only problem was that he had so far proved incapable of writing any.

He had begun quite a number of novels (mostly about love, for he was convinced that love and doubt were the best subjects for a virtuoso writer to tackle), but he had not managed to finish even one. As the perceptive Johnny had so rightly said, he had only written a few lines of each. He tried scrawling a few poems in his notebook – with no satisfactory result. There were so many beautiful lines floating around out there, in the air or in his head, but Francisco wasn't clever enough to catch them. He read Shakespeare's sonnets for the nth time. Oh God, Shakespeare! What a good poet Francisco would be if he had written Shakespeare's poetry.

Francisco had a degree in business studies, and for the last fourteen years, had worked as a business manager for various companies. On the first day of a new job he was filled with enormous enthusiasm. He took ambitious initiatives, thought up brilliant, daring plans which others were then charged with putting into action, and which achieved a rapid, effective and immediate increase in sales.

That was at the beginning. Francisco liked beginnings, they were his weakness. But just as happened with his novels (innumerable projects sealed with countless dazzling opening sentences), that initial energy rushed out of him in those first few moments, like champagne out of a bottle that has been shaken violently before being uncorked, and is soon exhausted.

He dried up. He would be overcome by a tide of apathy, by a paralysing indifference against which he could do nothing. He had no more to give. He really didn't. It was out of his control. It was the way he was, it was just his nature, Francisco would say, trying feebly to excuse himself.

The extraordinary thing was that he, a devotee of artifice (after all, isn't that what literature is in essence?), gave in so easily, without offering the least resistance, to the tyrannical caprices and rigid laws of the natural world.

What we can see is all that there is on earth, nothing more. But it's what we cannot see that brings things into existence, that makes them change and allows us to change, so that nothing is ever still. In Francisco's case, the invisible was also the counterweight that was destroying all that was visible in his life. As simple as that. And as traumatic.

When he married Laura – ten years ago and shortly after he had joined the world of work – he felt full of vigour and, in a very profound way, rooted in firm ground, just like an ancient tree; he was ambitious and bursting with self-confidence, surprisingly sure of himself in the arms of a wife so lacking in aspirations and so vulnerable.

She changed the sheets three times a week, did the cooking, got upset about the minor contretemps of daily life; and she was generous. He looked after her, and she looked after him. Francisco was Laura's little boy and her father. Laura was Francisco's mother and his little girl. Everything was perfect.

Whenever he lost a job, he always managed to find another one and to present it to his wife as being even better than the last. In between times, he allowed himself to sink for a while into the swamp of his lethargy, then splash his way to the shore, muddy and exhausted, to renew his search for another foul pool into which to plunge.

Then he made such a mess of his last job that they threw him out, and this time he failed to find one as good or better. Ever since then he had been collecting his unemployment benefit and coolly watching his marriage dying, as Laura found herself obliged to work ten hours a day as a receptionist in a hotel in the city centre, in order to pay the bills that Francisco's monthly unemployment benefit could not cover.

He watched Laura working and becoming gradually more distant. It was as if she were rowing towards some place that she alone knew. Ah, Laura, Laura . . . His beloved, long-time copulative conjunction. His other half.

It occurred to him that perhaps it was a good moment to throw himself into writing his novel. After all, he had always wanted to be a writer, for as long as he could remember.

'Do an outline of the novel and write the first chapter,' Laura had suggested. 'I'll find you an agent and you can start your career.'

Francisco agreed with his wife. That is what he would do: he would rough out a thrilling synopsis of his story, compose a first, sample chapter – nothing too definite, but intriguing enough to capture the heart of any agent or publisher in their right mind – and then launch himself upon the world of talent, even of fame, and doubtless of glory too.

Anyway, he had a feeling that his prospects were really not too bad at all. Especially bearing in mind the dangerous life situation in which he found himself. Especially bearing in mind – oh, most especially – his congenital weakness which, now that he was in his forties, hung over him like a cruel, constant scourge – namely an intractable sense of desolation which he had, for the first time, however reluctantly, begun to acknowledge as real.

But the months passed, and Francisco still did not finish his sample chapter, not even the outline of the superb novel he was planning to write.

Laura kept nagging him about it, becoming increasingly worried and suspicious. They began to have frequent bitter rows. Anything could set them off. A dark-roasted coffee stain on a pair of almost new trousers. Francisco forgetting to buy the bread again. Laura always feeling too tired to make love when her husband wanted her to.

'We haven't made love in ages,' Francisco would complain. 'It's driving us apart.'

Laura shrugged.

'I just feel totally shattered tonight, utterly drained,' she murmured.

'It will pass. Come to bed.'

'I said "No",' Laura insisted. 'Didn't you hear me?'

'I think you're going a bit far, Laura.'

'What do you mean "going a bit far"? In what direction?'

'We can't go on like this.'

'I agree.' Laura lowered her head and sat hunched and huddled in her chair. 'Let's put an end to this nightmare once and for all. Let's call a lawyer.'

'No, no . . .' Francisco went over to her, a look of powerlessness in his eyes. 'I didn't mean that.'

And Laura, thinking that the moment had come for her to begin taking care of herself, looked at him scornfully.

'You never say what you mean, Francisco,' she said in a soft, lazy voice, her words like a singsong refrain strung like beads on the air, 'and you never mean what you say. But since I doubt very much that you've got anything to say at all, how could you?'

Later on, she went to sleep in the children's bedroom, ready for the children they had never had, but whom they had been prepared to welcome from the moment they got married. Francisco watched TV for a while before going to bed. When he finally slipped between the sheets, he pulled the top one up over his head, and wept a little and gnawed at the pillow.

But his life took a different direction one afternoon when he was strolling in the Retiro gardens, with nothing better to do than throw pebbles at the ducks from the jetty of the boating lake, and his eyes met those of the little man. A small, wrinkled man, with no hope or life in his eyes. Wearing a pair of green trousers a few sizes too big, and a sour, miserable expression on his face – almost etched on it with a knife, you might say.

Skeletons in the cupboard

Happiness does not consist in joy or lust, in laughter or in mockery – which are the companions of frivolity – it resides more often in a sad firmness and constancy.

Marcus Tullius Cicero, *The Nature of the Gods*

'No, Mama, I haven't suddenly shot up – I'm forty-three years old,' said Jorge wearily, his lips brushing and moistening the mouthpiece of the phone.

'I'm sure you're not eating properly,' said his mother, at the other end.

Whenever she phoned, the first thing she said, after hearing her son's bored 'Hello', was: 'Jorge? Are you there?' And he sometimes felt like saying: 'No, I'm not, Mama. I've gone away.'

Though of course he never did.

'Then why are the new trousers I sent you in the post too short?' she enquired.

'It must be something to do with the brand,' said Jorge dispiritedly. 'Every brand seems to have its own ideas about what the word "size" means. And some make them shorter and some make them longer. That's all.'

'Are you sure you're getting enough to eat?'

'Yes, Mama, I'm sure. I'm a bit overweight actually, like most people these days.' He sighed, lying down on the sofa and stoically closing his eyes, meanwhile holding the phone clamped between neck and shoulder.

'You should eat better.'

'All right, Mama, I will.'

'You're just saying that to stop me worrying, but you've no intention of doing anything about it. It's very important to eat well, Jorge.'

'I know, I know. And I will eat well.'

'No, you won't.'

'I will, I will.'

'You won't, dear, I know you.' His mother uttered a small exclamation that came crackling down the line. 'You'll go on eating badly. As sure as two and two make five.'

'Two and two don't make five, Mama. Two and two make four.'

'Really?' There was a brief silence. 'Well, I wasn't far out, was I?'

'You're quite right, Mama. I should eat more fruit and vegetables. More soup and rice. More green things. But you know I don't have much time to cook. I have to eat out nearly every day.'

'Neither your life nor your meals have been right since that witch left you.'

'Now don't start, Mama.'

'All right, all right. . . I didn't mean to bring the subject up.' She cleared her throat, somewhat embarrassed. 'Anyway, leaving aside those two unimportant details, your life and your meals, how have you been since I phoned you last?'

She had phoned him two days ago.

'Oh, great. You shouldn't worry about me. What's the weather like in Santander? Has Papa been able to play any golf?'

'Of course he has. You know what he's like. It would take more than the elements to keep him shut up indoors.'

'Let him enjoy himself, now that he can.'

'He's always enjoyed himself. In fact, he's always arranged things so that he can do exactly what he wants.'

'And how are you?' asked Jorge, although he really didn't want

73

to ask his mother any such thing. He hated serving her up excuses on a plate in that stupid way. He immediately regretted having asked the question, but it was too late.

'Well, my right leg is a wreck, it's like an overcooked roast potato. My eyes can smell and hear, but I'm as blind as a bat when it comes to seeing anything more than half an inch away from my glasses. Not to mention other things, like freezing, for example.'

'Freezing?' groaned Jorge.

'Yes, freezing. You know how I've always loved *freezing* everything. I felt as safe as a little bear with all my provisions in. Having a freezer the size of a pirate's treasure chest made me feel secure, you know.'

Ah, yes. Jorge knew.

Some people discover one day that watching the rain makes them happy, others discover America or a gadget for de-pilling sweaters, and all these things can change people's lives. Long ago, Jorge's mother had discovered 'freezing'. For years she had frozen everything. Cheese, cream, oil. Carefully aged wine. Mineral water. All kinds of food and drink. Solid, liquid and gaseous. The half-alive and the (alas) terminally deceased. And so she would tell anyone who cared to listen. Freezing, for her, was like a major social coup.

She adored explaining in detail how she cooked vast quantities of food, even though there were only two of them at table (her and her husband) and even though they had a Cantabrian maid who had a golden touch when it came to stews. Whenever she wanted to introduce a little mystery into one of her long explanations of how to roast, brown, braise or marinade some foodstuff, she would always end up saying: 'And when I finished I had enough to feed twenty-five people – at least. So do you know what I did?' Then the other person, even after only a brief acquaintance, would venture the timid question: 'You didn't freeze it by any chance, did you, Olga?'

'So what's wrong with freezing, then? I thought you loved it,' said Jorge.

'I did until recently, yes. As you say, I loved it.'

'But you don't any more.'

'No, now I hate it. I like everything to be as fresh as possible. I'd change your father for a new model if I could, but even I know I've left it too late to do that.'

'Really? And what brought about this change?' Jorge hauled himself up off the sofa and shambled into the kitchen, still holding the cordless phone. He poured himself a glass of whisky and closed his eyes as he took his first sip.

He was afraid that, by the time this long-distance phone call with his mother was over, he would be completely drunk. Not that he was an alcoholic, it was just that his mother aroused in him a peculiar kind of anxiety that could only be overcome by a little light stoicism and a cheerful surrender to his dipsomaniac tendencies.

'Nowadays we don't really know *what* we're eating,' said his mother grimly. 'They feed farm animals on the most dreadful stuff and give them antibiotics instead of water, so that they don't die of cancer and things before being slaughtered.'

'But what's that got to do with anything?' Jorge felt obliged to ask. 'What's the connection between that and freezing food?'

'The other day, I saw a TV programme about the Yeti, the Abominable Snowman. There he was, a healthy young chap who had spent years and years frozen in the ice up in the mountains. And he looked *awful* . . .'

When he finally hung up, Jorge had a splitting headache which he didn't know whether to blame on the whisky or his mother.

He went over to the bathroom and opened the door. He approached the toilet bowl and cast a drunken, nostalgic glance at the toilet paper. Above it hung a little ceramic notice that his wife had bought in a bazaar. It was one of the few things that had fallen to him in the sharing out of their joint property. 'Use in moderation. It's your responsibility' declared the wretched notice that she had suspended from a pink cord above the toilet paper in the main bathroom of the house they had bought together in the country. Its pathetic advice was now on show in Jorge's pokey little Madrid bathroom.

He sat down on the seat and, when he had finished, was seized by a kind of obscure, wasteful, anti-ecological fury, and used up nearly the whole roll.

He pulled the chain three times and then went back into the living room. This did not take him long, because his was a small apartment, barely sixty square metres. It was already decorated and furnished when he rented it, and he was beginning to grow bored with seeing the same old pastel-coloured pictures, reproductions of graceless watercolours, framed in black plastic and hanging from the walls, looking rather ashamed of themselves, but neatly lined up, all in a row.

Perhaps he should buy a painting from Ulysses, Jorge thought suddenly. He would suggest it the next time he saw him. They were friends, after all, and Ulysses could probably let him have something a bit special. That way he would have something nice and lively to brighten up that succession of framed landscapes and anodyne, almost colourless bits of furniture that made him feel he was the only strident thing in the apartment, the only thing capable of movement and warmth.

What a good idea! Why hadn't he thought of it before? He would buy a painting from his friend Ulysses. Even, while he was about it, two.

He sat down at the small table that served as his office, turned on his laptop, clicked on Netscape and went to his Bookmarks.

Honestly. . . He disapproved of both his desire and his boldness, but really, it was no big deal. There was no reason to make a drama out of it. It wasn't as if he had any skeletons in the cupboard.

What did he do, after all. . .just spent every free moment he had visiting the Victoria's Secret website – panties, *culottes*, thongs and bras, pretty but cheap, and so affordable – or else dropping in on a highly amusing lesbian chatroom he had discovered a few months ago . . .

That was all.

It wasn't so very bad.

True, he might be suffering from False Lesbian Syndrome, but was he hurting anyone by spending a couple of hours every day chatting to other girls, passing himself off as a violently Sapphic buxom blonde?

Jorge thought not.

He switched on the TV with the remote control and on the screen appeared the David Feiss cartoon series *Cow & Chicken*. With the foolish, familiar background noise coming from the TV, he felt less alone, more confident, and ready to pretend brilliantly, to lie as sincerely as possible.

'Hi, I'm Marta, and today I feel so horny and so dirty that I could write lovely poems about my girlfriend's bum or make love for hours at a time just with my mouth, and bound hand and foot. I think you're all a lot of gutless whores too scared to come to my apartment and share with me my wickedest dreams. Or to go out into the street and let people see what you are. I think you're all talk and that, in fact, you hide away like timid little mice. You just have to count the number of personal ads in the magazines: "Boy seeks boy" – 84 ads. And beside that, "Girl seeks girl" – 4 ads. Either there are fewer of us lesbians around or we're far more cowardly. So, come on, show your faces, if you've got what it takes!' wrote Jorge and sent the message off to the chatroom.

He thought he should go to the fridge and get himself a cold beer and some olives before things got lively, before six or seven irate lesbians responded, as furious as young girls whose plaits he had given a good tug.

They should prepare themselves for more. This was just the first of a long string of insults he intended firing off.

He would give those dirty sows something to think about.

They were so sweet, so innocent . . .

He really loved them.

He enjoyed making them angry.

He hadn't had such a good time since he used to play rule-free soccer at school, apart from the few times he had coincided with that little man who used go to Vili's Academy. A fragile, tormented fellow who aroused the same feelings as a lizard – defenceless, lame and frightened – arouses in a snotty-nosed, eleven-year-old sadist armed with a lighter and a penknife.

When he was tired of 'chatting', and having failed to get a date with some sweet lesbian eager to be redeemed by a real man, he switched off the computer and the television and pondered the subject of his ex-wife.

Whenever he got a bit drunk, he always ended up thinking about her.

Carmen and Jorge had separated over a year ago, but for him, the separation was still as painful as it had been on the first day.

According to Jorge, long marriages – his parents' marriage was a case in point – could be defined in the same strategic terms as the military policy MAD, which stands for Mutually Assured Destruction.

The MAD policy had its absurd paradigm in the character of Dr Strangelove, played by Peter Sellers in the Stanley Kubrick film that Jorge so admired.

This was the policy that got Moscow and Washington to build

thousands of nuclear warheads during the Cold War. The idea was that a nuclear world war could be prevented by a process which guaranteed that – regardless of who started the war – the two rivals would both be destroyed, so there would be no winning side, just two losing (or rather obliterated) sides. Thus security depended on maintaining a balance of nuclear terror. Peace was guaranteed. A tense, icy peace reigned, but it was still peace.

It worked perfectly, in exactly the same way as long marriages did, thought Jorge. As long as he and Carmen – his ex-wife – practised a matrimonial MAD policy, things worked. Of course they did. Until one of the parties changed, and the situation became completely destabilized. That was his domestic version of the collapse of the Berlin Wall. The terrible consequences of this tense arrangement were then exposed to view: a broken marriage, an extremely expensive quickie divorce and thousands of resentments about to explode, like warheads scattered all over the planet waiting – when least expected – to fall into the unpredictable hands of some crazed megalomaniac.

He thought of Jorgito with a mixture of tenderness and unease. Because, of course, the worst thing was that Jorgito was caught up in the middle of this family cataclysm.

Jorge went back into the living room. He picked up the phone, which he had left on the TV, and dialled his ex-wife's number.

'Hi, it's me,' he said.

'Who's "me"?' asked Carmen.

'Who do you think? It's Jorge! I pay the mortgage on the house you're living in, remember?'

'Oh, hi.'

'Where's Jorgito?' Jorge asked. There was mingled envy and mistrust in his voice.

'He's outside, playing,' Carmen explained patiently.

'Outside? What do you mean "outside"? Outside what?'

'Outside. In the garden.'

'In the garden?' He was horrified. He gazed out of his one living-room window against which the rain was beating fiercely. 'Haven't you seen the news?' He went over to the window, in a state of shock. 'Sixty-knot winds in Rías Bajas. And torrential rain and storm clouds all over the place! Everywhere!'

'Didn't Rías Bajas used to be in Galicia or somewhere?' asked Carmen. 'Let me remind you that we live on the outskirts of Madrid, on the banks of the Jarama.'

'Yes, but. . .isn't it raining there?'

'A little.'

'How little?'

Carmen seemed annoyed.

'I don't know! A little!'

'And you let Jorgito go out at night in the pouring rain! He'll catch something!'

'As you know, he likes rolling around on the lawn.'

'I don't care what he likes. It's cold and windy, it's pouring with rain, and he shouldn't be out at this time of night. I just hope that next week, when I come to pick him up, he's not ill, because if he is . . .'

'He won't be ill. He'll be perfectly all right.'

'I can't believe you let him outside while the second Flood is taking place. I can't believe it, Carmen. I don't expect such behaviour from you. Life hasn't prepared me for such things.'

'He was whining and wanting to go out, so I simply opened the door,' explained Carmen.

'You're just incredible!' Jorge was furious. 'You treat Jorgito as if he's a dog!'

Carmen's long, weary sigh came to him down the line as if she had just breathed right into his ear.

'He *is* a dog!' she replied slowly.

Jorge suppressed a howl.

'Aha! I might have known. And is that any excuse?' He gripped the handset hard and roared down it: 'He may well be a dog, but he's not just any dog. He's Jorgito, remember? He's our dog. A very special white West Highland terrier. My Jorgito. And if you don't treat him properly, I'll have something to say about it. The courts made it very clear. I have the right to see him alternate weekends and half of all holidays. I can decide on important matters regarding his health, education and diet. And I'm telling you, Carmen, you go and call him into the house this instant. And make sure you dry him properly so that he doesn't catch cold! I'm perfectly within my rights. So go and do it now.'

When he got divorced from Carmen, Jorge had managed to get the judge to give him visiting rights to the dog. (Carmen and he had never had children.)

'All right,' she said. 'I'll call him in now. Anything else?'

Jorge was filled by a sudden, spontaneous lassitude. His legs went weak. He was tired and had had a terrible day. His head ached. He missed Jorgito. And he missed Carmen too, especially Carmen. He could imagine her sitting by the fire, or lying with her legs up on the sofa; he could imagine her slightly sleepy, freckled face, her wide hips sheathed in a pair of nice, warm tracksuit bottoms. She was a bit broad in the beam, agreed, but then he liked his women like that. He preferred the ones who looked as if they had a large matronly woman inside them fighting to get out and kill off the would-be top model and reclaim their round, flaccid place in the world. He much preferred them to those silicone-breasted, hard-buttocked women in the gym. Carmen was large and comfortable. As welcoming as a good home. She had very white teeth which looked as if they had been painted with Tippex every morning, rather than cleaned with ordinary toothpaste. She was a calm, curvaceous redhead, who recycled all her glass and paper, and when

81

summer came, ate ice creams, smiled and enjoyed life out in the open air.

He missed her *so* much.

'No, nothing else,' he said, feeling calmer now. 'What are you up to? If you don't mind my asking, of course.'

'Oh, I was just reading a bit before going to bed.'

'That's a coincidence,' he lied. 'I was reading as well, just before I phoned you.'

'Oh, yes? And what were you reading?'

'Well, a book . . .' spluttered Jorge. 'A story. It's about a woman who meets a fantastic man, but then he leaves her for someone else, and she commits suicide. Or maybe it's the other way round.'

'H'm, sounds interesting.'

'Oh, it is.'

'Anyway, I'll go and call Jorgito in now.'

'Yes, do that.'

'Goodnight.'

'Goodnight.' Jorge slowly put down the phone.

For a few seconds, he considered his existential situation. It wasn't as if he was asking for very much. He just wanted to lead a simple life full of small pleasures. That was all he had ever wanted. Nothing more. Instead, he had a hideous rented apartment, an old Barbie doll left over from Carmen's girlhood, and a tiny, punctilious wound – difficult to locate precisely inside him – which he seemed to be constantly inflicting upon himself.

He rubbed his face. He noticed that his neck was stiff and the roof of his mouth was sore. He needed to sleep for a few hours. He had drunk too much.

He picked up the doll from her usual place on top of the television, grabbing her roughly by her hair, and walked unsteadily over to the bathroom.

Watching the sparrows

The man who can talk to himself will not seek conversation with anyone else.

Marcus Tullius Cicero, *Tusculan Disputations*

October began and the weather barely changed.

The end of summer had been icy cold and the autumn gusted down the streets of Madrid, carrying before it drops of merciless and occasionally hail-bearing drizzle. The population seemed to have gone into some form of abrupt, personal hibernation. Urban life, in all its intensity, had slowed down in the same disquieting way in which certain chemical processes in laboratory experiments slacken their pace at precisely the moment when the person inducing those processes has given up all hope and merely waits, absorbed, idly presaging disaster, for a final violent descent into nothingness.

But it was Wednesday night in Madrid, and Vili's Academy was full of aficionados of happiness, of volunteers fleeing dull, soulless homes to cluster together around the philosopher's warmth.

La pensée console de tout?

Outside in the streets, the pavements smelled of pounding rain, and the bonnets of cars drummed beneath the liquid shrapnel of the storm.

The autumn, bringer of fruits, was thus pouring out its abundance over the city.

'You haven't got, you haven't got!' cried Vili, and everyone present watched him expectantly. He pointed at the small, slender person of Irma, who was standing up next to her chair. 'All you do is complain about what you haven't got, Irma! To look at you, no one would think that you lacked for so many things. What I see when I look at you is a capable, healthy, even beautiful young person. What can you possibly lack? Another hand perhaps? But what would you want with another hand?'

'We're all looking for perfection,' said Irma by way of an excuse. 'We all want to go a little further each day. We want a bit more and then another bit more. That, it seems to me, is progress.'

'Progress!' growled Vili softly. 'Do you really believe that progress exists?'

'Yes.'

'And how would you define the concept of progress?'

'It's an advance. It's something that makes things better over time.'

'Better for whom?'

'For everyone.'

'For everyone? Even for the five-year-old orphan, covered in nits and sores, who, even as we speak, is scrabbling about on some rat-infested rubbish dump in Lima, Peru? Or do things, perhaps, not get very much better over time for him?'

Irma pursed her lips, feeling awkward and somewhat troubled. Her neck went red and her shoulder blades relaxed. She was slightly embarrassed. She didn't like Vili using such arguments. It reminded her of her mother and of the catechism, of organized remorse as a form of moral control, of religion at its most antiquated. It smacked of repression and guilt.

And that is what she told him.

'All right. Let's forget about the little boy, but don't let's forget that he exists,' replied Vili regretfully. 'Because if progress is a general law that only fails in particular cases, then it doesn't convince me. It doesn't seem to me to be a real advance.' He paused and got up from his seat only to sit down again. 'And that is just in the sense of material prosperity, because as regards spiritual prosperity, do you really think, Irma, that human nature is so very different from what it was five, ten or even twenty centuries before Christ? I certainly don't. I think that we are the same as the human beings of yesteryear. Weak, tragic, violent, pathetic creatures with the same unhealthy penchant for suffering. Where is the progress in that?'

'Perhaps in our desire for that progress to exist, perhaps that is an advance.'

'I have no objections to that.'

'In our continued search . . .'

'Fine. But what are you searching for, Irma?' asked Vili, his eyes half-closed, as he chewed the top of his biro.

'I'm searching for my own private paradise,' said Irma. 'And in my private paradise there is a lot of love. It's full of love. But, above all, there is well-being, which, nowadays, means that there is money. That is my paradise, and that's why I still keep desperately searching for it. That's what I fight for every day.'

'You're searching for it desperately, searching for your own paradise, but why? What's wrong with our own little inferno down here? Do you know anything else? Do you know anything better?' Vili studied the faces around him.

'No-o . . .' the other people present said in a murmur.

'I know it from my dreams,' said Irma, who was beginning to feel uncomfortable, although not as yet unbearably so. 'It exists in my dreams.'

'Ah, but dreams are just dreams, isn't that right, Irma?'

'Yes, Vili, but they're beautiful.'

'Of course, but life, even without love and without money, is beautiful too, hadn't you noticed? Life itself, stripped bare, is the most beautiful and the best thing that could happen to us.'

'Not to me.'

'Not to you, eh? And who are you?' asked Vili.

'A woman,' answered Irma. Her platinum blonde hair glowed almost phosphorescent.

'And what is a "woman"?'

'A rational animal?' she asked, slightly hesitantly.

'Even she has her doubts,' whispered Jorge to the complete stranger next to him. (Ulysses was not there. Telemachus had a cold.)

'Is that all? Just a rational animal?' Vili sat up in his seat, a mocking smile on his lips, but with just a hint of camaraderie.

Irma glanced around at the other people, looking first to one side and then to the other. Everyone was looking at her, and although she didn't feel in the least embarrassed, she was starting to be aware of their eyes fixed on her, and this was preventing her from concentrating properly.

'Animal. Rational. And mortal,' concluded Irma, uttering a sigh of relief when she saw Vili nodding.

'And what use is your rationality? From whom does it differentiate you?'

'From the other animals, I suppose.'

'Including men!' yelled a female voice at the back of the room which Irma could not identify.

The audience was listening reverently to the dialogue between teacher and pupil despite the pounding rain and the wind rattling the window with noisy, pitiless scorn.

'From the other animals . . .' Vili paused to think, and made a few theatrical gestures with his hand, stroking his chin and then scratching his head. 'So the best you can do if you don't want to resemble the other animals and want to preserve the difference that exists, you say, between you and the wild beasts, all you can do is not behave like them. Don't behave like a she-goat or like a hyena. Don't behave like a goose or a dog or a sheep. Epictetus said that we are behaving exactly like sheep whenever we're moved by our stomach or by sex, when we allow ourselves to be governed by chance, when we behave in an indifferent or underhand manner. When we behave like that, then we are like sheep and we despoil the man, or, in your case, the woman, because we lose our rationality, Irma.'

'Oh, I often lose mine. It's just that there are things in the world I find hard to bear, Vili.'

'Really? And what do those things make you feel?'

'Anger, I suppose,' said Irma with a shrug.

'Anger. Ah, anger! When we are moved by anger, evil or violence, then we are behaving exactly like wild beasts. And some kill or beat their wives. Others smash plates and glasses because they're furious. Some of us are great murderous beasts, and others, who aren't quite up to it, are small, vicious beasts who take it out on the crockery and smash it to smithereens because we can't do anything else.' Vili opened wide his arms and examined Irma for a few seconds. 'Are you one of those small, malicious beasts, Irma, or are you a terrifying, bloodthirsty beast?'

'Oh, a small one probably.' She wasn't ashamed to admit it, for during the past few years she had done a lot of mental exercises and now found it easy to forgive herself for any venial errors committed – for there were no grave ones – and no longer allowed herself to be gratuitously weighed down by the lowering, baseless, omnipresent guilt of something like original sin. Now she was almost an expert in self-forgiveness. 'Small, but determined.'

'So, you're not a woman. At least not always.'

'Perhaps,' she agreed. 'Perhaps not always.'

'So why then would you have us believe that you're Jewish, when, in fact, you're Egyptian? Why do you want us to think you're blonde, when you're dark? Why do you tell us you're a rational woman, when you yourself have just admitted that you are, from time to time, a small wild beast?'

'Because I try to be!' said Irma vehemently. 'I try to be a good woman, an honest mortal; I try to make sure that an awareness of my own mortality doesn't prevent me from being rational at every moment of the day. I also try to have some love and some money in my life, but since we live in a brutal world, it's really hard to get the things I need.'

'Yes, possibly. Perhaps it is a brutal world out there . . .' Vili pondered for a moment, scrutinizing the greyish linoleum on the floor. 'So, according to you, we live in a cruel world?'

'Oh, yes.'

'I'm quite sure you're right, Irma, I'm sure the world is like that, of course it is, if we accept that it's full of people, like you, who are prepared to behave like wild beasts,' concluded Vili slowly.

The cockroach was already in existence when the dinosaurs became extinct. It didn't seem possible that so much time could have passed and that there the disgusting creature still was, an impassive, unmoving, repellent witness to Earth's obscure history. Would it watch us disappear too, we humans, as happened with the great saurians? Irma didn't doubt this for an instant.

She gazed down in disgust at this swarthy example of the Madrid cockroach. It was sidling nervously across the kitchen floor, having been surprised amongst the crumbs fallen from the seafood sandwich that Andros, her Greek boyfriend, had doubtless thrown together for his afternoon snack.

'Well, *you* won't live to see it,' she said, smiling cruelly at the bewildered insect. 'You won't live to see the end of the human race. Or even mine.'

When she squashed it with her boot (Seville leather, 3½-inch heels), she heard what sounded like a faint moan – although she might have been imagining it – followed by a feeble ker-runch. All that was left on the tiled floor was a sticky stain, a blackish, saffron-coloured pap, as if it were the remains of a small, sobbing quince crushed to death in the prime of life.

She cleaned it all up with paper napkins which she then threw into the bin. She washed her hands thoroughly. She disliked killing anything, even flies. Death seemed to Irma too surreptitious for human dignity, but she could not bear cockroaches. When it came to choosing between death and a cockroach, she always chose death, especially since it was, after all, only an insect, and she had the feeling that the act of killing an insect was something very minor and of not the slightest importance.

Although she wasn't always entirely sure. No, not always. Were the deaths of an insect and a person comparable? She was pretty sure that the death of a worm, for example, paled into insignificance beside, let's say, the death of a child. And yet sometimes . . .

Irma did not know if it was possible to compare the death of an animal with that of a human, or whether it should be the other way around. On the one hand, you ran the risk of raising the sanctity of life to ridiculous heights, and, on the other, of profaning it in the most abject, indecent way possible.

No, no, no. There was no room for doubt: caught between a laughable, albeit painful fact – the demise of an insect – and having to put up with the insect, she preferred to apply her heel to the spine of the creature in question and forget all about such animistic nonsense. Just as she did not hesitate when choosing between Shakespeare and Walt Disney. She always chose the latter, of course. Although, sometimes . . .

Irma could possibly have shared her kitchen with a cockroach. Who knows, the cockroach might have turned out to be good company. At least cockroaches know how to take care of themselves from a very early age, not like a child.

And speaking of children, Irma would like to have had a child. She still would, even though, to be honest, she was fed up to the back teeth with the children she looked after every day at the crèche where she worked from eight in the morning until five in the afternoon. But her own child, she was sure, would be different. Small, helpless, precious. Hers.

Thinking about death and children made her remember her own mother. She hadn't thought about her for a couple of weeks, until that evening's discussion with Vili. She poured herself a glass of mineral water – chilled with a few tap-water ice cubes – and added a squeeze of lemon.

She went into the living room, took off her boots and lay down on the sofa without even turning on the lights. She felt good in the darkness, which was broken only by the whitish glow of the lightning zigzagging across the rooftops, growing feebler and paler as the storm moved off.

Her mother had had an enormous influence on Irma's life. Yes, mothers always play an important role in anyone's biography, even when the mother is absent by virtue of being dead or simply because she has abandoned her child. However, it seemed to Irma that hers had been a special, almost casebook study.

She huddled up on the sofa and tried to recall her mother's frowning, aggressive face, her harsh, darting glances. Her Mama had taken her childhood and pared it down to the bone. Irma still felt bruised. When she was little and used to pray in silence, she never said, as other children did: 'Lord, have mercy', instead she would concentrate hard and ask tremulously: 'Mother, have mercy'. But mercy was not her mother's prime virtue. True, she never punished Irma by beating her or shutting her up in a dark room, or by using any of the usual, antiquated, sado-pedagogical correctives. She wasn't, thank heavens, that kind of person.

No, she was worse, thought Irma with a smile, in the nebulous night that was flooding the apartment. The earliest recollection Irma had of her mother was now only a faint impression, full of darkness and adorned with words that had climbed up her memory like a vine scrabbling up the defenceless wall of consciousness. It was the image of a grave-faced woman clutching a cast-iron saucepan full of green beans and bearing down on the child Irma had been and who was sitting very still on a kitchen chair. As a girl, she had enjoyed playing football – although everyone said it was a sport for boys and that she was a tomboy for wanting to play it – and that afternoon, during an improvised game in the street, she had slipped and fallen and grazed her right knee.

'You could have broken your leg! And have you any idea of the complications that can set in after you've broken a leg? Of course you haven't! You could have been crippled for life!' said her mother, waggling the saucepan up and down in front of Irma's terrified eyes. 'I would rather see you buried than see you with a broken leg,' she concluded, and returned the saucepan to the stove.

Irma, notwithstanding her liking for football, had been a delicate, sensitive child, and when, at thirteen, she had her first period, it did her no good at all to be told tartly by her mother what the blood and the uncomfortable feeling between her legs meant. 'I'd rather see you dead than pregnant' was how she summed up that painful, crucial female event. Irma heard all this, biting her nails and thinking how red and terrible the flux was that had spoiled her new knickers, almost as red and terrible as her mother's eyes.

Maybe the reason Irma still had no children, despite having been married for three years, was because her mother was still alive. The woman was, and would continue to be, as sad and dramatic as a natural disaster. She had the same effect on her daughter as an earthquake in India, or the unexpected sight on television of a dead foetus discarded amongst the rubbish in a plastic bag that still contained the sales slip from the last purchase made. Her mother's vision was as monochromatic as a blind man's. She was a bird that had never been able to fly. Her sole contribution to the world had been her sour face, not to mention her alarming and eccentric preference for the death of others over any event that might imply change, difficulty, joy or even simply living one's life. 'I'd rather have to prepare you for your grave tonight than see you in a discotheque at four in the morning surrounded by whores and no-good drug addicts,' was a threat regularly hurled at Irma during her adolescence, whenever she spent Saturday evening out with her girlfriends.

Irma, needless to say, did not go out much or have a great deal of fun during her adolescence and early youth. She managed to escape from her village, in the province of Cáceres, and from her mother's baleful influence, only after a year-long engagement and, finally, marriage, when she moved with her husband to Madrid, where he was stationed. Her now ex-husband was a sergeant in the Civil Guard. A good man, honest and irreproachable, but, alas, she did not love him.

When, one day, she went to see her mother during the Easter holidays, she mentioned that her marriage was on the rocks, and her mother – always true to herself – said: 'I'd rather have to visit your grave than see you divorced and know that everyone here was talking about you.'

Irma was nearly thirty; more than that, she was beginning to feel tired. Thirty years of accumulated maternal discouragement can weigh very heavily on one pair of shoulders, especially on such small shoulders as hers; so she got up from the brown imitation leather sofa, smoothed her skirt, went over to the sideboard in the living room and picked up her handbag where she kept her car keys. She looked at her mother and smiled at her silently, sweetly. She noticed that, outside the window, dozens of sparrows were fluttering about in a joyful whirl of wings and canticles, perhaps celebrating the arrival of spring; and she thought fleetingly how sad it would be if one of them were to die at that moment, in the midst of all that dizzy splendour and of the instinctive pleasure of being alive.

'All right,' Irma said to the woman, who was watching her with staring eyes anaesthetized by tension. And with a soft sigh, Irma murmured: 'I'll see you in the cemetery, then, Mama.' She went out into the street in her slippers, got into her car and drove back to Madrid, without even bothering to take with her the luggage she had packed to spend the week at her mother's house.

That had been two years ago. She hadn't seen or phoned her mother since. And her mother hadn't phoned her either. She got divorced from her husband and began making her own way in the world, with just what she earned from her work at the crèche. Surviving hadn't been easy. She took a sip of the lemon-flavoured water and toasted her mother, raising her glass in the air, intoxicated by the tenuous solitude there amongst the shadows of the room.

She had met Andros, her boyfriend, in a very noisy discotheque in Atocha, packed with an extraordinarily motley crew of people (Cubans, North Africans, South Africans, Poles and various other immigrants; groups of mature gentlemen from Madrid and environs, eager to pick up a nice thirty-year-old; unmarried office workers and hostesses; Spanish legionnaires on a night out . . .). It had been a Saturday, five months ago. She went there with Katia, her colleague at the crèche. That night her friend was dressed the way Madonna used to dress in the eighties, with a black leather bomber jacket, several tortoiseshell rosaries slung around her neck as necklaces, and a blue-grey top covered in sequins that twinkled so much they looked as if all the stars of some tiny, unstable universe had been squeezed on to her front. Irma, on the other hand, had put on a suit made of glossy brown poplin, with a waisted jacket and very narrow lapels. Her skirt reached just below her knees, and she was wearing a pair of spike heels that were absolutely killing her.

Katia was confiding in her about something or other when a man came over to them. He had a shaven head, although he had clearly shaved it to disguise his baldness, rather than to appear trendy. There were clusters of little black dots behind his ears and on the back of his neck, where a few hairs were still summoning up the courage to step out into the light of the capillary desert that was his skull.

'I thought when a man loved you, he would want to try and make you happy, but it turns out he's the sort that thinks loving you means making you cry. You know, the kind who beats you up when his football team loses, and then says that he's only doing it for your own good, as if the bloody stitches they give you at the hospital when they sew up your wounds were reward points at the bloody supermarket. Do you know what I mean?' Katia bawled at Irma, trying to make herself heard above the musical racket filling the place.

'Hello, sweetheart.' The bald man sat down next to Irma. He was about forty and was holding a glass in one hand and a cigarette in the other.

'How wrong I was,' Katia went on. 'There was me thinking that a guy who doesn't lay a finger on you except to take off your knickers, with your consent of course, or to give you a Thai massage, is rather nice company for a girl. And now I learn from this moron that real love is being, oh, I don't know, like one of those punch bags they have in boxing gyms, do you know what I mean?'

'And what did you say when he hit you?' asked Irma.

'Can I fill you up?' said the man who had just sat down next to her.

'Well, I didn't really *say* anything. I was out of that place like a shot as soon as he'd finished his poxy little speech and had turned his back for a moment. I haven't seen him since. And I don't want to either.'

'I said, can I fill you up,' said the bald man, lightly touching Irma's left arm.

Her feet were hurting and she didn't like the look of the intruder's face.

'You just try it and I'll slap *you* round the chops too!' Irma screamed at him.

'Look, I said "Can I *fill* you up" not "Can I *feel* you up",' said the stranger, much offended, and getting awkwardly to his feet.

'Coming from you, it's all the same, you dirty swine. Piss off!'

'There's no need to be so rude!'

'I haven't even started yet, dickhead!'

'Oh, I don't know,' Katia closed her eyes for a moment and seemed genuinely upset, 'with a man like that, with a real bastard like that I mean, you feel so . . .' she thought a little, all the while gesturing extravagantly as if trying to draw down from the air the words she was looking for, 'with a guy like that, you feel so . . . so . . . what's the female version of impotent?'

When the dazed Lothario had disappeared from view, swallowed up by the mass of restless bodies jigging frenetically to the rhythm of the music, the two friends stopped talking, looked at the dance floor and, in unison, sipped their blood marys through their straws.

Then Andros appeared in their field of vision. He sat down on an unoccupied stool, a couple of yards from where the two women were sitting. Irma gazed at him with satisfaction. He had dark, curly hair and, although Irma could not see his face very clearly, she could, nevertheless, sense a delicious symmetry and perhaps just a hint of an unusual masculine gentleness about his chin. Without quite knowing why, she imagined herself rubbing her cheek against his, and the thought provoked a pleasurable giddiness in her stomach.

He took out a cigarette and patted his pockets in search of a light. Katia also happened to be lighting up just then, and so the young man came over to them. He indicated Katia's lighter and his cigarette. She distractedly lit it for him.

'Δατ'ς βερι καïντ οβ γιου, θανκς', he said.

'God, I think I must be going deaf,' said Katia, turning to her friend. 'What did this nice young man say?'

'I haven't the faintest idea,' replied Irma, but she bestowed on Andros her most charming smile.

Irma and Andros had scarcely been apart since that night. At first, there were a few misunderstandings between them because, as Irma soon discovered, the only language the young Greek spoke was Greek. He couldn't even say '*Buenos días*' or '*Adiós*'. When they met, he had been in Madrid for a mere twelve hours, and it was his first time abroad. With much difficulty she managed to establish that Andros worked as a cook at the Greek embassy. In a despairing moment, she had begun to suspect that this man, who only had to look at her to make her insides turn over with sheer pleasure, was an escapee from an insane asylum, and afflicted with some strangely melodious form of dyslexia.

However, once this confusion had been cleared up, Irma began to enjoy their state of verbal non-communication.

'You're gorgeous,' she would tell her boyfriend, cuddling up to him.

'Γιου αρ σοου μπιουτφουλ, αï λαïκ γιορ χερ, αï λαïκ γιορ μαουθ, αï λαïκ γιου, σαλ γουι μεïκ λοβ εγγεν?' he would reply.

'What do you fancy for lunch today?' Irma would ask, stroking his chin.

'Αϊντ λαϊκ του ιντροντιους γιου του μαϊ μπος. Χι γουιλ μπι σοου ενβιους. Χις γουαϊφ χας γκοτ ε μουστας!' suggested Andros in his warm, mysterious voice.

'Oh, really? Well, that's great, because that's exactly what I fancy too.' And Irma felt as happy by his side as a sparrow in springtime.

Sitting in her small living room, she remembered fondly the four months she had spent with the young Greek cook.

Andros could spend hours and hours talking to her without once arousing disquiet, anxiety or terror in her troubled child's heart. They recounted their lives and thoughts to each other without understanding a single word and yet, despite that, the air did not tremble with foreboding, presaging who knows what terrifying tragedies. No alarm bells rang, darkening Irma's mornings. Life, for once, was all mystery and joy.

Yes, theirs was the perfect relationship, Irma thought gleefully, because she and Andros – and this was no small thing – never quarrelled. They agreed because agreement was neither a condition nor a necessity. Since they had no word in common to describe agreement, it didn't even exist in the world they inhabited.

Yes, utterly perfect. A wonderful relationship. Or at least it had been until very recently, until, to be precise, the fateful night three weeks ago when Andros came home from work at midnight as he always did. Irma had been lying on the sofa, as she was now, dully watching a TV programme about sex and tranquillisers while she waited. He opened the front door with his set of keys, closed it again and smiled jubilantly. And there was nothing in his dark, round, smiling eyes that gave a hint of the cataclysm to come: his delightful, full lips contracted and stretched in the effort to form the awful sounds. Irma felt almost sucked in by them, drawn towards that tunnel of linguistic horror. She almost fainted and cried out as if she were being torn limb from limb by a murderer.

'Bue-nas no-ches, a-mor mí-o,' he said slowly and clearly. *Good evening, my love.* And he appeared to feel a certain childlike exultation or perhaps pride.

A home for Araceli

Someone once said to a wise man: 'I'm sixty years old,' and the wise man replied: 'You're referring, I presume, to the sixty years that no longer exist?'

Lucius Annaeus Seneca, *Philosophical Treatises*

How hard it is to resist flattery! Flattery will use any means at its disposal to achieve the aims of whoever is doing the brown-nosing. It exploits other people's weakness and depression, it even resorts to untruths (embellished with truths, of course). Araceli was wondering how she had allowed herself to be won over by such a simple, senile seduction technique, as cloudy as her eyes, as full of aches and pains as her old body. And yet she had. She had tried to place a door between herself and the flattery, but, as usual, she had left that door ajar. Anselmo, naturally, did not knock before coming in, he kicked the door open, thus breaking down her defences once and for all. Perhaps that was why Araceli had surrendered almost without a struggle.

She felt suddenly afraid, a subtle fear that tickled as it ran up and down her spine, just like the tremulous caress of a hand as decrepit as her own. She recalled some words which were now drifting about in her memory: 'If you want to fear nothing, think only that you have nothing to fear; look around you and you will see how little it would take to destroy you. Why fear an earthquake when a bit of phlegm could choke you?'

How much truth there was in those few words! So she, who

wanted to fear nothing, tried to fill herself with courage by thinking that there was nothing to fear, in the words of . . . well, she couldn't quite remember whose words they were. That was how it was these days: she would read something or hear it on the radio (only very rarely on television, a diversion more suited to old fools) and then the words would sail up and down inside her head until they finally ran aground and she could no longer remember where they came from; and she would find herself attributing to Flaubert a quote from Ronald Reagan and to Ronald Reagan a quote from Mickey Mouse. And who lost out most in the process? Why, Mickey Mouse, of course!

Anyway, what did it matter at her age if she couldn't necessarily remember the finer points, when the truth was that it took her such a long time to get up in the morning simply because she needed someone to give her a good reason to do so.

While she was thinking about her fear and her need to avoid that feeling, Anselmo was sitting opposite her in her room (she dreaded to think what some of the neighbours along the corridor would be saying at that moment), looking at her tenderly and smiling like an imbecile intent on displaying each and every one of his new teeth.

'God, those dentures!' she thought somewhat warily. 'I can even imagine what his skull will look like.'

At that moment, Anselmo started reciting some kind of poem or folk song or piece of doggerel. Who could say? She knew him well enough, though, to know that whatever nonsense he came out with was probably of dubious origin. 'When it comes to high fashion I don't have a clue but, Mariamanuela, is that dress really you?'

Anselmo again unfurled that broad, breathless smile of his. He obviously couldn't believe his luck at finding himself alone with Araceli in her bedroom. The door was locked, or, rather, as closed as any door in any old folks home ever can be, and they were sitting down facing each other, each shaken by very different feelings. They were both nervous, although they were doing their best to hide it.

'Regarding your letter . . .' Araceli cleared her throat and, leaving poetry aside for the moment, tried to begin a more or less coherent conversation with him. 'I really must thank you, it was very nice. All that business about you wanting to make curtains out of my eyelashes and how you'd like to bathe in the depths of my eyes is . . .' she coughed and took the opportunity to sigh deeply, to pause for breath, 'it's really very sweet of you, Anselmo.'

She studied him carefully over the top of her glasses. Arrogant and, in a way, valiant too. A plucked peacock in a pair of green terylene trousers and with eyes like two eager skylights. Anyway, she thought, having gone this far . . .

She wondered if there was still life in the life of an 83-year-old woman like her. She straightened up and gave her companion a shy smile.

Yes, there she was, sitting opposite a man ten years her junior. A man who claimed to love her madly – and, given their joint ages, 'madly' was the right word. There she was, sitting opposite a man who was doubtless hoping to be able to change position after half an hour of insignificant chatter. A man in her room. The only man she knew who could chew a natural yoghurt.

'Oh well. It's better than nothing,' she thought mischievously. 'At least he's a man. Not that you'd notice, mind; there's almost a yard and a quarter of material in his trousers from waist to crotch. At least he's alive, though. I can even hear him breathing.'

'Araceli, may I speak frankly?' he said. 'It seems only logical now that I've opened my heart to you and declared my love.'

'Of course, Anselmo, of course,' Araceli managed to say.

He stared down at his slippers for a few seconds and sighed.

'We're behaving like children, you know. We're both grown-ups.

And I love you,' he murmured, pressing one hand to his heart.

Was he asking her for something?

'Yes, you're quite right, that is how we're behaving, and we're certainly neither of us children any more.'

'I have the feeling you don't really like me enough, Araceli. But if that's the case and you're only stringing me along, I'd just like to say that, at our age, we really don't have much time to lose.'

She nodded and shifted awkwardly in her chair.

'You're quite right,' she said. 'We have medicines and pots and pans and tempers to lose. At our age one loses nearly everything. But time is something we don't have much of, either to lose or enjoy. You're quite right.'

Araceli did not want to appear to be a cold woman. Suddenly this was important to her. Her husband (she hoped God had taken pity on his soul, always assuming he had a soul) had been a notary. He was so dapper and glossy and attractive, he looked as if he were made of artificial ingredients. But in bed – she blushed to remember it – he was insatiable, so much so that it had begun to be a bit of a bore. One night, he reproached a surprised Araceli, who had just alleged a headache in order to avoid having to consummate the sacrament of marriage for the second time that day: 'You know, my dear, if you were ever to go to the Antarctic, the temperature would drop five degrees as soon as you set foot there.'

She suspected that he had a lover, possibly several. And it was probably her fault, because she was too cold.

The last thing Araceli wanted was for Anselmo to think she was a frigid old woman. Although, as regards her husband, it really didn't matter any more. She didn't think there was any point now in having regrets.

Anselmo made an old-fashioned bow which, given that he was sitting down, looked more like a spasm or an involuntary twinge brought on by persistent lower back pain.

'Excellent. I'm so glad you agree,' he said. 'So . . .'

'So . . . what?'

'Exactly. So . . .'

'I don't know what you mean.'

There are some hard women who have no sooner been wounded than they're healed. Araceli knew she was not that kind, although she would like to have been. She was the exact opposite, the sort who nurture a wound their whole life, not in order to help it heal, but to keep it open. At eighty-three, was it worth having an affair with a man whose stomach touched the walls before his hands did? Was it worth exposing oneself to the sorrows of love at an age when it's more important to look after your bladder than your conscience? And what if he went off with someone else afterwards? And what if he didn't like her breasts, which hardly deserved the name any more? And what if he wasn't satisfied with the way she moved? She wasn't as manoeuvrable as she had been at forty.

O to be forty again! It's odd how when you're young, you think you'll always wish you could stay twenty-five for ever, that you'll spend your life longing for that quarter-century. And yet, once you're past sixty, the age you remember with most pleasure is forty. When your body has ripened, like the fruits in season; when your brain works easily and rejects all the little things that cloud your spirit. Forty. Araceli would give all her sleeping tablets just to be forty again – even if only for a few hours.

'You know what I mean. It's absurd for us to start worrying about appearances now,' exclaimed Anselmo, and he stood up. Araceli started when she saw him coming towards her. 'Obviously we can't get married, because you'd lose your widow's pension, and, besides, it would hardly be appropriate, but we can . . . we can still . . .'

Araceli touched her wedding ring and looked at him very seriously. Anselmo stood beside her, tenderly took off her glasses, placed his lips on her ear and kissed her. It was a warm, soft, dry kiss, not full of the sort of sticky, refrigerated moistness that one might expect from the mouth of an old man with halitosis. It wasn't unpleasant, far from it. She even had the feeling, after receiving that kiss which melded so naturally with her rather worn, yellowish skin, that something in the world had changed for ever.

Araceli calculated that it was at least . . . well, it was years . . . thirty perhaps . . . even more . . . She'd been a widow since . . . Of course, she had never . . . Her husband . . . Oh, to hell with it.

When Anselmo offered his hand to help her out of the chair so that they could go over to the bed together, she noticed that he smelled good, as if he had prepared himself to pass inspection. His round, wrinkled face was smiling, and his teeth were barely visible. Even his breath smelled all right.

To be honest, she wasn't in love with this man – nor, it must be said, with any man – but making love with him (or whatever it was they had done) was not as pathetic or as awkward as Araceli had thought, although, of course, no one at the time would have mistaken them for movie actors, the sort who have long, slender legs and skin so bronzed and taut it looks as if their bodies have been coated in thin, shiny plastic. 'It's never too late to begin a career of liberation, promiscuity and wild abandon,' she thought with a chuckle, covering herself with the sheet.

Outside, the deluge, the furious deluge continued. The window positively sizzled with water as a salvo of liquid pellets struck the glass panes, which nevertheless let in a surprisingly grey, hostile glow.

Anselmo was sleeping like an angel. He wore a distinguished, circumspect expression. She was aware of his peaceful proximity in the bed, saw the comic bulk of his round belly and the bluish shadows under his closed eyelids. He wasn't even snoring. He could turn out to be an excellent companion. He barely seemed to be breathing. It was good to sleep with a man like that.

Perhaps she had been missing out on something during all those years of celibate, solitary widowhood. Company, perhaps. Conversation. The comforting certainty that old age was not something that only happened to oneself.

She moved tentatively nearer to Anselmo's body. Perhaps it wasn't too late. They would make a good team, they would joke about the puddings served in the dining room and would be the talk of the home. She would learn to smile with the same intensity and frequency as he did, and they would stroll around hand-in-hand, showing off their expensive dentures to the whole world.

She studied Anselmo's forehead, pearled with moisture, and struggled to sit up in bed. He still wasn't snoring. She could not even hear him breathing. His eyes were sunken, and almost all the colour had drained from his face, apart from those navy blue circles under his eyes.

'Oh God!' she cried. And as she feebly shook him, her hands trembled even more than usual. 'Anselmo, wake up! Wake up, wake up, wake up! Please, wake up!'

When Ulysses arrived at the home, Araceli was sitting in her armchair, as shrunken as a ball of yarn used time and again to knit and re-knit the same sweater. She looked small, sad and old, yet still capable of holding inside her a grief so profound it made her breathe more heavily.

'Hello, my dear,' she managed to say.

'Hello, Araceli. Are you all right?'

'No, of course I'm not, my dear.'

'Would you like to come home and live with me and Telemachus?'

She looked at him, and then, after a moment's hesitation, asked:

'Where is Telemachus? What have you done with him?'

'I phoned a friend of mine, Irma, who works with children, and asked if she'd stay with him at home while I came to fetch you.' Ulysses crouched down in front of her, took her hands affectionately in his and gave her a kiss.

He looked very noble and determined, Araceli thought, like one of those pedigree dogs whose hackles rise at the slightest change in the wind. Ulysses was a strong young man, quite remarkable really, although he did sometimes look overly solemn, even surly.

'Of course, of course . . . It's best if he doesn't come out in this weather.'

'Yes, and, as you know, he's had a bit of a cold too.'

'Yes, so you told me on the phone the other day.'

'Shall I help you pack your bags?'

'Bags?' asked Araceli, puzzled. 'Where are we going?'

'Home. With me. I've spoken to the manager and the doctor. I've got a taxi waiting outside.'

'I can't go home with you, my dear. I can't.'

'Why not?'

'I'd be a bother to you and the boy.'

'Yes, you would.'

'Well, then . . .'

'But what's life's without a bit of bother now and then?'

'Paradise?'

'I don't think so. Especially when the bit of bother can cook as well as you can. Come on. Wrap up warm, though. When we get home, you can help me make some croquettes for Telemachus.'

Araceli tried to stand up, reaching out her hand so that Ulysses could grasp it firmly and give her and her exhausted body the impetus to stand up.

'Anselmo's dead, did they tell you?'

'The nurse told me when she phoned.'

'Yes, he's dead. Do you remember how he was always smiling?' She leaned forwards, her shoulders rigid from the effort of getting out of the chair. 'Well, after he died, his smile disappeared. Completely. It disappeared completely.'

I have a fig tree

Philip wrote a letter to the Lacedaemonians threatening to lay siege to them on all sides, and they replied: 'What, and will you forbid us to die as well?'

Marcus Tullius Cicero, *Tusculan Disputations*

Mireia Amorós, seated regally in the centre of the small amphitheatre of chairs grouped around Vili, crossed her legs and shot a defiant look at Jacobo Ayala, who did not return it because he had been blind since birth.

'But I could . . . that is, I think it's quite possible. It seems perfectly logical to me,' she said with a snort. She had slightly protuberant eyes and used a pinkish foundation that gave her a rather strange appearance, as if her skin were made of chewing gum.

'Of course it seems logical to you,' bawled Jacobo, who tended to get overexcited . 'It's just that your idea of what's logical doesn't strike me as being very logical at all.'

'I think she's got a point, though. It could happen,' said Martín, who had only just turned twenty and sometimes accompanied his cousin Jacobo, acting as his guide through the now damp, slippery streets of the city. He spoke so modestly that his voice dropped a tone with each word.

Jacobo had brought a blind friend of his to the Academy for the first time, one Manolo Erice, whose eyes were constantly flicking from side to side, and who seemed to be scrutinizing everyone present with voluptuous interest and making them all feel terribly nervous, even though they assumed he could see nothing. Martín had brought them both, walking along between them, holding an umbrella, while they clung on to either arm. It occurred to him that it was lucky for them that he wasn't much of a drinker. Two blind men guided by a drunk through the slippery, sodden streets of central Madrid would not have been the best way of improving the flow of traffic.

'You're not going to start agreeing with her as well, are you?' Jacobo said to his cousin.

Martín shrugged.

Vili remained seated in his armchair. He had hardly said a word all evening. He seemed serious and abstracted, as if trying to decipher some coded message written on the smoke-filled air.

'Hang on a minute, Jacobo . . .' commented Manolo Erice, his neck swinging round so far and fast that everyone was afraid it might never stop turning. 'The lady's probably right. A generous heart has room enough for many great loves.'

'Oh, come off it!' exclaimed Jacobo sarcastically. 'You don't really believe that! You'd be lucky to find room enough for one love, and not even a great love either. That's quite enough for anyone. And that goes for her and for all of us who live in the broad light of night.'

Manolo cleared his throat, then said: 'But there isn't any light at night.'

'How would you know?' Jacobo retorted, with a scornful wave of his hand.

Mireia wrinkled her nose in annoyance. She couldn't understand what all the fuss was about. She was a grown woman. She was forty-three, for heaven's sake. She was the successful manager of a large branch office of a bank. She had chosen not to have children, although she didn't rule them out in the near future. If David, a homosexual and a man, had been able to do it, she didn't see why she shouldn't be allowed the same luxury. Was it forbidden by nature, religion or science? And if she couldn't have her own, she would adopt one of those malnourished children with dark, suspicious eyes, dying a slow death in some far-off country.

She had a right to make her own family, to have a family made in her own image. That was what God had done, although according to some people, the stories in the Bible were just so much ancient gossip torn to shreds by the passing of the centuries. Of course she had the right to live with her husband and her ex-husband under the same roof. When she divorced the latter, she did so on the best of terms, simply because of the new relationship that had arisen with her present husband. But they remained in touch. They still loved each other. They had lunch together and saw each other at least once a week, and always on public holidays and birthdays. She was there by his side when he lost his job – he was the manager of a big department store which suddenly went bankrupt and closed down, leaving more than four thousand unemployed, most of them mature people, stunned by what had happened and facing a very uncertain future on the job market. She lent him money. She encouraged him.

One day, when she saw that, despite all his efforts, he was getting nowhere, it seemed only natural to suggest to her husband that they invite him to stay with them for a while, until he got over this bad patch and found another job. Mireia's present husband worked under her at the bank (he was two rungs below her on the promotion ladder) and had known her ex for years. Her husband was a delightful man, tolerant and open-minded, with lovely pewter-grey eyes. He agreed at once, and so it was that Luis went to live with them. At first, it was just a temporary arrangement, but Luis was so attentive and affectionate that they grew fonder of him by the day. He did the washing and even ironed their underwear, placing it in the drawers all neatly folded and perfuming it with little lavender sachets made of linen. He made wonderful low-calorie meals (he had learned to cook while he was unemployed). Fresh pasta with lobster and shallots. Tender haricot beans with clams, almost fat-free. He dusted all the places that the cleaning woman never seemed to have time to tackle – under the television and round the door frames, and so they got rid of the cleaning woman. Luis took charge of the house and confessed that, for the first time in his life, he felt happy.

When she and Pedro (her husband) got home after work, the table was laid with an embroidered linen tablecloth and adorned with aromatic candles. Soft music would be playing in the background, and Bach provided the soundtrack to their evenings. It was not long before Mireia was sharing Luis's bed again. On the first occasion, she told herself it was out of gratitude to someone who, on a daily basis, was making her life easier and more pleasant. On the second occasion, she thought, well, it was just for old times' sake, but on the third, she felt overwhelmed by guilt. Guilt is greenish-grey in colour and burns like a bee sting in the very depths of the heart. But Pedro, her husband, wasn't in the least upset when she told him what had happened. 'The flesh is nothing but flesh, my love,' he said, looking at her sweetly with the slight squint that she had always found so irresistible. 'We spend our lives giving importance to things that aren't important at all, confusing the price of a pound of flesh with the value of a pound of soul.'

When Mireia told her best friend, her friend said: 'God, you're lucky. I really envy you. You've married a mystic – well, either that or a fool.'

Now the three of them lived under the same roof, happier than they had ever been. Mireia was convinced that this would be an excellent time to have a child, and that it really didn't matter which of her two husbands was the father. Luis could look after the child while she and Pedro worked. Surnames and genes were the least of it.

III

These were her major concerns at the moment, the goals on which she pinned her future happiness, and yet, when she had finally got up the courage to talk about them in public, an irrascible blind man, dishevelled and retrograde, had the nerve to call her immoral and to accuse her, and anyone else who thought like her, of not having room in her heart – basing himself on who knows what mysterious parameters of anatomical architecture – to give comfortable lodging to both her husbands.

That wretched man Jacobo had made her feel for a moment like Judith or Salome or some other lascivious pervert. Like a praying mantis who has suddenly turned into an atheist bulimic. She could almost hear the bells around her hips tinkling rhythmically in the air as she performed the lewd, pulsating movements of an old harpy.

She gave him a rancorous look. Jacobo had tiny eyes, filled with darkness, as if, over the years, someone had stashed all kinds of things away in them, until they had finally overflowed. He sniffed the air around him with the determined, eager curiosity of a terrier puppy. His nails were the colour of the inside of a very old kiln.

Blind or not, he was a boor. And he was so ugly too.

Mireia had always thought that ugly people, so as not to make themselves still more unpleasant, did their best to be really nice. But Jacobo disproved this theory. He obviously had no idea how hideous he looked, and clearly no one close to him had yet been brave enough to tell him. But then what can you expect from someone who believes that God made the night as a salve to the blind who resent the sighted?

'Oh, forget it,' said Mireia, feigning indifference. 'I don't want to get into a fight with anyone.'

'Well, I do, I want to fight!' cackled Jacobo. 'That's dialectics, that's life! In life you have to fight!'

'Yes, because it's life, but I've no intention of discussing questions of morality with you or with anyone else.'

'Of course not, because you know you'll lose, because what you're suggesting – one woman living with two men – is disgusting. It's as true now as it's always been.' Jacobo was breathing hard. 'Do you happen to know anyone who lives like that? Do you have a friend, perhaps, who lives with her present husband and her ex and goes to bed with them on alternate nights?'

Mireia had not told them that she was the woman she was talking about.

'That's none of your business, Jacobo,' she replied, thinking: 'And you're not bloody well going to find out either, you creep.'

Gabriela Losada put up her hand; she was a 28-year-old baker, blonde and sensual, with eyes the colour of aquamarine. 'Perhaps if it was a man living with two women, a Muslim for example, or a Mormon, no one would be so very shocked. In fact, there are some countries where it's legal,' she said. She had a low, attractive voice with a slight Andalusian accent.

'Absolutely!' shouted another woman. 'Men really are the limit. We women should all have at least one spare husband at home. What are we waiting for?'

'I didn't say that . . .' Jacobo shook his head angrily, not knowing to whom he should address his reply. 'The way I look at it . . .' He tried to explain, but the murmurings around him gradually increased in volume until they were a barely contained clamour.

Vili, who was still sitting in his chair saying nothing, stood up. He looked half bored, half ashamed. He had to shout in order to make himself heard. 'All right, all right . . . will you all just pipe down!'

When the shouting began to diminish, and most of the comments had petered out, he announced: 'We'll take a short break now and continue in about twenty minutes with those of you who want to stay a little longer. Otherwise, to those who are leaving now, see you next week.' He walked over to the chair where Ulysses was sitting in silence, listening with amusement to his friend Jorge Almagro.

Vili passed a group of people who were getting up and stretching, all the while talking, smiling and arguing or else frowning, as if they had been deeply wounded by the words of either Mireia or Jacobo respectively.

A depressed, lonely-looking man was still in his seat, next to Francisco de Gey. Francisco was a man permanently at odds with the world, and always had the look of someone studying the scene of a recent crime in which all those around him were potential suspects. He appeared, thought Vili, to be one of those people who find it very hard to receive affection.

The little man beside Francisco glanced at Vili, who stopped, half expecting the man to open his mouth and say something to him, but when this didn't happen, Vili continued on his way. He greeted Jorge and then Ulysses. 'Do you fancy having a coffee downstairs?' he asked Ulysses.

'Yes, sure,' replied Ulysses, saying to Jorge: 'We'll be right back.'

They went out into the street.

Torrential rain was falling. No one could explain where all this water had come from nor how it had managed to reach the sky above Madrid. The two men zipped up their waterproof jackets, Ulysses opened a small collapsible umbrella and, keeping close to the buildings, they walked together along the pavement as far as Calle Cuchilleros. They entered Casa Botín, first brushing the rain off their shoulders, then went over to the bar and ordered coffee.

'Decaffeinated for me,' said Vili. 'With just a drop of milk, please.'

'And you, sir?' asked the smiling waiter.

'Oh, anything will do,' Ulysses said, shrugging.

The waiter eyed him suspiciously. 'What do you mean by "anything"?' he asked, rather anxiously scratching his greying beard.

'Do you want coffee with a dash, espresso, latte, capuccino, Irish? You must have some idea what you want.'

'Come on,' said Vili, dabbing at his forehead with a paper handkerchief. 'Stop playing the fool and order something from this gentleman.'

'I don't know . . .' said Ulysses.

The waiter matched the decor in the restaurant. He wouldn't have looked out of place in nineteenth-century Madrid or, indeed, during the days of the Republic. He had a kind of timeless quality: the greying, slightly thinning hair, wetted with cologne and combed neatly back; the immaculately trimmed beard; the malevolent, intelligent eyes; the ears very close to the skull; and the determined, rather fastidious look on his face. He was beginning to grow impatient.

'What's got into everyone tonight?' Vili shifted uneasily on his feet, moving the weight from one leg to the other, and leaning one elbow on the bar. 'Give him a coffee with a good dash of brandy in it. And thanks.'

The barman shot Ulysses a defiant glance, then turned away in a dignified manner and set about getting their drinks.

'Where's Telemachus?' Vili asked.

'At home with Grandma Araceli. It was too cold to bring him out tonight.'

'Ah, yes, Araceli, my dear mother-in-law.' Vili sighed. 'How is she after . . . after . . . oh, you know.'

'Much better. Looking after Telemachus keeps her pretty busy.'

'I hope she doesn't have any mishaps, I mean, with the boy and all that. She is getting on a bit . . .'

'Don't worry, he was asleep when I left, and she was comfortably ensconced on the sofa, reading,' Ulysses explained. 'Telemachus sleeps well now, and hardly wakes up at all in the night. I'll be back by the time he needs to have a pee.'

The waiter returned with their order, and they each sipped their respective drink.

'Do you really not mind having her with you?'

'No, not at all. I just have to remind her when it's time for her medicine and which colour pills to take. Besides, she's a really nice lady.'

'Yes,' said Vili sadly. 'She's the only female in her family who's still in her right mind. Because her daughter, Valentina . . . well, you can imagine. And Penelope . . . ah, my little Penelope. What's wrong with her? Why is she so confused? I ask myself what's got into them, both mother and daughter.'

'It will pass,' said Ulysses reassuringly.

'I'm not so sure it will. It's like this rain – interminable. Whatever it is, it won't pass yet awhile. And I'm talking about Valentina now. I have confidence in Penelope, I always have had, she's my daughter and she's never let me down yet. I hope she doesn't do so now. But sometimes she seems so very far away, she's distanced herself from me so much that . . . Oh, I don't know, Ulysses.'

Ulysses slowly shook his head. 'Perhaps you just have to give them time.'

He noticed that Vili was looking tireder than usual, and was in such a state that sometimes his thoughts lagged behind his words, giving the impression that his conversation was full of ellipses.

'It seems so sad to me that my wife can't get on with her mother . . . I haven't had a mother for a long time, and I wouldn't mind having one now, when I might be in a better position to understand her. But there you are.' Vili took a sip of his coffee and muttered something about it being too hot. 'Araceli could be living with us. There's no reason why you should take on an old lady. I know you're not exactly awash with money.' Vili took out his cheque-book, scribbled down an amount, then signed the cheque. 'Here you are, this should cover a few immediate expenses. If you need to get someone in to help you with the housework and so on . . .'

Ulysses nonchalantly took the cheque from him, without even looking at it and without going through the pantomime of rejecting it. He didn't say thank you either.

'I'm not rich, Vili, but I'm not poor either. Don't worry.'

'How did that exhibition go, the one you told me about, the one in Valencia? Did you sell much?'

'Enough to keep me going for a while.'

'I'm glad.'

'Yes,' said Ulysses.

When they went back to the Academy, almost everyone was still there. Jorge had kept guard over Ulysses' seat for him.

The air inside smelled damp, though it wasn't cold. The atmosphere in the room was stuffy and smoke-laden, just like it used to be in shambling, high-ceilinged, university lecture halls, with flaking, cracking plaster around the bargain basement light fittings, skimpily whitewashed walls – as if they had been watering down the paint as the money ran out, leaving paler areas near the skirting boards – and, under the seats, endless blobs of chewing gum, with all the colour sucked out of them.

'How are you doing?' Ulysses asked Jorge, once he had resumed his seat.

'Not too bad.'

'Do you think a woman can find happiness living with two guys at the same time?' Ulysses asked with a wink. 'Have you come to any conclusions during the break on female polygamy?'

'Yes.'

'What's that then?'

'I've come to the conclusion that there's no God and that the art of conversation is dead.'

Ulysses' hands felt sticky. He wiped them on his jeans.

'Shit,' he said.

'There's no need to get annoyed, I was just quoting Raymond Carver.' Jorge yawned and glanced at his watch.

Ulysses gazed at him in amazement.

'I didn't know you read.'

'A bit, but then I'm on my own, you see. I have plenty of time for everything, even for a fascinating sex life. With myself, of course. It has the advantage that I never have to give myself stupid explanations about what I've done and where I've been. And, needless to say, I never go behind my own back.'

'Sounds like a good arrangement.'

'I do what I can.'

'Well, the stuff we learn here must have its uses, don't you think?'

'Absolutely, I've learned a lot of things here.'

'The Academy's not such a bad place,' said Ulysses.

'Of course it isn't. Besides, I don't know anywhere else in Madrid where you can go at this time of day and have someone listen to you and not have to pay a penny for the privilege. It's much better than a pick-up joint, and you never leave drunk.'

'That's why there are so many people here, because it's free.'

Jorge smoothed the knees of his trousers as carefully as if he were folding his breakfast napkin.

'Mireia's gone,' he said.

'That's a shame. I like that woman. I think it's delightful that she should defend female polygamy.'

'You like all women, Ulysses.'

'And you don't, I suppose!'

'Not *all* women, no.'

'But most of them.'

'Yes, perhaps most of them.'

'Well, there you are.'

'Anyway,' said Jorge, closing his eyes sleepily, only to open them again wide when he became briefly aware of the presence of a small, miserable-looking little man, 'you won't get anywhere with Mireia, my friend. I'm telling you this so that you don't go wasting your time. She wouldn't let you touch her even if you sterilized your hands first in the deep-fat fryer. She's well and truly married.'

'But, Jorge, she's an ardent defender of polygamy. Her husband and I might be able to come to an agreement,' joked Ulysses.

'Oh, well, in that case . . .'

The session resumed. They chose a different topic for discussion. Mireia was no longer there, and Jacobo, after downing three gin and tonics in a nearby bar, in company with his friend Manolo and his cousin Martín, had pretty much lost interest in his crusade against female polygamy.

But everyone was still edgy.

'But, Vili . . .' A woman stood up. She was plump and not particularly old. She had a very red face and was wearing a water-proof hat which, perched on top of her head, looked like the cap of a mushroom. 'I can't achieve happiness by good means or bad. My husband's been paralysed for the last five years.'

'Oh, good heavens!' said the person next to her. 'Was it a traffic accident?'

'No, no,' she replied, 'he broke his neck on the stairs at home while we were trying to make a funny home video for a competition on TV.'

'Oh, I am sorry.'

'Not as sorry as I am.'

'Did you win the competition though?'

'Yeees,' said the woman slowly. 'They gave us the prize, but it wasn't very much, and my husband lost his job and I had to go out to work. He was a truck driver, you see. And now I'm a cleaner and get paid by the hour. He spends all day at home, and I'm out working all the time. And happiness? Where's that?'

'Oh no, not another personal tragedy!' howled Johnny Espina. 'Look, let's just stick to the topic under discussion and forget about people's private lives, because if I were to tell you *my* story . . . I mean, the way my homeland was plundered by Spain, the mother country, who looted, raped, exploited and generally shafted it . . .'

Someone said that they were sick to death of listening to Johnny's whingeing, and if he hated Spain so much why didn't he just go back where he came from and stay there.

'Who said that?' Johnny got furiously to his feet and scanned a few faces. 'Who was it?'

Hipólito Jiménez stood up.

'It was me,' he said simply.

'Oh, I should have known. Our very own son-of-a-bitch.'

Hipólito emerged from behind a row of chairs packed with people who were looking at the two rivals with expressions of startled interest on their faces, just like the bronzed spectators at a tennis match.

'Hi, Johnny,' said the young man.

His shoulders looked even broader than they actually were beneath the chunky green woollen sweater he was wearing. He was like a peasant lost in the middle of a city in which there was only noise, indifference and greed.

Sitting in his chair in the centre of the room, Vili closed his eyes, disheartened. What was wrong with them all lately? Was it the rain? Would the foul weather end up sending them all barking mad?

'I might have known it would be you!' clucked Johnny. 'Pay the debt of history once and for all! Give back everything you stole from us!'

'I didn't steal anything from anyone,' roared Hipólito. 'I'm a painter and decorator, you know. I was born in 1969.'

'Of an unknown father.'

'I wasn't there when bloody Christopher Columbus discovered America.' He sighed and swayed threateningly over to where Johnny was standing. 'I wish to God the bugger had just stayed where he was and not gone anywhere! That way, I wouldn't be here now, paying for his bloody navigational cock-ups.'

'What? Just pay the debt of his –!'

'Yeah, that way I wouldn't have to put up with you!'

'Stay where you are,' ordered Johnny. 'Come any closer and I'll call the police.'

'Go on, then, call them. As long as they don't arrive in a boat, or should I say caravel?'

'That's a low blow, you bastard,' boomed Johnny.

'About the right height for you, though, dickhead,' someone behind him said in a shrill, hysterical voice.

Vili intervened before a real fist fight broke out. He bawled at them at the top of his voice, threatening them with a lifetime ban from his Academy, stamping on the floor and clapping his hands just like a ringmaster at a circus for unruly children.

Almost half an hour later, when things had calmed down and everyone had returned to their places, the atmosphere in the room was heavy with gloom and with a thick, malodorous rancour that had been waiting in the wings for some time and was now fouling the air.

'Life stinks,' said Miguel Acebo, who worked at the Ministry of Agriculture and was a regular at the Academy.

'Yeah,' said most of the others present, 'life stinks.'

Then Vili got really angry. It was the first time anyone there had seen him so enraged. It seemed to him, he was thinking with pounding heart, that Valentina, his wife, had given him a roasting before he left the house that evening and now, at the Academy, they were all taking it in turns to baste him. He couldn't stand it any more. He was beginning to be well and truly sick of it. What was he, after all? A philosopher or a poor ingenuous fool? He felt a nervous spasm in his voluminous belly. The pain made him double up.

What the hell was he doing? He was rich, he could go wherever he wanted to, do whatever he pleased. He could dump his wife along with all her baggage of neurotic bitterness and disappointment. The only obligations he had were those he himself had created. No timetables, no bosses. Not even his own children. He could travel more, eat at exotic restaurants in far-off countries, sit by the Sea of Japan reading Seneca, he could stop trying to seek dialogue with others and try talking to himself instead.

'So life stinks, does it?' he roared, and there was absolute silence. 'Why go on living, then, if nothing pleases you, if you can't find happiness and life isn't in itself sufficient reward? What are you doing here, then?'

They were dumbstruck and watched him as intently as if they were guarding him.

'Listen very carefully, because I'm going to tell you a story. It's a story I learned from Plutarch. In the olden days, to which I always refer you when I want you to learn something about yourselves, there was a citizen called Timon who decided one day to address the tribune.' Vili took out a crumpled paper handkerchief from his trouser pocket and wiped his neck with it. He was sweating, and his hands were trembling. 'A great silence fell, because it was most unusual for Timon to speak, so everyone held their breath and listened. And Timon said to them: "I have a plot of land, O Athenians, and on it grows a fig tree whose fruits many citizens have enjoyed. Since I have now decided to build on that plot of land, it seemed wise to make a public announcement first, so that anyone wishing to hang themselves could do so before I tore down the tree."'

Vili paused and looked around him at the serried ranks of grave, perplexed faces. 'Well, this Academy, my friends, is my fig tree, which you have all enjoyed during the two years that it has been open, but today, this very night, I have decided to close it, to cut down my tree. Before that happens, here it still is. If anyone wishes to hang himself, please do so now. Tomorrow it will be too late.'

Tomorrow, he thought, he would pack his bags and take a plane to the other side of the world. The farther away he was from Madrid and the Academy, from Valentina and the rain, the better.

Yes, the farther off the better.

He turned towards his seat. He felt tired and depressed, a desert island in the midst of a hostile sea, an island eroded by salt and wrapped in the murky light of lonely, greenish sunsets.

He did not even see the little man who, behind his back, was getting up from his seat and advancing fearfully and clumsily, but with a determined look in his eyes, threading his way through the seats around him, and who, when he was less than two yards from Vili, proclaimed in a soothing, almost feminine voice:

'Thank you for lending me your fig tree, sir!'

Then he took a tiny revolver out of his raincoat pocket, a gun so small that it looked like a toy, and before almost anyone had an inkling of what was going on, he held it to his right temple.

Vili turned round when he heard Gabriela scream. The hysterical note of alarm in her voice made him start.

The little man closed his eyes and pulled the trigger.

But the bullet did not exit through the stranger's left temple, as he must have intended. Nor was its path blocked by some evil thought or by some unusually robust bone inside his small head.

None of this happened. There was no spilled blood, no irreparable tragedy. No death. Although there was a crime: attempted suicide (does the law in some countries punish this offence with the death penalty?).

No, none of this happened, because another hand closed swiftly and firmly around the would-be suicide's hand and deflected the bullet up to the ceiling: a hand at the service of a quick eye.

II. *What we have*

Guilt

Penelope believes that life is a hand-to-hand struggle with guilt, duty, anxiety, fear of the unknown, dependence, the desire for justice, dread, worry, procrastination, lack of self-love and the absurd tendency to live in the past which afflicts everyone from time to time.

All that and a few other things too.

In order to combat all these enemies in her personal and professional life, she follows the rules laid out in Gracián's manual on the art of prudence, *The Oracle*. When she was sixteen, her stepfather had given her a copy, but she had been unable to extract any teachings from the book – or, indeed, from any other book – until twenty years later. As a teenage girl, she knew nothing. She may not even have known how to read. Or, rather, she did not know what she was reading, nor what her eyes were seeing or her hands holding. She was not really aware of anything. She was possessed by the wild existential gluttony of youth, in which appetite, longing, extravagance and sleep are everything.

Now, however, she does know. Penelope knows a few things. Not everything, but that doesn't matter. She knows enough to get by. She knows the importance of choosing your friends and enemies well and knowing how to make the best use of both. She knows that one should always behave as if one is being watched. That one should leave other people wanting more and never ever give them too much. That she must never have illusions about herself or about anyone else. That she should know her own faults and never explain herself too clearly, because most people do not value what they understand, but are prepared to worship anything they cannot decipher.

Penelope has learned the art of dissembling, because being transparent in a pitiless world is death: that is why it is often necessary to go in disguise. In the jungle, the most fragile insects live camouflaged amongst the vegetation, the green insects blend in with the green leaves, and the carrion-coloured ones with the dead leaves.

Penelope has learned good sense. A grain of good sense, said Baltasar Gracián, is worth more than mountains of intelligence. She has learned to show taste and care when doing things, to be brave, conscientious and sensible. And, above all, to know how to wait.

Oh, yes. Penelope knows a thing or two now.

She arrived back from Paris only a few hours ago. The Paris of the Seine and Christian Dior, the elusive Paris of ragged, grey silk skies draped elegantly across the sun. She spent six days there in her role as the new wunderkind of Spanish fashion, trying not to stare at the immensely tall models, trying to appear as disenchanted, tough and visionary as everyone expected her to be. The shows were a success. Her designs speak the language of flowers and have a natural grace that goes beyond the purely contemporary. The long jackets in white cotton, the little shantung boleros, the embroidered silks, the lamé of shirts with plunging necklines, the faille and the organza, all floated about the models' figures, clinging, provocative and daring, creating the illusion that these were not so much clothes as vaporous feathers or skins born to fit the wearers' bodies.

A stylist working on French *Vogue* asked her where she had done her training. At Nina Ricci or Balenciaga perhaps? Penelope's boss pursed his lips and gave the woman a withering look. Now Penelope smiled at the memory of this insult tattooed on his old face. Thoughts of murder hovered in the air about him until the woman wisely decided to move off and talk to someone else.

Paris had been unanimous: her creations are unique, even thought-provoking, because Penelope knows what she's doing: 'These days, when we've seen almost everything, not just in the world of haute couture, but in all the arts,' a famous chronicler of Paris fashions wrote in her daily column, 'the only thing that still manages to capture our imaginations is intelligence, which is why it's such a rare occurrence. Penelope Alberola Gordón, dear readers, has more than enough intelligence to do just that.'

Perhaps it wasn't a matter of intelligence at all, Penelope thought at the time, but good sense, *her* good sense. And she felt proud of herself.

The last six days had been very intense, but she had still found time for a brief fling with a large, blond, rather distracted 'cool-hunter'. His name was Jeremy and he was ten years her junior. He had spent the last two years working in Milan, where his company was based, and he had just flown in from Tokyo. He smoked a lot, took photos constantly (he hardly put his camera down even on the three occasions when they went to bed together, and afterwards she had stolen three rolls of film from him while he was asleep), and ended up spilling cognac down the lovely sky-blue shirt she was wearing. Penelope began to think she was going to bed with a slightly upmarket version of Mr Bean or Mr Magoo, and she didn't like the idea at all. When she returned to Madrid, she didn't even bother to say goodbye.

Since she left Ulysses, none of the men she had been with had lasted very long. She had known several. None of any importance. If she thought hard, she could see them all, including Jeremy, the last in her collection, lined up and looking very serious, arms hanging by their sides and a guilty smile on their open lips, waiting for something. It was as if she had unwrapped them as soon as they had arrived from wherever it was they had come from, and they were now waiting their turn on Penelope's desk, like unanswered letters.

There have been quite a few, it's true. Eleven to be exact. But she, nevertheless, remains alone. Not that she really minds. It was what she wanted throughout her marriage. You can always rely on being alone, she tells herself.

She has read somewhere that, after the age of thirty, lesbian women tend to be monogamous, but that this charming propensity is reversed in heterosexual women, who tend instead to seek other sexual partners, especially if they have been married or have lived with the same man for more than five years.

That's probably the case with her. One way or another, she has spent more than half her life with Ulysses. Perhaps everything that has happened in the last two years, between the ages of thirty-three and thirty-five, has been nothing but a series of manoeuvres perpetrated by that fluid instinct of hers, so attuned to the latest trends that it would naturally tend to support the reliability of statistics on female sexual behaviour. It's perfectly possible. As everyone knows, life is made up of a combination of atavism, abundance and iniquity.

Or perhaps her post-marital affairs are just a way of avenging herself on Ulysses. Oh, what does it matter anyway?

She looks at herself in the bathroom mirror and thinks about the flight back from Paris. It wasn't exactly pleasant, but it was at least short. There was a lot of turbulence, the air-conditioning was set at permanently chilly, the flight attendants were rude, rather like bored, inattentive waitresses who know that no one is going to leave them a tip, and the noise of the engines, even in the first-class cabin, was deafening. So loud was the clatter that she couldn't even daydream about her recent triumph in Paris. And as if that wasn't enough, her assistant, Jana, had a sudden desire to confide and ruined the whole journey with her complaining and her displays of gratuitous emotion. She entirely monopolized Penelope's attention, not leaving her a second to wallow in the glorious memory of her fashion shows.

Penelope hates having such a strong sense of reality. It can be really irritating sometimes.

She should have known that the black clouds brushing the wings of the plane and smearing them with a gritty dampness augured no good. And so it was, as she found out shortly after setting foot back in Madrid.

But then, as she was flying over France through the grubby smoke of the heavy rain clouds coming in from the North Atlantic, she thought only of the satisfaction of a job well done and Jana's tearful chatter. They were served glasses of champagne so cold it was almost frozen. The first sip set her teeth on edge and the pain immobilized her tongue. 'Are you trying to give us all pneumonia?' she asked the attendant angrily, indicating the drink.

The woman smiled. Her smile was so broad it could have wrapped around her whole head. Her expression was one of resigned, slightly disdainful tolerance, despite the near bow she gave as she replied that if the passengers mutinied and things got really ugly, they would just have to stick the bottle in the on-board microwave for a few seconds. Then she gave a bright little laugh, which sounded to Penelope positively ghostly.

'That was a joke,' the attendant said, still smiling. 'Sorry.'

'H'm.'

'If you like, I can bring you a coffee.'

'No, thanks. Don't bother.'

Jana took a sip of her drink, then downed it in one and stared out through the window. She had lovely eyes from which one could have collected pounds and pounds of honey. She started blowing her nose, and soon the tears were flowing down her perfectly made-up cheeks.

'Oh, come on, Jana . . . It's not that bad,' said Penelope. 'You can order a fruit juice or a coffee. Even a whisky. Although . . . wait a minute. It's still only . . . good grief, it's still only midday and here we are knocking back the booze – what do you think of that?'

'Seems a great idea to me. I wouldn't mind getting drunk. Or high on drugs. Perhaps a bit of crack would go down well before lunch.' The girl sighed. 'Or peyote.'

'Don't talk such nonsense! What on earth's the matter with you? Crack, for God's sake!' Penelope tried to stretch her legs, but couldn't.

'Oh!' was Jana's only response.

She started crying in earnest then, emitting two parallel streams of tears that could not have emerged more quickly and abundantly if they had come from sprinklers hidden behind her eyes.

'There, there,' said Penelope consolingly. 'Calm down, Jana. The gentleman in the next row of seats is staring at us,' she whispered, crouching down a little as she spoke.

'Well, he can go fuck himself!'

'Sh! Lower your voice, will you?'

'That nosy old guy over there . . .' Jana pointed an accusing finger.

The man saw this and tried to feign indifference by immediately looking back down at the newspaper he was holding in stiff fingers. His skin was the colour of overcooked veal, and he displayed a sudden intense interest in an article in the *Financial Times* which made him plunge his nose in among the pages, thus covering his face completely.

'Him and anyone else,' Jana went on. 'As far as I'm concerned, they can all go fuck themselves.'

'For heaven's sake, Jana!'

'Oh, Penelope!'

'What's wrong?'

'I had a row with Mauricio.'

'Oh, so that's what it is.'

'Yes, that's what it is.'

'Was it a big row?'

'Well, it was just before I left for Paris, the day before. I've had a terrible time, I felt so guilty and . . . You'll probably say you didn't notice a thing, but that's because I'm a real professional. When I work, I work – I just change the chip and that's that. Goodbye, personal problems, hello, work problems.' Jana dried her eyes and placed her hand on her breast, as if trying to slow her pounding heart. 'It was all my fault. At least I think it was. I could do with another glass of champagne.'

Penelope summoned the attendant and ordered another glass.

'Well, my fault and the horoscope's.'

'The horoscope's fault?'

'Yes, you know, the one in the newspaper. "A bad day for Taureans, you can expect some unpleasant news at the office" or "The sun shines bright on Geminis today. You will be more sexually active than ever, more attractive, enterprising and bursting with ideas . . ." That kind of thing.'

Penelope was staring into space.

'Don't you ever read your horoscope?' asked Jana.

'Yes, well, now and then. It's not something I bother with much.'

'Well, I take horoscopes very seriously indeed.' Jana paused for breath, took a small hand mirror out of her bag and started retouching her make-up as she spoke. 'The fact is I genuinely believe in astrological prediction. It has a very calming effect on me, reading my horoscope each day. It's really good karma. I'm not religious, as you know, I don't go to Mass and I haven't become a Buddhist like almost everyone else I know . . . So, I think I have the right to read my horoscope every day, don't you?'

'Absolutely.'

'I'm not one of those silly superstitious women, but I just think it's best not to tempt fate. I'm not an ignoramus, far from it. You know me . . .' She put the powder compact back in her bag. 'I mean, I've got a degree, for God's sake. I can recite the names of the twelve most recent Nobel prizewinners in biomedicine and physics. Not everyone can do that. It's not the same as remembering who won the last Nobel Prize for Peace or for Literature. Nobody knows the winners of the science prizes. But I do.'

Penelope raised one eyebrow.

'Don't you believe me?' asked Jana, as if she were about to start crying again.

'Yes, of course I do.'

The attendant arrived with more champagne for Jana, who thanked her with a brief nod.

'No, I can see from your face that you don't. Well, listen, I'll recite them to you. David Baltimore, Renato Dulbecco, Walter Gilbert, David Hubel, Arthur Kornberg, Joshua Lederberg, Susumu Tonegawa, James Watson, Sheldon Glashow, Steven Weinberg, Leon Lederman and Murray Gell-Mann.' She intoned these names solemnly, as if declaiming some difficult, highly experimental poem. 'You didn't think I could, did you?'

'Yes, I did, Jana. There was no need to . . .'

'All I'm trying to say is that I'm a sensible, competent woman. I do my job well, don't I? You can testify to that, because not only am I your assistant and your secretary, I also bring you cups of coffee, make sure your income tax form is in on time, that you always have a spare pair of tights at the office and, if necessary, I buy your Tampax. I'm perfectly capable of having mature, balanced romantic relationships with men.'

'I'm sure you are.'

'But for me my horoscope is a bit like . . . well, like my daily spiritual guide. I even stopped smoking because of my horoscope.'

'Really?'

'Yes. One day, four months ago, I opened the paper, as I do every morning, and I read: "Gemini, isn't it about time you gave up smoking? Today you will consider the possibility of giving up this filthy habit for good, and you'll succeed too, because you always achieve what you set out to achieve." So I said to myself, why not? I mean, smoking is the pits.'

'It causes lung cancer.'

'Well, it's not so much the lung cancer, I just couldn't put up with the bad breath a day longer. I mean when you think about it, cigarettes really make your breath stink.'

'They do.'

'So I stopped smoking there and then. When I'd finished my breakfast, I simply didn't have my morning ciggie. And I haven't had another one since. And now I honestly don't know how I could ever have smoked. My breath smells of roses every day now, rather than like a blocked chimney.'

'Well, that's great, Jana.'

'It consoles me, Penelope – the horoscope, I mean. Life is so uncertain that if, when I got out of bed to go to work every morning, I couldn't read my horoscope and find out what's going to happen to me during the day, I'd have a fit. I would die dunking my biscuits in my morning coffee. I've never liked surprises.'

'Really?' Penelope smoothed her blouse and tried to accommodate her knees under the tray.

'No, I don't, because they tend to be really nasty surprises. Most of them, anyway.'

'That's a bit of an exaggeration.'

'Well, the thing is, as you know, Mauricio and I have been living together for five months now.' Jana took a sip of her drink. 'He's so handsome, so considerate, so . . . Of course, he's a Virgo with Leo in the ascendant, which means he combines orderliness with animal strength. He's as confident and independent as I am. When we met, we hit it off straight away. I really loved living on my own, and so did he, so we decided to live together. Up until now, that is. Well, up until twenty days ago . . .'

'What happened?' asked Penelope resignedly.

'Disaster struck, Penelope. I mean it. The thing is this, ever since I've been with Mauricio, as well as reading my own horoscope every day, I also read his. And that dreadful morning, I got up feeling full of the joys of spring, as I do nearly every morning apart from when my period's due. I opened the newspaper and read my horoscope, which said nothing out of the ordinary. Then I read his. And that was when the tragedy occurred.'

She paused to create dramatic tension.

'So what happened?' Penelope felt obliged to ask again.

'Do you want to know exactly what it said?'

'Yes.'

'Well, it said: "Virgo, if you have a partner, you might well consider leaving him or her today or, at the least, being unfaithful to them, because you will meet someone who will draw you into a wild passion such as you have never experienced before. In matters of love, your time has come. This person will be the most important person in your life, so much so that they could turn your head if you're not very careful." That's what it said.' Timid tears once more filled Jana's large eyes. 'I nearly fainted over my Winnie-the-Pooh mug.'

'But it was only indicating a possibility. It did say "might", after all.'

'Yes, it did,' agreed Jana, who seemed like a small, helpless child in a world of malevolent giants. 'Mauricio is a model, and that day he had a fashion show in New York. You know the kind of world models live in. Most of the time they're surrounded by perfect bottoms, lewd looks and girls with six-foot-long arms that end in claws. They're very fragile. Anyone who lived that kind of life would be. And Mauricio is so handsome. I've always thought how lucky I was to have such a handsome boyfriend who wasn't gay. Anyway, I just went crazy. I phoned him in New York, but of course he wasn't at his hotel. I don't even know what time it was there. I spoke to him the next day, when he phoned me at home, very late, I suppose it must have been six o'clock in the morning where he was, which means that he hadn't even been to bed yet.'

'He probably had jet lag. Those four-day trips back and forth across the Atlantic can ruin anyone's sleep patterns,' Penelope said to calm her down.

'Either that or he was cheating on me with someone.'

'When you have various options to choose from, I recommend choosing the best one. Don't always plump for the worst. It will only cause you unnecessary suffering, and why suffer unnecessarily when we have quite enough real suffering to deal with already?' Penelope flicked back her lovely blonde, almost waist-length hair.

'Anyway, I was almost mad with jealousy, and by the time he came home three days later, I was in a state of near hysteria.'

'No.'

'Yes. I was horrible to him. I kept making ironic references to the affair he'd had. He pretended not to understand, and kept saying: "Jana, are you all right? Shall I call a doctor?" A master of pretence.'

'Perhaps he wasn't pretending.'

Jana shook her head sadly.

'Then I decided to pay him back in kind. But I didn't feel like going out and picking someone up just to spite him. I *have* been unfaithful to him once, at the beginning, when our relationship was still a bit uncertain. But I didn't do it out of desire, which I didn't feel at all, more out of weakness really, just to have a bit of fun, and because I felt flattered by the guy in question, who was really something. An American photographer. But those quickie flings with complete strangers are really not my scene, I don't enjoy them at all.

'When you've been with a guy for a while, well, you trust him and the sex is so much better. You can say to him: "Yes, just there. Oh, yes, I like that." Or: "No, you're barking up the wrong tree there, sweetheart. Don't touch me there, you're making my hair stand on end and it's no fun at all."

'But when you make love with someone you've only just met, or someone you know, but have never been to bed with, oh God, you have to put up with all kinds of fumblings and horrible, creepy things that he thinks will send you wild with pleasure when, in fact, you just feel like telling him to piss off. You have to pretend and make all kinds of stupid moaning noises just to make him think that you've come, in the hope that he'll come too and stop bothering you and . . . well, all that happens is that you get a reputation as a randy slut who's always up for a quick fuck.'

Jana pulled a face. 'In short, I hate casual sex. You can't just flit from prick to prick, because in the long run, it turns out to be a very exhausting game of snakes and ladders that will end up giving you some nasty infectious disease.'

'H'm.'

'Don't you agree?'

'Well, I . . . Yes, I do actually.'

Penelope quickly reviewed some of her recent conquests. Jana was quite right. But she had been so taken up with the game of seduction, which she needed badly, that in nearly all cases she had relegated her own pleasure to second place, or even to no place at all.

'Anyway, since I didn't fancy going out looking for a date, I decided to invent one.'

'*What!*'

'I invented one. An imaginary lover is much less bother than a real one. And I didn't have to go to bed with him. The person I wanted to go to bed with was Mauricio. He's fantastic and he knows me so well. He knows what I like. He's so tender and he's got a lovely body – supple as a reed. I love him, for God's sake. And that's all there is to it.'

'What do you mean by "imaginary"?'

'Well . . . I started sending myself love letters signed by a certain Pablo. I wrote them on the office computer. Then I'd leave them lying around so that Mauricio would see them, but always giving the impression that I had hidden them in places where he wouldn't look. I refused to make love with him, saying that I was tired, but with a look on my face that said "I don't need it, thank you, I'm being served already". Like when you eat in a good restaurant before going home so that you've got no appetite for the family meal that's there on the table. I used to spray myself with Eau Sauvage before leaving work. And I persuaded Jaime, the delivery boy, to leave a few messages on the answer machine, in which he just had to say in desperate tones: "Jaaana, Jaaana, darling . . ." and then hang up. Things like that.'

'Good heavens!'

'Until, one day, of course, Mauricio exploded. It was the day before we were due to fly to Paris. He had to go to Tokyo that same afternoon. And just before I phoned for my taxi, he told me that he wasn't prepared to put up with my infidelity any longer. He said he was a faithful guy, and expected to be treated the same. And that when he got back from Japan, he would come by the apartment to pick up his things, and that he'd prefer it if I wasn't there, so that he didn't have to say goodbye to me. He told me how he had loved me like crazy, but that I had responded by simply acting crazy.' Jana subsided into tears again; one tear rolled delicately down as far as her upper lip, and she licked it up with the tip of her tongue. 'Isn't that sweet? Anyone else would have said I'd behaved like a whore. But not him. He just thought I was mad. And he was absolutely right.' She uttered a low sob. 'It was only then that it occurred to me that the horoscope might have been wrong, or that he might have been an exception. It could happen.'

'Didn't you tell him the truth? I mean, didn't you tell him that you had sent yourself all those letters and the whispered messages and everything.'

'No, I called a taxi, picked up my suitcase and went downstairs. He stayed at home in front of the telly. With the telly switched off.'

'Oh, Jana.'

'He'll be back tomorrow. He'll have to come by to pick up his things.'

'Tell him the truth, tell him everything.'

'Yes, that's what I should do, isn't it?'

Duty

When they arrive at Barajas airport, Penelope takes the newspapers she had stuffed into the pocket of the seat in front where they always put the instructions on what to do in case of emergency. Remove the parachute from beneath your seat and do not open it until you have put it on. Do not leave through the emergency doors if blocked. Make sure you have your seatbelt fastened and that your seat back is in the upright position before leaping into the void. Do not bother the flight attendants if you feel a heart attack coming on: they will not be able to help you and they will simply become even more flustered than usual. When the plane explodes, very carefully place the mask over your mouth. If you do not have any oxygen, please do not breathe.

She hasn't even had time to glance at the papers. She will do so when she gets home. There might be something in the Arts section about her Paris success. She still does not know that what she reads is not going to please her at all.

The company chauffeur comes to pick them up. The sky is the colour of a gigantic half-eaten coffee caramel, and a persistent drizzle is falling, although less energetically than on previous days. Jana gives the chauffeur her address and he drops her off first. Half an hour later, Penelope opens the door to her apartment. It smells of wood polish; the maid must have only left a short while ago.

After showering and changing her clothes, and thinking about her fashion shows (the glamour, the flashbulbs, the bouquets of flowers), she removes from the fridge a cold pasta salad left for her by the maid, pours herself a glass of white Alsace wine and goes over to the sofa in her study. She won't go to the studio or the office this afternoon; besides, she has work to do at home. While she picks at her food with a fork, she finally gets to look through the newspapers. The incident makes the headlines in all of them.

She dials her parents' number. Her hands are shaking, but after a few seconds she manages to control them. No one answers. What state will Vili be in? He is the only father she has ever known, and although he is not her biological father, this detail has never worried her. She calls a taxi, rummages in the wardrobe for a raincoat and prepares to wait for the cab to arrive.

The new maid, thin and middle-aged, opens the door. She has an air of general despondency, as if she has given up hope of ever achieving something for which she has long been trying. It makes one sad just to look at her, and Penelope hopes that her mother does not spend her time pursuing her around the apartment clutching a fistful of hairs, the kind that block up the plughole in the bath.

'Hi, Roberta, is my mother in?'

'She's gone out with her friends.'

'And my father?'

'He's in his room, but . . .' she hesitates and rubs her hands on her skirt, at thigh level.

'I've come to see him.'

'He said that nobody was to bother him. He doesn't . . . Journalists and all those other people who keep phoning . . .'

'But I'm not nobody. At least not that kind of nobody.'

'All right. Go through.'

'Don't bother to tell him I'm here. I'll find him.'

Penelope takes off her raincoat and gives it to the maid. She strides across the hallway and down the corridor, crosses the library and the small living room, and walks past her old bedroom, which she doesn't even notice.

When she's outside Vili's study, she knocks softly on the door, listening for any noise coming from within.

'Leave me alone, Roberta! I told you I didn't want to be bothered!' says Vili's angry voice.

'It's me, Penelope.'

There is a kind of buzz. A clink of glasses. Vili's slow, hesitant footsteps across the creaking wooden floor.

'Ah, my dear . . .' says Vili when he finally opens the door, then he embraces her so hard it is almost as if he is, in fact, collapsing on top of her.

When her daughter walks into Thalia's living room, Valentina gets up from the armchair and kisses her on both cheeks, exclaiming: 'What a surprise, sweetheart!' Her voice sounds like a faint, disheartened grunt.

Her friends, Euphrosyne, Aglaia and Thalia, stare at Penelope so hard that she fears that from now on they will carry her concealed in their retinas until the end of their days, that she will somehow remain engraved on the eyes of those three women, her muscle, bone and cartilage, all reduced down inside them.

For some inexplicable reason, she feels embarrassed, as if they have just stolen something very personal from her. But she is used to penetrating looks, to all kinds of looks – envious, lustful, murderous, indulgent. A look cannot harm you even if it wants to, and she knows that; a look is just someone's eyes focusing on some point in space, seeking out and rubbing up against things with the aid of light.

She says hello and puts on a sweet, seductive, child-like smile. You have to know how to behave whatever the situation. To have an ordered, discreet, far-sighted approach. Besides, to her certain knowledge, a little elegance never hurt anyone.

'Old harpies,' she thinks as she kisses them one by one, trying not to touch with her lips the ladies' overly made-up cheekbones – cold, slightly damp and as fine as tissue paper; almost, one might say, on the point of tearing and revealing something far more intimate and terrible than mere raw flesh beneath the mature skin. She has known them since she was a girl. She has watched them hardening and ageing, seen the touch of desperation edged with incredulity and resentment that can make them at times seem pathetic, even wicked, and, why deny it, occasionally delightful. She doesn't know if she likes them or loathes them. It's odd, she thinks, how sometimes we're not sure what we feel about certain people. Or even if we feel anything at all.

'Oh, Valentina, it's your daughter, the model. We haven't seen you for ages, my dear! You're always so busy. But you look lovely, absolutely wonderful! And your bust has got bigger too. A whole cup size bigger, or even two. I don't know why girls these days are so obsessed with their boobs. The bigger they are, the harder they fall later on. In the end, you have to be careful where you put your feet in case you trip over them, believe you me.'

'Those won't drop. Silicone sets as hard as concrete. And anyway she's not a model, she's a fashion designer,' whispers Aglaia, leaning towards Euphrosyne, who was the first to speak. 'She does look like a model though. She's so pretty. We see you in all the magazines, Penny.'

'I haven't got silicone implants. My bust got bigger when I was pregnant and . . .' says Penelope.

'Ah, I see. Yes, of course, the little boy. H'm . . . but he must be about two now.'

'No, I didn't mean that, I just meant that I liked the way I looked then.' Penelope smiles seductively. 'And to be perfectly honest, I've been using padded bras ever since.'

'Sit down here with us. I'll ask the maid to bring you something to drink.' Thalia, the owner of the apartment, indicates a small divan by the fireplace.

'You carry on with your conversation. I just came to be with my mother for a while and to take her home afterwards. Of course, if I'm in the way . . .' Penelope sits down.

'Not at all! What would you like to drink?'

'A martini, please,' she says. She flicks her hair back over her shoulders and smooths her skirt over her knees.

'Great, now we'll have another person's point of view. The view of a modern young woman,' says Thalia, whose lips spread into a prissy smile. 'We were talking about prominent pubises.'

'About what?'

'Prominent pubises. Pubises that are too bulky.' Euphrosyne lowers her voice when she notices that the maid has come into the room. Then, as soon as they are left alone again, she goes on. 'I'm talking about fannies, fannies that are too fat.'

'A doctor told Euphrosyne that her pubis was too prominent and that she should have liposuction on her mons veneris,' explains Valentina.

Penelope notices that her mother's eyes seem distracted, colder and bluer than ever. Like two pieces of sky plucked from outer space and immediately stuck, in a rather slapdash manner, in the middle of her face.

'A doctor told you that?' Penelope looks at Euphrosyne, amused; she sips her martini. 'And how would anyone know? I mean, are there statistics on the subject?'

'The surgeon is a man. What would he know about fannies?'

'What can a man know about anything?'

'Nothing really, but they have opinions about everything.'

'How many fannies has he got up close and personal with to know how big they ought to be?' asks Aglaia, and sets the gold bracelets on her wrists tinkling. 'Good grief, the man's a faggot!

And a boor too. A butchering boor who's making a real mess of you with all that cutting and pasting. If you go on like this, you'll need to use a remote control in order to pee.'

'He's making a mint out of your gullibility,' adds Thalia.

'Cutting and pasting?' Penelope shoots her mother a questioning glance.

Her head fills with images so innocent they seem alarming. An angelical pubis, a pair of children's scissors for cutting up card and the cut and paste icon from the screen of her Macintosh.

'She's had some reconstruction work done down there. Well, that's what the doctor calls it.' Valentina seems subdued, she bites into an olive and stares at the carpet. 'He's reduced her labia majora and menora. He told Euphrosyne that they would have a more youthful appearance like that. Like a schoolgirl's fanny. But now he thinks her pubis is too high and too fat.'

'Appearance? Who thinks about appearances when you turn out the light and let your husband's beer belly heave itself on to you and crush you?' Thalia asks Euphrosyne accusingly.

'Well, this is the first I've heard of such a thing,' Penelope says and takes another sip of her drink. She feels as if her teeth, like the martini, have just emerged from the ice. 'And in the kind of circles I move in, you hear all kinds of things that . . .'

'Is this why we fought a sexual revolution?' Aglaia gives a nervous little yelp and fidgets in her seat on the sofa. She's thin and, thinks Penelope, beautiful in a way, despite looking as if she has been recently rubbed down with a damp cloth. 'Why did we go to university and then carve out a career, meanwhile allowing ourselves to be felt up by a load of sex maniacs with spots, bad breath and grubby little cocks, and all because of that poxy, so-called revolution? For this? To end up letting some scalpel-happy cretin slice up and liposuction the origin of the world?'

'The what?' asks Euphrosyne.

'The fanny. *The Origin of the World* is a painting by Gustave Courbet,' explains Penelope earnestly, 'a painting of a black hairy fanny.'

'Ah, for a moment . . .'

'Is that why we have reconstructed and re-reconstructed ourselves and bankrupted ourselves paying some wretched psychoanalyst who never came up with any answers anyway? To end up being mutilated again? How much longer are we women going to go on being as stupid as women?'

'Ah,' said Penelope in a hoarse voice. 'Oh, ah . . .'

'We are what we are, right?' Thalia gets up and paces the room. She looks distractedly around for a clean glass, then finds one on the sideboard and smiles as if she has just stumbled upon some lost treasure.

Euphrosyne is seated comfortably, looking half-stupid and half-mysterious, and she doesn't seem particularly embarrassed, despite the telling-off she has been getting.

'And what about oral sex?' she asks. She looks mischievously at each of her friends, and finally at Penelope.

'Anal?' Valentina asks, bewildered.

'No, no, oral. Oral sex.'

'Oral sex? Heaven help me!' Aglaia wrinkles her brow and her pupils narrow like a cat's eyes. 'Your beast of a husband probably thinks oral sex is having a quick chat about it before he gets down to business. Something along the lines of: "Euphrosyne, do you fancy a bit?" That's all oral sex means to Eugenio.'

'Yes, but . . .'

'Well, then, it hardly merits having origami performed on your labia majora and menora,' Thalia says.

'You're quite right,' says Valentina. 'I absolutely agree.'

'Christ almighty.' Penelope takes another sip of her drink. She has almost finished it. She could drink another one. Or even two.

'But . . . what if you had an affair and you found someone who wanted to practise *real* oral sex.'

'To be perfectly honest, I hate oral sex.'

'Why?'

'Well, not *all* oral sex. I don't mind a man performing cunnilingus on me, but not since our bloody sexual revolution, definitely not. I had quite enough of that at the time.' Aglaia shakes her head. 'I never enjoyed being a cocksucker. I absolutely hate fellatio. In fact, I always have, even then, when it was revolutionary to do it and we all felt obliged to say how much we liked it. I hate it.'

'Why's that?'

'I get hysterical if I see so much as a hair in my bowl of soup.'

'All I'm saying . . .' insists Euphrosyne.

'All you're saying is that you should be free to treat your fanny as if it was the hem of your skirt, constantly turning it up and turning it down again. Just stop it, Euphrosyne. Stop committing acts of terrorism on your own body. Because, to be perfectly honest, I really don't think the results are worth it.' Thalia inspects her fingernails while she says slowly. 'You're setting a bad example to the female sex. Women should be the opposite of what you are.'

'Yes, but . . . I mean . . .'

'Euphrosyne, when will you learn?'

'I just mean that, even though no one sees it, what we've got inside our knickers is still quite a big deal.'

'Less and less so in your case.'

'Oh, I don't know . . .' Euphrosyne sighs and says in a sing-song voice: 'I *like* the way it's turned out so far. And when it's a little less bulky . . .'

'Yes, but . . .' Aglaia gets to her feet. She lifts up her skirt.

She is wearing waist-high knickers in pink lace, expensive and good quality, but old-fashioned. She's so thin, she looks as if she hasn't got any hips, as if someone has sliced them off for her.

Penelope thinks of a legless doll, all torso, a long plastic torso, crammed into a pair of horrible, old-fashioned, pink lace knickers.

Now what's she doing? She's not really taking off her knickers, is she? Aglaia's skirt slips down over her knees again and, for a moment, Penelope can see nothing more. But Aglaia decides that the skirt is in the way, so she undoes the zip and slides the skirt down to her ankles, trampling on it with her feet before kicking it to one side. Now that she is free of her skirt, they all watch as she rids herself of her knickers, which go flying off to land near the vast glass-topped living room table. They lie crumpled and discarded near the table leg, as if saying accusingly to Aglaia: 'I can't believe you just cast me off like that, without consulting me, and when I'm not even dirty.' They can all see Aglaia's surprisingly bushy mons veneris, in the form of an inverted isosceles triangle, in which the predominant colour is black, streaked with an increasing number of silvery brushstrokes, growing thinner over the actual pubis, as the gaze slides downwards towards the vertex of the triangle.

'So, tell me, what's wrong with this, eh?' Aglaia indicates her crotch with one stiff, trembling forefinger. In the middle of the living room, she spreads her legs wide as if she were riding a horse.

They all look at each other.

'Nothing,' they chorus.

Penelope can see Aglaia's slack but still elegant bottom and a few complicated folds of scrawny skin adorning her waist, as if they were the prematurely aged remains of a slab of dried meat long exposed to the elements.

'Unappealing? Doesn't lubricate itself as well as it used to? Urine leakages? Minimal levels of oestrogen and progesterone? Dryness? Tightness? Pain?'

'Nooo . . .'

The worst of it is that Aglaia is not drunk or high on drugs or anything. The best of it is that this is the real Aglaia. And she doesn't seem grotesque or mad or obscene. Penelope realizes how difficult it must be to walk gracefully across a room full of people, even when they are old friends and the daughters of old friends, wearing only a waist-length polka-dot blouse, medium-heeled shoes, a bare bottom and some silver earrings. She has seen models do it and appear incredibly crude. And they were girls of fifteen or maybe seventeen. Twenty at most. Beauties in full bloom. None of them was fifty-six or likely to be so in the near future. None of those little dolls could have done what this woman standing before her now has done, with all the pride and insolence of daring to be herself reverberating through her skin and her face, beautifying them and endowing them with a fine, almost fierce dignity. No, none of those girls could have carried it off.

Penelope realizes then how attractive that old witch Aglaia is, how truly captivating. She is suddenly aware of Aglaia's sensuality, her femininity, and she feels intoxicated, jealous. She is a desirable woman. So desirable. So feisty, uninhibited and unexpected. She seems utterly clean, she appears not to be concealing any lacerating wound, either inside or out. Penelope realizes that she wants to be like her when she is her age, she wants to be like her now, and would like to have been like her in the past too. At seventeen and at twenty. She wishes she could always have been like her.

'You've got a gorgeous fanny,' says Thalia, coming closer to get a better look.

'You really do,' says Valentina. The last few times they have met, she has not been exactly talkative, and this afternoon, even less so. As soon as she opens her mouth, therefore, everyone looks at her almost spellbound, expectant. 'Yes, really.'

'It's just a fanny, but it's the only one I've got and I like it. And it likes me,' says Aglaia, sitting down.

When she does so, the air seems to grow thick with particles of time. Penelope wishes she would stand up again and walk up and down the room. If that woman would only stand up again, she would be able to breathe more easily, she thinks with rapt nostalgia.

'It's awful,' exclaims Euphrosyne.

'What is?'

'Oh, I don't mean your fanny, which is lovely and untampered with, not like mine,' she explains, and for the first time that afternoon she seems slightly troubled. 'I mean it's awful knowing that one is fifty-six years old. I mean, it's terrible. When I think of all the things I won't ever be able to do again! Discover love, lose my virginity, die young . . . I mean, it's terrible knowing that you are the age you are and that however hard you try and however much calcium-enriched milk you drink every day, your legs are never going to grow any more.'

'Nor is your fanny, so stop letting them chop bits off. It's not a starfish,' says Thalia, taking out a cigarette. Penelope asks for one too and they light up together. 'Show it a little respect. It's given you three children and a great deal of pleasure. Don't even think about having liposuction.'

'Oh, I don't know.'

'And be cheerful. You may be fat, ugly and menopausal, but what does all that matter compared with the fact that, one day, you'll have to die?'

'Show it to us,' Aglaia says to Euphrosyne. 'Show us your fanny.'

'Well, I . . .'

'Drop your knickers and show it to us. We want to see what that moron has done to you. We could denounce him. We could slag him off on telly. We could cause a scandal.'

'Honestly . . .' Penelope takes a long drag on her cigarette; the smoke gets in her eyes and she rubs them to relieve the stinging. 'I haven't seen anything like this since I went to see a season of films from Uzbekistan . . .'

'We'll make your fanny an international star. We'll post a photo of it on the Internet to serve as a warning to all those millions of menopausal women throughout the world who are as crazy and as rich as you are.'

'Or you could have the same thing done, because it really hasn't turned out too badly . . .' says Euphrosyne, but immediately regrets what she has said and falls silent.

None of the other women takes any notice.

'Come on, show us.'

'No, I won't.'

'Come on, don't be such a wimp. If you can show it to that charlatan, why can't you show it to us?'

'It's not the same.'

'No, it's better. *We're* not going to poke around inside you.'

'We're not going to cut you or sew you up. We're not going to do anything to you.'

'All you've got to do is take your knickers off. You can close your eyes if you don't want to see us looking at you.'

Penelope thinks about female circumcision. She thinks about school playgrounds. She touches a small pimple that has appeared near her top lip.

Come on, you sissy, take off your bloody knickers before the head teacher catches us, she thinks, feeling a kind of convoluted joy, and stroking her right thigh with one anxious hand. We want to see what you've got down there. How did they bandage you to stop the bleeding? Did they fit a catheter so that you didn't have to pee while you were convalescing? What did it feel like the first time you masturbated after the operation? Does it feel the same as before? Can you feel anything? Can you feel?

Penelope thinks about female circumcision and cosmetic surgery, minimally invasive or reconstructive or destructive or whatever. She thinks about female circumcision and the Third World. She thinks about cosmetic surgery and the First World. About young bodies. About wild sex. About babies.

She misses her son. Her small, soft son.

She remembers Ulysses' body in the mornings when things were good between them; she remembers that substance which seemed to stay stuck to her skin after making love with him and which didn't, in fact, exist, but which was light and fragrant, and wrapped her in a tangle of sweetness.

Ulysses, that son-of-a-bitch.

Penelope feels like screaming. She doesn't know why she's thinking all these things at once. They don't mix well inside her head.

She wishes Euphrosyne would just take off her knickers.

'Come on, do it, don't be embarrassed,' she says, lowering her voice to a whisper. 'It'll be all right.'

'All right,' says Euphrosyne, getting to her feet. 'I'll show you.'

They all utter relieved sighs and prepare to observe her closely.

'I'll show you mine if you'll show me yours,' she adds, a triumphant look on her face.

'You've been looking at mine now for ages,' complains Aglaia.

'I didn't mean you, but the others.'

'I don't mind,' says Thalia. She lifts up her skirt and lowers her knickers.

Thalia is a widow, but she's wearing a black thong which, Penelope suspects, belongs to the category of lingerie that can only be bought by mail order or in sex shops. Aha, she says to herself, aha; *almost* all of us women want to get married, but absolutely all of us want to be widowed at least once. Thalia has managed to achieve this perverse dream. The delectable harpy. She's buried her husband, who died a natural death (are there also unnatural deaths? isn't it natural to die sooner or later of something or other?), and now she buys thongs that look like strips of linoleum dreamed up expressly to inflict pain on the crack in the bum of whoever is wearing them. And she has shaved her pubis . . . from top to bottom. Smooth and bald as an orange.

'I don't believe it,' exclaims Aglaia.

'Not bad,' says Valentina. 'Very innovative.'

'Oh I say, darling,' giggles Euphrosyne, winking at her.

Penelope is coughing like a little girl with a bad cold.

'Honestly, I . . .' she splutters, but does not finish her sentence. She hadn't actually considered joining in herself.

Euphrosyne urges her on, come on, it's her turn now. Penelope hesitates for a moment, but . . . what the hell. She doesn't think hers is any worse than the others.

She takes off her clothes as if she were performing a striptease for a group of Japanese businessmen on holiday. Valentina and her friends cheer her on until she is standing there completely naked. She has taken off everything. Her padded bra, her lilac silk briefs with their slightly damp, creased pantyliner, her tights and her dress. She doesn't feel cold or embarrassed. In fact, she thinks she should do this more often.

'Oh, it's ginger,' says Aglaia. 'Of course, I'd almost forgotten that you were ginger-haired when you were little, especially since now you dye your hair blonde.'

Valentina is looking at them, smiling.

'We're mad,' she says, 'absolute nutters.'

'Yes, we're a load of horny old nutters.'

'We're not doing too badly though.'

'It could be worse.'

'It certainly could.'

'Come on, Valentina,' says Euphrosyne. 'It's your turn now; into the fray. We're really kicking over the traces today.'

'No, not me.' Valentina shrinks in on herself, she folds her arms over her chest as if hugging herself and shifts uneasily on the sofa.

'But we've seen you before, a long time ago, mind. Don't you remember? At university? And when Penny was born and you . . .'

'Look, I said no and I mean no.'

'But why?' screeches Euphrosyne. 'If you don't all do it, then I won't either. Besides, you've got a great figure now. You've lost loads of weight lately, not like me. You look really good, you're so slim and . . .'

'I've got cancer. I often bleed,' says Valentina. 'Cancer of the womb.'

'Oh, really? Well . . . it really suits you . . .' Euphrosyne swallows hard. 'Will you excuse me, I think I've just seen someone . . .'

Aglaia gets to her feet, picks up her knickers and carefully smooths them out. She goes over to Euphrosyne and makes her sit down again.

'Please, Euphrosyne, shut up, will you,' she says. 'And keep your foolish remarks to yourself, all right, sweetheart?'

Penelope is completely naked, half lying on the couch. Her skin is like that of a summer fruit, there are small brown freckles on her shoulders and reddish marks left by the underwear she has just removed. Her gaze – she has her mother's bright blue eyes – is absent. Her hands are resting on her stomach (there the skin is perfect, unmarked by pregnancy, her belly is firm and rounded, a beauty made for pleasure); her hands are placed modestly one on top of the other. She is not wearing any jewellery. Her long, blonde, dishevelled hair half covers her breasts, partly concealing her rosy nipples, so tender they look like two fleshly shadows made of peaches. She could be a virgin in a Flemish painting, a child virgin, much younger than her actual age. She resembles a sweet young girl painted before she lost her innocence for ever. Her legs are nonchalantly spread, revealing the origin of the world. On some nights, the inside of that narrow cleft covered in reddish hair and brimming with solitude has the texture of lard and tastes sweet.

Penelope's bare feet are on the carpet, one foot slightly twisted, in an uncomfortable position which she does not bother to change. Her mouth is slightly open and her teeth shine like little bits of pure white paper that contrast with the red of her lips.

Anxiety

Mother and daughter are sitting next to each other in the car, in the back seat. Penelope had made various calls ('Oh, dear God,' Jana moaned, 'there's your mother with cancer and me with a broken heart. Who's going to heal us all, Penelope, who?') and then phoned for the company chauffeur to come and pick them up. They drive quietly through the streets of a muffled, rainy Madrid. Their bodies do not touch; they stare out through the car's steamed-up windows at the puddled pavements outside.

What an odd feeling, thinks Penelope. Thinking that your mother is going to die soon, perhaps now, right here, beside you.

She takes a deep breath, strokes her left wrist, then presses her nose to the area of skin beneath which her pulse is beating. She likes touching herself when she feels anxious or worried, running her hand between her bare thighs, over her shoulders, her waist, her arms, smelling herself. She knows that it's a childish form of self-consolation, but it calms her. When she was a little girl and was upset for any reason, she would hurl herself down on her bed and root and snuffle amongst the sheets, rolling around in them, sniffing them, and finding relief in recognizing her own smell. All very animal, she thinks, and she cannot suppress a sad, fleeting smile.

'Oh, God, Mum,' she says at last.

'Don't let's start,' replies Valentina.

'Why didn't you tell me before?'

'What was the point? Would it have cured me or just made you ill?' Valentina turns to look at her daughter. 'You've got your own problems. You're busy. I couldn't do that to you. I didn't want you to suffer for my sake. I know I'm not the perfect mother, but . . .'

'Neither am I.'

'. . . but I've always tried to make sure you suffered as little as possible. And now was no different.'

'Life . . .' Penelope feels like crying, but can't. She wants to say something, but doesn't know how. 'Life changes. It has changed. It changes every day. Although things aren't any different from what they were. I mean that this has been going on since the world began. I mean that people die every day, and never the same ones. It's bound to be our turn at some point, isn't it?'

Valentina smiles. A luminous and, for once, maternal smile. She reaches out and touches Penelope's dress with the tips of her fingers.

'Don't make such a big thing out of it. I'm not the only one who's dying, I'll just do it more quickly.'

'But you should, you should . . .'

'Oh, come on, Penny, don't start that. I've seen all the doctors I need to see, I've compared all the opinions I need to compare, and I've visited all the clinics I need to visit. I have no illusions about what's happening to me, and the doctors haven't been feeding me any illusions either, and I'm simply not willing to submit myself to some form of hospital torture just to gain five months of mineral, not even vegetable life. Plugged into a machine and full of rusty holes, just like a battered tin can on a shooting range. With exactly the same degree of mobility and the same kind of life as a battered tin can, only capable of leaping when it receives another hit, a new dose to lengthen your life, but which, at the same time, takes away another bit of your body, makes another hole for your soul to escape through. Who wants that? Obviously not the people who've got it. It just doesn't seem like a good idea. Don't forget that we're talking about me here, that I am that tin can, and I don't want to be stuck on some shooting range. I'd rather go straight to the rubbish heap once I'm empty.'

'But why haven't you explained all this to Vili, why have you been tormenting him instead of telling him everything and having him on your side?' Penelope takes her mother's hand, which releases its grip on her dress and enters into shy contact with hers. She doesn't know quite what to do. It has been a long time since she has held her mother's hand, since she has touched her at all. Only kisses that leave a broad expanse of air between lips and cheeks, an embrace that involves no contact, the odd pat on the shoulder. Nothing. She no longer knows what it means to touch her mother.

Penelope thinks of Telemachus and feels a stab of pain in her stomach. Her little ray of sunshine. So fair and so abandoned. She tells herself that he's still too small, that soon she'll take him back and teach him to slip his hand in between her breasts, and to keep doing it as long as she lives, and to hell with the family psychiatrist, that friend of Vili's who, years ago, nearly drove her mother round the bend.

'We've been together a long time, Vili and me.'

'Exactly. He loves you. He's always loved you.'

'But I don't want his compassion, and that's all I would get if I told him. I'd rather be a complete bitch than a poor woman with a terminal disease. At least that lack of affection gives me life. Pity makes me feel like dying, and in my situation, you can imagine . . .'

'I think you're underestimating him, Mum.'

'Maybe, but I don't want him to know, all right? Besides, this is a bad time for him, what with everything that's happened. That chap who tried to commit suicide at the Academy. Let's just be grateful he didn't succeed, even if it means, if you'll allow me, being grateful to Ulysses. Anyway, it's an unpleasant business. Vili's very down at the moment. I don't want him to know anything about my illness. I never have, still less now.'

'If that's what you want,' Penelope sighs.

The car stops outside the building where Vili and Valentina live. The chauffeur takes out an umbrella and opens the door, letting Valentina lean on his arm in order to get out. It's spotting with rain. Penelope feels like crying and assumes that, more than anything, it must be because of the rain. The blasted rain and its tendency to fill up the tear ducts of pretty young women like her who go out into the street accompanied by their dying mothers.

'Look at me, will you?' Valentina asks anxiously. She touches her own face and passes her hand lightly over her cheekbones. 'Have I got many wrinkles?'

'Yes, but only in your trousers,' replies Penelope, and her lips tremble.

'Oh, you're so sweet.' Her mother kisses her on the lips and encounters with her own lips (wan and bare of lipstick) a small, stray tear that has rolled down as far as her daughter's mouth. She drinks it up as if thirsty.

They go in through the front door. One behind the other.

Nowadays, Penelope says to herself, the alternative for a woman who doesn't know how to wiggle her arse is to wiggle her brain, although she would advocate, if at all possible, mastering both disciplines. And she dances. She likes reggae. 'Impossible Love' by UB40. Old tunes. Her old records, her old, adolescent bed, her yellowing posters, her old smell. She is dancing alone in the middle of her bedroom, in her parents' apartment. She gets up on to the bed and sways her hips in time to the music. She jumps up and down (this time her mother won't tell her off), just as she did when she was a child.

Oh God, Penelope thinks. Oh, God.

I'm dancing, fighting tooth and nail just to get by.

She closes her eyes as she dances and can see a darkness full of precious stones. Chrysoprase, chalcedony, beryl. Turning and turning without cease in the sparkling blackness that she can find only behind her closed eyelids as she dances.

Oceans of water are falling outside her balcony window, and she has the impression that decades have passed since she got back from Paris. And yet she only landed a few hours ago and it's just beginning to grow dark. The sun is setting, hidden behind the muddy sheet of clouds brimming with rain. In the street, the air is an enigmatic, malevolent colour.

Does it presage imminent destruction?

The vice of dreaming is the sanest of the mental illnesses, whilst that of remembering is the most futile. But Penelope is remembering. At this moment, she feels the need to remember, now when her mother is dying (she was always dying, as she herself says, but she might do so now from one moment to the next), now that the woman – the woman from whom came the original cell from which she herself sprang – is about to vanish, leaving behind only her bloodless body, her empty shell.

She is fifteen years old and has feminine curves, crazy ideas, a lot of freckles (which resemble the remnants of another, browner skin that someone has crumbled over her), night-time imaginings, not an ounce of cynicism, and the keen sense of smell of a young dog.

And there is that boy, Ulysses, standing in the playground. The older brother of Héctor (the charming, handsome boy who is in the same class as Penelope and who, unbeknown to her, is almost identical to the son she will one day have with Ulysses).

That, of course, would be in the future, and Penelope wasn't thinking about the future then. The future did not exist then because, quite apart from anything else, it never has existed.

There is Ulysses, a tall, serious boy, with slightly untidy hair, who always looks at her in the same way (at first, Penelope thought she was the only girl he looked at in that way). He is about to finish secondary school; next year, he'll be going to university. They say that he boxes at a gym every afternoon after school; they say he paints well, that when he picks up a paintbrush, the colours simply do as he tells them. Her girlfriends say that everyone says he'll be a great artist. Soon. Very soon. He's already sold a few drawings. He's already been in exhibitions with important painters – very important and very old – and he's only seventeen.

He is seventeen, but his gaze is much older. Like the gaze of someone very old who has seen everything. The origin of the universe and of the world. The final explosion. As well as everything that happens in between. In other words, everything. A tireless gaze that embarrasses Penelope, makes her feel stupid and occasionally ugly, and sometimes so beautiful she thinks she's the belle of the ball.

That's why everything is so strange.

Vili says that what's happening to her has to do with proteins. That she needs to eat loads of protein all the time. He says that, for the moment, she shouldn't even think about boys because they're all bastards, that she should wait for a few more years, until she's strong enough – inside and out – to be able to defend herself from them, with her bare fists if necessary.

But she thinks about Ulysses as often as she can. She does so unwittingly. Sometimes, she wakes up in the middle of the night, sleepy and disoriented, goes to the bathroom to have a pee, and his face appears in the middle of an enormous empty space that opens up in her thoughts like a midnight flower.

And that sort of thing happens all the time.

Penelope is talking to Héctor about mathematics – they have an exam next week; they are gossiping about the teachers and their classmates too, and they laugh uproariously like children, which is what they are. Héctor is always smiling, unlike Ulysses, who has the air of an animal lying in wait. Héctor – his eyes alight with

162

desire and urgency – says that when he's older, he wants to be a traveller and see the world. In class, everyone calls him 'The Pilgrim'. Héctor says that when Ulysses gets angry, he sometimes comes out with German swear words (really, really bad ones). She wonders if he often gets angry.

They are sitting on a bench when Ulysses joins them. He speaks tenderly to his brother. Penelope would never have imagined that anyone so surly and unfriendly – sometimes, from a distance, he resembles an indignant bird of prey – could show even the tiniest bit of sensitivity.

Then he falls silent and sits down on the ground, facing Héctor and Penelope, and looks at them with interest. He observes them with an exasperating degree of concentration.

He's a little owl, thinks Penelope. No, he's not, he's a barn owl. No, he's an eagle owl on heat, just flown in from the marshes, eager to eat raw flesh and fly freely through the night. No, he's a fierce wolf out of some dark fantasy, standing his ground, vigilant and wild.

Penelope notices that her body is shrinking as he looks at her. Héctor is still talking to her, oblivious to his brother's presence, doubtless accustomed to his eccentric behaviour, but she is trembling, although she doesn't want either of them to know that she is. She is profoundly disturbed, in the grip of some terrible neurological change, as if control of her brain has passed from the left hemisphere to the right in a matter of seconds. Her material self is suddenly shaken, and, concentrated in her body, she feels all the hatred in the world, all the evil in evil, all the virtue in vice, all the sickness in the world, the beauty of horror, the pleasure of pain and all the love in the world.

She feels almost dizzy. She closes her eyes tightly, wrinkling her nose in the effort. I feel awful, she thinks. I've never felt so well in my whole life, she thinks.

Héctor asks if anything's wrong, and she says no, shaking her head so that her hair ripples and glows like old gold. She feels like peeing. Whenever she feels nervous or excited, she has to race off to the toilet. Her bladder is burning, an agreeable stinging sensation that extends as far as her pubis and distracts her with its pleasurable tickling. She bursts out laughing, then shrugs her shoulders. She doesn't know what to do or say. She doesn't know anything. Not that she cares.

There is such wisdom, such pure instinct in the moment she has just experienced that the sensuality of it will last far beyond it.

How wretchedly, how impeccably Penelope fell in love with Ulysses that morning at school, without even knowing that she had.

When the bell announcing the end of break rings, she and Héctor get up.

Ulysses does the same. He approaches her and says he'd like to walk her home that afternoon, after school.

She agrees – well, what else could she do?

Penelope and Héctor head off to their class.

Ulysses stands motionless in the playground and watches them leave.

Procrastination

Once (a long time ago), Vili read Penelope a passage from Confucius: Those ancestors who wanted to bring lustre to the virtue of the whole kingdom, first put their own estates in order. Since they wanted to put their own estates in order, they first sorted out their families. Since they wanted to sort out their families, they first tried to cultivate them. Since they wanted to cultivate them, they first amended their own hearts. Since they wanted to amend their own hearts, they first tried to be sincere in their thoughts. Since they wanted to be sincere in their thoughts, they first broadened their knowledge as much as possible. This broadening of knowledge involves the investigation of all things.

Penelope did not really understand this at the time, but she was very struck by the passage and noted it down in her adolescent diary. She learned it by heart.

That was what Vili was like, *is* like: rather than teaching you a prayer, or giving you a slap or a piece of hackneyed, fatherly advice or a bundle of notes, he would read you something from Plutarch or recite a Chinese poem. A few words that nail themselves into your senses and find their destiny there, as if they had spent centuries looking for you and for your senses.

The investigation of all things. It sounds so . . . potent.

She is beginning, within her limitations, to understand what it means.

She turns the idea over in her mind as it grows dark and her mother fiddles around in the kitchen, making some hot rolls. They are, in fact, pre-baked; Valentina has never been – nor has she ever needed to be – what one might call the perfect housewife, the sort that chops the wood, lights the fire, roasts the meat, scares off the wild animals and carries water up from the river. She is also slicing a pineapple which will go off if they don't eat it tonight.

Penelope goes over and over the idea, while Vili remains shut up in his study (although he has agreed to come out for supper; he shouted at the maid to make sure that she heard; for some reason, he believes Roberta to be deaf, although no one knows where he got this idea from).

Since Penelope wants to bring lustre to her virtue, she has first tried to put her own estate in order, her own small kingdom: vanity, wounded pride, independence, a broken home, an abandoned child, a dying mother, a father experiencing depression for the first time in his life, a career in a cut-throat business where you always have to keep one step ahead.

It's exhausting and very complicated having to put all that into some kind of order, but she has, at least, managed to make a list. It's always a good idea. 'Make a list,' Vili used to say to her when she was little. 'You won't forget anything if you make a list.'

Since Penelope wants to put her own estate in order, she has first tried to sort out her family. Just over half an hour ago, she told her mother:

'You must speak to Vili. Tell him everything, ask him for his love and his companionship. You can't die like this.'

'Oh, piss off, will you, sweetheart,' her mother replied.

She phoned Ulysses.

'I want my son,' she said. 'Bring him to my mother's apartment tonight and he can stay with me from now on. Then you'll be free to chase after all the women you want.'

'He's my son,' Ulysses replied. 'He doesn't even know he's got a mother. He's only seen you four or five times since you left home.

I've brought him up. I love him. You have no right to take him away from me.'

'Bring him here anyway. I need to see him. I want to see my son. We can discuss it properly later,' said Penelope and hung up.

Since Penelope wants to sort out her family, she has first tried to cultivate herself. 'Vili, have you got any books that might interest me?' she asks her stepfather from the corridor, pressing her lips to the tightly shut door of Vili's study. 'I've read nothing but magazines for a whole year now . . .'

Since Penelope wants to cultivate herself, she must first amend her heart by being sincere in thought. 'Ulysses, you vile, faithless liar. You great son-of-a-bitch. Ulysses, my love, oh, your hands, my love, your hands . . .' she says to herself, silently moving her lips, even though no one can see or even hear her.

Since Penelope wants to be sincere in thought, she first tries to broaden her knowledge by investigating things.

And although it seems about as useful as a pendulum in the sea, she once more turns to memory.

Penelope is eighteen and is ready to make love with Ulysses for the first time, her first time (she's not sure about him, although they've been together for three years: a whole lifetime).

She has followed him to the faculty of Fine Arts. Ulysses has another year to go before he graduates, although he would have left on the very first day if his father hadn't stopped him. She would follow him to hell itself. She may well have to do so, although she does not know this yet.

Héctor is in Seville, studying to be a naval architect. Sometimes he sends Penelope postcards in which he says things like: 'The Guadalquivir has eyes the same colour as yours', or, 'My brother is a lucky bastard', or, 'I'm bored with studying, I just want to travel, to live', or, 'Today all I've had to eat is a cheese sandwich, and it's stuck in my teeth'.

'Let's make love,' she says to Ulysses one evening. They have talked about it before, many times.

'What a great idea,' he says. 'I'll put my penis on.'

They are sitting outside a café, near the Temple of Debod and the gardens of Ferraz. A soft early summer breeze is blowing. The sultry weather has not yet assailed Madrid. Soon the unbearable heat will arrive, and everyone will experience a strange difficulty in breathing, a certain tedium. They get up and start walking. Ulysses puts his arm around her waist.

'You're like a peach,' he says and nibbles her ear.

Penelope enjoys the intense, luminous shiver and lets it travel slowly down her spine.

Down.

And down.

She notices a tiny trail of translucent saliva that lingers between Ulysses' lips and her skin; they are linked by a liquid, indestructible spider's web, entwined for ever. That string of saliva is her engagement ring. Exquisite, valuable, unique in the world.

The saliva cools from her ear down to her throat as they walk along. It is very fine, the slenderest of threads.

It's not fair, Penelope thinks.

She feels like crying. It's not fair, it's not fair.

Suddenly, she is afraid. Of pain, of disappointment, of loss. Perhaps it isn't a good idea after all. They shouldn't go to bed with each other just yet. They should prolong indefinitely this state of strange innocence in which they find themselves. Kisses that are events in themselves. His hand inside her knickers, and fantasies and music and desires and nothing else. She doesn't want to stop being a child (she never will want that, but she herself doesn't know this now). She doesn't want her vagina to stretch after sex until it is as big as a tunnel, so big that anything can enter it – trains, fugitives, anything. Oh, no, not anything, please. She doesn't want that. She doesn't want to become dissolute or impulsive or mature.

She wants to stand still in this moment of her life. A frozen forest, a nature reserve. Motionless, unchanging. Like a postcard, a perfect photograph. That is how she wants things now, when there is still so much she knows nothing about, when she is still inopportune, awkward and alive. She wants to preserve herself intact, asleep on one of the peaks of paradise, and to remain like this for ever and ever so that everyone can see her and marvel.

'What's wrong?' asks Ulysses and lets his hand slide slowly down her back, past her waist, a little further down, further.

What *is* wrong with her? Childish nonsense? Fear? Confusion? Vertigo, perhaps? She would like to phone Vili and ask him his opinion, but he would probably just get annoyed with her and tell her that's she's over eighteen now and can do what she likes, that he'd rather not know, and then, for months and months afterwards, he would keep glancing at her strangely, in sulky silence. Besides, Ulysses wouldn't let her phone him. He would kiss her on the ear again, ask her to forget about Vili, and she would.

'Come on, Penelope . . .' That hand moving further and further down. It's difficult to walk along the street like this; people will start to stare; anyone behind them will be able to see her underwear. 'Are you afraid?'

'No.' She is filled by a paralysing panic.

'My father isn't home, he won't be back until Monday. We can go to my room. There's nothing to be afraid of. I'll put some music on and I've got . . . well, you know . . .'

'No, I don't know.'

'You know, protection.'

'Ah, yes, we must protect ourselves.'

Although love cannot be protected.

She finds it hard to walk properly, she can barely take a step without feeling that her legs will buckle and she will fall on her knees in the middle of the pavement, like a newborn foal. She stares at the faces of the people they pass. They all seem to be afflicted by terrible suffering.

Ulysses kisses her neck, and Penelope looks rather sadly up at the stars. Ulysses is enjoying her neck, planting little sucking kisses on her clean, perfect skin. She can feel his soft, blond stubble scratching her, irritating her, slowly and provocatively.

'I could eat you up,' he says. 'You're like a peach. I would bite right through to the stone and gnaw at it like a hungry dog.'

They keep nearly colliding with the people walking in the opposite direction. Why is it that, when you're in love, everyone you meet seems to be going in the opposite direction?

'Why don't we take a taxi?' Ulysses suggests.

'Really, I don't . . .' Penelope is starting to feel faint, she would like to run home and just leave him there. 'To hell with boys,' as Vili says. 'Stick their willies in the mincer.'

'We'll get there more quickly – I don't want you to get tired or too nervous.' Ulysses disentangles his fingers from the her small cotton briefs and takes his hand out from under her skirt.

'Really, I don't need one, in fact, I think, I think . . .'

Ulysses moves away from Penelope, steps out into the road, scans the street for the green light of a taxi. He's so handsome and has such a determined air about him that looking at him is unbearably sweet.

'I don't know, whenever you need a taxi in this bloody city, you can never find one,' he says, and mutters something under his breath in German.

Penelope goes over to the wall of a nearby building while she waits. She needs to lean her back against something. Something solid that will stop her falling over. Something that will keep her awake and in a vertical position.

She can't believe it. She can't believe that she feels so ill and weak and terrified, when she was the one who suggested it. Ulysses has never tried to put any pressure on her, has never hinted that they should hurry up and do it; he says that he doesn't even think it's particularly important. She knows this is true, that he's not lying or pretending. She knows that he will wait for as long as she wants. But she is afraid that he might look for someone else. She knows he will, that he either already has or will soon start to consider the possibility. She suspects that he has another girlfriend. Or other girlfriends. That he has a multitude of girlfriends between the ages of fifteen and seventy-five (Ulysses is not really bothered about women's ages), that he has at his disposal any number of passionate women who would make much less of a fuss about things than her. Women who enjoy his body and know how to pleasure a man. Yes, he's got them hidden away somewhere, he's got all those eager, jolly, happy-go-lucky girls somewhere, licking their lips, legs permanently spread.

She doesn't think he is a virgin like her; Penelope finds it hard to imagine that he is.

'Boys have more freedom than girls,' Vili tells her, adding that he was a boy once and so he knows what he's talking about. He says that all men think about is scattering their seed far and wide and that they don't much care whether it falls on goddesses or paralytics, on cows or in the middle of a field full of poppies.

Ulysses and Penelope have grown up together, they have kissed, rolled about on the floor, legs entwined, they know each other's bodies and tongues, every corner of each other's flesh, have linked thoughts and hands thousands of times, so why then the need to perform an act so carnal and implacable, to inflict this irremediable wound on her body, if it were not because she was afraid of losing him?

It's all right, thinks Penelope, it's all right. I won't lose him, I can't lose this man. He is my man and I'm not going to lose him.

Ulysses finally manages to hail a taxi and he opens the door so that she can get in first.

He lightly touches her bottom as she gets in and sit downs. The taxi smells of cigar smoke, and the radio is tuned to a sports channel.

He takes her hands in his as he tells the driver the address. He counts her fingers one by one; they are trembling slightly.

'How are you?' he asks. 'Are you all right?'

Penelope gives a barely audible moan. She would like to smash reality to smithereens, to tear at it with her nails as if it were a glossy paper poster, and then stamp on it accusingly, uttering war cries.

'I don't know . . . my . . . my mouth is dry,' she says.

'When we get home, I'll get you a drink. A nice cold Pepsi, with lots of ice.'

'Yeah, great.'

The taxi stops outside the apartment building, Ulysses pays the fare, gets out and goes round to Penelope's door. Penelope is still seated and has not made the slightest move that would indicate her intention of getting up and leaving the taxi.

'Come on, my little peach,' he says, opening the door and smilingly holding out his hand to her. He does not often smile so broadly. Why, then, does Penelope not appreciate this smile to the full?

When they go in, the apartment is in darkness and he turns on a little Chinese lamp on the sideboard in the hall.

His room faces on to the street, but it is a quiet street, with only the occasional car passing, and they are on the seventh floor. The light from the street slips feebly into the bedroom and forms blurred yellow lines that seem to be watching Penelope like avenging bolts of divine lightning.

Ulysses puts on a record and turns the volume way down until the music is just a caressing, muted murmur.

'I'll get you that drink,' he says, kissing her on the cheek. 'Do you want to go to the bathroom? I don't want you saying afterwards that you're dying for a pee. I know what you're like.' He winks and gives her another kiss, this time on the mouth. He goes to the kitchen.

Penelope knows this room as well as she knows her own. She has been here on countless occasions. She has made sandwiches for herself and for Ulysses' father, revised for exams, posed in her bra for Ulysses to paint her, sought refuge here from her mother's bad temper; she has even, on more than one occasion, slept in that bed.

Now, however, she feels that she has entered an unknown and unknowable space, full of dangers. A space as profound as the cosmos. This is the dragon's cave. The fox's lair. The serpent's hiding place. Every corner is full of gloomy presentiments. The air she breathes here burns her lips. She feels dazed. Perhaps she should have drunk something. A whisky. German beer. Sangría. A couple of litres of something that might get her in the mood.

She goes to the bathroom, lifts up her skirt, takes down her knickers and sits down to pee. Should she wash herself? Should she use the bidet like a French tart or would it be better to have a shower?

She smells her armpits, then takes off her knickers and sniffs them as if she were looking for a trail; she rubs her nose against the damp crotch which, only a second before, had been next to her pubis. It doesn't smell bad – it smells of something tender, fecund and hidden – but then, of course, it's her own smell, so her opinion doesn't really count. She decides to have a shower; whatever happens, a shower will do her no harm; the water on her skin will pacify the volcano of madness and disquiet she is feeling.

She turns on the shower and gets undressed. Water is so purifying. Hot water sweeps away the dirt, however deeply in-crusted it is. She feels dizzy; she closes her eyes and imagines that the water is a stream of boiling lava, that she is a tree about to burst into leaf in the spring.

'Penelope, where are you?' Ulysses comes into the bathroom, puts the glass down on a shelf and slowly draws back the shower curtain. 'I knocked on the door, but you didn't hear me.'

He looks at her naked under the shower. He looks at her as he always does, the way in which she thinks he only looks at her and at no one else.

'You're shivering. Is the water cold?'

'No, no, it's not cold.'

'You're afraid,' he says. 'We don't have to do anything if you're afraid. If you don't want to do anything, we don't have to, I've told you so before, loads of times.'

Penelope turns round to the wall, stands face to face with the tiles decorated with seaside motifs. Yachts. Oysters with pearls in them. Little waves. The water gets in her eyes, and everything seems to her undulating and aquatic and unstable.

'No, I want to. I want to make love with you. I don't want to put it off any longer. I want you to be the first. And the last too,' she says, still with her back turned to Ulysses. 'I love you. I . . . I've chosen you, you see.'

Ulysses steps into the shower beside her and stands under the water. He is fully clothed, black streams gush from his shoes as the dirt from the soles dissolves in the hot water. Penelope's feet, licked by this stinking mess, grow grimy.

'My love, my love,' he says.

He takes her face in his hands and kisses her eyelids, runs his tongue slowly over her eyebrows and then down as far as the little upturned curve between nose and upper lip. Then he kisses her on the mouth. Her mouth, fragile, vehement, seeks his.

Ulysses gets undressed, pulling off clothes and shoes, which fall and block the drain within seconds. They turn off the water and get out. He searches the cupboard for a clean towel and slowly dries Penelope off. Hair, armpits, groin, feet. Just as if she were a doll. Then he picks her up and they go out into the corridor.

He is strong. She knows he is strong. She loves him for that.

The ceilings of this old apartment are very high.

'Are you all right?' he asks.

'No. Yes.' She is still wet, her hair is dripping slightly, and every time a drop hits the floor, the wood seems to creak or sizzle, as if it were about to go up in flames.

'Don't be afraid, I love you and I won't hurt you. I would never hurt you, you know that, don't you?'

'Yes. No.'

How our senses deceive us. How the great lie of mortal flesh is set in motion. Penelope snuggles her head into Ulysses' neck and tells him in a whisper that she loves him. That she loves him and loves him. A shiver runs through her. Her blood is young and ardent. She loves him and loves him. That is all it is, nothing more.

Ulysses lays her down on the bed, lays her down there to dry. A drenched dream with red lips. Young and pretty, and as frightened as a fawn.

He kisses her toes. He counts them as he counts her fingers, but he does it with his tongue. One, two . . . five. And again, one, two . . . five.

'You're tickling me,' says Penelope. 'Stop.'

He makes his way up her legs. His tongue, his tense muscles, waiting for something. His young boxer's shoulders. His hands. There can be no other hands like his in the world. What is he doing with his hands? Where did he learn all this? Certainly not in books. Not everything is to be found in books. Books can only contain a tiny part of everything that exists, of everything that is, that was, that has ever been. Where has Ulysses learned to do all this?

She is collapsing. She is filled by a whirlwind of equivocal

175

thoughts. She wants to move, to help him, but she feels absurdly paralysed by the excitement, overwhelmed by what is happening to her. She should do something. Touch him, caress him. She has often caressed him. She has even on occasions touched his penis – long, pink and shy, a strange creature that she has never known quite what to do with – she has kissed his back, his waist, his balls. But now she can do nothing. Immobility is her refuge in the midst of this storm of feelings. She remains alert to every touch of his tongue, to every change in pressure of his fingertips, savouring everything.

Have minutes, hours, days passed since they have been alone in this room? At any rate, some immense length of time.

He kisses her breasts. He plays on her nipples with his lips. They have shrivelled up to become two small, insolent buds.

She is breathing hard.

'I could eat you up,' says Ulysses, 'but I won't.'

Ulysses raises her hips with his hands. His fingers, where are his fingers? Penelope cannot see, she cannot distinguish who is who. Erratic ecstasies, over and over. Her thoughts are full of smells and that is all. His cock is just an imaginary space which – gently, very gently – penetrates her body, another imaginary space.

The pain – discreet, persistent, humiliating – does not stop Penelope from giving a long, satisfied out-breath. She is living a fantasy so dense it seems real. She cannot separate pain from pleasure, cannot put them into two neat little piles: black beans and white beans.

He suddenly leaves her body.

'There, I didn't hurt you, did I?' he asks, his mouth on her mouth; they are both breathing hard. 'It's all right, it's all right . . . This is what love is.'

And she doesn't know that what he is saying is true.

Ulysses has not come, and he will not do so afterwards either.

He doesn't want to satisfy himself, that isn't the point. He just wants her to know what love is and is prepared to teach her.

He puts his head between Penelope's legs. What is he up to? No one has ever put his tongue there before. No one in her entire life. It's such an inaccessible place. The highest peak and the deepest chasm. What a tender, vulgar sensation! Penelope is a green, juicy grape, and Ulysses is sucking her, squeezing her, eating her up. She grabs his head and presses it to her belly.

Ulysses is tenacious and will not stop until he has found what he is looking for. When he finds it, her whole body contracts, she closes her legs about his head, rocks back and forth and howls like a cat. Very quietly.

Lost. From now on, she will be lost forever in a secret garden. She will never get out of there, not even in order to find the person she was.

Lost completely and for ever.

Ulysses has the look of a satisfied lover.

She loves him and loves him and loves him.

He moves closer to her mouth and kisses her and she tastes her own taste on his teeth. A few select drops of blood and moisture, the sap of a water flower.

She returns his kisses.

And there is great sweetness.

Dependence

Penelope knows that she is lucky. That's important for a woman, to be lucky with her first man. She met Ulysses, and he was a man, he really was. Not all women are as fortunate, she thinks. She remembers her girlfriends. By the way, where are her girlfriends from childhood, adolescence, early youth? Where have they gone? She hasn't seen any of them since. Is that her fault? She tells herself regretfully that it probably is.

She had a friend who lost her virginity when she had just turned fifteen. She went with a boy from school, in the back seat of a clapped-out Renault 5 that someone had dumped in the Casa de Campo. He pulled down her tights and her knickers, stuck his skinny little red thing inside her, moved it around for thirty seconds, dribbled all over her blouse and when he had finished, said that since she obviously knew the score, they could see each other again if she liked.

Another friend did it with a colleague of her father's with whom she was obsessed. He was a lawyer like her father. He's so mature and virile, she said before she went to bed with him. Shortly after he had broken her hymen, she discovered that *he* was the obsessive. He tied her hands behind her back with a scarf. He bound her hands, raped her and then wiped his bloody penis on her face.

She was seventeen, and that afternoon, in her father's friend's apartment, she learned of the existence of films depicting Japanese sado-bushido, films that excited him. As well as films showing bondage, candy-burning, choking, spanking, pissing, hard-raping, shaving, enemas and shit-eating. That afternoon in her father's friend's apartment she learned that he had a predilection for very young girls whom he took by force and that, although he admitted it did perhaps hurt some of them, he believed, nevertheless, that they went on 'to develop a real taste for it'. That is what she learned that afternoon. She had never before even imagined such things could exist.

For this reason, and for many others, Penelope knows she is a lucky woman. Very lucky. She should not squander that luck.

She goes looking for her mother. She isn't in the kitchen. It smells of hot bread, and on the work surface is a large salad made of Roquefort, chopped apple, endive and olive oil.

She picks up a bit of apple and licks her lips as she eats it.

'Mama,' she calls, but no one answers.

Roberta comes in and says that her mother might be in her bedroom, having a rest before supper.

'She does sometimes have a lie down about now,' she says.

Penelope goes to her mother's room and knocks on the door. She raps lightly.

'Mama?'

The door isn't locked, so she goes in. There is a heavy, sour, medicinal smell in the room. They should air it a bit, even if it means the rain coming in and drenching the curtains. A hurricane would be a good thing, she thinks, or a tropical cyclone that would fill the room with the wild smell of rough seas and sweep everything away.

Her mother is sitting on the bed with a strip of rubber tied tightly around one thigh. She is concentrating on sticking a hypodermic needle into her flesh.

'Mama?'

'Oh, hi. Come in,' she says and finishes injecting herself. She unties the strip of rubber. She does up her dressing-gown. Her legs never used to be so skinny, and suddenly that thinness seems to Penelope the saddest thing she has ever seen.

'What are you doing?'

'As you see, I've become a junkie.' Valentina smiles. 'It's morphine. Very pure. Sometimes the pain becomes unbearable. I very much fear I've become an addict, like the young Sherlock Holmes. But the doctor told me not to worry; there'll be no need for me to go to a special clinic to detox.'

'But . . .'

'Because, my dear, I'll die first. Now don't upset yourself.' She lies down on the bed, her head on the pillow, and closes her eyes.

Is she at peace? Does what was hurting no longer hurt, or is the pain still there, hammered like a nail into the same place? Where does it come from, all that pain, with its very precise way of expressing itself? Does pain know what it is doing, does it know that it hurts, does it realize?

'Mama . . . We hardly ever talk now, well, not much,' Penelope says. She lies down beside her on the bed. 'It's been ages since I told you that I loved you.'

'Same here, but that's life, don't worry about it. Far more things don't get said than do get said, but it doesn't matter.'

Penelope is waiting for Ulysses to arrive with her son. She is looking at herself in the mirror of what used to be her bathroom and carefully retouching her make-up. She wants to look beautiful. Not just so that he will see her and suffer, but because she knows that, one day, time will scatter its loud, macabre laughter over the ashes of what she is now. Her skin, her youth, her strength, her self. She wants to be truly beautiful, not just to look beautiful.

She studies her profile; she removes a loose hair that has got caught on the side of her dress and throws it down the toilet. She is wearing a low-cut black dress that sets off the warm gold of her skin. 'You're not white, you're golden,' Ulysses used to say to her. The dress suits her, which is hardly surprising since it is her own creation. Black, simple, made-to-measure, devastating. Like death. Ah, yes, black is a good colour.

She remembers a client of hers, an old Italian aristocrat who confessed to her once in Milan, after one of her fashion shows: 'Cara, black is always a good choice. That's why I liked your collection. Black is the ideal colour. I even had a black lover once, cara mia, because he went so well with everything.'

It's true. Black and death are rarely out of place; when it comes right down to it, they are never inappropriate.

She feels like crying, like smashing the mirror with her fist. But she doesn't, she knows she won't do anything, that she will merely go on looking at herself and go on waiting. More than anything else, more than tears and shattered mirrors and sadness, she wants to be desired.

Her mother is dying.

There is a small jewellery box in the bathroom cabinet. It still contains the jewels she wore as an adolescent. Silver earrings, cameos, bracelets made from tiny pebbles, and a real pearl necklace that Vili gave her one birthday. When he gave it to her, Vili had winked and said: 'Wear a pearl necklace and you'll always look like a lady.'

Perhaps she should put it on.

She unfastens it and places it around her neck, holding her hair to one side. She thinks better of it, takes it off and replaces it in the box. To hell with it. Who wants to look like a lady, especially in front of Ulysses? What she wants is to look like a real whore.

The doorbell rings, and Penelope hears Roberta walk wearily down the hallway.

It's almost supper time.

'Ask who it is before you open the door!' she hears her mother say. She has got up intending to look for a good wine to go with the lobster and the salad.

'He says he's Ulysses, your son-in-law – shall I let him in?' Roberta shouts from the other end of the apartment, holding the phone in one hand.

Ulysses has arrived. Will he have brought the boy with him? If he hasn't, Penelope will kill him, and then they won't have to argue about the child any more. Or about anything else.

'Let him in,' orders Penelope.

She click-clacks over to the door and prepares to wait for Ulysses. The lift up to the penthouse is slow, old and slow. She is impatient. She opens the door wide and stands on the threshold, hands on hips, while she struggles to impose some order on her desires. It is a broad landing, adorned with heavy nineteenth-century furniture; theirs is the only apartment on that floor, and the front door and the service entrance are at either end of the landing.

At last, the lift rattles and wheezes its way to the top, like an old fossil made of iron and cables. Ulysses opens the door with some difficulty. He is carrying the boy in his arms, a ball of straw-blond hair nestling against his father's chest. The child is dressed haphazardly. He is wearing the expensive, tasteful clothes provided by Penelope, but it is clear that Ulysses makes no effort to ensure that they match. Telemachus is sleepy, and she hopes he didn't catch cold during the drive in the taxi. Surely Ulysses will have come by taxi, won't he, although he's perfectly capable of having dragged her son through the Madrid public transport system despite the bad weather and despite the bacteria and coughs and grime that Penelope imagines must necessarily pervade any piece of municipal equipment: unsuspected perils for the innocence and health of her little one. If he has come by bus or by metro, Penelope will have yet another reason for killing Ulysses at the first opportunity.

'Hello,' says Ulysses. 'I have to say that this is hardly the best time to have me bring Telemachus out. He's only a baby, after all, and he should, by rights, be asleep in his cot.'

'How did you get here?'

'What do you mean how did I get here?'

'I mean, did you come by metro, by bus?'

'No, I took a taxi, and I expect you to pay the fare, sweetheart. I asked for a receipt. I've got it somewhere in this pocket.' He feels clumsily in his pocket with one hand while clutching his son's little body to him with the other. Telemachus stirs and moans softly.

Penelope gives Ulysses a searing look. Or rather, she tries to, but the attempt fails, for he's still standing there, a few paces away, examining her mockingly as he searches for the bit of paper. Angry, contemptuous, arrogant.

His arrogance, however, usually conceals a large dose of despair; it's just a mask, and she knows it, which is why she can smell his dejection beneath that outer wrapping of disdain. A chocolate filled with layers and more layers of contradictory emotions, spurious and real, vague but utterly lacerating. Does it hurt, Ulysses? What is it that hurts? Does it hurt you often or only now and then? Is the pain very deep? Does it hurt as much as it hurts my poor mother? What is your morphine, Ulysses?

'I think it's time we sorted our situation out in the courts. For Telemachus's sake,' he says.

Ah, if only she could murder him right now.

'Give me my son,' she says, holding out her arms.

'He doesn't even know who you are, love,' Ulysses says with a half-smile. His voice is soft; he never shouts even when he's really angry. 'What are you talking about? *Your* son? You've only seen him a few times since you abandoned him, when he still needed to be breastfed, and you dare to call him *your* son.'

'Of course he's my son. My little boy. Give him to me!'

She is beginning to raise her voice. She always tries to remain calm in Ulysses' presence. She tries, she really does.

They are on the landing, separated by about nine feet. By millions of miles of outer space packed with crazed heavenly bodies, with no fixed orbit.

'He's my son. Mine, mine, mine, do you understand?'

'No, I don't understand, because only Cinderella's stepmother could fully understand you. But I have a vague idea what you're getting at.'

Telemachus is woken up by the argument; he turns and opens his eyes. What bright eyes! He rubs them with one small, disoriented fist. Then he puts his fingers in his mouth. All of them. He looks at Penelope curiously. He hasn't seen her for at least three months. She has been busy. New York, Rome, Tokyo, Paris. She hasn't stopped for a minute these last three months, going back and forth, like a top spinning round the world and transforming every square inch of floor space into beautiful, orderly piles of banknotes.

'He doesn't even recognize you,' says Ulysses, putting Telemachus down.

Penelope opens her arms to him.

She crouches down so that she is on the same level.

Mute, silent, what can she say to him?

'Maaaama!' exclaims Telemachus, with a huge smile which evolves in a second into an anxious pout only to be transmuted immediately back into a smile. A lament that comes out through his nose and makes him choke. And then a long, nervous, guttural chuckle: 'He, hua, guha, huhu, hum.'

He lurches towards Penelope, like a bow-legged doll whose batteries are starting to run out.

'You little squirt,' mutters Ulysses. 'Traitor. Midget. Womanizer.'

Living in the past

The flesh is weak, but the spirit is even weaker.

Perhaps, as Mark Twain said, life would be infinitely happier if we could be born at eighty and live backwards until we're eighteen. Of course that isn't normally how it happens.

The first time Penelope caught Ulysses with another woman, they hadn't even been married a year. In an attempt to find some excuse for such ignominy, she thought to herself, oh well, the flesh is weak.

What had Ulysses got out of it? Pleasure. An orgasm. A fuck. Easy as pie. Post-coital lassitude. Physical release. Then: clear off, sweetheart.

What had Penelope got out of it? Wounded pride. Jealousy. Rage. Hysterical crying. Murderous desires. Permanent mental problems.

So it was her spirit and not Ulysses' flesh that had shown greatest signs of weakness. Penelope was young, she had not yet lived for eighty years, how could she have behaved in any other way?

Penelope is not an octogenarian, she is an impulsive 26-year-old. She feels rejected, she thinks of the forbidden pleasures of lunatic asylums. Yes, she should just let herself go, get lost once and for all along the tortuous paths of reason. If she – for she is not as good a draughtsman as Ulysses – had to draw a straight line representing rationality, she would draw one full of curves.

She'd really like to be a nutter. Being mad has so many advantages. You don't have to go to prison or explain yourself when you kill or rob or kidnap or wound someone or go to bed with the first person who comes along. You don't have to work because no one will let you. And if you insist on working, you can always gain a few extra Brownie points by claiming learning disabilities when you sit the entrance exam for lowly civil service posts. Then there are the discounts at museums and theme parks. You can test positive for cocaine or phenobarbitol or Valdepeñas at police checkpoints. You can smoke, get fat and insult people in the street. You can think what you want and do whatever you like and no one will find it odd that you, being the way you are – i.e. barking mad – also form part of the evolutionary process.

It's obvious: going mad can only be to her advantage.

'I think I'm going to go mad!' she screams at Ulysses. 'You go to bed with your models, you pig! So these are the pictures you paint, are they? What do you paint them with, your prick? How long has this been going on? How long have you been deceiving me? How many women have you had in my bed? Is that why you bring models home? Where do you find them, in the personal columns? Or do you pick them up in the red-light district?'

She focuses on her fury.

It tastes good.

She can almost chew it.

She realizes that he has just given her the right to eat him alive.

Perhaps she will.

Liver in herbs cooked very rare.

Lightly salted testicles: twenty minutes in a preheated oven and they're ready to serve.

'How *could* you?' she moans. 'Once I've finished at that godawful university, I spend the rest of my time at that godawful college, studying patterns and darts and industrial design. *And* learning to sew! You have no idea how frustrating a needle can be. Meanwhile, you . . . *you* . . .'

They are in the kitchen of the apartment that was Vili's gift to them both, and on which Penelope spent two years getting the decor just right before they actually got married. Ulysses is naked, he seems calm and collected, as if his vulnerable physical state were no obstacle to being so. It probably isn't. At least not for him.

She is looking distractedly around for the carving knives, but can't remember which drawer she keeps them in. She is extremely upset. She doesn't even know why she is looking for them. The lovely Japanese steel knives she bought on the shopping channel.

The model had retrieved her knickers from on top of the paint-spattered easel and had finished getting dressed in the corridor. She was very tall, at least six foot, no kidding. And very serious. She didn't proffer any excuses, she didn't say anything. She left as quickly and discreetly as she could. She had a distracted look on her face as if she had forgotten something. She had big, porcine lips. Obviously a cocksucker. Penelope is sure she was drooling when she left. Pig. Whore. I hope you die on the stairs. In the street. I hope you get run over by a car. I hope a bolt of lightning strikes you and splits your fanny in two.

'Penny, I love you. You're the only woman in my life.'

Penelope starts pacing about like a caged animal. She goes into the living room, into Ulysses' studio, then back into the kitchen. She looks tired, she can't breathe properly. She has climbed a mountain of eight thousand metres, with no Sherpa, with no one to help her carry her pack, and she is showing signs of physical wear and tear, she is going to die of exhaustion. She shouldn't have climbed so high. Every step she takes provokes a wave of nausea, like when you lift your foot in the darkness to place it on a step, and then there is no step, no rung, nothing, just the smooth floor and an unexpected dizziness, a mental pirouette that turns the stomach upside down.

She's dying. She can't even breathe.

She just about manages a juddering out-breath.

'Penny, my love . . . My love, my love . . .'

Penelope feels as if her eyes have turned the colour of dirty water.

'Penny, my love . . .'

Oh, please.

She paces back and forth. She will die in the attempt. But what is it she's attempting? She can't quite remember.

She wants to stop and look at something, to concentrate on something. Some object, a chair, the blank television screen. She can't do it. She has to keep moving, to follow the rhythm that only she can hear.

Sex. An evanescent frippery.

Love. All loves are basically monstrous. They all have something perverse about them. The desire to possess, to be the only ones to enjoy and endure their puerile pornography, their horrific intimacy. A waste of energy imposed by tradition and biology. That's it.

Who would have thought it?

And disloyalty? Well, that too. Cursed be the cretin who first mixed up love and honour.

Kill him. Cut him into pieces.

How noble Ulysses would seem once reduced to mincemeat. How innocent and manageable.

'Anyway, how could you go to bed with someone like that? The woman's enormous!' sobs Penelope. 'She could have eaten you alive. She's a whole head taller than you.'

'Well, yes, possibly. But it was because she's taller than me that I was worried about having her pose standing up, so I asked her to sit down and . . . well, one thing led to another,' says Ulysses, and he says it in a very formal, very serious way.

Just to make matters worse.

'Meaning?' asks Penelope.

'Meaning exactly what I say, whether I actually say it or not,' he replies. 'It's only sex. Don't make such a big thing about it. Anyway, I'd taken precautions.'

'But with . . . with that creature . . . How could you?' Penelope is crying. 'You can tell a mile off that she's one of those women whose clitoris practically hangs down beneath the hem of her skirt!'

'Penelope! There's no need to be rude, my love.'

'Rude? How despicable, how sadistic, how . . .'

'Don't say such things, my love . . .'

'How could you, you disgusting pig?' Penelope roars and even she is taken aback by how loud her voice sounds. 'Haven't you ever seen *Fatal Attraction*? Good God, they've been showing it on telly for years now. Don't you know what happens to married men who have affairs? That . . . that . . .*woman* who just left with her bum in the air could be another Glenn Close!'

As Bonnie Tyler said, the world is full of married men; unfortunately for Penelope, Ulysses is married to her. As Bonnie Tyler said, they do it, they do it, they do it, married men, they do it, they do it again and again.

'My love, you're the best thing that ever happened to me. I mean it,' says Ulysses.

'And how would *you* like it if *I* went out now and picked up some guy and had sex with him in your bed? In my bed. In the bed we both share. What would you think if me and him . . . if him and me and me and him and me . . .' What a lot of people, she thinks. She is distraught.

'It wasn't in our bed, Penny.'

'She was lying with her legs apart in the middle of your studio; that's the same thing,' Penelope says.

'It's not the same thing,' protests Ulysses.

'For me it is.'

'My love, my love . . .' he tries to touch her, but Penelope pushes him away. 'You're so full of possessive preconceptions.'

'Of what?'

'Unjustifiable jealousy.'

'God! Unjustifiable . . . Possessive preconceptions. You talk like a bloody judge.'

'My love, my sweetheart . . . Come here. Let me embrace you, let me . . .' says Ulysses.

'Like hell I will!' replies a furious Penelope, who bursts into tears, adorning her pain with long, mournful howls.

They're having tea with Aglaia, her mother's friend. (Her mother has such strange friends, so very similar to her.) Ulysses and Penelope are sitting on a sofa opposite Aglaia, and the stuffed figure of Aglaia's husband is standing in a sunny corner of the living room, next to a ficus. Both man and plant seem to be enjoying the late afternoon sun coming in through the balcony, although the plant is the more effusive of the two. Aglaia's husband is a solidly built fellow, although not in the way Ulysses is. Ulysses has biceps and triceps and a whole series of other well-defined muscles, honed through long years of boxing at a gym, whereas Aglaia's husband is merely big and fat.

Penelope knows she is dreaming, but knowing this does not in any way diminish her disquiet. It seems to her that things in Aglaia's living room are not quite what they should be. They shouldn't be like this. At least, she doesn't think so.

'I always feel so sorry for dogs,' says Aglaia, who is dressed like a dominatrix: long black leather boots, black leather bra, black leather suspender belt and not much else. Well, nothing else really. 'I always feel sorry for them because, poor things, it seems to me so sad that they should live in the strange world of human beings and not even speak the language.'

'Absolutely,' chorus Penelope and Ulysses.

Aglaia gets up and goes over to her husband, who remains

standing stiffly at his post, revealing a little of his cadaverous dentures, and with an inconsolable look on his face (well, it must be hard being sent off to a taxidermist's just to please your wife and make life with her more pleasant).

'And you can shut up too!' Aglaia screams at her husband's stuffed corpse; then, addressing the two lovebirds, but mainly the lady lovebird, she says: 'You must never let men get away with anything.'

Aglaia rubs at her husband's snout with a black leather handkerchief. She scrubs energetically and determinedly at his half-open mouth, the way one might rub away at a stubborn bit of grime on a mirror.

'One of these days, I'll have to call in the removal men and have them take him to the dentist. To Dr Morillo at the Rosales clinic,' she says as she continues with her polishing. 'His teeth need scaling.'

Ulysses stands up and approaches the eccentric couple. He bends down. He takes a long look at the husband's face.

'Is that yellow stuff between his teeth tartar?' he enquires with some interest.

'Of course.'

'Oh, I'm so sorry!' Ulysses gives a desolate cry. 'I thought it was urine.'

They sit down again. Aglaia clutches her tea cup. Her fingernails are painted with black leather. How did she achieve this weird effect?

'The mouth is a very intimate thing,' says Penelope, pointing to her husband.

'Yes, in that sense, it's very like the arse,' Aglaia replies.

'Yes, in that sense and in many others,' agrees Ulysses.

'Anyway, going back to what I was saying, I've decided to set up an organization,' concludes Aglaia, more to herself than to anyone else.

'What organization is that?'

'The Association for Sexually Exploited Dogs.' Aglaia pronounces the words with such emphasis that they receive each syllable in their ears like a whiplash.

'Are there dogs like that?' Penelope asks. 'I find it hard to believe. What kind of a world are we living in?'

'Well, it's true, my dear.'

'And who exploits them?'

'Well, there's talk of an Aragonese mafia, of disreputable property developers, of dissatisfied housewives . . . But what we're talking about here is mostly zoophilia and porn movies.' Her voice becomes reserved, caressing. 'You can't imagine how many rackets are involved, the underworld, the shady deals, the money, the power, the people in the high places . . . You simply can't imagine.'

'We could if you explained it a little more clearly,' says Ulysses, and Penelope shoots him an angry look for having spoken out of turn.

He shrugs.

'And what are you doing about it?' asks Penelope.

'I've formed this Association.' You can hear the capital A when she says the word. 'I founded it. I preside over it. I direct it. I raise funds. I make a fuss about what's going on. I blackmail a few people into donating money to pay for my campaigns. I take in dogs and give them psychiatric help, food and a happy home where they can heal the wounds inflicted on their innocent, canine souls.'

'Where do you get the dogs from?'

Aglaia gives a sideways glance at her husband, who remains impassive by the ficus. A fly is walking calmly about on his right iris, doubtless depositing its detritus there.

'Did he move?' asks Aglaia anxiously. 'I'm sure he did.'

'I don't think so.'

'Did he move or didn't he? Should I go over there?'

'He didn't move,' says Ulysses.

Penelope gives him another baleful look.

'You were explaining how you find the dogs . . .'

'Oh, yes . . . Well, I have my contacts, and . . .' Aglaia turns all her attention on Penelope. Suddenly, she swivels her neck round to look at her husband, hoping to surprise him.

'Really, he didn't move.'

'Don't underestimate him,' murmurs Aglaia venomously.

'So you take in these dogs and . . .' Penelope is wondering why she is suddenly so interested in sexually exploited dogs. But there's no denying it, she feels an intense curiosity.

'See, he did move.' Aglaia pulls a surly face; she angrily purses her lips.

'He didn't,' insists Ulysses. 'Your husband . . . what's your husband's name?'

'Gordon, Flash Gordon!' Now it sounds as if Aglaia were admonishing a frisky colt.

'Well, it's a very appropriate name . . . very appropriate,' says Ulysses. 'But he hasn't moved.'

'Our marriage is a hell. Although less so now.' Aglaia points at him with the whip that she keeps by her chair. 'Pig. He used to go to bed with me and then refuse to pay me what he owed me.'

'But didn't you say he was your husband?' exclaims Ulysses.

'Exactly, my dear. You see what I mean.'

'Anyway,' puts in Penelope, 'we were talking about dogs . . .'

'Yes, of course. I've got contacts, you know. Producers of hardcore movies. They use the poor little creatures and when they can't perform any more, they get rid of them. They just kick them out and tell them to get lost. All that awaits them then is the municipal dog pound, the male menopause and an undignified, needy old age. Discarded sexual objects. Worse than used condoms. Much worse. I don't know what the world's coming to,' says Aglaia. 'I take them in. I give them love and company.'

'Do you also free them from their fornicatory duties?' asks Ulysses ghoulishly.

'Oh, they're quite free. If they want to, of course, then it's up to them. But we never speak here of duties or enslavement. There are no chains. I don't even put a collar on them.'

'But wouldn't it be, oh, I don't know, easier, more acceptable to devote yourself to orphans or something?' Ulysses refuses to keep his mouth shut. He opens it and takes a large gulp of tea.

'I don't see why,' replies Aglaia.

'And where do you keep them?'

'Keep what?'

'The dogs.'

'Here, of course. I wouldn't put them in a separate apartment, it would completely ruin the restorative therapy. They're very damaged creatures, they've had a really hard time and I need to have them with me, so that I can care for them and heal them, however long it takes. Why do you ask? Do you want to see them?

Penelope knows she is dreaming and that she shouldn't let Aglaia show her the dogs. She shouldn't see them. She doesn't want to and she shouldn't. Well, she probably does want to, but she shouldn't.

'I'd love to,' she says and claps her hands.

Aglaia agrees, gets up and walks majestically over to a side door, keeping one eye on her husband, so stiff and still and sad.

'If you so much as think of moving . . .' she mutters.

She flings open the door, and the room is immediately filled with the sound of joyful barking. It fills up with dogs of every imaginable breed and colour. Several of them approach Penelope's legs, and she keeps a close eye on their pelvic movements. Disgusted, fascinated.

'Well, they don't look to me as if they've suffered very much.' Ulysses, for once, has to raise his voice, to make himself heard above the hubbub made by the hundred and one mutts. 'It strikes me that they've scored even more often than I have.'

It is then that Penelope begins to study the dogs properly. She kicks them away from around her legs as soon as she realizes what is happening.

She gives a terrified scream. She is sweating.

She screams again. She climbs on to the sofa, trying to escape from the dogs. She looks at the dogs once more, and sees for herself the horror, utter and complete. Disturbing and alluring, as are all terrors written on the heart by an unconscious, tormented imagination: the dogs all have Ulysses' face. Every one of them. The same damp, hairy snout. The same round, questioning eyes. The long dangling tongue, lolling several inches out of their mouths. The big, pointed ears, listening to everything. The same greedy, swinish . . .

'Penelope, my love, what's wrong?' Ulysses is shaking her gently, trying to wake her up.

'Aaaargh! Aaaargh!' she roars, drenched in a cold sweat.

'Wake up, Penelope, my love . . .'

'A dog! You're a dog!' she pants indignantly, slapping the air.

'Oh, sweetheart, when are you going to forget all about that business with the model? How often have I got to tell you that it didn't mean anything,' Ulysses whispers sadly. And he tenderly strokes her hair, as she trembles.

The desire for justice

Tac, tac, tac go Penelope's heels as she walks through the apartment, holding her son. He's so heavy this little boy, but she can manage, she's strong enough, she has to be. While her mother is dying before her eyes, Penelope wonders what it is that she has always wanted from life. She answers that she has always wanted from life exactly what the public demand from television: excitement, reality, involvement, popularity, comedy and drama, something to talk about.

Has life given her that? Well, she may have had a little of all those things, but she doesn't yet feel that every one of her expectations has been met. She's not asking for much: she's not as ambitious as Ulysses, for example.

Ulysses devoted himself to painting because he loved it; he had so much talent that he succumbed to the lure of permanence. He believed that by painting amazing pictures he would eventually be transformed into an enduring myth. Penelope, however, cannot even understand the concept of eternity. How could she when she is a mere mortal?

Tac, tac, tac . . .

She knows that canvases rot in museums, despite being resuscitated every so often – reworked, recomposed, remade. She knows that in art – in life, and in general – there is always more than enough artifice, vanity and dissipation. She does not believe in eternity; she puts her trust in fashion alone, in the endless passing show.

That is one of the ways in which she and Ulysses differ: Penelope knows that collecting clocks will not make her immortal.

Oh, Penelope knows. And the more she knows, the more everything she does not know weighs heavily upon her. But so what?

She is carrying the boy in her arms, walking with great determination, clutching him to her as if he were her captive. Her little boy. She hasn't seen him for three months, and he's her son, dear God, her little baby.

But he's so heavy.

Tac, tac, tac, her heels tap nervously across the old floorboards.

Penelope is a Delavayi magnolia that has closed its petals about the small insect that has landed on her. She is an intrepid explorer bravely facing the unknown: a long corridor, the rainy night, the domestic jungle, an elusive, treacherous husband, an innocent child, a mother. Penelope is a mother. A mother with a mother who is dying, who has always been dying.

But how heavy her little boy is. He's grown a lot, he's quite the little man. Telemachus clings to her neck. His firm flesh smells of quince. She walks through the apartment carrying him as if she were walking through the night. Her steps, every step she takes, are a reaction against unease. She will reach the kitchen even if she were suddenly to become asthmatic, paralytic and hunchbacked.

'Let me carry him,' says Ulysses. He is walking behind them, his eyes fixed abstractedly on Penelope's waist.

'No.'

'He's really heavy.'

'It doesn't matter.'

'Mama!' screams Telemachus, and he gives her a kiss, as he puts his arms about her neck.

Penelope's impeccable black dress now has a bit of mud on the skirt where the boy has scuffed it with his shoes.

'Sweetie,' Penelope says, and rubs noses with the child.

'Love you,' says Telemachus.

'Who loves me?'

'*I* do,' and the boy again embraces and kisses her. He is a child of love, and the only happy creature in that apartment. A child is a life sentence, she thinks. What a delightful sentence, though, here, now, with him in her arms, plunging his sticky little fingers into the warm space between her breasts. In full bloom, bursting with life and health, they walk along together, his small body pressed to her body. Keeping each other company and exchanging kisses. Flesh of one flesh. True love come to fruition. *Tout n'est pas dégout et misère*. She will reach the kitchen without putting him down to let him walk on his own – regardless of much he weighs.

'Telemachus!' Valentina comes to meet him, unexpectedly, though somewhat feebly, clapping her hands. She must be tired. 'Hello, Ulysses,' she says rather less enthusiastically. 'How's my mother?'

'Hello,' says Ulysses. 'Oh, she's fine. She stayed at home, though. It's not really the weather for coming out at night with children and old ladies.'

'No, she's better off staying at home. Telemachus . . .'

'What?' says the little boy, smiling and tugging at his mother's hair.

'You're here!' says Valentina.

'Supper,' replies the boy.

'Hasn't he had his supper yet?' Penelope demands of Ulysses, frowning.

'Of course he has,' he replies, 'but I had to give some reason for dragging him out of the house at this hour, in the pouring rain, and living as we do in a part of town which, after about eight o'clock at night, is overrun with drug dealers, junkies and other forms of low life.'

'You could just have told him you were bringing him to see his mother and his grandparents,' retorts Penelope, carefully depositing Telemachus on the floor.

Valentina holds out her hand to him. She has dark circles under her eyes and her irises are slightly cloudy, but she smiles at the boy and is glad to have him there. Does the thing that hurts her still hurt? She looks ill. But then she is ill.

'I've got something to show you,' she says in a mysterious voice. Children are fascinated by mysteries – and by everything else.

'What?'

'Aha! It's a secret. But, if you come with me, you'll find out,' says his grandmother.

The little boy agrees and lets himself be led away by her, although he keeps turning to look back at his mother; he doesn't want her to disappear again the way she always does. Valentina leads him over to a corner of the kitchen and rummages around in one of the cupboards.

'What should I have told him then? "I'm taking you to see the mother who abandoned you when you were three months old, the one you only see every few months?" Because you are the mother who abandoned him, and no one else, or have you forgotten that?' The opening salvo from Ulysses. Ulysses takes out his guns. This is war. When it is necessary, war is just, according to Livy. As are weapons, which are innocent when they become the only hope.

Ulysses is a son-of-a-bitch, but Penelope appreciates this quality in a man. She smiles at him as if she were trying to seduce him. Is that what she's trying to do? Why not? She has thought about all this beforehand; she knows the advantages of thinking ahead. Thinking about tomorrow today, and the day after tomorrow tomorrow. And so on every day. But she doesn't know if she has thought correctly, if she has thought of everything she should have thought of. Her heart is beating, nothing strange about that, of course, but it troubles her that she can count the beats so easily, without trying and without feeling her pulse. Anyone could count them, they are echoing through the whole apartment, with the thunder of irregular drumbeats. Ulysses is probably counting the beats and knows that they're too fast, as if they are in a hurry to do whatever it is they have to do to keep the body functioning and for her not suddenly to become another empty vessel.

'Do you mind coming into the library? I don't want Telemachus to hear us arguing,' she says, breathing deeply and exhaling mouthfuls of air as carefully as if they were bits of fiery phlegm that she had to expel from her body without burning her throat. She inhales and exhales. That's it. Gently does it.

Ulysses indolently follows her. He looks at her waist, at her buttocks beneath the caressing fabric of the dress, at the two halves formed by her glutei, left and right; doubles, twins, good and evil, instinct and reason. His eyes snake down her body to her ankles, her heels. Tac, tac, tac.

Roberta passes them and greets them with a timid nod, muttering a glum 'Good evening'.

'I no longer know whether you're my wife or my ex-wife. I don't even know who you are any more,' Ulysses says to Penelope. 'That's why I think we need to go to a lawyer and start divorce proceedings, and get things clear as regards Telemachus. I've had enough. I'm not prepared to let you do whatever you like any more. I need to remake my life. If you don't want to do it, then I'll do it on my own. I don't even think I need you in order to go to a lawyer and ask for a divorce.'

'Don't ever say again that I abandoned Telemachus,' Penelope says bitterly. 'Don't say it again, because it isn't true: I left you, not him.'

'Ha!' Ulysses runs a hand over his hair and looks away.

Rows and rows of books, on floor-to-ceiling oak shelves painted white. Too many books. Vili is always buying books. Does he really have time to read them all? Who can possibly have so much time that they can afford to squander it on millions of dead letters printed on plain bound paper?

'What do you mean by that?'

'You left him in his cot. He was crying when you finally slammed out of the apartment. It was his feeding time. You should have breastfed him. And he was crying. And you'd left all that rat poison in the fridge; I even had to throw away the baby's bottles that were in there. All of them. They could have been contaminated by the poison you left us as a present. I had to scrub the fridge out with hot water and bleach, and I nearly choked in the process. I had to grab the baby and race off to a pharmacy in search of milk and new bottles. I had to ask the pharmacist how to make up the bottles. She didn't have a clue. Can you believe that – she didn't have a clue. She didn't have children herself, had only graduated two months before and was working in her father's pharmacy for the first time. It was her first day at work. We had to open the packet of milk, the packet I bought, and read the instructions from start to finish with a starving baby crying in my arms.'

'Ulysses, I don't think that . . .'

'That was you, Penny. That's the kind of woman you are.'

'I suppose that if, even once, you had deigned to make up a bottle for the baby, even if it was only mineral water and sherry, it wouldn't have been quite so hard for you to fend for yourself when you had to.'

'Oh, of course, and I suppose . . .'

'And I suppose that, if it hadn't been for your continual infidelities, and all those years of putting up with your adulteries and your affairs, I wouldn't have left you, and I wouldn't have made you that toxic supper for rodents.'

'The thing is, Penelope . . .'

'You can't say I didn't fulfil my duties as a good wife: I left you your supper ready prepared. It's your problem if you decided not to eat it.'

'But what about the baby, Penny? Didn't it break your heart to leave him like that? He was so small.'

'I left him with you to buck your ideas up, to teach you a lesson, to make you understand what it means to have a child. Having a child means having a duty to bring him up, feed him, wash his bottom, bathe him, treat any illnesses he gets and try to ensure he doesn't get any more. It's struggling to keep him alive, to protect him. And that's hard, you know. Having a child isn't spending the day swanning around, going to bed with models and gallery owners, hatching murky business deals and rolling home in the small hours to plant a little kiss on the cheek of a baby who is, by then, sleeping peacefully because someone, i.e. me, is there to look after him.'

Penelope pauses for breath. Her pulse is beating fast. Be careful. You have to be careful with anger, and not allow it to take you over. Anger and madness are sister substances. A moment's inattention, and the one puts down roots in the other. You have to rein in the heart. And the pulse.

Cicero advises getting to know people before venturing to love them. Penelope knew Ulysses when she decided that she loved him. She never deceived herself about him. But all that love eventually proved too painful. She doesn't regret having left him. Nor having loved him. She doesn't even regret loving him still.

'I told you thousands of times that my affairs meant nothing.' Ulysses sits down in an armchair, puts his hands together and watches Penelope. 'There was never any other woman but you. And there still isn't,' he adds, staring down at the floor now, as if talking to himself.

Penelope doesn't even blink.

Ah, male love, always ruled by such a liberal regime. This guy gives himself so much leeway, he's always so generous when it comes to dealing with himself. The bastard.

'And what about all those paintings, the ones you were forging for years behind my back, the ones that your friend, that loony Belgian art dealer, sold for you? Some of them, I believe, can be found in large American museums, whilst the originals are hanging, much to their astonishment, in the private rooms of some multi-millionaire who doesn't know his Picasso from his Matt Groening.'

'Don't start on that. I've moved on since then,' says Ulysses. 'I've cut all my ties with Jacques. He's retired. I don't forge paintings any more. The truth is that, since you left me, I haven't even had time to paint my own pictures, let alone find the energy to plagiarize Goyas and medieval Flemish panels.'

'I'm very glad to hear it, darling.' Penelope beams, and sits down on a cherry-red leather sofa. 'I'm really pleased for you. It's good that you don't have time for certain things. I'm delighted that the child takes up all your time.'

'Well, almost all.'

'You're a philanderer.'

'*What?* I've always been faithful to you. I only know one way of being faithful to you and that's by loving you. And my love for you has never faltered. If you deny that, you're a liar.'

'You're a criminal.'

'That's not true. It's just that my point of view doesn't always coincide with that of the law.'

'And a sex maniac.'

'That's not true either, Penny. You know, better than anyone, that isn't true. Even you would admit that I'm the most loving and devoted man you've ever met. And I'm still devoted to you, even though it's all over between us.'

'Yes, it is,' Penelope confirms. Does she really believe that? Who knows when something is really over? What does it mean when you say something is really over? Does it mean anything?

'But what about the boy?' stammers Ulysses.

Roberta knocks on the door, even though the door is open. The skin on her face is the colour of a fresh egg yolk.

'Excuse me, but your mother says to tell you that supper is

served in the big dining room,' she whispers, as if she were ashamed to announce such a thing.

'We're just coming,' says Penelope, getting up.

'She also said could you tell Señor Vili.'

'Yes, of course.'

'Why aren't we happy?' Ulysses suddenly asks.

Roberta looks at him, perplexed. Is she supposed to answer this question? She pulls a comical face, shrugs and puffs out her cheeks, as if about to give a response.

'I don't know,' says Penelope.

And off she goes. Her steps are muffled as she crosses the thick Persian carpet, until she reaches the corridor. Once there, the refrain resumes, that feminine tap-tapping.

Tac, tac, tac.

Lack of self-love

Trust.

The secret of all loving relationships must be trust, thinks Penelope. She doesn't mean, as therapists usually recommend, that there should be no secrets in a union.

Union: what a terrible word – it sounds so impressive and definitive, as if it were a terminal illness. Cancer of the heart. Metastasis of the feelings.

Secrets and lies. Deep drawers full of time bombs lodged in memory and recollection. Deceptions. Betrayals. No, she doesn't mean that. She doesn't mean that between a couple – assuming they want to strengthen their bond – there should be no secrets, no mutual evasions.

No, quite the opposite. She thinks that an excess of trust is dangerous and prejudicial to love.

Penelope suspects that, children and a few select friends apart (although she's not even entirely sure about them), with the other people in one's life – husbands and wives, lovers and loved ones, fiancées and fiancés – it is best to adopt the same strategy as one does when driving: always keep a safe distance in order to avoid catastrophic accidents.

This is the prudent measure taken by calm, cautious folk. The kind of people who love themselves and the other person enough to want to avoid a fatal collision.

Roads made slippery by the rain. Oily surfaces. Adulteries.
Speeding. Monotony.
Fog and smoke. Deceit. Resentment.

Once she asked her grandmother, Araceli: 'Why did you and Grandpa never fight?' Araceli replied: 'Because I never trusted him enough.'

Therein lay the problem: too much trust.

That had been the case with her and Ulysses. Vili and her mother (especially her mother) had likewise overdone the trust. Penelope imagines trust as a small handicapped girl who is easy prey to lollipop thieves, someone with plaits you can tug, someone you can kick, then run away. Poor trust.

True, her grandmother's marriage was hardly perfect, but no marriage is, and at least they didn't go on at each other like two foul-mouthed louts. They never behaved like a drunken sailor and a prostitute who hasn't been paid.

Shouts, insults, betrayal and crime.

She and Ulysses, her mother and her father, had all done just that.

Does that mean they love each other more?

'I'm not going to eat much,' says Vili, sitting down at the table, trying hard not to seem upset.

'Why not?' asks Valentina.

'You know perfectly well why not.'

'Look, you can't go on like this,' insists Valentina. 'Nothing really happened. Nothing important. The man was paranoid, and he happened to pick on you; he could just as easily have picked on the fellow from the bar on the corner.'

'Yes, it could have been the fellow from the bar on the corner, but he picked me. Anyway, I'm not hungry.' Vili places his napkin on his lap. He fiddles with his fork.

Roberta serves the salad.

Telemachus is excited and fidgets in his seat. He doesn't usually eat with the grown-ups. He's not hungry, he's sleepy, but he's nevertheless determined to try a little of everything, just to see what it's like.

'Don't start to eat until we all start,' Ulysses says, sitting down next to him. On the other side of the boy sits Penelope.

'Not start?' asks Telemachus.

'Because it's bad manners.'

'Bad manners?'

'Yes, it means you're not being a good boy.'

'Aaah,' Telemachus nods sagely and continues, very seriously, to eat.

'Leave him,' says Vili. 'Don't pester him about it now. It doesn't really matter if he eats before or after us. The table isn't an orchestra, after all; there's no need for us all to be perfectly synchronized. Let him do what he likes while he can. Isn't that right, champ?'

'Yes,' says the boy.

'What a sweet grandson I've got. I couldn't have found a better one even if I'd looked, not even on the telly,' says Vili.

Telemachus nods contentedly several times.

Penelope is also beginning to chew her food. She looks at Ulysses out of the corner of her eye, and it seems to her that a kind of shadow crosses her eyes at that moment. With the endive and the apple in her mouth, releasing their juices and mingling them with her saliva, she is filled by a strange feeling. The feeling that all of them, without exception, are innocent. It strikes her as so simple and so extraordinary that she cannot understand why she didn't realize this before.

She observes her son, who hardly uses the cutlery to eat with, although he manages very well with his fingers, and she wonders if this way of life is right for her. If it is really the most appropriate life for her.

Why are they so unhappy? Why, why?

Valentina is terribly pale.

Has she started to die already? Will she be able to last until they have all finished eating? Death, after all, is not like the desire to pee. Although, who knows?

'Isn't it a bit late for the child to be up?' asks Vili.

'You bet.' Ulysses speaks with his mouth full, doubtless unable to contain himself.

'Everyone stays up late in Madrid. It's not so terrible,' says Valentina.

'Exactly.' Penelope finishes her mouthful of food. The salad is superb. A salad made by the hands of a dying woman. Dressed by her mother's hands and tossed by her trembling, dying fingers. It's delicious, the salad. 'In Madrid people go to bed late and get up early.'

'True,' says Vili, who merely moves the salad about on his plate with his knife, without tasting a morsel. 'But I have the feeling that those who go to bed late are not the same ones who get up early.'

Vili rubs the sockets of his eyes.

She should tell him that her mother is dying, thinks Penelope. She should tell him tonight. But is it right to flout the wishes of a dying woman? Is it correct? Will she be punished in some way if she doesn't? An avenging meteorite; a small plague of locusts in her kitchen; a terrifying wind that will steal away her son's soul; the kind of thing that tends to come from the other world. She's not superstitious, like Jana, but she would prefer not to think about it.

The processing centre in the brain is located in the lateral pre-frontal cortex, which exists in both hemispheres and is situated above the eyeballs. The very parts that Vili is furiously massaging at this moment. (He is frantically rubbing his eyes and his eyebrows.) That is the area where information is organized and collated, then transmitted to other parts of the brain as necessary. Penelope read this somewhere, although she can't remember where. All she can recall is thinking how odd it was that one could almost brush against the brain's processing centre – even disturb it – by a simple movement of the lashes.

'Papi,' (Penelope always calls Vili 'Papi', never 'Papa', and now she wonders why) 'what's wrong?'

'I've got a headache, but it's nothing serious. I'll take a paracetamol. Would you mind calling Roberta?'

As if she had heard them, the maid appears at the door.

'Would you mind bringing a paracetamol for my father?' Penelope asks, and looks with sad, supplicant eyes at the sad, supplicant eyes of the maid.

'Of course,' says Roberta and turns to go out through the door she came in.

'Thank you, Roberta.'

'That's Madrid for you.' Ulysses seems cheered by the food and the wine; he fills his glass and takes an appreciative sip. How long has it been since they all had supper together? 'Where we live . . .' he shoots Penelope the briefest of spiteful looks, only a second, and then immediately grows cheerful again. 'I mean where Telemachus and I live . . .'

The child smiles at his father when he hears his own name. He is beginning to grow bored with the meal and he too is rubbing his eyes. He is tired. He puts his arms on the table and puts his head close to the tablecloth.

'Mami . . .' he says and closes his eyes. 'Mami.'

Penelope strokes his hair and takes the exhausted hand held out to her.

'Hello, sweetie.'

'Anyway,' says Ulysses, 'there's this Chinese restaurant near our house, which I just love. They do home deliveries, and I can call them up at one o'clock in the morning and they're always happy to bring me something. They just defrost a few Peruvian prawns, or a few fillets of cat, or whatever, and they bring it round to the house, with a look of pure delight on their face too,' says Ulysses. 'That's what I like about Madrid. I don't mind people staying up late. As far as I'm concerned, people can do what they like.'

'That isn't what you were saying earlier on,' says Penelope.

'What was I saying earlier on?'

'You said the area is full of yobs and drug addicts, and that you didn't like bringing Telemachus out at night.'

'Well, that's true, but what's that got to do with what I've just said?'

Roberta enters carrying a glass of water and a tablet on a dish.

'Here you are.' She sets it down in front of Vili and removes his plate. He has hardly eaten anything.

'Thank you!' cries Vili.

'There's no need to shout,' says Valentina, 'she's not deaf.'

'Isn't she?'

'No, I'm not.' Roberta gives a half-smile and takes away a few knives and forks and used glasses.

'Well, I was convinced . . . I don't know why, but . . .'

'It's not good to be convinced about anything,' Valentina says, and raises her glass to Vili.

He puts the tablet in his mouth and drinks the water.

'You're not drinking as much,' he says to Valentina, pointing at her with his empty glass. 'You haven't had a drink for days. This last week the level in the vodka bottles hasn't been dropping like the River Nile as it usually does. Is something wrong?'

'I don't feel much like drinking.'

'Don't you feel like smoking either or having a go at me?'

'Stop it, Vili.'

'You're right, I'm sorry. My head hurts.'

'I have a friend who only ever drinks in bars,' Ulysses says. 'Unfortunately, he's a bit of barfly and drinks an awful lot, even though he never drinks at home. And . . . Oops, Telemachus has dropped off. I knew he wouldn't make dessert,' he says to Penelope.

'We should put him to bed.' Penelope gently draws Telemachus towards her, head and shoulders first, sliding him off his chair and on to her lap. She rocks him in her arms and sniffs his hair. Does Ulysses wash it often enough? Does he do it well? Does he rinse it thoroughly with plenty of warm water?

'Poor little thing. Put him in your room,' Valentina suggests.

'Yes, I will.'

Dread

Penelope would like to know what marriage really is.

Oh, she knows that it is, first and foremost, a bureaucratic process which, once two people have been through it, facilitates routine administrative procedures and ensures a certain degree of social consideration, even respect, from family, neighbours, friends and civil servants.

But marriage does not seem to be much more than a practical evolution of administrative law, which, in the modern world, has come to include even bonds of affection, given our incurable fondness for ridiculous ceremonies, for all kinds of ceremonies, and given our fondness for adorning all kinds of ceremonies with all kinds of feelings induced and provoked by the ceremonies themselves.

(Football.

First Communions.

Weddings.

Parades.

Birthdays.

Graduations.

Funerals.

State investitures.

Television interviews.

Terrorist attacks.

The Oscars.

War.)

Marriage is just a means of facilitating the transmission of private property, and is usually sealed in a registry office or a church, in front of some bored official, accompanied by a secretary badly dressed for the occasion, or a parish priest who is thinking more about the food and drink at the wedding reception than serving God in the strictest sense. What service are we doing the Divine One by arranging carnal pairings-up and subsequent relationships in such an unimaginative way? The only people who really gain – from the income tax on child support – are the Inland Revenue.

Or so Penelope fears.

Because, whichever way you look at it, the one thing marriage doesn't give the bride and bridegroom is a certificate of feelings. So it fails to deliver the essential thing. No 'lifetime guarantee'. No guaranteed clause that declares categorically: 'The emotion you are feeling now will never go wrong because it was made in Japan by a 100 per cent automated industry using cutting-edge technology.' No chance.

Affections are born, grow, get old and die. They are as alive as the people who feel them. We do not feel today what we felt yesterday, nor will we feel tomorrow what we feel today, because, be it yesterday, today or tomorrow, we are never the same person. Indeed, we rarely know who we are.

According to Vili, Gide said: 'I am never who I believe I am, and that changes all the time.'

Sometimes, Penelope feels afraid – of failure, illness, poverty, of arousing hatred and violence in others, of losing for ever the adolescent she was, the girl she was, the young woman she had been. She liked those three little women. Carrot-topped and smiling, voraciously gulping life down. Absurdly ignorant, and perhaps happy. Now Penelope is a different Penelope. Should she be afraid too of the Penelopes she will become in the future? Ah, Time, that wretched beetle making its insistent little balls of filth out of flesh and feeling.

*

213

She lays the child down on the bed. He may only be small, but he's still a heavy weight for her lower back which has grown unused to the more humble tasks of motherhood.

Into the bedroom, through the window, slips a pale, disorderly light that seems to be constantly collapsing like a golden house of cards. The rain is getting worse again; it sounds like the tiresome echo of a madman's prayers. Sha sha sha. Never stopping. Never taking even a brief respite in order to gather the strength to carry on.

Telemachus is asleep, oblivious to everything. He doesn't care about the bad weather or people's problems, he isn't afraid that the sky will break over his head and that everything will end. He is like a small animal whose one aim is to grow, to offer himself up to life and then gollop it down in great mouthfuls, laughing and laughing as he does.

She hopes he manages it, she hopes he does drain life to the dregs with the same smile on his face that he is wearing now as he dreams his child's dreams.

Someone opens the door.

'Do you want any help?' Ulysses asks.

'No, thanks.' Penelope is untying the laces on Telemachus's shoes, which she takes off and puts beside the bed.

'You don't need to cover him with the sheet.' Ulysses touches Telemachus's forehead. 'He's sweating. He always sweats.'

'Ssh! Don't talk so loudly, you'll wake him up.'

'Children always sweat.'

'Lower your voice.'

'He's not going to wake up.'

'All right, but speak more quietly, will you?'

'I'm telling you he won't wake up. He sleeps like a top, he really puts his all into sleeping. He wouldn't wake up even if you put a bomb under his bed.'

'Don't talk like that?'

'Why, what did I say?'

A bomb under her son's bed, is he mad? It's hardly a pleasant image for a mother, however bad a mother she might be.

Ulysses opens his mouth, then closes it.

'Don't say such a thing again.'

'Why?' he says. 'It's just a manner of speaking.'

'Well, I don't like it.'

'All right, but don't cover him up. I don't want him to sweat. He'll only catch a chill when we leave and then I'll be the one who has to nurse him through a cold.'

'He's not going to leave.'

'What? What are you talking about?'

'I mean he's going to sleep here with me.'

'Oh, no he's not.' In the darkness, Ulysses' eyes take on a hard glint. 'If you believe that, you've got another think coming.'

'But why not? He's my son.'

'Your abandoned . . .'

'I didn't abandon him. And please don't say that again; one day he might understand you.'

'You should have thought of that before.'

'Look, Ulysses, we've already talked about . . .'

'Not enough, it seems.'

'All right, we'll go to the courts, as you suggested. We'll see what they decide.'

Penelope goes over to the bathroom door. She goes in. She switches on the lamp above the carved pine dressing table. Ulysses follows her. She closes the door and sits down on the lid of the toilet. They whisper.

'Shut up,' she says.

'No, you shut up,' he says.

'I don't feel like it. I want my son. I warned you the last time we met that the situation with Telemachus might change soon, but you didn't want to listen.'

'Oh, of course. . .you warned me. You warned me and then the next day you jumped on a plane and disappeared off to. . .where was it? Tokyo? Paris? Fuenterrabía? I don't remember and frankly I don't give a toss. The fact is that the boy was left with me, and he's going to stay with me.'

'I had . . .' Penelope begins. 'It was the height of the . . .'

'Don't come to me with any more of your excuses,' Ulysses looks at her. He goes over to her. He examines her lips. Not a trace of lipstick, it must all have rubbed off on the napkin while she was eating the salad. Her lips are slightly dry. She should lick them. Perhaps if she wet them with a little saliva. . . 'I don't want to hear any more of your second-rate superwoman excuses.'

'Of course not, you've got more than enough of your own "great man" excuses – ah, yes, the great man brought low.' Penelope smiles. She feels nasty, vicious. She likes the feeling. 'The artist *extraordinaire*. The Velázquez of the post-modern age. The latest great arsehole never to be hung in the Prado.'

'Shut up!' Ulysses goes over to the mirror and rests his hands on the sink.

'No, you shut up.'

'You're . . .'

'What? What am I? Does it bother you that I'm a success while you're living on the money I give you for Telemachus's keep?' But what is success, Penelope thinks but does not say. Nothing fails like success. There's nothing to be learned from success, she thinks but again does not say. 'Is that it? Is the great man unhappy, does he feel humiliated? Did the great man think that, when I left his house, I wouldn't know what to do and would return to the fold the next day, to put up with his forgery rackets and his little flings, again and again? Is that what the great man thought? Well, in that case, the great man was, above all, a great fool. And it's hard for him to admit it now, the poor great man, the stupid great idiot.'

Ulysses goes over to Penelope, who is still seated. He grabs her by the shoulders and grips hard. She can smell the violence emanating from his body. The tense forearms of a boxer who hasn't trained for ages, who only takes time out now to rock the cradle. She can even see a foreshortened version of his thoughts. That little bit of hatred, crouched and naked, like a ball of fire in the middle of his pupil. But that fire doesn't burn her; on the contrary, it restores her spirits. Screw him.

She isn't afraid of him, and she smiles again, this time sweetly. She is pretending. And she grinds her teeth as she pretends to be smiling.

'What am I, then?' she insists. 'Does it bother you so much that I have managed to do in two years what you have been trying to do your whole life?'

'No.' Ulysses removes his hands from her shoulders, very slowly, as if they had been connected to her by deep filaments of living nerves which it now takes an enormous effort on his part to uproot from Penelope's body. 'No, I don't mind, I'm pleased for you. I hope you've got what you wanted. But . . .'

'But what?'

'According to the proverb, he who makes his fortune in a year should probably have been hanged twelve months before.'

'You don't say.'

'No, I don't say anything, that's what the proverb says.'

Ulysses goes over to the chest of drawers. He picks up a hairbrush. It's hard and fibrous; he runs the bristles over the palm of his hand, he strokes himself with them. They are rough, unpleasant, like strips of dried monkey skin.

'Your hair needs brushing. Let me brush it for you.'

'Put that brush down at once,' she orders.

'Why do you dye your hair blonde? I much prefer your natural colour. Tell me, why do you do that?'

'Because I'm starting to get a few grey hairs,' says Penelope, looking him straight in the eye.

'Really?' And he gives a mischievous smile. 'Is the princess getting old? Sound the alarm! What a tragedy! And what will become of the princess when she's an old lady?'

'She'll turn into a queen. Now put that brush back where it belongs.'

'Why? I just want to brush your hair. You're not looking quite so glamorous after your close encounter with Telemachus. Look, your dress is all stained and creased; your hair's all over the place and your lipstick's come off. What would your boss say if he could see you now? Or your secretary. Or your lovers.'

'Put the brush down. Please.'

'I'm going to brush your hair.'

'Don't come near me. Put it back where you got it from.'

'I can smarten you up a bit; after all, we've got to go back into the dining room and finish supper. Your parents deserve to see you looking . . .'

'I said, put that brush down!'

Penelope goes over to him and wrenches the brush from his hands.

He doesn't resist. He smiles. And he raises his arms as if she were pointing a gun at him. Why doesn't he resist? Why doesn't he put up a fight? Why doesn't he ask her if she wants to make love with him so that she at least has the chance to give him a kick in the . . . ? Oh, who cares?

The fact is that Penelope has won. She has the implement in her hands. She puts it back in its place. It is a hairbrush, her hairbrush, it is in her possession, she has won. She has won a fool's victory.

'Let's go and finish supper,' she says and sighs loudly.

When they leave the bathroom, Ulysses turns out the light and follows her.

'Have you put the boy to bed?' asks Vili. He has a bored expression on his face and is gripping his wine glass hard, as if he wants to shatter the fine Bohemian crystal with his fingers. Perhaps he thinks that the glass, which looks rather like a chalice, represents some kind of wall or fortress, which he feels obliged to breach, tearing it down with his own hands.

'Yes, he's asleep,' replies Penelope, returning to her chair.

'If you go on squeezing your glass like that, you'll break it,' Valentina warns Vili. His eyes are half-closed. He's pondering. Weighing up in his mind good and bad ideas. Letting his mind wander. And why shouldn't he?

When she was little, Vili always used to buy Penelope ice creams. She loved ice creams. Now, suddenly, she doesn't feel like continuing with the meal. Despite the wild weather outside, she would rather be eating an ice cream. A Frigodedo. A Cornetto. A Calippo. Or, even better, a Dracula, her all-time favourite, from the days when Vili was in charge of buying her ice creams.

'Childhood is our only paradise. Let the child enjoy it while he can,' says Vili, taking a sip of wine.

'Do you think so?' Ulysses gobbles down a few scraps of salad before Roberta removes all the plates. 'It's odd, but I don't imagine paradise like that.'

'And how do you imagine it?' Penelope looks across at him over the chair that Telemachus has left vacant between them.

'You're my idea of paradise, my love,' says Ulysses, and she doesn't know whether he's being serious or not. 'Quiet and sunny, but right next door to hell, like one of those houses in the country they build nowadays. With just a partition wall between you and hell, so that you can hear all the noises from next door.'

'Oh, very funny.'

'My father,' Ulysses continues, 'used to say sometimes that for him paradise was simply a place where you could always find a parking space.'

'He might have been right.'

'And I knew a gallery owner once for whom paradise . . .'

'A gallery owner? Which one of the many?' asks Penelope scathingly. She knows she should have kept quiet.

'Annetta, the one who . . .'

'Annetta? Ha!'

'And what does "Ha!" mean?' Ulysses looks at her, frowning. He is still chewing. He wipes his mouth with his napkin.

'I never liked that woman. Her breath smelled funny.'

'What do you mean, "funny"?'

'Oh, I don't know.' Penelope tries to catch her mother's eye in search of complicity, but she finds neither, neither her mother's eye nor the desired complicity. Valentina seems to be entranced by a stain on the table cloth. 'I don't know . . . it smelled of . . . what was it? Penis?'

'Penelope, for heaven's sake!' says Ulysses.

'Are you still in touch with her? Tell her, as Martial might say, to stuff her knickers in her mouth.'

'Penelope, sweetheart . . .' Vili takes another sip of wine and leans back slightly so that Roberta can put a clean plate in front of him.

Roberta is looking at them all out of the corner of her eye. It's impossible to know whether she feels shocked or perhaps excited by the snippets of conversation she picks up. She probably couldn't care less.

'You were the one who told me about Martial, Papi. Don't you remember? You used to read me all those rude poems and make me laugh, and now you're saying . . .'

'Penelope . . . sweetheart,' Vili says again.

'You're so crass,' says Ulysses, 'so bitter.'

'Penelope . . . Look, I mean . . .' Vili shifts about on his chair. 'Whatever you do, don't underestimate the power of sex.'

'I wouldn't dream of it, Papi.'

'Quite. Sex is important,' Ulysses adds.

'Oh, I agree,' says Penelope, 'but not because you say so. Your opinion isn't exactly worth much, bearing in mind that you're one of those prize idiots who believes that the world is always a slightly better place once they've had a quick fuck.' She has lowered her voice to a hiss aimed at Ulysses. If it weren't for the fact that she was speaking so softly, anyone would have said she was screaming.

'Come on, Vili,' urges Ulysses, speaking out of the corner of his mouth like a gangster. 'Tell her what Cicero has to say on the subject, or some other smart-arse. Go on, tell this clever dick here.'

'If it were not for sex, we human beings would not even go anywhere near each other, and we would have long since become extinct,' says Vili.

'What a loss for the universe in general and for us in particular.' Penelope is turning her plate round and round, as if she wants to screw it into the table.

'We are animals, and in the animal kingdom, proximity equals danger. If sex didn't make us seek each other out, who would ever bother to approach anyone else?'

'Annetta would approach Ulysses because of his art. She's crazy about artists, isn't she? And Ulysses is one of them.'

'Oh, drop it, will you?'

'Valentina . . .'

'Can you bring the lobster in, Roberta?' says Valentina and bestows a lacklustre smile on everyone present.

'Valentina, are you all right?' asks Ulysses.

'Yes, of course. I'm just not feeling very energetic. I'm a bit tired, that's all,' she replies with a wink. Or an attempted wink. 'At my age, you know, people are like television sets: they work best when they're plugged into some energy source.'

'What do you mean "at your age"? You're beautiful,' says Ulysses.

Valentina is grateful that he doesn't say 'but, you look great' or 'why, you don't look your age at all' or some such nonsense, which would only make her feel older and even more ill. No, Ulysses would never say anything so commonplace – domestic ideology for the petty and the exasperated. Ulysses is different. A dark night as clear as day. He knows that 'you are' is better than 'you look'. He knows that 'beautiful' is the appropriate adjective to use.

Penelope eyes him from the side. She has to admire his talent. Render unto Caesar the things which are Caesar's. As long as he is Caesar.

'God, what a life,' she says.

Her mother is dying. But when someone is on the brink of death, ladies and gentlemen, that *is* life.

'Oh, yes, terrible. Everything tends to chaos, as proven scientifically by Tom and Jerry cartoons,' retorts Ulysses, and he purses his lips as if blowing her a kiss.

'Where do you live, Ulysses – through the looking glass?' Penelope picks up a bit of bread and starts pulling it apart, making out of each crumb still smaller crumbs. And even tinier ones out of those. She wants to reach the atom. To count the neutrinos. She makes a little pile of crumbs. She cuts them up with the point of her knife. Then she squashes them together again.

'Life isn't terrible,' Vili says wearily. 'It never has been. At least not as terrible as we tend to think. What's terrible is us. And I know that sounds . . .'

'Right,' agrees Ulysses, interrupting him. 'Shall we attack the lobster?'

'There's venison too,' Valentina says, indicating another dish.

'Great.' Ulysses allows Roberta to place a generous helping on his plate. 'Come on, Penelope, eat something. You're too skinny.'

'No, thanks,' says Penelope. 'I don't like eating the flesh of dead animals.'

'Oh, really?' Ulysses picks up his knife and fork. 'I don't mind in the least, as long as I didn't know the deceased personally.'

'Come on, Penelope. I thought you liked seafood,' Vili says.

'But you're not eating anything, and no one's criticizing you. Besides, I'm full. I'm not a child any more. I know when I want to eat and when I don't.'

'Don't get angry.'

'I'm not getting angry, I'm just not hungry.'

She could eat an ice cream, though. A chocolate ice cream.

She wouldn't mind some chewing gum either. She loves chewing gum. It's so. . .trusting.

'Mama, is there any ice cream?'

'There might be some in the freezer. I'll ask Roberta to look.'

'Thanks. I just fancy an ice cream.'

'Fine, but wait until the rest of us have finished eating, all right?' says Ulysses.

'I'll wait, don't worry.'

Of course Penelope will wait.

'Not that I'm criticizing you, Penny.' Ulysses is eating and talking at the same time, addressing Penelope and lowering his voice as he turns to speak to her. 'I would never dare to criticize you, my love, especially since I never understand a thing that you do or a word that you say.'

'Thank you, it's very sweet of you to admit it.'

Penelope has been to bed with twelve men in her lifetime, including Ulysses. She went to bed with the last eleven out of spite and in the space of a little over eighteen months, since leaving her husband. She has been to bed with each of these men (she imagines them – a small army, erect and defiant), has made love with them all – well, she has really only made *love* with Ulysses – and for some reason she can't fathom, she has not yet learned to think well of them.

She examines Ulysses with interest. Men are a mystery. All except Vili, of course. Men are an enigma which she associates with a multitude of absurd, pathetic, sinister rituals.

'Does anyone want more wine?' asks Vili.

Ulysses is the first to hold out his glass.

Worry

Worry is a cultural malaise of epidemic proportions. As soon as we are born, it spreads out in ever-widening circles from the cradle into infinity; it takes only the slightest touch of a pebble or a mote of dust on the passive waters of our consciousness, and that's it, worry invades and conquers us. It is a lustful, carnivorous beast. It seduces and devours us and not always in that order.

It's such an exasperating, gratuitous complaint.

Absolute poison to reason.

(Really shitty.)

Penelope had spent her whole pregnancy worrying, while she was decorating her son's room with pastel drawings of animals inspired by Dürer. God, she was worried.

What if her child was born dead? What if he was mentally handicapped? What if he had a great red mark on his face that would make him feel ashamed for the rest of his life? What if he didn't put on enough weight and then caught all kinds of diseases and died slap-bang in the middle of kindergarten? What if he had cancer, like Ulysses' mother? What if he was very short? What if he was really ugly and no one loved him, not even his own mother? What if, when he grew up, he suffered from a flaking scalp because of seborrhoeic dermatitis or psoriasis that caused dandruff and terrible itching? Or what if he was morbidly obese? What if he became a criminal or a miserable clerk? What if he died in a traffic accident? What if his wife left him and he went mad? What if he had Siamese twin daughters joined at the hip? What if, when the time came, he didn't get his old age pension because the social security system all over Europe had gone bankrupt? What if he got old? What if he then died of old age?

She worried about all this and more, but she'd rather not remember.

Now Telemachus is three months old. He's just like a little doll with a very white face. Quiet and fragile. Penelope has breastfed him, but her milk is beginning to dry up. She has to give him a couple of bottles of formula milk every day. (Is the milk you buy in chemist's good? Yes, but is it *really* good?)

She has arranged to have coffee with a friend. Well, she's not really a friend (she met her at that awful college where she studied design after graduating); they're not bosom pals, but Marta has contacts in the fashion world and she's a cheerful soul. Penelope will use it as an excuse to take the baby out, although this is, in fact, a real pain, because it's not easy getting from her apartment to the street door down three flights of stairs with no lift, carrying a small baby and a buggy.

She does it backwards, very slowly, step by step, placing the rear wheels of the buggy on a step, then sliding them down on to the next one, while she acts as a counterweight so as not to throw the front wheels off balance and send the three of them – buggy, baby and her – flying.

When she finally gets to the front door, she is sweating from the effort and the tension. They could so easily have fallen. Her heart turns over at the mere thought. Outside the air is warm, there's the sound of work being carried out on a nearby building, or perhaps they're mending a street somewhere. Madrid will be a really beautiful city, Penelope says to herself, once they've finished building it.

She'll walk down Calle Atocha to Puerta del Sol. She's still got time, and she would never, of course, take her child on the Metro, not even if her life depended on it. Nor in a taxi. The child might hear things. Radio stations. Conversations with other taxi drivers over the radio transmitter. Mediocre music. Babies are very sensitive, and who knows what might get imprinted on their tender little brains. Besides, the child needs to get some sun, even if it is Madrid sun. If she had left home earlier, she could have gone for a walk in the Botanic Gardens, but she's always in a hurry. Newborn babies take up so much time. The hours whizz by before you know it. A baby empties a mother's head of all thoughts, leaving space only for things like food, milk, detergent, poo, sleep, baths, and so on.

She bumps along the pavements. Building under refurbishment. Suspicious, resigned policemen (you have to earn a living somehow, but really . . .). People in a hurry. People with unhealthy, suffering eyes, standing still as statues. People waiting for something, quite what they don't know, and who turn and turn on themselves until they're dizzy. People selling things, cheap toys, cheap lycra tops, cheap drugs. People begging, carrying babies younger than hers on their hips and shamelessly displaying their child's small, sad, sorrowful eyes to passers-by, then holding out the dirty palm of one hand and murmuring something in the unmistakable tones of the outsider.

Things are so badly organized for a woman taking her child for a walk in the city centre.

She should have used the sling someone gave her, and put the baby in that. She could then have carried him pressed against her chest like a mother kangaroo. She'd make faster headway. But it's too late now to go back home, swap things over, take the baby out of the buggy (she'd have to check, of course, that his nappy wasn't wet) and carry that bag, that enormous bag where she puts everything she might possibly require to cater to his needs. Including bandages. A bottle of mineral water. Antiseptic. Plasters. Make-up. Two magazines. No way. It's so heavy, that bag. It's better stashed under the buggy than slung over her shoulder.

Whenever she's walking anywhere, Penelope behaves exactly as she always did even in her pre-baby life. She thinks that the shortest distance between two points is a zigzag, avoiding the obstacles which, had she gone straight ahead, she would have bumped right into. That is why she crosses the road every few feet, taking an eternity to reach Puerta del Sol and walk up Calle del Carmen to the café near El Corte Inglés in Callao, where her friend is expecting her.

At least it's not too hot, although she is, nevertheless, sweating. She is aware of dampness above her upper lip and that her black silk blouse is sticking to certain parts of her back.

Telemachus is asleep.

Perhaps that is the best image she can come up with as her idea of happiness: seeing her son asleep. Safe. Peaceful. Breathing perfectly.

Penelope is worried, but she doesn't want Marta to notice. Worry and guilt have a particular musty odour that sends people scurrying away from anyone who gives off the tell-tale stench. They have quite enough worry and guilt of their own.

She is worried because she has known for some months now that Ulysses does not spend all his time painting his own pictures. That's why he's always having whispered conversations, locking his studio door, attending important meetings and scooting off on suspicious trips.

Shortly after the birth of their son, he paid an enormous amount of money into the bank. Money from the paintings he'd sold at his last exhibition, he told Penelope. But that was impossible. Not at the prices Ulysses commands.

In the end, she learned the whole truth.

Dodgy invoices, dangerous friendships, notes, papers, phone calls, nonsensical receipts, sketches of terribly familiar images, too unlikely to be mere pictorial exercises, stupid lies, easy money. It was all there, and it all fitted.

At the time, Penelope occasionally thought, it's better not to know. Not to know anything. She begins to doubt that knowing serves any purpose at all. If it is only in order to live so little, what is the point of knowing so much, wrote the Mexican poetess, Sor Juana Inés de la Cruz.

Ulysses, Ulysses . . .

He finally confessed, proffering excuses and grotesque promises of change and hope. Penelope cried, and there was more shouting. A huge row.

She and Ulysses had such a vulgar tendency to melodrama. And the worst thing was that this ridiculous talent was growing by the minute.

'Marta!' Penelope cries, as she struggles – as best she can with the buggy – into the agreeable darkness of the bar.

Dusk is coming on. Marta looks like a beautiful cat, aloof and with an abundance of black curly hair. She is sitting at a table near the window, smoking and drinking something that appears to be water with a slice of lemon in it, but which is undoubtedly not.

'Darling!' Marta stubs out her cigarette in the ashtray on the table next to her – oblivious to the vindictive look bestowed on her by the gentleman sitting at that table drinking his vermouth – and embraces Penelope. 'Goodness me, no one would think you'd just had a baby. You haven't got a tummy or anything. You don't look like you're considering suicide either. And your bust . . . And your . . . turn round. You haven't been treating yourself to a few sessions of mesotherapy have you? If you have, then tell me all about the beneficial effects. I think I'll put my name down for some as soon as I leave this ghastly place.'

'It's great to see you. You look gorgeous.'

'Have you noticed how vulgar Madrid has become?' Marta points out of the window at the people passing by. 'The moment you land at Barajas Airport, you feel like some peasant with blackheads on your cheeks and a dewdrop dangling from your nose. And then there are those loud-mouthed taxi drivers who take you on a detour via their own house just so that they can pop in and slap their old lady around a bit before dropping you off at the address you originally asked for. And the useless traffic police, who make you drive the wheels of your Lotus through the mud left behind by the roadworks . . . By the way, why are there *always* roadworks here? Did I miss something? Was there an earthquake perhaps? I thought we didn't get earthquakes.'

Marta pulls out a chair to allow Penelope to sit down, pushing the chair gently in towards the table as she does so. Real ladies are the only gentlemen left nowadays, thinks Penelope while she thanks Marta. 'Now let's have a look at the little angel.'

'Don't say things like that about the taxi drivers and the police. Madrid wouldn't be Madrid without its policemen and its taxi drivers,' Penelope feels obliged to say.

'Fine, it's all the same to me.'

Penelope removes the hood from the buggy. Telemachus looks like a perfect, very healthy rag doll. He is asleep and gives a peaceful, silent sigh.

'Oh, I could eat him up!' Marta tenderly touches one of his little hands, which is closed in a fist, as if he is holding firmly on to the thread of life. 'He's adorable. I'm so jealous.'

'Don't be! I don't get a wink of sleep at night.'

'But why don't you hire a nanny? Any woman who can't afford a nanny shouldn't have children. They should forbid it by law, don't you think? But you could afford it, your father's rich, not like mine – he's just a GP.'

'Yes, he is rich, but he doesn't live like a rich man, and he doesn't expect me to live like a rich woman at his expense.' Penelope signals to the waiter. 'Vili's a philosopher really.'

230

'H'm . . . He is a weirdo, I'll grant you that.'

'Anyway, how are things with you?'

'Well, Penny, my love, I don't like to appear presumptuous, because it's in bad taste, but things couldn't be better.' Marta smiles coquettishly. 'I have everything I could possibly want in life. The perfect job, freedom of movement, excitement, travel, interesting friends, Treasury bonds . . . And an Italian boyfriend who's dyslexic and a millionaire.'

'Really? Oh, that's great.'

Penelope involuntarily touches her nose. Is there a dewdrop dangling from it? Suddenly her black silk blouse seems terribly coarse and inappropriate even for having coffee in the late afternoon in a bar in Callao. Marta is wearing a purple Gucci dress and snakeskin boots. If Penelope was a man, she would be feeling intimidated, fascinated and cowed, and her one thought would be how to woo Marta.

She wonders if she's missing something in life – perhaps she's letting something slip from her grasp while she's busy squabbling with Ulysses, buying disposable nappies and polishing the floor.

She drums her fingers on her waist.

She's nervous. Worried.

She puts her hand into the left pocket of her jeans. She takes out a piece of paper and sneaks a look at it. It's a shopping list. Envelopes. Listerine. Orange juice. Actimel. Sherry. Sanitary towels. She rolls it into a tight little ball and throws it on the floor, hoping that Marta won't see it. Has she got blackheads on her cheeks? She *is* still rather sweaty. She wipes a paper napkin over her face, knowing full well that this will ruin her makeup.

Living is a suicidal act.

'Haven't you ever tried again, Penny? Oh, sorry . . .' Marta turns towards the waiter, who is ready to take their order. 'What would you like to drink?'

'Um, water, I think. Yes, water. Carbonated. Vichy, please.'

'And I'll have the same again,' says Marta.

'Yes, madam.' Like Penelope, the waiter too feels subjugated by Marta. He races off to the bar and from there shoots her sultry, surreptitious glances.

'Good grief,' Marta whispers, pulling a disgusted face. 'Did you notice the waiter? Heavens, doesn't he ever watch the telly? Doesn't he see the adverts? Hasn't he found out yet that body odour is preventable? I thought everyone could afford deodorant nowadays.'

'Well,' says Penelope in his defence, 'he does spend all day working inside . . .'

'We all work, my dear, make no mistake about it. Apart from my boyfriend, that is, who is as rich as your father, except that he has a really easy life. He's about as much of a philosopher as I am a lama, much as I love the Dalai Lama, of course.'

'Of course.'

'His only defect is this weird dyslexia-type thing he seems to have. He can never get my name right. He calls me Tamara and Tita, and anything else that occurs to him, the poor fool. And when you get into bed with him, don't mention sixty-nine because he might break your hip. Numbers just bob around in his head like the numbers in one of those drums they have at bingo, and sixty-nine and nine plus sixty are all the same to him. You could dislocate yourself. And if you ask him how old he is, well, instead of saying thirty-nine, which he's just turned, he'll blithely tell you that he's ninety-three. Oh dear.' Marta closes her eyes, laughing. 'But no one's perfect, and I've always wanted a boyfriend who didn't have to work to live or live to work. He's in India at the moment, can you believe it? He's in India and I'm in Madrid, stuck in a lousy bar full of sweaty people. At least I'm with you, though, sweetheart . . .'

'Would you like us to go somewhere else?'

'No, no, it's perfect here now that you've arrived.'

'Oh, Marta.'

'It's true. You're the most talented designer I've ever met, and that includes Tom Ford and me, not that I have any talent myself, but then I don't need it because I perform other functions in the world of fashion. You should go and see a friend of mine,' and she carefully enunciates the name of the person who will one day be Penelope's boss. 'I've heard a few rumours, and I have it on good authority that he's looking for someone. New blood, because he needs a daily transfusion nowadays. I think he'd like you, really I do. Go and see him and say that I sent you – I've done him a few favours which I'm sure he'll remember. I reckon your designs will end up on display in the Costume Institute of the Metropolitan Museum in New York, and in Ivana Trump's wardrobe, even in the wardrobe of the girlfriend of that sweaty waiter who's been serving us. You know how to give a touch of class even to clothes intended to be worn by cooks. You know how to dress cooks as if they were ladies, and ladies as if they were cooks, which is what you have to do in this business, it's what all the really big names do. And I can say that because I'm not the envious sort. Haven't you tried to get work?'

'I've got a bit bogged down what with one thing and another, although I still draw and do sketches, mainly to amuse myself, but what with Ulysses' work commitments and his business trips . . . and now with the baby . . . I don't know, it just feels like I've left it too late.'

'Oh, come off it, Penny, I'm five months older than you and I don't think of myself as over the hill. Women don't reach their peak until they're in their thirties. They're the best years of our lives. You just have to turn on the engine and roar off down the track, because, believe me, your car is running at maximum horsepower. Come on, give us a smile. You've become a real little mother, haven't you, but there is life for women beyond motherhood. Oh, look, he's getting restless.'

'He's hungry. It's time for his feed.' Penelope bends down to pick Telemachus up.

By the time they leave the bar, it's getting dark; the air is warm. The street is full of bustle. A pair of young men are performing juggling tricks, watched by a circle of curious onlookers who occasionally drop a coin on to a plate on the ground. The jugglers are very young; they have white-painted bodies, bare but for loincloths that look as if they are made out of strips of old sheet. They leap and strut, taking turns beneath the misty blue pinnacle of the evening sky. They are the remnants of some puppeteer's imaginings plonked down in the street, set free, all strings cut for ever. They caper about, jump, slide and jump again, then suddenly stand utterly still, turned to stone in the middle of Calle Preciados, while the people around them murmur and coo admiringly. They are so young and so lithe. Like vivid operatic figures – Pierrot and Fantasio – so terribly alive. The people watching them seem, in comparison, random figurative smudges whose sole purpose is to accompany them and to make them stand out against the seething darkness that is beginning to descend on the street, newly fallen from the skies.

Penelope is afraid they might stumble and injure themselves.

'I've got a car waiting for me in Puerta del Sol. If you like, I can give you a lift home,' says Marta.

Penelope nods, then thinks better of it.

'Actually, would you mind dropping us in Calle Velázquez? Ulysses has got an exhibition on; it opened the other day, and he was meeting some clients there tonight. Could you drop us outside the gallery? Or are you in a hurry?'

'Whatever you want, I don't mind at all. I'll take you wherever you like.' Marta strides decisively along. She is no ordinary woman and is not easily daunted; each step she takes confirms this, increases her allure, attracts more glances.

The car draws up alongside the parked cars outside the gallery with its all-glass façade, which allows passers-by a good view of many of the paintings on show in the first room.

Penelope gets out of the car and walks round to the back, her child in her arms, while she waits for the chauffeur to open the boot so that she can retrieve the buggy. Marta gets out too; her eyes are shining and she chatters on about all the things they should do, all the things that she does, about all the things still to be discovered and experienced. When Penelope glances towards the gallery, she sees only Ulysses and Annetta, the owner of the gallery, and no one else. She is almost on the point of smiling and waving at them in case they haven't noticed her. Then her husband takes the gallery owner's face in his hands, as tenderly and carefully as if she were a fragile doll, and places a long kiss on her lips; he slides his hands down to her waist, then further down. He buries his face in her neck, he clasps her to him, almost as if they were dancing, dragging his fingers across Annetta's body, squeezing.

Penelope looks away, embarrassed. She tells Marta she has changed her mind and would prefer to go home. After all, it's getting very late for the baby, she still has to give him his bath. Marta doesn't mind, and the chauffeur puts the buggy back in the boot of the Mercedes.

Penelope knew it, she knew Ulysses was being unfaithful to her – she could smell it, if you like – but she had never caught him red-handed (with his hands on the flaccid, doubtless dirty and lustful, suet-coloured flesh of a female behind), not since that time with the model, years before.

Now she is full of bad thoughts; they are, she realizes, obstructing her mind; they are as pointless and bothersome as water that refuses to drain out of a bathtub. Now she sees again what she saw, as well as what she couldn't see, which is even more unbearable than what she could.

Fornication and murder, she says to herself.

Lust and wickedness, she thinks.

Adultery and betrayal, she suspects.

She remembers Dante.

> *Tu stesso ti fai grosso*
> *col falso imaginar, sì che non vedi*
> *ciò che vedresti, se l'avessi scosso.*

You make yourself stupid with false imaginings and do not see what you would see if you discarded them.

That same night, several hours later, Penelope tries to sleep. She is alone in a room in a cheap hotel. Without Telemachus, her helpless little boy. With her eyes puffy from crying. She slowly ponders her rage. She knows no moderation, can find no possible consolation.

She really is an excellent housewife, she thinks, flailing around for something positive to hold on to while she bawls her eyes out in the most ridiculous fashion, almost comic in its excess. What a talent for melodrama Penelope has. She's creating a real ruckus in that small hotel in Paseo de las Delicias even though she knows perfectly well, because Ulysses has told her over and over, ad nauseam, that sex is nothing but sex, which is, after all, only sex and only as important as sex is . . . By the way, how important is it? Perhaps it *is* only as important as you make it. And if that is so, how can anyone ever agree on how important or unimportant sex is?

She is a housewife, she thinks proudly, wiping away the trails of mascara running down her cheeks. She has seen to every detail. She has bathed the baby and left the supper ready for her husband: a large bowl of rat poison *au naturel*. She likes cooking simple dishes. She has no intention of going home again.

Fear of the unknown

Valentina is chewing her food with gentle determination. She doesn't feel much like talking and so is not the most ebullient of companions.

'What do you want for dessert?' Vili asks her.

'Nothing,' she replies.

'Fine, I'll have the same,' says Vili.

'Mama,' Penelope says.

'What?'

'Do you want anything? I mean, do you need . . . ?'

'Eat your food, dear.'

'I didn't have any food. I'm waiting for the rest of you,' says Penelope, and she looks at the tub of chocolate ice cream that Roberta has left on a tray to soften.

'We should take a look at Telemachus,' says Ulysses, still picking at his lobster. 'Sometimes he turns over and falls on to the floor; he's not really used to sleeping in a bed yet. He falls asleep clinging to the bars of his cot, like a prisoner.'

'I'll go.' Penelope gets up and leaves her napkin on the tablecloth, neatly folded beside her plate.

She goes to her bedroom and recalls the evening when she told Ulysses that she wanted to have a child. She had a sense that she had waited a long time before reaching this decision. The thought of having a child filled her with panic, but she knew that if she didn't, she would spend the rest of her life regretting it, missing it. How can you possibly miss someone you've never met, who has never existed because you never gave them the opportunity to exist? Well, it happens often enough, and Penelope did not ever want to experience anything so terrible.

Ulysses didn't care whether they had children or not, although, given the choice, he would prefer not to.

'Yes,' said Penelope, 'but I *do* want a child. It's up to you whether you collaborate or not. I'll perfectly understand if you don't want to participate, and I'll just go shopping at a sperm bank.'

She was absolutely serious. Who did he think he was?

Ulysses considered for a moment.

'All right, but there's no need to go to a bank. Why would you want to do that? We can dip into our savings,' he said smugly, looking at his crotch.

Now Telemachus is sleeping placidly, with the look of total abandon and unconcern that sleep paints on children's faces. Nothing troubles him. There is no spectre organizing his dreams. He is lying face down, his head where his feet should be and his feet on the pillow.

Her little one. No one will ever take him away from her again. She has already interviewed various prospective nannies. Penelope goes out again, closing the door carefully behind her.

Ulysses is a lover determined to teach her how to love love. When his wife comes back into the room, he winks at her and gives her one of those half-smiles of his that never quite evolve into a full smile, like flowers that have got stuck in the middle of a process which they are unable to complete.

Penelope feels like grabbing hold of his cheeks and tugging them upwards, towards his ears, to force him to burst out laughing; she feels like slapping him around the face and breaking two of his teeth. But she doesn't do or say anything; she sits down.

'How is he?'

'He's asleep.'

'I knew it!' Ulysses drops his knife on to his plate. 'Has he fallen out of bed?'

'No, he hasn't.'

'Oh.'

'Were you expecting he would?'

'Well . . .'

'You don't have much confidence in your son, do you?'

'I. . .I mean . . .'

'What?' asks Penelope.

'What do you mean "what"?' Ulysses shrugs and looks at Valentina. His lips say nothing, but his face is saying: 'See what I have to put up with? See how unbearable your daughter is? Why did you make her like this? Couldn't you have tried a bit harder?'

'What are you trying to say?' insists Penelope.

Ulysses thinks for a moment.

'I think you're making a mountain out of a molehill, although, to be honest, I don't even know what the molehill in question is,' he says.

'All I'm saying,' says Penelope, 'is that it's obvious Telemachus would be better off with me, because I, as well as being his mother, and not his father, will always expect him *not* to fall out of bed. Unlike you.'

'Oh, dear God . . .'

'Please,' mutters Vili, 'don't argue.'

'We have to clear up what to do with Telemachus once and for all, Papi.' Penelope shakes her head and then points an accusing finger at Ulysses.

'Why don't we have some ice cream,' Valentina suggests.

'All right, just a little bit for me.' Penelope notices the scalloped edge of her napkin, and the embroidered daisies there fill her with a sudden sense of relief.

'Of course we have to sort out what to do with Telemachus.'

Ulysses lets Roberta serve him a generous portion of ice cream. 'For once we agree.'

'Yes, more than anything, you should be thinking about the child,' mutters Vili.

'Children should be with their mothers,' says Penelope, addressing an antique sideboard in the room.

'You should have thought of that before – before you abandoned him,' Ulysses retorts.

'Me? Abandon my child? Oh, please! I abandoned you, you imbecile!'

'That isn't how I understood it at the time,' says Ulysses, eating a spoonful of ice cream.

'Well, you have difficulty understanding anything,' says Penelope reproachfully. 'You are living proof that stupidity is, along with hydrogen, the most commonly found element in the known universe.'

'Why didn't you sue me for divorce as soon as you left?'

'Why?' Penelope hesitates. 'I had . . . I had things to do, more urgent things. I wanted to get on, I wanted to establish myself before Telemachus . . .'

'Oh yeah. Don't give me that, sweetheart.' Ulysses polishes off his ice cream. 'The truth is you didn't even consider it. You thought you'd leave me on my own with the child, that you'd teach me a lesson, that I'd bring up your little one, that I'd learn the error of my ways, and you'd have your revenge, but meanwhile everything would be there for you at home, just the way you like it, waiting for you to come back to reclaim Telemachus or sweep up my ashes from the floor of my studio, or to do whatever it was you wanted to do. You never had the slightest intention of divorcing me. In fact, you couldn't give a damn about getting divorced. You're just an egotist. But you can't play around like that with the life of a child.'

'That's a pack of lies,' says Penelope coolly. 'A pack of lies. What about you? Why didn't *you* ask for a divorce, since you're so keen on it? Why didn't you sue me for desertion? Why?'

'When you've got a baby to look after, it's not that easy to go chasing after lawyers asking them for divorces and other such nonsense. They're too busy running their own little rackets.'

'Ha!'

'Calm down, please!' begs Valentina

But they won't. They can't calm down because neither Valentina nor Vili, nor Ulysses' parents, nor their teachers at school or at university or anyone else has ever given Penelope and Ulysses the slightest hint of a sentimental education. No, no one, and they haven't managed to pick it up on their own either.

That is why Penelope is sitting with arms folded, looking at her husband out of the corner of her eye and realizing that the more she looks at him, the more she is conscious of the feeling that someone is scraping away at her flesh with a metal lemon zester, and that whoever it is grating furiously and meticulously away at her flesh is getting closer and closer to the bone. Since when has reason been able to educate the emotions?

'You'll traumatize the child,' Ulysses says, wiping the chocolate stains from the corners of his mouth with the lovely embroidered daisy petals on his napkin.

'I see nothing wrong with having a few traumas,' Penelope says by way of an excuse. 'People have to make the most of the occasional minor trauma, those abrasions to the soul that force us to grow up, that make us tougher and just a little perverse, in other words, more human.'

'You'll never change, Penny,' says Ulysses, tut-tutting.

'Oh, so you don't think I'm good enough as I am, do you?'

Vili looks at her and slowly shakes his head. No one could know for sure whether he is shocked or whether he approves of every word his daughter has just said.

'H'm,' Vili says. 'H'm.'

Penelope remembers the night she left. Her first thought had been to kick Ulysses out. After all, the apartment was hers, a gift from Vili. At first, her plan had been to make a huge pile out of Ulysses' things, rather like a funeral pyre, and hurl everything down into the street from the balcony, including his paintings full of female faces, none of them hers, and all the bottles of paint thinner and other dangerously flammable substances that surrounded his various painting implements. She would throw it all out into the street, pay the fine for doing so, and leave Ulysses in the midst of it all, alone and bewildered in the middle of the street. She started to do this, but soon realized that she couldn't remember who owned what in the house. They had lived together for so long that she could no longer distinguish her belongings from those of her husband. She could not even remember who was who. And so she decided to leave instead, before the confusion grew to still more terrifying proportions.

'Pass me the water,' Penelope says with suspicious haste, raising her glass. 'I need some water.'

'Cold? Hot?' asks Ulysses. He languidly picks up the jug from near his plate on the table. He puts it down for a moment on the spot which, a while before, had been his son's place. He dries his hands on his napkin.

'Are your hands sweating?' Penelope gives a muffled giggle. He's nervous, she tells herself, and she licks her dry lips, glad to think that he feels uneasy, that he is not entirely imperturbable.

Where is the usual Ulysses, the dazzling, radiant, glowing, benedictory Ulysses? Where, in which crease, in which line in the palms of those sweating hands? In the life line, the fate line, the love line?

'Yes, sometimes my hands do sweat.'

'How vulgar. My hands never sweat,' says Penelope with a smug smile, like a foolish girl, proud of her silly-little-girl nonsense.

'Of course not, my dear. But then I'm real, you see.' Ulysses picks up the water jug again and fills Penelope's glass. To the brim.

The dream of their past lives takes place, very slowly, on other rainy nights, just like this rainy night, depositing its bitter mysteries on a tablecloth covered in wine and chocolate stains and lovely embroidered daisies.

'So what do you think you'll do, then?' Vili enquires.

Roberta asks if they would like coffee.

'Decaffeinated for me, with a tiny bit of milk, just the tiniest drop,' says Penelope.

'Espresso for me, with not even the tiniest drop of milk and with plenty of caffeine, as much caffeine as you can muster, thank you, Roberta,' says Ulysses.

'I won't have any coffee,' says Valentina. 'Could you make me a camomile tea, Roberta?'

Roberta nods vaguely.

'I'll have . . .' Vili hesitates for a moment. 'I won't have anything. So what are you going to do with the child?'

Valentina stands up. Her gestures appear very slow and calm, but Penelope knows that this is because the illness and the pain make her clumsy and muddleheaded.

'If you like . . .' she says, looking at them coldly from the other side of her pale, sunken eyes, 'we can have coffee in the library; we'll be more comfortable there.'

Penelope imagines her mother is engaged in a titanic struggle with a dark force that fills her with fear. She assumes that her mother is suffering, that she is making a great effort, that she hates to hear her daughter squabbling with the father of her grandson – just as, lately, she has been arguing with Vili; she imagines her mother is dying, that she is fighting against death, that she is in pain and that all these things together are too much for her. Or for anyone. And that this is why she is not more agile when getting up from the table.

Penelope imagines that everything we imagine is always real, and that this is why the imagination is a mental artefact which, at times, is unbearable, hateful, obscene. With her imagination Penelope can see Valentina's inner face. Small, shrunken and frightened, gradually, secretly consuming itself, spurred on by the disease. She does not like to see this face, and so she looks away, ashamed, terrified.

They make their way to the library. Vili picks up his glass of wine in one hand and with the other lights a cigar. He hangs back a little, blowing out lazy coils of grey smoke that look like a child's drawings of pleasant ghosts.

'So . . .' Ulysses says to Vili.

Penelope has gone back into her bedroom to make sure Telemachus is all right, and Valentina has excused herself for a moment, saying that she has to fetch something from her room. Ulysses is lounging in a comfortable old armchair.

'What?' asks Vili in turn, sprawled on the sofa.

'Are you better? How do you feel after what happened with the would-be suicide and all that?'

'Oh, you know.' Vili fidgets as if trying to uproot himself from the place where he is sitting. 'I feel just like the lobster Valentina served up for supper – alive, but thoroughly cooked.'

'You're not considering opening the Academy again, then?'

'No, I'm not. Screw them. Screw the lot of them.' Vili sighs and takes a sip of wine. 'I'm tired, Ulysses. Nothing but a lot of neurotics, hysterics and then, to cap it all, suicidal maniacs and slurs in the press on my integrity and my intentions, that's what I get for my efforts. After all these years of teaching philosophy, I read in the newspapers that I might be the leader of a sect. A sect! Can you believe it? It's too much. The matter is in the hands of my lawyers. No, no . . .'

Vili pauses, gazing abstractedly at the fire in the hearth, then remarks: 'Fire is rather like a delirium, don't you think? No, Ulysses, there's very little room for philosophy in today's world. People don't understand that philosophy is the art of living, of living well. People don't know what philosophy is, or what anything else is for that matter. And I feel like an old, weary philosopher. I'd like a bit of peace, that's all. No, I won't be going back to the Academy. Perish the thought!'

He takes another sip of wine, but this time he spills it down his shirt front in his attempt to drain his glass.

'Damn that Melanos!' he exclaims, brushing frantically at his shirt. He fishes a paper handkerchief out of his pocket and rubs ineffectually at the stain.

'Who's Melanos?'

'Eh? Oh, he was the first idiot to have the unfortunate idea of adding water to wine,' he replies, still rubbing at his shirt and managing only to make the stain still bigger. 'It never goes amiss to curse him now and then.'

'But, you know, Vili, I think you've helped a lot of people with the Academy,' Ulysses insists.

'To be perfectly honest, I think the only person who really helped at the Academy was you. You were the one who grabbed that fellow's hand and stopped him putting a bullet from that gun in his brainless brain. That's what I call helpful. The rest is just a lot of hot air.'

'Perhaps you've been deflecting a lot of bullets from brains without even knowing it.'

'H'm,' says Vili, slowly blowing out an aromatic cloud of Havana cigar smoke. 'H'm. Who knows. Obviously I'd like to think so, but really I'd rather think the exact opposite, that there was never any need, that the people who came to the Academy never required that kind of help from me.'

'But it might have happened, Vili, and you . . .'

'No, Ulysses.'

'You're doing exactly the opposite of what you taught us, Vili. You're running away.'

'Don't say that. I'm just resting. I've always preferred actions to words, the strong arm to the tongue, but I've also always known that the tongue can mobilize thousands and millions of strong arms. At the moment, both my tongue and my arm are tired and it really doesn't matter what I want now because neither of them feels like moving. And I'm resigned to that.'

'Vili . . .'

'No, no more "Vili". By the way, I don't think I've thanked you properly for what you did. You prevented a death. Thanks to you my arm and my tongue will some day move and speak again. They're just resting now, but if that man had died, my arm and my tongue would, in some way, have died along with him. So, thank you, on behalf of my arm, my tongue and myself. And thank you too in the name of that poor idiot whose life you saved.'

'You're welcome.' Ulysses bows his head.

'You're a real hero, although I don't think you're conscious of it. Nor of anything else, if you don't mind my saying. You are, in general, dear son-in-law, conscious of very little. But anyway. . . Do you need anything?'

'You mean money?' Ulysses strokes his cheek thoughtfully. 'You know I never say no, but the truth is that I'm all right at the moment.'

'I'll write you a cheque.'

'Whatever.'

'You'll need a bit of extra money. Because of Araceli, I mean . . .'

Vili sighs affably. 'I'd like to have her here, but Valentina and her mother have never. . .you know . . .'

'Later on, perhaps.'

'All right.'

'Anyway, there's no reason why you should feel bad about what happened,' Ulysses says, returning to the main topic of conversation. 'You're not responsible for what that man tried to do, you're not responsible for him or for any of us.'

'I know,' agrees Vili.

'So why are you feeling so down?'

'Too many things at once, Ulysses. Even I have my limits. Lately, most of the people who've been coming to the Academy have really been getting on my nerves. Sometimes I used to feel like a swineherd, tending the pigs day and night, feeding them on my philosophy, which they would gobble up along with the mud and the drool; talking and walking amongst all those snuffling pigs; and, of course, cleaning out the pigsty at the end of the day . . .' Vili yawns languidly. 'And then, what with that nutter and Valentina, who is driving me mad with her . . .'

Penelope comes running into the library.

Tac tac tac.

Her hair is dishevelled, it glows as if it were surrounded by the luminous halo cast by a lantern lighting it from behind. She is frowning and gripping one arm, digging her nails into the soft black fabric of the dress before she speaks.

'It's Mum,' she says; some kind of profound sorrow keeps her propped against the door frame. 'It's Mum. We've got to get her to hospital.'

'But what . . .' Ulysses leaps up.

'Or else call a doctor . . .' Penelope goes on. A tiny, greasy tear slides down her left cheek. She finds it hard to cry, to externalize her grief.

'What's happened? Has she had a fall? Has she . . . ?' Vili stumbles to his feet, half stubs out his cigar in a brass ashtray that trembles beneath his nervous fingers and is on the point of sliding off the table on to the floor.

'No, don't worry, she hasn't fallen over or anything,' Penelope says, and gives a feeble laugh. 'She's just dying. She's dying. That's all.'

III. *What we are*
(Final odyssey)

The British economist Andrew Oswald and an American colleague have come up with a formula for how to be happy (which belies the saying that money can't buy you happiness). The formula is as follows:

$r = h (u (y, z, t)) + e$

r = the happiness that one considers oneself to enjoy and which is equivalent to a mathematical constant (h)

u = real level of happiness

y = real income

z = personal and demographic characteristics

t = time factor

e = changes in opinions and preferences

With the discovery of this mathematical formula, something long desired by humanity, Oswald concludes that a long marriage brings as much personal happiness as an extra payment of $96,000, while the loss of a job costs, in terms of happiness, $64,000.

From the newspaper *Levante*, 6 November 1999

Ithaca

When you set out on your journey to Ithaca,
pray that the road is long,
full of adventure, full of knowledge.
The Lestrygonians and the Cyclops,
the angry Poseidon – do not fear them:
You will never find such as these on your path,
if your thoughts remain lofty, if a fine
emotion touches your spirit and your body.
The Lestrygonians and the Cyclops,
the fierce Poseidon you will never encounter,
if you do not carry them within your soul,
if your soul does not set them up before you.

Pray that the road is long.
That the summer mornings are many, when,
with such pleasure, with such joy
you will enter ports seen for the first time;
stop at Phoenician markets,
and purchase fine merchandise,
mother-of-pearl and coral, amber and ebony,
and sensual perfumes of all kinds,
as many sensual perfumes as you can;
visit many Egyptian cities,
to learn and learn from scholars.

Always keep Ithaca in your mind.
To arrive there is your ultimate goal.
But do not hurry the voyage at all.
It is better to let it last for many years;

and to anchor at the island when you are old,
rich with all you have gained on the way,
not expecting that Ithaca will offer you riches.

Ithaca has given you the beautiful voyage.
Without her you would have never set out on the road.
She has nothing more to give you.

And if you find her poor, Ithaca has not deceived you.
Wise as you have become, with so much experience,
you must already have understood what Ithacas mean.

Constantine Cavafy

The call of adventure

Unlike Penelope, you – Ulysses – never look back. You know that you cannot change the past.

Every day, when you wake up, you feel the call of adventure, you sense that life is a state of mind and that the mind is a form of life. You are a new man with each new day that dawns. You have never felt defeated because it has never occurred to you that anything could defeat you.

Vili says that you're irresponsible, that you lack awareness, that this very lack of awareness is both your greatest virtue and what makes you dangerous. He says that you're brave because you don't know that you're brave, and that if you did know, you would immediately stop being brave. He says that in this world without heroes, you suffer the same fate as the heroes of old, who are so daring they frequently end up behaving like complete idiots; so greedy they find it hard to grasp that the only things of real value they can store away during their lifetime are the very things that no one can steal from them; they even risk death and do occasionally die, because in their ignorance as living beings, they have become incapable of fearing what they do not know.

Vili says that, instead of covering your ears so as not to hear the songs of the sirens, you sometimes cover your ears so as not to hear that there are no songs, that there are no sirens. Because there are none.

It's April now, and it's not raining. It stopped raining months ago.

You remember that it was in October that the rain suddenly

ceased. Then the black sky split open, like a rotten fruit, and stopped squandering its energies on frenetically spewing out muddy water and lightning bolts on the helpless city.

And the sun came out. A glorious sun. The freezing winter that followed was dry, bitterly cold, but without heavy showers or other such things. Now, the sun preens itself on having studied Fine Art while the clouds were in the way. The king of the stars lights the world as never before; the proud possessor of urban landscapes, it colours everything with its incessant activity. It shines brightly, and the people in the street are like the sun's flocks which the sun pastures and carefully watches over.

So real it seems unreal, the good sun. So far away that it probably is.

Today will be cool and the air quality relatively good. So the sing-song voice of a woman on the radio says, a woman whom you imagine to have no body. No legs, no lips, no age. Just a female voice floating out from the void, whispering sweet nothings to you as you awake.

It's half past seven on the morning of Penelope's birthday. Unlike Penelope, you don't care much about birthdays, you never have. Their glitziness and their unreasonable punctuality. Their monotonous rigour. The phosphorescent paper wrapped around the cheapest and most improvised of surprises. The tuneless songs sung around a sugary cake. No, birthdays and anniversaries don't really excite you.

Still, you'll have to buy her a present.

You ask yourself what.

Perhaps she'd like a novel. Jorge recommended a writer to you. He said to you one day: 'They say the guy writes with his cock and fucks with his pen. As you can imagine, he's really good.'

H'm, possibly, although some expensive perfume might be more suitable. The more expensive the better.

Today is also the first day of your exhibition, your first exhibition in over two years. You've painted a lot in the last six months. Eighty new paintings, as fevered and dazzling as the sun. Not bad for such a brief period of work. Your dealer couldn't believe it. The gallery owner is clearly expectant and hopeful.

This time the gallery owner is a man, a mature man, well-shaven and sensible, who smells of vetiver and the right kind of people. This time there is no sexual tension between you crying out to be resolved.

Just as well, because you have never liked tensions and tend to resolve them as quickly as possible.

You can't help it, it's your nature.

Besides, like St Augustine, you want to give up sex.

But, again like St Augustine, not yet.

It's just as well the gallery owner is a prudent man. Fortunately, on this occasion, he's a businessman whom you do not find in the least attractive or, indeed, feminine. The thing is, gallery owners, the female variety, always have some problem stuck to their skirts that ends up attaching itself to your trousers.

Ah, women. That's just the way they are. You ask all of them to make love with you because, even if they don't want to, you're sure they're glad to be asked.

You flit from one woman to the next almost without realizing it and, the moment your attention slips, you find yourself caught between Scylla and Charybdis. Quite unwittingly and without knowing how or why.

The worst monsters all tend to be feminine in Spanish – *la muerte*, *la enfermedad*, *la tragedia* – death, disease, tragedy. That's mostly how it is. The greatest pleasures too – *la aventura*, *la pintura*, *la amistad*, *la sensualidad*, *la marihuana* – adventure, painting, friendship, sensuality, marijuana.

You obstinately cling to your pleasures.

Not, of course, that you think about it much, nor about anything else. In fact, you don't tend to think much at all. You do. You're a man of action, not abstraction. (And that's all there is to it.) You can paint, of that there's no doubt, although you would rather not define the what, how or why of it. You can talk, and sometimes, when you stop to listen to yourself for a moment, you wonder with some amusement who it is who is talking on your behalf from inside you. You like walking, not mapping out possible paths you know you will never walk.

Neither are you overly concerned about the matter of happiness, which everyone these days seems to drone on and on about. You're fed up with obligations. You've never liked impositions of any kind, and feeling obliged to be happy seems to you the height of social perversity. A pure collective delusion. The great terrorist joke of the Western world. The end of the individual. A stupid formula dreamed up to keep people occupied and anxious, and eternally dissatisfied. You're happy when you're not aware of being happy, and, anyway, what does it matter? You're happy when you're not constantly asking yourself whether you are or are not.

You just want to be left to drift, to paint, to travel, to suffer and enjoy, as you wish. In short, you want to live, isn't that right, Ulysses? That's all it is. Nothing else.

You remember with glee one evening at Vili's Academy, when someone asked an elderly man who always sat in the same seat and who never spoke: 'Are you happy?' and the old man replied: 'It's not a question I've ever thought to ask myself, my friend.' 'So what are you doing here, then?' asked his colleague, curious. 'Well, it's like this,' replied the pensioner, 'I come here because my wife sends me. She says I'm always at home, getting in the way.'

Ah.

There were some memorable evenings and nights at the Academy. Sometimes you miss it. You know how it hurts when your sparring partner catches you in the side with a right hook. And although you would be unable to explain what pain is, you tell yourself that it must serve some purpose and, in any case, its existence certainly doesn't depend on you.

'Papa, bweakfast!' Telemachus climbs up on to your side of the bed and thumps the pillow – symbolic stones thrown up at the window to catch your attention.

You sit up very straight, leaning against the bedhead, your legs straight and relaxed, and you take him in your arms. You throw him up into the air, and his little body goes hurtling towards the ceiling. He weighs a ton. You tense the muscles in your forearms when you catch him. You've started boxing again at the gym, and you notice with a thrill that your tissues and muscles are much more flexible, much more defined.

The boy does a somersault in the air, shrieking with joy, and his eyes flash.

'You little rascal. You greedyguts,' you say to him.

Telemachus roars with laughter. You tickle his small hungry stomach until he screams with pleasure. Again you hurl him up into the air, absorb with your eyes his excited, triumphant face and store it jealously away inside you.

'We want to eat!' croons the boy softly.

Sunday. Today is a sunny April Sunday.

Crossing the threshold

When you go into the kitchen, you immediately feel Araceli's absence; you notice that, although she was only small, there is a huge hole in the place where she should be, but isn't. Since her death, it is as if the apartment has been razed to the ground. Oh, everything is quiet and in its place. The light filtering in through the windows is yellow and almost tangible, falling directly from the sky on to the furniture and giving form to your silhouette and that of your son. The apartment seems to be at peace. But she's not there. The first thing you feel when you wake in the morning, that lurch in your stomach when you get out of bed and start work, is called nostalgia.

The evening she died, you were sitting together in the living room of your apartment. You were talking about wars, the Gulf War to be precise. You can't even remember why the subject came up. You used to talk about all kinds of things. She was the perfect companion. Araceli knew how to be quiet and to say nothing when she didn't know the answer.

'The Gulf War?' she asked you vaguely. 'Heavens, my memory gets worse every day. The Gulf War, the Gulf War . . . I can't remember now . . . Who started it?'

'Oh, the usual people, I imagine,' you replied.

'I don't know.' Araceli shook her head. 'I don't know, but it seems to me that, when it comes to wars and all that, I'm beginning to lose my memory. That other one, for example, the war in Yugoslavia, you know the one . . . It was quite recent, wasn't it?

Well, I can't for the life of me remember what they were fighting about.'

She went back to her work. She was crocheting a small tablecloth, and you found it relaxing to watch her.

After a time, while you were doing some charcoal sketches of her, she told you that she had come up with a fantastic idea for a business. Her eyes shone with an intensity that may well have been a harbinger of the coming catastrophe; the light in her eyes perhaps signalled the beginning of the end.

'Grandparents for hire,' she said with a mischievous grin. She put her work down in her lap and pointed her crochet hook at you. 'What is it that modern life offers us in abundance, my dear? A load of old people abandoned in residential homes like so many dead rats, and an equally large number of children with no grandparents, and children really need grandparents. Anyway, the idea would be to establish links between schools and residential homes. For a modest monthly sum, a bunch of old crocks could be trundled off to schools to spend a bit of time each week playing with the children, giving them a few cuddles and listening to them. I think it would be a terrific extracurricular activity.

'Parents would be queuing up to enrol their children. Can't you just see it? "Tuesdays, music. Thursdays, grannies and granddads." I think it would be rather a good idea. That way the children's parents wouldn't feel so bad about having abandoned their own parents at a petrol station; the children would have adoptive grandparents to go to when no one else would listen to them; and the old dears could set up a social fund with the money they earned from the schools to buy the kind of food and treats that never figure on the menus in old people's homes. And everyone would be happy. Don't you think it's a good idea, Ulysses? I think I'll sleep on it. No, I won't, I'll just have a little doze right here, if that's OK with you. Right here on the sofa. You don't mind, do you, dear?'

No, you said, of course you didn't mind if she had a nap; she could put her feet up if that would be more comfortable. You yourself took off her slippers and lifted her legs on to the sofa; so that she wouldn't get cold, you covered her up with that green travel rug that's always hanging around in the living room and that Telemachus is so fond of. Araceli settled down and sighed contentedly, then she slowly closed her eyes and never opened them again.

No, Ulysses, you don't think about things that much, you're not afraid of death. You're brave. Or else a complete fool. You hope to meet it face to face one day, to settle a few old scores: your mother, Araceli. Not to mention John Lennon, Fofó the Clown, Elvis Presley, The Novel, Lady Di, Félix Rodríguez de la Fuente, Art, Bambi's mother, God.

Your encounter will prove therapeutic, but until then, you prefer not to think about it. There is no stormier or more stubborn life than death's. Constantly taking the bread out of our mouths, taking our dreams. Always bugging us. No, you're not afraid of death. But you can't deny it, you – like Yeats, like all the human beings who have ever lived – you too feel humbled by your own mortality. Don't deny it, Ulysses.

You fill a large cup with milk for the boy, pour it into a saucepan and heat it over a low light.

Telemachus scampers about the living room and the kitchen in his pyjamas. His vital presence lightens the morning gloom that awoke with you.

'Clean your teeth!' you tell your son when he has finished his breakfast. And then, after a dramatic pause: 'Every single one of them!'

It's already half past eight by the time you leave the house. You step decisively across the threshold. The child is in your arms. Dressed in a new navy-blue outfit and with his hair just combed, he is a restless, playful chiaroscuro figure who stands out against your chest. The sacred image of your religion of life.

There are a few small, white, fluffy clouds lined up above the rooftops. They are the Elysian Fields of the Madrid spring sky.

'Isn't it a lovely day?' you say to your son.

'No,' he replies confidently.

You don't take much notice, because lately he tends to say no to everything.

You trip over a broken litter bin, lying in the middle of the pavement, with its filthy contents – vegetable, mineral, animal, aerial and aquatic – scattered to left and right.

You curse litter bins. You curse the ones broken by the night-time vandals and those as yet unbroken, because, being intact, they prove an irresistible provocation to the vandals who like to kick them to pieces each night.

You curse in German and in Madrid slang.

Telemachus watches you in silence, taking a sudden interest in the movements of your mouth.

Another curse – on the health of the town hall, on municipal taxes, on the common good.

You don't believe in the common good, you believe, rather – like that jovial Archpriest of Hita, Juan Ruiz – in communal pleasure.

You push your way through the people in the street and disappear off into the smells and colours and sounds of this city that never seems to rest, which has not got up early because it has not yet been to bed.

The dragon flower

You, Ulysses, know the secret of making a woman happy. You know that the knack lies in accepting her child's heart, whatever her age, even if she is over eighty, as with your beloved Araceli.

Once these foundations have been laid, the rest is simple. At least it is for you, although it might not be for everyone. And any *madamigella* realizes at once that you do it very well. You do, Ulysses. You always do it very well.

After spending just over three hours finalizing details and signing documents with your dealer and your gallery owner – two sensible men of business – you delicately kiss the gloved hand of the special client they have introduced to you. She knows your earlier work and is, they tell you, very interested in your new work. She bought one of the etchings you showed at the Dokumenta in Kassel four years ago. She is rich and does not like to mix with other people. People, en masse, are so terribly vulgar (the rich can allow themselves the luxury of thinking like that). She preferred to have a look around the collection on her own, before the official opening that evening.

The highly circumspect but sensitive Señor Tamisa smiles voluptuously whenever he says the woman's name. Odón Tamisa, the gallery owner, possesses a lush, burgeoning garden in which he grows clumps of impatient green banknotes. It is hardly surprising that he should smile so approvingly at the lady.

What can one say about the charm of art, about the strange marvel that engenders hopes beneath the terrible, empty sky? What can one say about you, Ulysses, the artist, about the immodest dignity of your gaze? How consummately you will embellish this lady's rooms with your paintings. How attractive you look, with your tousled hair and your eyes like those of a hurt child, in the white morning light filling the room.

She's not at all bad, actually, and she obviously feels a certain fearful attraction for you. Her whole being shines, as if she had been given a few thorough coats of varnish before leaving home.

No, she's not at all bad. Although, when have you ever thought any differently about a woman? She buys three large oil paintings and signs a cheque with a lot of zeros on it, which your dealer – depending on the time of day, he hovers between vacuousness, dementia and usury – snatches up with his bony fingers, the very same fingers which he gives a daily work-out on an ancient calculator, as a way of keeping his digital muscles in trim.

Telemachus runs from one side of the room to the other pursued by Señor Tamisa's long-suffering secretary, a woman of a certain age and with hair dyed a shade of aubergine. The little thug might send the poor woman mad if she has to look after him for very much longer. Although, of course, you quite like madwomen. They have a certain something. (In fact, there is only one category of women that you really like: the living. You've never been interested in the others.)

You cast a sideways glance at Telemachus, then at the new owner of three of your works. With a silk-gloved hand she holds out her visiting card to you. Then she thinks better of it, and slowly removes her glove and brushes your hand with her bare hand as you take the thin card gripped between her fingers. A shiver runs down your spine, a shiver of embarrassment, possibly of desire. You had never thought of a hand being able to undress itself. You had never taken on board the fact that normally we all have bare hands. Women are always teaching you new things.

You promise to paint her portrait in exchange for another cheque similar to the one she has just signed. She will call you to discuss dates. She click-clacks towards the exit. Her chauffeur opens the door and stands aside to let her pass before closing it again behind him.

Women. Like the pistils of the dragon flower. How they move. Bless them.

'How old do you reckon she is? Seventy, nineteen?' asks Ramón, your dealer, and he blows softly on the still wet ink on the cheque.

'Shall we go to lunch?' suggests Señor Tamisa. 'It's a quarter past two.'

Telemachus walks over to your legs and puts his arms around them. His cheeks are the same colour as the secretary's hair. There is a sweet little dimple in the middle of each one. He is tired of running around, he is sweating, reeking of happiness. There is something about him, something unique to childhood, that proclaims to the four winds that he cannot possibly stop.

'Sweet little boy you've got there,' says Ramón.

'Fat! Ugly!' Telemachus bawls in reply, and gives a wild laugh.

'And so friendly,' adds Ramón laconically.

'Telemachus!' you say angrily. 'If you're rude like that again, I'll smack you. Now stop it!' Meanwhile, your son continues to laugh loudly right in Ramón's face!

You give him a smack on his bottom which doesn't seem to have much effect, but which does at least silence him for a moment and diverts his attention to a pencil on the table.

When you turn to speak to Señor Tamisa, you hear your dealer, Ramón Correa, mutter spitefully to Telemachus: 'Listen, you little wretch, you may not know it, but you're dying too, just like everything else under the sun.' Telemachus, however, who is painstakingly chewing the end of the pencil, is sitting on the floor, well out of earshot.

Even if he could hear him, he wouldn't understand what Ramón

267

meant. Telemachus still does not understand the concept of death, if death is a concept. It would be completely incomprehensible to him, or, at the very least, unacceptable, however often you tried to explain it to him. How could you prove to a child that life, while it may appear to be an ongoing performance, is merely the fiery spectacle offered up by the endless dying of all that is? And why try to frighten a child in that way?

You think it is perhaps time you changed your dealer. Your son is right. Ramón *is* fat and ugly. He's always frowning, like a victim who, furious at his own victimhood, but incapable of doing anything about it, is consequently filled with resentment, even against little children who don't know what they're saying (although Telemachus does always seem to know exactly what he's saying). He's too easy on his own weaknesses: poker, chocolate bars and perverse blondes – male and female – who've overdone the peroxide. His words betray him. His face betrays him. Even his bum betrays him. And you will betray him too at the first opportunity.

'Yes, let's go and eat.' You put Telemachus under your arm and follow Señor Tamisa to the door.

According to the Talmud, a man without a woman is not a human being. You can testify to the fact that any woman, in the same circumstances, turns into a ravening beast.

Ah, love. A trick thought up by some fool with no understanding of biology, but who believed that such a thing as love was possible.

Admit it, even you were slightly taken in.

Some people believe in reincarnation, so why shouldn't there also be lovers, who have far more reason to put their beliefs into practice? Your love for Penelope, for example, must be true because it's survived adolescence, marriage and infidelity (hers, for you know she has had her moments since she left you). Your love for her has withstood both the bidet and abandonment. Your love for

Penelope is one of the few things of which you can be sure, you tell yourself, and cast an approving eye at the waitress's bottom as she moves off, bearing the money for the bill on a small silver tray and swaying her hips the way Telemachus would shake a rattle.

You close your eyes for a few seconds and think of Penny. The *delectatio morosa* of her skin, her breasts, the hollow between her neck and her shoulders. Her hair, tawny and alive, bathed in silky light. You miss her smell, and more especially her colour, lying beside you every night and every morning. It must be love. It must be the effects of the overly generous dessert you've just eaten. The profiteroles they gave you were cold inside and warm outside, like the heart of your son's ungrateful mother. Shouldn't it be the other way round for both hearts and profiteroles? You are not quite sure. (You shouldn't have drunk those three glasses of grappa.)

Perhaps you should have eaten a lighter lunch, bearing in mind that soon there will be a reception to go to – the catering staff were arriving at the gallery just as you were preparing to leave; you will eat and drink still more and be all too aware of these excesses when you go back to the gym the day after tomorrow.

'Leave Señor Tamisa alone,' you tell Telemachus in thick tones. 'No, he doesn't want to see what would happen if you poked that pencil in his eye. Besides, we've got to go now.'

Lost in the night

À propos des fleurs, there's your friend Jorge. He was one of the first to arrive and here he is now elbowing his way towards you, displaying an anxious and imperfect mastery of the space he is walking through, as if he is trying to gulp down all the air around him. He pushes past the waiters and some of your fellow painters, those who felt obliged to drop in and say hello and who will be the first to escape the hustle and bustle of the exhibition once they have cast an eager, but critical eye over all your paintings.

'Ulysses!' he cries breathlessly.

'Jorge!'

'Congratulations, my friend. I can see you haven't been wasting your time.' He shakes your hand, smiling, and then gestures around him at the walls bedecked with your paintings which reflect the glare from the spotlights positioned on the ceiling. 'Hi, Telemachus.'

'Hello, Jeje . . .'

'Why does the wicked little shrimp always call me Jeje rather than Jorge?' asks Jorge. 'Is he making fun of me or what?'

'He just can't speak very well yet.'

'Oh yeah. He can't pronounce my two-syllable name, but he can manage to say "penicillin" and "ridiculous". He's just making a fool of me.'

'Penicillin! 'diculous!' yells a delighted Telemachus. 'Pennn-Nnnniiiiciiiilin!'

'Anyway, how are you?'

'Pf!' says your friend. 'I hate this bloody city. It's full of cars.' He pauses and grabs a glass of sparkling wine from the tray of a passing waiter. He takes a sip and licks his lips. 'It's full of streets and pavements. It's outrageous. When you're walking along you don't feel like a person, you feel more like a bollard, like another piece of street furniture.'

'Well, I don't think . . . But speaking of people, how are things going with Carmen? And how's Jorgito?'

'Jorgito's fine, thanks, although he's had a a bit of a cold lately. And things with Carmen . . . well, the usual. Awful. We're divorced now, if you remember, and we sleep together even less than we did when we were married. But you know all about these things.'

'Oh, don't talk to me about divorce,' you say, fending off the subject with a lift of your chin. You stroke Telemachus's hair.

'The best years of a man's life, Ulysses, my friend, are when he's single. No doubt about it. You have a girlfriend, take her out to the cinema, the country, the theatre, the railway station . . . You're just getting to know each other, and the girl is so eager to please that you think you've won the lottery of nymphomaniac wives-to-be. You actually believe there are such things as nymphomaniac wives. You think that's what life will be like from then on: passion and potency, going out at night, having meals in restaurants, having sex in car park toilets. Happiness, my friend, pure happiness . . .'

You take a few steps into the crowd which is beginning to pack the gallery. You, Ulysses, say hello to various people with your best host's smile, nodding and waving. 'But as soon as you marry them, that's it, women change. God, it's frightening how they change! Well, they're pretty frightening the moment you marry them actually. Of course, before you were married there weren't all those little things getting in the way and constantly coming between you. Snoring and morning halitosis, not to mention farting and having to think about what to eat every day. Hairs blocking the sink, dirty dishes, dirty underpants, stains in the toilet bowl, her periods, her mother, the weekly shop at the supermarket, the crumbs you leave on the floor under the table after eating, her smudged mascara, which stings her eyes because she's crying, and she's got more than enough reason to cry, but mainly it's because you don't pay her enough attention and because there's football on the telly and her mum's got terrible sciatica . . .'

Jorge pauses for breath. More breath. 'You wonder where all these disgusting, horrible things were before you got married, why you didn't notice them, because there they are in front of you, messing up your life, leaving her cold as ice and you mad as hell. Where were all those daily miseries before you were married and everything was sex and cinema and sex and wanting to see each other and sex . . .' Jorge stops suddenly and raises his hand to his chest. He seems to be trying to locate his heart.

'What's wrong?' you ask, alarmed. 'Is something wrong? I mean apart from everything else that's wrong.'

'No, it's nothing. I didn't mean to chunter on like that. It's your big night, after all, and I shouldn't be bothering you with my problems and ruining your party. It's just that we haven't seen each other for weeks and I, well, that's it really, I don't have that many friends I can talk to about my problems.'

'I've been really tied up sorting out the exhibition, as you know.'

'Of course, of course. I'm not trying to make you feel bad or anything.'

'Don't worry about it, we're friends, aren't we?'

'Anyway, to sum up, if it's fucking you want, then stay single,' sighs Jorge nostalgically, taking sips at his wine like a particularly perfidious, thirsty bird, 'and if it's wanking, then get married.'

'And what about divorce? No, don't tell me . . .'

'If you want to feel really depressed then get divorced. Do you know, sometimes, at night, I feel like one of those little orphan boys Murillo used to paint. When the moon comes out, I get so bored and restless. I get sozzled while I chat on the Internet, passing myself off as a lesbian, and no funny comments from you either, you bastard, I know what you're like. Then I pick up Carmen's favourite Barbie doll – she's had it since she was a kid, but it belongs to me now . . .'

A tiny tear apears in Jorge's right tearduct, but immediately disappears. Perhaps his eye is crying inside. 'I stole it from her when we divided up our worldly goods. She thinks the removal men lost it when I left home,' he explains in dull tones. 'It's a lovely doll, with red hair just like Carmen. Anyway, I pick it up by the hair, take it to the bathroom, place it lovingly in the bathtub and I pee every drop of the whisky I've drunk that night all over her. Then I sleep like a baby. I can tell you, it's more relaxing than a good back massage.'

'Jorge, I had no idea . . . Do you need . . . ?'

'What are you suggesting? That I need help? No, thanks. And don't look at me like that. Is it so awful that someone should spend their chaste nights peeing all over an old Barbie doll?' Jorge manages to grab another glass of wine and to deposit the earlier one, now empty, on the tray of another harassed waiter. 'My liking for the booze is much more serious than those monstrous – but very pleasant – nocturnal micturations. I'm keeping it under control though. The drinking, I mean.'

'So I see.'

'Oh, come on, Ulysses, this is only sparkling wine. It turns straight to piss.'

'Of course it does. Especially in your case, champ.'

'Besides . . . but why the hell am I telling you all this?'

'Because we're friends. You're quite right to tell me anything you want to. We haven't had a good chat for ages, although I don't know that we're going to have much of one this evening. Let's get together next week, eh?' you say, running your hand over his bowed, sunken, office worker's shoulders.

273

'I wash it afterwards.'

'What? The bath?'

'No, damn it! The bloody doll.'

'Ah.'

'I wash her hair with white nettle shampoo. I leave her to soak in a special Barbie bath that I bought in the toy department in Eroski's on a visit up to my parents in Santander. I brought the wretched thing back with me in my briefcase, all the way from Santander to Madrid. I just happened to see it and it was love at first sight. I add a pinch of bath salts to the water; they contain essential oils of bergamot, orange and sandalwood, which combine all the pleasure of a good bath with a deep anti-stress action. I put her clothes in the washing machine. I do a special wash just for them. Well, sometimes I do stick in my week's worth of underwear too, because one shouldn't really waste water,' says Jorge gravely. 'I always feel terrible about doing what I do to her, but I feel relieved too, I won't deny it. Along with the contents of my bladder I empty out the darkness in my heart, if I may put it in such Conradian terms. I can't see anything wrong with it myself.'

'You obviously have some very entertaining evenings,' you say with a sigh, holding tight to Telemachus's hand so that he won't escape and get lost amongst all those legs. 'Has your doll got a name?'

'Yes,' Jorge says reluctantly. 'She's called Carmen. Carmen Carmen Carmen.'

'Oh, Jorge.'

'Anyway, let's change the subject. I came here today to give you moral support and to congratulate you, and, more importantly, because I want to buy one of your paintings.'

'Do you mean it? Well, I'm really touched.'

'I need to get rid of those horrible prints I've got on the walls. They keep the women away.'

'But not dear Barbie Watercloset.'

'No, she takes whatever you throw at her, poor thing. She's the ideal companion for a lone wolf like me.'

'Well, if you're determined to buy something, we can make a reduction on the price. My dealer won't like it, so you'd better drop by my apartment and choose one of the paintings not included in the exhibition, the ones I've got in my studio. We can reach a gentleman's agreement.'

'Oh, no. No way. I'm going to buy a painting here, in the gallery. Like a proper buyer. Deals on the side aren't my style. You've got to sell the paintings you exhibit, and I intend to get tax relief on every penny I spend, so don't you worry.'

'All right, if that's what you want.'

'Well, as Tolstoy would say: the main thing, Excellency, is not to think about anything.' Jorge cranes his neck to get a glimpse of the heads crowded round the tables of canapés. 'You've got most of Vili's ex-students here tonight. It's a shame about the Academy. We've all been a bit disoriented since it closed. I drink more; you paint more and see your friends less; Jacobo, the cantankerous old blind man, bumps into more doors . . . Actually, I saw him around here somewhere a while ago. He's got a nerve. A blind man at an art exhibition.' Jorge's throat gurgles as he takes another sip of his drink. 'But, as he himself says: "We've seen everything anyway", isn't that right? Oh, and there's Irma, who gets blonder by the day – and she was the one who, when she was at the Academy, claimed to be such a passionate lover of the truth, but now she's always dousing her hair with peroxide. And there's David, who looks poovier by the day . . . Whoops, speaking of the Holy Family, here he comes. Hi, David, you old son-of-a-gun.'

David comes over to you. He smells so good, looks so elegant, attractive and refined that Jorge fidgets uncomfortably in his suit.

'I feel like peeing whenever I see this guy,' he says to you in a low voice, at the same time holding out his hand to David. 'David, I haven't seen you for ages.'

'Yes, it's been far too long. But first of all, Ulysses, congratulations on the exhibition. It's ab-so-lute-ly brilliant. Real genius, real talent. There's so much light in your pictures! My husband and I – my husband's over there somewhere – are interested in buying a couple of them,' says David, and you thank him, eyes downcast, slightly overwhelmed. 'But it's a shame, isn't it, that we no longer meet up at the Academy. How is Vili, by the way?'

You shrug. You have nothing to say on the matter. Vili's choice.

'Well . . .' you mumble, and make a vague gesture that could mean anything.

'I miss our old teacher so much,' David goes on. 'Do you know I've even had to join a gym. And all because, whenever it was time to go to the Academy, I'd realize there was no Academy to go to, and I'd get depressed. I just didn't know what to do with those hours, how to fill them. I'd get edgy, my neck would itch and my ears would buzz. "Withdrawal symptoms," said Óscar, my husband. "You need to do some exercise to get over it." He thinks you can get over anything with a bit of exercise, he's one of those men who can solve any problem, a family drama, for example, with a good long jog around the park. And if, when he gets back home, the drama is still there, he nevertheless thinks it's not quite as dramatic as he thought. He is a fervent believer in physical exercise. Anyway, I let myself be persuaded and the hours I used to spend at the Academy, I now spend at the gym. Instead of moving my brain, I move my . . .'

'Arse,' suggests Jorge quietly, but David seems not to hear.

'. . . body. Sit-ups, weights, the whole lot. I can't honestly say it has the same effect. Cicero, Epicurus, Plutarch, et cetera, aren't a patch on a series of stupid exercises that leave you feeling a physical wreck by the time you get into bed. Vili, though, did manage to make me believe that I'm normal, that we are all, without exception, normal. That was a great feeling, you know. I really miss him.'

Telemachus starts to cry.

'What's wrong, you little rascal?' Jorge asks him.

'Shit, shit, shiiit!' moans Telemachus and bursts into furious crying. The people nearby turn to watch; they cast mistrustful glances at you, as if they suspect that the three of you have been inflicting pain on him in some cruel and surreptitious way and are now clumsily trying to cover up the damage done.

'Shit, eh? I couldn't have put it more clearly or concisely myself.'

'Don't be so rude,' you say to Telemachus, and then to your friends you add: 'He's tired.' You pick him up. 'We've been out and about all day. It's too much for him. And it's starting to get really smoky in here now, and noisy too.'

'Maybe he's frightened,' suggests David. 'My little boy doesn't like crowded places either. We've left him at home with the nanny. Crowded places aren't good for little kids. They feel even smaller than they are and that scares them.'

'I haven't got a nanny,' you say.

'We're all afraid of something,' says Jorge.

'Oh now, really. You're from the Inland Revenue, Jorge: what have you got to be afraid of?'

'The dark, loneliness, women . . .' Jorge recites wearily. 'Et cetera, et cetera.' He raises his glass as if giving a toast and drains it to the dregs.

'Would you like me to hold him, to see if he'll calm down?' asks David.

'I don't know . . . oh, all right.' You hand Telemachus over to him. Telemachus screams and gives great disconsolate sobs, clinging to David's neck, fumbling clumsily with David's spotted bow tie and succeeding in undoing it. 'I should put him down for a while

277

in his buggy and let him have a bit of a sleep in Señor Tamisa's office. His secretary can keep an eye on him. I've still got to have a word with a couple of art critics and a few other people . . . I don't know . . .'

'It's OK, I'll do it.' David moves as if performing a gentle dance. Telemachus is still clasped to his chest. 'If you tell me where the office is, I'll take the boy there; I'll sing him a few lullabies until he falls asleep, then I'll leave him with the secretary. "Hush now, hush now, little dark-skinned boy,/Your mama's working in the fields,/Working, working, working so hard,/Yes, working for nothing at all." My little son loves that song.'

'Thanks, it's on the left down the second corridor. The door marked "Private". Tell Señora Gómez that I'll be there soon to check on him. The buggy's in there, and it's already in the reclining position. Oh,yes, and if Señora Gómez isn't there, there's another girl, I can't remember her name, she's from public relations. And there are a couple of other people too. Ask one of them.'

David nods his agreement.

Telemachus is crying more quietly, he occasionally closes his eyes and presses his little face covered in sweat, tears and saliva into David's shoulder. 'Shhhit!' he says. But he is gradually calming down under the influence of David's singing.

'He pronounces his "sh"s really well, doesn't he?' you say proudly. You give your son a kiss and murmur something in German, then: 'You have a little sleep now and Papa will be with you soon, all right?'

David turns to leave, but before he has gone more than a few paces, Jorge calls to him:

'Hey, David!'

David stops and wheels round.

'Yes?'

'Are you happy?' Jorge asks him.

David shrugs and tenderly strokes the now sleeping Tele-machus's hair.

'Yes, I think so, most of the time,' he replies, after thinking for a few seconds, then he disappears, baby in arms, amongst the people filling the rooms.

Jorge and Ulysses look at each other.

'Bastard!' exclaims Jorge.

'Come on, Jorge, don't be so envious.'

'Well, well,' says Jorge, pointing to his left, 'here she comes with her husband and her lover. The subject, verb and predicate. All three of them.'

'Who? What?'

'Mireia, from the Academy, don't you remember? I've got a colleague at work who knows her really well. Surely you haven't forgotten her apologia for female polygamy? It was a classic!' Jorge clicks his tongue and gives a crooked, mocking smile. 'She's a stalwart defender of female polygamy. She lives with her husband and her ex-husband, and apparently they rub along brilliantly. On alternate nights, one hopes. Some people get a lot and others get nothing at all. Great!'

Mireia comes over to you, flanked by her two husbands. She is wearing a radiant smile. Her smile is like a trophy won from life which she likes to show off. Her smile is full of a wild, private pleasure, which prettily dimples her cheeks.

'Ulysses . . .'

'Anyway, champ, I'll say goodbye. I'm going to have a word with your gallery owner about a painting I saw over there, and then I'll dash off home,' Jorge says. 'I'll call you next week and we can have supper or go to a pick-up joint or something.'

'I've got tickets for a boxing match,' you say, winking. 'The Lavapiés Kid versus the Basauri Bull.'

'Terrific! Hard punching, blood, shouting, sweat, testosterone.

Just what my life has been crying out for, only I wouldn't listen.' Jorge picks up a fake caviar and cucumber canapé, then bows briefly. 'Good evening, Mireia. And to your companions.'

'Good evening,' the ménage à trois respond in unison.

'Take care of your bladder.' You slap Jorge on the back and give him a hug. You feel foolish, awkward and fraternal. And the feeling doesn't seem to you entirely bad.

In the belly of the whale

'Ulysses.'

'Mireia.'

'Considering that we hardly know each other, it was really sweet of you to invite me to your exhibition. I think it's magnificent.'

'That's all right. Thank *you* for coming. It's lovely to see you here. I was hoping that tonight all the people who used to go to Vili's Academy, or nearly all of them, would be able to be here with me.'

'Well,' says one of Mireia's husbands, whether the first or the second you don't know, 'we're thinking of buying one of your paintings, aren't we, guys?' He looks eagerly at the other husband and at Mireia

'Yes,' they chorus.

'Oh, forgive me, Ulysses, I haven't introduced you to my husband and my ex-husband.'

She tells you their names, but you immediately forget who is who. You have the impression that they look rather alike. But what does it matter – Mireia can probably tell them apart, even in the pitch dark.

The atmosphere around you is as gay, frivolous, multiform and sultry as the atmosphere in an old brothel. The air is growing warmer and thinner, full of smoke, sophistication and schmaltz. You can just make out the figure of the industrious Señor Tamisa moving ceaselessly back and forth, handing out cards, noting down numbers, bestowing smiles and making deals. He'll soon be coming over to find you and then you'll have to shake sweaty hands and appear friendly but enigmatic (you are, after all, an artist), and allow yourself to be photographed; you'll have to greet people loudly, make promises and create illusions.

'The exhibition was already a success with the purchases made by our special client this morning . . .' Suddenly, Señor Tamisa is by your side, whispering smugly into your ear. His breath smells of cough drops and has a slightly narcotic effect on you. 'You know, my boy, I think we're going to sell the lot. And I've got some of the best art critics in the land who are just *head over heels* with pleasure at what they're seeing. I'll leave you alone with your friends a while longer, but don't run away afterwards, all right?'

The gallery owner disappears once more behind various restless bodies, all dressed in their party best for the occasion. No one would think that, at this moment, a single one of these bodies contained an iota of sadness.

Mireia's husbands excuse themselves politely, leaving you alone with her. They haven't had a good look at all the paintings yet, they explain with a certain shy amazement.

'Oh, no!' says Mireia. 'It's him again!'

'Who?'

'That wretched blind man. Jacobo Ayala. I mean, look at him. He's staring at the paintings as if he really can see something.'

'Well, that's a good attitude to adopt in life.'

'It's more as if he's sniffing them. He'll leave them all covered in little drops of cold saliva.'

'H'm.'

'I bumped into him in the toilets just now.'

'Really?'

'Since he can't see a thing, he'd gone into the ladies by mistake.'

You remember Jacobo's eyes. You saw them close to one evening at the Academy, when he took off his dark glasses for a moment and wiped the bridge of his nose – damp with perspiration – with

282

a paper handkerchief. There appeared to be something like the skeleton of a leaf drawn on the inside of each of his pupils. The garnet-red and blue leaf of some absurd tree, the product of an inflamed, devilish, botanical imagination.

'Although I have my doubts . . .' Mireia goes on, wrinkling her nose as she talks. 'It may not have been a mistake at all, because, when I went in, he had his trousers down around his knees and – wait for it – underneath his flannel trousers he's wearing pink stockings and a pink satin suspender belt. The old transvestite!'

'God!' you say. Your mouth hangs open. But who knows, Mireia might well be lying. You seem to recall that the two of them didn't get on very well. It's a terrific idea, but she's probably making it up to annoy Jacobo.

'Isn't that incredible? There he is, the perfect phallocrat, and it turns out that, underneath, old Tiresias is all dolled up in a rather sexy little lace number.'

Good old Tiresias. The same Tiresias who was blinded by Athene because he saw her bathing naked. On the other hand, the goddess did give him the gift of longevity and the ability, in hell, to preserve his mental faculties intact. (You, in Tiresias' skin, would not have scorned the importance of that last mercy, even here, on earth.)

'He probably is Tiresias,' you say, smiling. You imagine him in his undies, wearing silk petticoats.

'He might be.'

'Tiresias was both man and woman. The gods were always punishing him for something or the other. The goddess Juno, for example, took great exception to him announcing to Zeus that women got more pleasure from sex than men. He could say such things because he had been both.' You provide this little explanation to Mireia, although you suspect she doesn't need it.

'Well, this particular Tiresias,' she says, pointing with a scornful finger at Jacobo, who is only a few yards away, his nose pressed against one corner of a large oil painting, 'this Tiresias spends his life denying women their most elementary rights.'

'But he wears pink tights.'

'Yes, I suppose that is a point in his favour, isn't it?' Mireia suddenly opens her mouth and adopts such a strange expression that, for a second, her features seem to fuse, as if they are about to disappear and dissolve into the corners of her face. 'Oh, dear God, I think he's sniffed you out. I think he's coming over here. Right, I'll leave you. I just wanted to congratulate you and to ask after Vili . . . oh, and can I give you a piece of good news?'

'I love good news.'

'I'm pregnant!' Mireia walks backwards away from you, smiling. Her smile is a small and now clearly defined amber ellipse. 'I know it's of no importance to anyone else, but I'm happy. If you see Vili, tell him that, will you?'

By the time you are clasping Jacobo's hand, she has disappeared from view. She has probably rushed off in search of her husbands, who will be waiting for her in some corner of the vast gallery, impatient to pamper her, each holding a glass of sparkling wine. Eager to plunge back into the belly of the whale.

'Jacobo! Thanks for coming.'

'It's a remarkable exhibition, my boy.'

'How are you?' you ask.

'Excellent, if it wasn't for these tights, which itch like fury and have been bothering me all evening,' Jacobo says.

The elixir of the gods

You have gone to see how Telemachus is. He is asleep with one fist stuffed in his mouth. Señora Gómez has left the office in darkness. Your son is sleeping, resting with impunity like a small, exhausted animal. This, for you, is happiness, seeing him there, safe and untroubled.

After rushed greetings, hugs, two or three quick interviews for the radio, introductions to Señor Tamisa's contacts who will soon be your contacts too and who crush both your hand and your nerves, and after false smiles and genuine ones, snatched conversations, photos for a major woman's magazine who are going to write an article about you, meeting people whom you recognize but don't know from Adam, and who seem to you like smug, foolish shadows moving about against the pale backdrop of the walls, you finally manage to return to the middle of the main room.

It occurs to you that the surrounding panorama would be much more beautiful if everyone would just stop for a moment so that you could contemplate them calmly. Looking is one of the carnal pleasures you most appreciate. You would make a bad blind man. But no one will stay still, because they're all real, and yet you, like Goethe, and like most people, prefer a fixed error to a shifting truth. You would prefer them framed in one of your paintings, unstirred by fear or desire. Nice and still. Very good. Very quiet.

The next thing you know, you have been talking to Johnny Espina Williamson for at least ten minutes. And you cannot remember a word of what has been said, even though you are vaguely aware of having held a more or less coherent conversation.

'My problem is that I've loved too much, you see. That's been my main defect,' Johnny says, his eyes sad and bright.

'Oh, I don't know,' you say, 'I don't think that loving too much can be seen as a defect.'

'No, what I mean is that my love has rarely been reciprocated. That's been the defect.'

'Ah, I see.'

'I've sacrificed my life for success,' Johnny goes on. 'Social success, literary success, success with women. And now here I am, a fifty-year-old expatriate, and I find that I have neither a life nor success. That's why I'm so glad that you, a good friend, should triumph in this way, and that I can be here to see it. Cheers, my friend.' He takes a sip of his drink; he means it.

'Cheers.' You drink too – after all, why not? 'Thanks, Johnny.'

'The worst thing about fame is that everyone knows you,' declares Johnny, leaning against a wall. He seems tired. 'But you're on your way, I can tell. A real star. The new Picasso. Anyway, take my advice and enjoy it. Despite the drawbacks, success is much better than failure. More comfortable, if you see what I mean. Your current account, your reputation, the women dying for you to look up their skirts. That's what success is. And failure, what's failure? I'll tell you, my friend: a piece of shit on a stick. Girls these days don't go chasing after guys who wander about with nothing but a piece of shit on a stick to hold on to. That's where my generation went wrong. We idolized failure. We thought failure was somehow aesthetic, honest, right – do you know what I mean? The fact is that most of us were just a bunch of losers, which is perhaps why we gave such importance to failure. But at this stage in the game, as far as I'm concerned, you can screw failure.'

'But didn't you just say that you had sacrificed your life for success?'

'Yes,' says Johnny, nodding vigorously. 'But I always *said* I was on the side of the underdog and all that. It just wasn't on to say otherwise. When I arrived here in Spain, fleeing the butchers in my Latin American homeland, I was a trendy young lefty. That was the only way you could get your leg over in those days. I still *am* a trendy lefty.' Johnny coughs, takes a loud gulp of his drink and lights a cigarette. 'Only now it makes no difference if I'm a trendy lefty or an Albanian, because I never get to screw anyone anyway. Oh dear, I seem to be ever so slightly pissed. It's this wine.' He hiccups. 'I love free wine. The elixir of the gods.'

'Well, I think there's plenty more where that came from.'

'By the way, have you seen that bastard?'

'Which one?'

'Who do you think? Hipólito, of course. Hipólito Jiménez, the painter. The house painter. Not like you, of course,' says Johnny with an affected smile. 'I've missed him like mad, the bastard, ever since Vili closed the Academy.'

'There he is.' You point to a group of young people. Hipólito is amongst them; he waves and comes over to join you.

'Ulysses, my friend! Quite a crowd you've got here. Really impressive. I hope you don't mind, but I brought a few friends with me,' says Hipólito.

'No, on the contrary. Have you all got something to eat and drink?'

'Yes, we're fine.'

Hipólito and Johnny eye each other warily, but say nothing. Johnny douses his cigarette in the half-empty glass in his hand, then stamps on the floor as if he is stubbing it out with his shoe.

'I haven't seen you for ages.'

'I know.'

'I'm really glad things are going so well for you,' Hipólito says.

There is a kind of current in the air, invisible but very strong, that binds Johnny to Hipólito and Hipólito to Johnny. It is as loud as a cannon-shot. It oozes resentment, masochism, romanticism and a cosy nostalgia. An atmosphere so thick you can almost chew it.

'Thanks. And how about you, Hipólito, are you happy?' you ask, just to say something and to try to distract them from each other, from their shared passion for each other.

'Good grief,' you think glumly. 'These two are like Pepsi and Coca-Cola. They're practically identical, but they hate each other's guts.'

'Well, I was, at least until I saw the spic here,' says Hipólito, pointing at Johnny.

'Who are you calling a spic!' yells Johnny, and as he steps angrily forward, he spills a little of the wine and cigarette ash mixture. He pauses, calms down and leans back against the wall again. 'I may be a spic, but at least I know who my father was.'

'Oh, very funny, dickhead.'

'At least I've got a dick.'

Hipólito flushes. Ah, yes, the pleasure of the fight stimulates the circulation. Crossing swords, brandishing the keen machete of the word. We are all by nature impure and savage.

'Oh, you think you're so smart, so witty, don't you?'

'That's because I am,' says Johnny, and he takes a sip of his stinking ash-filled drink, then drinks it down, including the soggy, sticky cigarette end, which gets stuck in his teeth. He spits it out. 'You said it.'

'Oh, yeah,' Hipólito smiles languidly. 'You're always saying how intelligent you are, but since you take care never to give any evidence of it, we just don't know, do we?'

'He's like a character out of Gogol, this guy!' Johnny laughs loudly. 'Although you've probably never read any Gogol, have you?'

'What's that got to do with anything?' retorts Hipólito uneasily. 'At least I'm not a Uruguayan.'

'I'm not a Uruguayan either, you moron.'

'Well, whatever it is you are.'

'Anyway, what have you got against my Uruguayan brothers?'

'All right, enough is enough.' You look at them gravely, slightly downcast. You put on your angry face. Penelope used to say that when you got angry you looked like someone whose soul had died.

'I'm sorry, Ulysses.'

'Yes, me too.'

'Why don't you just make peace once and for all? Why don't you get drunk together? I'll pay for the drinks. Or better still, why don't you go to bed together? That would probably be the most worthwhile and the cheapest solution for all concerned. Or why don't you just go outside and punch each other until your teeth fall out?' you say without once raising your voice. You know that a reprimand has much more impact when delivered in a low voice. You're like Don Corleone. A harsh, hoarse, very Sicilian Mafia boss.

'It's just that . . .'

'I . . .'

'I'll leave you two together.' You slap them both on the back. 'Love one another. Enjoy my party. Enjoy life, brothers.'

And you walk off in the opposite direction.

The shadow line

You're heading for the exit. You're hot. Your linen jacket is bothering you. It's too heavy. You could do with a breath of fresh air. You'd like to gulp down the darkness of the night sky, its infinite shadow lines. April has you by the throat and, if you're not careful, flowers might spring from your mouth.

You tell yourself that the night is perfect, that you're lucky to be alive.

Soon, too, you'll have money in your pocket. Isn't that what you wanted, Ulysses? You've taken up the reins of your career again, in the words of that brainy TV critic – so gruff and formal – with whom you were chatting for a while and whose permanently windswept hair looked as if it had been sown with threads of electrified silver.

When you go back into the gallery, you run straight into Francisco de Gey. You've never liked the look of him. His cunning eyes create chasms all around him, open up cracks in the ground he walks on. He has the appearance of a half-felt emotion, of a snail with a fractured shell, trying desperately to conceal the shape of its exposed body, and leaving a furious trail of slime behind.

He sways about in front of you. He's obviously drunk, although he talks lucidly enough and with a certain faux meekness.

'We artists,' he says, 'are bloody geniuses. We all want to be artists because we all want to be geniuses, and for other people to recognize it and to shout it from the rooftops. But only a few of us are real geniuses, eh, Ulysses? And we're amongst them, aren't we, Ulysses?' He takes your hand and clasps it or, rather, shakes it.

'What would become of the world without us artists, eh, Ulysses? What would become of this vale of tears without the consolation of art, without the business of art, eh?'

'You tell me,' you say coldly.

'It would be buggered. Completely buggered. You know that, you sense that. You're like me. We both know the same things. We are the chosen ones. We are both fortunate enough to be able to devote ourselves to art. You paint, I write.'

'Oh, you write, do you? Since when?'

'Well, I've been writing for a long time, but now I'm officially a writer. I've just finished my first novel, and it's going to be published.'

'I'm pleased for you,' you say, looking distractedly around you.

Suddenly Francisco grows sad. Or confidential. Or . . . Well, who knows what snails feel?

'My novel is based on real events,' he says into your ear. For a second, his lips brush your skin. An icy shiver prickles the back of your neck. You nervously wipe away some invisible filth from your ear.

'Really.'

'It's the story of a guy, a man a bit like the one who tried to kill himself at Vili's Academy, do you remember?' His mouth opens wide in satisfaction. His mouth is an inert space which his tongue only just manages to stir into life as it moves sinuously to speak. Very sinuously. 'My hero is a poor sod who has lost everything, even the will to live. And it's based on real events, do you see?'

'No, not really. Explain it to me better. I'm a bit slow on the uptake.' You're beginning to be interested in this little chat.

You beckon to the waiter and pick up another glass of whisky for Francisco. You put his near-empty glass down on the tray. You pour yourself a drink too.

'My publisher thinks it's a really meaty book. He's very excited about it. He says you can see this man's changing emotions as if you were watching them from the side of a boat. Those were his very words. He's really excited.'

'Wonderful.'

'That's where the artist's talent lies, isn't it, Ulysses? In knowing how to draw conclusions from reality.'

'And you have, have you?'

'I think so, yes. When I met him . . .' He pauses to take a sip of his drink. 'When I met him in the Retiro park, as soon as I saw him, I knew he was a lost soul.'

'You knew him? But no one at the Academy knew him.'

'I did. I was the one who took him there.'

'Really? You should have told the police. But you didn't – or did you?' you ask.

'No, I didn't. What was the point? They would have carted him off to the psychiatric hospital anyway. What did it matter if I knew him or not? He's locked up in the loony bin now, although he'll be out soon enough. All the crazies end up back out on the street nowadays. The State doesn't want to take responsibility for the insane or for criminals or for difficult young people. In fact, it doesn't want to take responsibility for anyone who's got problems. That poor man never harmed a soul. He just wanted to die. OK, wanting to die is a form of madness, but it's just as legitimate as wanting to live. In my novel, he does die.' Francisco gives a crooked smile; there is a yellowish gleam to his teeth. 'That's the only thing I've changed in his story. You have to draw the reader in, and death makes more of an impression on us than life.'

'Does it?' you say. 'How odd. With me it's exactly the opposite.'

'You could say that you changed *his* story when you stopped him killing himself with that gun.'

'His story, yes.'

'And my story too.'

'I'm sorry if I changed your story, but not his, if that's what you mean,' you say. 'If someone wants to commit suicide, they should do it in private; that way no one will stop them.'

'Everyone said you were a hero. The newspapers all talked about your quick reactions, about how you were a boxer and a painter, and really good-looking too. I confess I even felt a little jealous when I read that. After all, I was the one who took him to the Academy, not you.'

'Really, to me . . . I mean, I spend my whole life looking. I make a point of noticing things, and I noticed him taking out a gun. Anyone else would have done the same, they would have stopped him firing the gun at himself or at someone else.'

'No, not anyone. I wouldn't have. I was bogged down in my novel and in my marriage. Laura . . . she's my wife . . . well, as you may or may not know, things weren't going well between us.' He half closes his eyes and concentrates as if trying to commit something to memory. 'I knew the man was quite likely to do something of the sort. He'd told me so several times. I even knew he had a gun on him, but I didn't do anything to help him. He was . . . well, being with him was like watching a film, a drama being played out just for me; it made me forget my own problems. For weeks, that man gave meaning to my life. Real emotion and pain, albeit gratuitous and vicarious. When I met him, I felt compassion at first, but then disgust. I felt like trampling on him, or slapping him. His weakness, his pleading eyes, his puny body . . . He brought out the worst in me. He brought out the cruelty we all have inside us. The same thing that makes us squash an innocent worm when we see it dragging itself across our path.'

The same thing you feel when you look at Francisco, for example. That is what you think as you listen.

'I started talking to him the first time we met in the park. The kind of banal, conventional phrases two strangers might exchange

293

– well, you can imagine. But you could tell a mile off that he wanted to die, you could sense the depression and the despair, all the things that drive someone to want to kill themselves.'

'Go on,' you say.

'Then we met the following afternoon in the same place, and this time I had my tape recorder with me. I just took it along in case I got some ideas for my novel. I find it easier to talk than to write. I thought I might make more headway if I recorded any ideas that came to me while I was out for a stroll. When we met again, he started to talk, and I found it interesting and decided to record it. He talked and I recorded his words. We saw each other often after that, and I always did the same thing. At night, Laura, my wife, would transcribe the tapes. The novel is written in the first person.'

'How clever of you. Would you like another drink?'

'Yes, please. I could do with one. I'm celebrating the start of my career. The occasion deserves a proper libation.'

This time it is a waitress who fills both glasses.

'My wife has left me. She's gone,' Francisco tells you, his eyes flashing. 'Laura has left me.'

'A good blend,' you say, savouring the whisky. 'Do you know yet what your next novel will be about?'

'No, not yet.'

'Perhaps you should start thinking about it,' you suggest.

'The man was very alone. He lived with his wife and son.'

'I thought you said he was alone.'

'Exactly. That's the very worst way of being alone – in company. That's something I learned from being with him.'

'Listen, Francisco, have you ever heard of the morality of snails?'

Francisco looks straight at you, confused, and shakes his head.

'No, never.'

'I'm not surprised. Because, as far as anyone knows, they don't have one,' you say softly. 'Goodbye, Francisco.' And without more ado, you go to meet Señor Tamisa, who is hurrying towards you, muttering 'Excuse me, excuse me', as he elbows his way through the throng. From his face you can tell that he has been looking for you for some time.

'You and I are the same, eh, Ulysses?' shouts Francisco, his voice slurred.

There is a lot of noise in the room. You don't hear him. Perhaps that is why you don't reply.

Emerging from the kingdom of fear

The night progresses, and the social duties imposed on you by your gallery owner and your dealer (with journalists, organizers of international exhibitions, advertising people, wealthy collectors, two executives from a multinational, a pop singer with a passion for painting . . .) are beginning to weigh on you. All these obligations and the constant deployment of your social skills, and all just to earn an honest living, have a depressing effect on you.

As you once found out for yourself, earning money illegally doesn't take nearly so much effort.

Your mouth is beginning to ache from having to stretch your lips, urging them into a smile, then you spot a group of three women only a few feet from you. You mumble an excuse to the circle of important people surrounding you and sidle over to the three women.

As you approach, for a fraction of a second you have the terrifying feeling that you have, at one time, slept with all three of them. You savour the idea, the overall vision of that delicious trio, who are chatting calmly away about who knows what. Their words emerge from their respective painted mouths as if wrapped in ribbons of smoke.

But no, you have never shared anything with Jana that could not be shared over the phone, or by registered post. She is Penelope's assistant, and your relationship has, up until now, been limited to receiving orders, demands, reproaches and cheques from your wife through her.

'. . . for another woman – fancy leaving me for another woman!'

you hear Jana say with a slight tremor of the lips, raising her voice above those echoing around her. 'Can you believe it? That pig of an ex-boyfriend of mine. He must be out of his mind. He goes and shacks up with some old, retired model and has the nerve to tell me that they're going to get married in Las Vegas and have five children one after the other. Possibly in Las Vegas too. They do everything so fast over there. He even had the cheek to suggest that she might still be able to get work modelling maternity clothes. Apparently, Versace is preparing a really stunning collection. I can just see the scrawny old hag now, wearing a transparent blouse with holes in it for two huge great nipple shields.' She moans softly. 'In the most recent photos of her, she had so much cellulite, she looked as if she'd been upholstered. Oh well. Abandoned, that's what I feel! The cow is older than me, more stupid, and richer, too. I can't understand Mauricio. I can't understand men at all. They should all be forced to undergo some kind of annual psychological test, and if they're found wanting, if they don't pass, then the same thing should happen to them as happens with cars – off to the scrapyard with them.'

You lurk behind a couple of young men with a lot of hair who are holding what appears to be a crude but impassioned debate about art, and from there you continue your eavesdropping.

You love women's conversations.

They're *so* educational.

'Absolutely,' agrees Irma, who is listening to Jana with rapt attention. Does she envy Jana's bright, youthful beauty? Or is she ashamed of her own cheap hair dye?

Next to Jana, Irma seems vulgar and brash, a painted woman, more suited to furtive, unmentionable desires than to true love.

'Sorry, ladies.' Jana takes a paper hanky out of her bag and blows her nose delicately. 'I know we've never met before, and that I only stopped to ask you for directions to try and find my way around this dump, because I've got to give a message to my boss's ex-husband, but . . . it's just that . . . you're not going to believe this, my horoscope today says that complete strangers will turn out to be my guardian angels, that they'll offer me understanding, kindness and protection. That they will open up to me a whole new world of relationships and work opportunities that I had never even imagined. By the way, what do you do? I'm probably . . .'

'I'm a housewife,' says Luz and smiles expectantly.

'I work in a crèche,' says Irma, wrinkling her nose, slightly on her guard.

'Ah, I see. Yes, well . . . And are you happy in your work?' Curiosity replaces the look of disappointment on Jana's face in a matter of seconds. 'I say "work" because I think being a housewife is one of the hardest jobs there is. Mostly because, at the end of the month, where do you go to pick up your wages, eh? There you have it. Anyway, how do you find it?'

'As you'd expect,' admits Luz. 'No prospect of promotion on the horizon.'

'Oh, I get by. The kids,' says Irma, 'aren't too bad. Well, they're a pain in the butt really, but they're not too bad because, at their age, they still can't talk very well. I think that's what spoils men, the fact that they can talk . . . and talk and talk . . . If they didn't know how to talk, we would never have rows with them, don't you agree?'

'Exactly,' says Jana.

'Yes, you might have a point there,' concedes Luz.

'When someone can talk, they can say the most terrible things, and I don't want to hear terrible things. For example, my boyfriend's Greek.' Irma gesticulates wildly when she says the word 'Greek'. 'At first, everything was perfect between us because Andros is very handsome and affectionate and a marvellous cook and I didn't understand a word he said. But then he started going to night school. He signed up for classes in Spanish for foreigners.'

'And?'

'And?'

'The moment he learned to say "the cat sat on the mat", I felt as if something had broken between us. Something very important.'

'Really?'

'Yes. I felt so bad that I was even unfaithful to him a couple of times, well, seven actually. Out of revenge, you see.'

'I'm not surprised.'

'I'm normally very faithful, but I was still reeling from the effects of that emotional blow. It infuriated me that Andros had begun to be able to read the names of the streets, the label on the rice packet and my name on the mailbox on the landing. Little things like that can put a strain on a relationship.'

'So how are you getting on now? Or have you split up?' asks Jana.

'No, no, we haven't,' Irma says, smiling. 'He's still as handsome and affectionate as ever, not to mention his cooking, which is fabulous. No, we haven't split up or anything. We're fine now. After all, life doesn't give you that many chances, so why throw this one away? Although I still think it would be better if he didn't know a word of Spanish.' She gives a wry shrug. 'But, as we all know, nobody's perfect. Every morning, when I wake up beside him, I have the odd feeling that I've just emerged from a black hole. As soon as I wake up, it's like I'm gasping for air. Then I look around me and I see Andros there asleep and the room all quiet and starting to fill up with daylight, and I just feel a sense of enormous relief.'

'And what's your love life like?' Jana asks Luz. 'Do you get on well with your husband?'

'I suppose so, but I'm not sure really,' replies Luz. 'I probably do, because this is probably how it is for everyone. At least, that's what I tell myself every day, that it's the same for everybody, that this is just how things are, and it's not that bad really.'

'How long have you been married?'

'Nearly twenty-three years.'

'That's great. Nowadays it's like everyone gets divorced. If they haven't got a reason, they invent one, but absolutely everyone breaks up with their partner over something or other. It's terrible, it's like no one can stand long relationships any more, let alone marriage,' declares Jana.

'That's true,' says Luz, laughing loudly. 'Even the ones who don't split up can't stand it!'

The witches and death

As if in a moment of illumination, you recall the image of your smiling mother, arm-in-arm with your father, when you and Héctor were children. You miss your mother and your father and your brother. You hardly ever stop to think how much you miss them. Henriette, your mother, is dead, although on some mornings, you see her eyes there in the mirror, while you're shaving. Your father has gone back to spending most of his time in Zurich, and Héctor is somewhere a long way away. At the Pole. In the Antarctic. You wouldn't be able to pinpoint it on a map. You've never asked him if he's right on top of the world, or right at the bottom. You're not even very clear that the world has a top and a bottom, because it probably depends on how you look at it. Or from where. In any case, Héctor lives and works on one of the polar ice caps. When you last spoke to him on the phone, he told you that he had an Eskimo girlfriend. 'An Eskimo?' you said. 'Do you mean "an eater of raw flesh"?' Your brother replied smugly: 'Yes, I had high hopes of her in the oral sex department.'

You are suddenly aware of an admonishing hand on your shoulder. Your instinct makes you grab it hard and hang on to it.

'Ow!'

When you turn round, you find Aglaia's face contorted with pain. Beside her is her friend Thalia, looking at you with a disapproving frown.

'He's a real bulldog, this boy. At least, he would be if he looked any fiercer,' says Thalia, tut-tutting.

'Let me go, you beast!' moans Aglaia. 'It's bad enough that we had to find out about your exhibition from the newspaper . . .'

You gradually slacken your grip on her hand. You raise it to your lips and plant on it the lightest of kisses. Your silky lips are hot, burning.

'Forgive me, Aglaia,' you say. 'You startled me.'

'Well, you certainly startled me, you great fool.'

'You didn't even invite us. You sent invitations to every Tom, Dick and Harry in the Madrid phone book, apart from us three,' says Thalia reproachfully.

'Three? Of course, where's Euphrosyne?'

'She couldn't come. She's just had an operation and her stitches hurt when she walks.'

'Nothing serious, I hope.'

'No, she'll survive. She'll be a few ounces lighter, but she'll get by.'

'Yes, on the grand scale of things, it's pretty trivial,' agrees Thalia.

'Well, I'm pleased for her.'

'She sends you a big kiss.'

'Tell her I send it back.' You think for a moment. 'Not that I don't want it, of course. I'm just sending her a different kiss back. Yes, a different one.'

'Don't worry, we'll tell her.'

'Nice party,' says Aglaia.

'You're both looking more beautiful than ever,' you say. And the worst of it is that you mean it.

'Flatterer!' they chorus.

'I'm really glad you came.'

'Well, as you know, we're two old witches with plenty of free time and no men planning our days for us.' Aglaia puts her arm through yours. 'We wanted to see you. It's been ages since we saw you.'

'Not since Araceli's funeral.'

'You were an absolute hero. We all know how hard it was for you. And without Valentina . . .'

'It doesn't matter, really . . .'

'Yes, it does.'

'I did what I could. I loved Araceli,' you whisper shyly. 'We lived together.'

'Ulysses, you say that as if . . .'

'Oh, no, there was nothing sexual between us, if that's what you mean,' you say.

They look at each other. They can't decide whether you're an innocent, a joker or a pervert.

'Um, yes, of course.' Aglaia clears her throat.

'And we wanted to see how well you were doing, to see your paintings. And we wanted, above all, to have an excuse to go out.' Thalia looks around at the other people, who are growing fewer by the minute.

The party is coming to an end. At last.

'And to ask about Valentina,' Aglaia concludes. 'Have you heard from them lately?'

'Vili sent me a postcard from New York a week ago,' you say.

'New York! Are they still there after their trip to Barbados?'

'Yes. He said that Valentina is feeling weak, but no more than she was, say, a month or so ago.' You look at one woman and then at the other. 'He said that they're happy. "Each day that passes is a gift from time," he said. He said: "I don't know how long it will last, but then, who does?" That's what he said in his postcard. I believe Valentina phoned Penelope the other night, and that they had a long chat. You could ask her. You could even phone Valentina. Penelope can give you her number.'

'Yes, we'll do that, my dear, we'll do that,' Aglaia assures him. 'We'll ask and we'll phone. We might even go and visit her.' And after a pause, 'Valentina, I mean. If she'd like us to, of course. Besides, we've been talking for a while now about going on a little jaunt, haven't we, Thalia?'

Strangers in paradise

When you and Jana arrive at the building where Penelope lives, it is almost half past eleven at night. Jana has the keys and she opens the door to let you in. You enter carrying the sleeping Telemachus.

'He didn't have his nap today,' you explain to Jana. 'He's exhausted, poor thing.'

Telemachus opens his eyes when Jana turns on the hall light, and abruptly closes them again.

'Shiiit . . .' he murmurs.

'Haven't you got another topic of conversation?' you say softly. 'Go on, go back to sleep. Papa's going to put you on your potty and then pop you into bed.'

Afterwards, you give him a kiss and leave him in his room. You tiptoe out, trying not to make any noise.

On some nights, when Telemachus still used to live with you, you couldn't even leave him alone in his room. You used to stay beside him until he fell asleep. Then you'd get up and walk to the door as quietly as you could. But your ankles would always crack – you've done a lot of sport in your time and sport leaves these little souvenirs – your bones sounded like someone tramping over dry sticks in the middle of a perfectly silent night. Telemachus would immediately wake up and leap to his feet. He would watch you accusingly as he clung to the bars of his cot. Even though, in the darkness, you couldn't see his eyes, you could sense his bitter, childish reproaches in the damp, troubled rhythm of his breathing, as if he were calling for help. You would return to his side. You would stay there, sitting on the floor, next to his cot, until you were the one who fell asleep.

Now, on the other hand, Telemachus has no problem sleeping. He doesn't protest. He doesn't complain. He's tired. And he lives with his mummy. As far as he's concerned, you can go wherever you like.

You feel betrayed. You retrace your steps and go back into his room; you bend down over his small huddled body and give him another kiss.

'See you next weekend, sweetie,' you say. 'Although I might come and see you sooner.'

You go back into the living room. Jana is standing up, ready to leave. She is holding the keys in her hand and keeps fiddling with them nervously.

'The nanny won't be here until eight o'clock tomorrow morning,' she tells you. She runs her hand over her hair and pushes it back over her shoulders. 'Penelope said to tell you that she'll be home soon. Could you wait with Telemachus until she comes back? I'd wait myself, but I'm meeting someone for a drink. It's only our second date, and he's a Libra. You know, balanced, orderly, suspicious, et cetera, et cetera. I don't want to arrive late and have him think that I'm always like that. Especially since it isn't true.'

'OK.' You flop on to the sofa and rub your eyes. 'But your boss should know that, according to our agreement, I'm supposed to hand over Telemachus at eight o'clock on Sunday night, and it's almost midnight now.'

'Yes, well, you'd better talk to *her* about it.'

'I might just do that.'

'Anyway, I'm off. I'll take the keys with me.'

'Have fun.'

'Thanks. The stars are in a favourable conjunction for me tonight, so I probably will,' Jana says as she waves goodbye with a tinkle of keys and keyring.

You hear the front door close with a metallic click. You go into the kitchen and prepare something to eat. You're hungry. The canapés you managed to cram into your mouth tonight at the gallery didn't fill you because you weren't even aware you were eating them.

Just as you are about to fall asleep on the sofa, you hear the front door open again and Penelope bursts into the living room encased in a dress that does not even look like a dress. It's as if she had made a kind of sleeve for her body. Much too close-fitting in your opinion, if anyone cares to know. Scandalous. After all, she *is* the mother of your son. You're perfectly within your rights to feel bothered. If you'd seen her in the street and not known who she was, you would have thought she was a very elegant hooker.

You sit up on the sofa. You look at each other without saying a word.

The *diableteau*. The *marionnette*.

Frozen there, face to face. Such opposites.

You consider the social function of sadism (it must have one).

You've never liked love songs. Call me, and I'll come running. I love you madly. I love you desperately. I think only of you. No one but you, just you and only you. You have always suspected love songs of sending people sad, depressing messages. No one should love anyone madly or desperately. Nor should they think only of the beloved. People should be perfectly capable of living, and living well, without anyone else. That's why your favourite songs are those written under the influence of drugs. LSD, for example, produced some magnificent results. 'Lucy in the Sky with Diamonds', for one.

Penelope in the sky with diamonds.

And yet you love her.

You have submitted your love to a highly imaginative and variable system of metrics. But it is love that you feel for her, because you can see her now. Penelope. Alone. Beautiful. In the sky. With diamonds. Sex. That's what you're thinking about. You can't help it. It's your nature. But with diamonds. You think that, when it comes to sex, women are like aerosols, you have to shake them well before use. Penelope is standing in the middle of the room. No, no. She's too still.

'Are those real diamonds you're wearing round your neck?' you ask when you finally manage to speak. You get up and go over to her.

'No, they're fake. Good costume jewellery,' she replies. 'It was the launch party tonight. A designer friend of mine makes them.'

'Ah.'

'Is Telemachus sleeping?'

'What do you expect a child to be doing at this time of night? This is hardly a decent time . . .' you begin.

'I'm sorry.' Penelope is very beautiful tonight. Was she this beautiful before? Was she? 'The nanny doesn't get here until eight o'clock tomorrow. When you have Telemachus, she has the weekend off.'

'Yes, I know. I don't give a toss about your nanny's timetable. I don't think that a good mother should . . .'

'What?'

'That a good mother should go gadding about at all hours knowing that her little boy is waiting for her.'

'What are you saying?' Penelope takes off her shoes and looks at you grumpily.

'Nothing that I haven't said to you before.'

'No, tell me what you mean.'

'What you do doesn't seem to me appropriate behaviour in a good mother. It's late. Look at the time. I have a right to demand that you take care of the child at all hours. I don't give a damn about your friends' parties, sweetheart. You took my son, and I have a right to expect you to be by his side just as I was when you chose not to look after him any more and you abandoned him.'

'*What* did you say? No, tell me, what did you say?' asks Penelope. She looks smaller without her shoes on.

'Oh, nothing. Happy birthday.' You suddenly smile, you decide to give in, you move closer. You don't feel like fighting. And what a surprise. You smell her smell again. 'Although your birthday's nearly over now.'

'It is over. It's half past midnight,' she says, looking at her wristwatch.

'Didn't you celebrate?'

'Are you joking?' Penelope looks at you incredulously. 'In the circles I move in people don't celebrate birthdays, just as they don't celebrate catching a venereal disease.'

'I wanted to bring you a present. I didn't know what to give you.'

'There's no need.'

'I've painted your portrait. It's in acrylic. You'll like the colour. I've got it at home. At my home. Your home. Well, in the apartment in Calle Santa Isabel. I can bring it round some time. I didn't know if you'd want to have one of my paintings here. That's why I thought about buying you a book or some perfume, but it's been a hellishly busy day, and I didn't have time.'

'H'm. How's the exhibition going?'

'Oh, pretty well. We've sold everything. I'm going to be taking part in a couple of collective exhibitions in Berlin and Chicago soon. And there are a few other things too. I can't complain,' you say phlegmatically. 'I don't think I'll be poor for very much longer, although oddly enough it doesn't matter to me as much as it used to.'

'Ha. You and money make a fine pair.'

'No, really, Penny, it's true.' You study the colour of her hair. The tone is different from when you last saw her a week ago. A subtle change that cannot, however, escape your trained eye. 'Come on, let's not quarrel for once. It's been a big day. Can I give you a kiss?' you ask cautiously. 'A congratulatory kiss?'

She frowns. She seems nervous. She is beginning to get worked up. That's good. Or so you think.

'How long has it been since you kissed me, since we kissed each other, you and me?' asks Penelope distrustfully.

'I don't remember.'

'I do,' she says.

You kiss her on the lips, placing one hand on her waist. As you recall, she used to like that.

Shake her up a bit, you tell yourself.

Penelope repays you with a punch in the eye. The ungrateful woman. It stings. It was a good, solid, well-aimed blow. Surprising. Spot on. Tears fill your eyes. You don't get clobbered like that even in the ring at the gym. At least not every day, and you're usually wearing protective headgear.

Pain is always a surprise. As ancient and persistent as life itself. Never out of fashion, displaying the perfection with which it establishes its cruel thresholds.

Penelope blows on her bruised knuckles. She shakes her right hand furiously.

'Ow! You're, you're . . .' she howls with pain. 'You're an animal!'

'Honestly, darling . . .' you say, as you rub your wounded brow and eye socket. You look at your fingers, there are a few intensely red drops of blood mixed with something that looks like water. 'Honestly . . .'

A few hours later, you are tossing and turning in bed, sleepy and confused. Where exactly is the profit and where is the loss, you wonder. But there are some things it's better not to know, so you reject the answers, if there were any, or if any were possible.

'I think I should go home,' you say to Penelope, who is lying face down beside you, asleep. 'It's really late. I'll phone for a taxi. Don't get up, love.'

Your eyebrow still hurts. It's still bleeding. But you haven't got blood anywhere else on your body.

There are some things one should never forget. When life wounds you, it does so in an instant, without warning, so that the blow can't be blocked. Life lives in the moment, which is why no one can get the better of it.

'Stay here the night, if you want,' Penelope says. She turns over. She is sleepy. Tired and tranquil and grateful. You have always been generous with women. Perhaps that is the secret of your success.

'And tomorrow?' you ask foolishly.

Tomorrow? Tomorrow, who knows, Ulysses.

Love and life, unlike pain, are very inexact.

'Do you want to stay?' Penelope asks.

You slide under the sheets again and feel your way towards her waist.

'Yes, I do,' you say. 'Yes.'

Appendix

Eudemonology
(A Brief Treatise on the Art of Being Happy)
Notes for an impossible book
by Viliulfo Alberola

That in the beginning when the world was young there were a great many thoughts but no such thing as a truth. Man made the truths himself and each truth was a composite of a great many vague thoughts. All about in the world were the truths and they were all beautiful.

The old man had listed hundreds of the truths in his book. I will not try to tell you all of them. There was the truth of virginity and the truth of passion, the truth of wealth and of poverty, of thrift and of profligacy, of carelessness and abandon. Hundreds and hundreds were the truths and they were all beautiful.

And then the people came along. Each as he appeared snatched up one of the truths and some who were quite strong snatched up a dozen of them.

It was the truths that made the people grotesques.

The old man had quite an elaborate theory concerning the matter. It was his notion that the moment one of the people took one of the truths to himself, called it his truth, and tried to live his life by it, he became a grotesque and the truth he embraced became a falsehood.

You can see for yourself how the old man, who had spent all of his life writing and was filled with words, would write hundreds of pages concerning this matter. The subject would become so big in his mind that he himself would be in danger of becoming a gro-tesque. He didn't, I suppose, for the same reason that he never published the book.

Sherwood Anderson, *Winesburg, Ohio*

A happy life is that which, objectively speaking, is absolutely preferable to non-existence, to never having existed.

Be cheerful.

Strive for tranquillity of spirit.

'The prudent man does not aspire to pleasure, but to the absence of pain.' (Aristotle)

Avoid envy.

'Love cannot be taught.' (Seneca) Learn from experience what it is that you want and what your capabilities are.

Remember that there are some things about which you can do nothing.

No one misses what they have never had. The poor man does not miss the great possessions of the rich man. What we cannot see does not trouble us. Nowadays, when everything is laid before us by the mass media, we tend to be troubled by everything. When this happens to you, stop looking for a few days.

In the absence of great sufferings, minor annoyances will torment you.

In difficult times, you must remember that all things pass. And in times of great happiness too.

Do what you can with a good will, and have a strong enough will to put up with suffering.

'Live not as you would like to, but as you can.' (Fleischer)

Always bear in mind that everything is subject to chance and error.

'Submit to reason if you want to submit entirely.' (Seneca)

When some misfortune occurs, do not think that things could have been different, because they couldn't.

Speak little with other people and a great deal with yourself.

Open your door to happiness and do not ask yourself whether or not you have any real reason to be happy.

Do not live in the past or think too much about the future. Work in the present for the future.

Keep calm. Be aware that your misfortune might be but a small portion of the disasters that could have befallen you.

Don't spend your life tormenting yourself with thoughts of possible imaginary happinesses. Enjoy your bearable, painless, tranquil present.

Try to avoid pain, even at the expense of rejecting pleasures.

Remember that showing anger or hatred in word or gesture is useless, dangerous, imprudent, ridiculous and vulgar.

The things in life that affect you are unconnected and fragmentary. Organize your way of thinking about them in the same way: detach yourself, think, prepare, enjoy and suffer each thing as it happens, nothing more.

Do not mourn for lost pleasures: they are lost chimeras. 'Only pain is real,' said Voltaire. Avoid it.

Use your skill to improve on what chance offers you.

In the first half of your life, you will anxiously seek after happiness. In the second half of your life, you will seek tranquillity and absence of pain. That is when you will feel most satisfied.

Do not think how happy you would be if you had all those things you do not have. Think what would happen if the things that you have were taken from you.

The only really important thing you have is the thing that no one can steal from you.

Restrain your desires, your appetites and your anger. Human beings can attain only a small part of all the things they desire.

'Do not allow yourself to be tormented by fear and hope over futile things.' (Horace)

If you believe you are suffering, then look at those who are suffering more than you, not at those who are enjoying themselves more.

Do not think that there are no joys or pleasures in old age. All pleasure is relative; if you fulfil a need, pleasure disappears along with the need.

*

'Some desires are natural and necessary, others are natural and unnecessary. Others are neither natural nor necessary, but are born of vain opinion.' (Diogenes Laertius) Epicurus made the same distinction regarding possessions.

Working and struggling against something that resists you is one of human nature's basic needs. Overcoming obstacles is a pleasure.

Do not be guided by the images conjured up by your imagination, because they will not satisfy you and will vanish as soon as you touch them. Be guided by concepts which fulfil their promises.

Take care of your health. 'Nine-tenths of our happiness is based on health, because our good humour depends on it.' (Schopenhauer)

What can be seen is much stronger than any product of thought or reason. Do not allow what you see to blind you.

Our life is the product of a series of events and of another series created by our own decisions. Both forces pull in opposite directions and thus shape the course of our existence.

Be aware of the transformations that time works on you. Do not persist in things that are no longer suitable for your person and for your age.

'The surest means of avoiding unhappiness is by not desiring to be too happy.' (Schopenhauer) May the demands of your pleasure – possessions, rank, honours – be moderate. 'Tall towers have far to fall.' (Horace)

*

Always remember: 'Stupidity only grabs hold of one corner of life, but that one corner can be very pleasurable.' (Schopenhauer)

Each person lives in a different world depending on his mind. Do not aspire to the possession of material goods, aspire rather to having a happy, cheerful temperament and a sane mind. The 'state of mind' is the only thing that lasts, all the rest is transient. It is 'what we are' that matters, not 'what we have' or 'what we represent'.

Consider that everything that happens is necessary. Anything which can actually happen is 'possible'. Everything that is real is necessary, and in the factual world there is no difference between reality and necessity.

For reason, on the other hand, necessity, reality and possibility are separate things. Treat them as such.

When you think about different possibilities, consider the bad ones and take measures to prevent them. Vain hopes will only bring you disappointment.

Do not make 'ample preparations for life'. Life is too short to accommodate all your plans.

'Why force your weak spirit into eternal plans?' (Horace)

Never forget, though, that the false belief that life is long has its good side: without it, we would never achieve anything of importance.

Your ease and your dis-ease lie within you.

*

One can only enjoy oneself. 'If the "I myself" is not worth much, then all pleasures are like delicious wines in a cold mouth.' (Schopenhauer)

There are two great enemies of human happiness: pain and boredom. Against pain, joy. Against boredom, the mind.

Sometimes joy and the mind are incompatible. 'Genius is related to melancholy.' (Aristotle) 'Joyful natures only have superficial spiritual abilities.' (Cicero) Whatever the truth of the matter, the happier you are, the better you will withstand pain. And the livelier your mind, the more you will enjoy your leisure.

'My mother had a marvellous sense of humour, and I learned from her that the highest forms of understanding we can achieve are human laughter and compassion.' (Richard P. Feynman)

'The philosophical life is the happiest life.' (Aristotle)

'A seventeenth-century nobleman had inscribed on his castle in Saxony: *Amour véritable. Amitié durable. Et tout le reste au diable.*' (Schopenhauer). Friends are one of your most precious possessions.

'Happiness belongs to those who are sufficient unto themselves.' (Aristotle)

'The greatest good fortune is a good character.' (Goethe)

Do not think that your happiness depends on your fate and on what you might acquire. Your fate might improve, but if you are a fool, not even a favourable fate will stop you being a fool.

*

'All the luxuries and pleasures represented in the dull consciousness of a fool are as nothing compared with the consciousness of Cervantes when he wrote *Don Quixote* in a comfortless prison cell. What you have for yourself, what accompanies you in your solitude and which no one can take away from you, is far more important than everything you possess or are in the eyes of others.' (Schopenhauer)

Always remember that your happiness depends on you, on what you are, not on what you have or what you represent.

Author's note

Contrary to appearances, happiness is not the art of resigning ourselves to our lot, although it might well be the art of learning to enjoy what we are, rather than what we have, and not worrying too much about what we will clearly never be or never have. For example, I know someone who, when she was a child, wanted more than anything in the world to be a bird and to be able to fly. It took this woman a long time and much unhappiness before she understood that she would never have her own wings and that, besides, a bird does not even *know* it is flying. When she realized this, she at last began to enjoy the enormous dignity and privilege of being a human being. Neither more nor less.

The novel you have in your hands, dear reader, is, in a way, the product of my reading of certain philosophers, who are mentioned (and quoted) where appropriate. Personally, few things in life have given me as much joy as reading these philosophers; they have always helped me to understand – to understand other human beings, the world and myself.

I should point out that the story is divided into three parts – 'What we represent', 'What we have' and 'What we are' – in honour of Arthur Schopenhauer, because, according to him, these are the three points that constitute *The Fate of Mortals*.

To write the Eudemonology (or *Brief Treatise on the Art of Being Happy*) which concludes the book, I used, and abused, another text by Schopenhauer, made up of various fragments and collected together under the Spanish title *El arte de ser feliz* (*The Art of Being Happy*, Herder, Barcelona, 2000), which I strongly recommend.

I think the old master would have given me permission to explore his thoughts as much as I wanted. Schopenhauer is one of my favourite thinkers (along with Marcus Aurelius, Montaigne, Seneca, Cicero, Epicurus, etc., etc.), despite the fact that he is not exactly famous for his optimism. He was, as Jean Rostand put it, a philosopher who felt 'very optimistic about the future of pessimism'. Nevertheless, following the model of Gracián, he demonstrates with his 'doctrine of happiness' that 'metaphysical pessimism is perfectly compatible with the struggle to lead a happy life' (according to the preface by Franco Volpi, in the Spanish edition mentioned above).

Translator's acknowledgements

The translator would like to thank Ángela Vallvey, Annella McDermott, Palmira Sullivan, Mary Argyraki and Ben Sherriff for all their help and advice.

Z470505